THEIR PASSION KNEW NO RULES

It had seemed so natural, the way he came slowly towards her to rest his hands on her shoulders. But Kerry began to tremble, as always, at his touch. She could hear him behind her, so close, his breathing heavy, ragged.

Suddenly he reached for her, drawing her against his chest as he pressed his lips to her forehead. "You didn't figure into my plans, green eyes," he said huskily. His lips covered hers to sear and possess, but only for an instant as he paused to whisper, "Tell me to stop, Kerry, because, God forgive me, I want you."

She was not thinking about the right or wrong of it. All she wanted, needed, was here and now in his arms. . . .

BOOK YOUR PLACE ON OUR WEBSITE AND MAKE THE READING CONNECTION!

We've created a customized website just for our very special readers, where you can get the inside scoop on everything that's going on with Zebra, Pinnacle and Kensington books.

When you come online, you'll have the exciting opportunity to:

- View covers of upcoming books
- Read sample chapters
- Learn about our future publishing schedule (listed by publication month *and author*)
- Find out when your favorite authors will be visiting a city near you
- Search for and order backlist books from our online catalog
- Check out author bios and background information
- Send e-mail to your favorite authors
- Meet the Kensington staff online
- Join us in weekly chats with authors, readers and other guests
- Get writing guidelines
- AND MUCH MORE!

**Visit our website at
http://www.zebrabooks.com**

MY IRISH LOVE

Maggie James

Zebra Books
Kensington Publishing Corp.

http://www.zebrabooks.com

ZEBRA BOOKS are published by

Kensington Publishing Corp.
850 Third Avenue
New York, NY 10022

First Printing: December, 1999
10 9 8 7 6 5 4 3 2 1

Printed in the United States of America

Chapter 1

It was a day all golden, blue, and green, the Irish landscape kissed by the gods above to make for splendor to stir the spirits and lift the soul.

Kerry paused in her chore of dumping trash behind her father's pub to gaze out at the sprawling field beyond. The yellow daffodils danced and swayed in the gentle breeze as though cavorting with mystical leprechauns.

Grunting beneath the weight of the heavy barrel, she emptied it into one even larger.

She turned once more towards the field and thought how wonderful it would be if leprechauns really did exist and could grant wishes. If so, she would have but one— that she and her mother could escape the misery of their existence and start life anew somewhere else . . . away from her mean-spirited father.

Kerry did not love him. She told herself she should feel guilty but to no avail. After all, she could not recall hearing a gentle word from the man in her entire life. And the sad reality was that he acted as though he hated her. He cursed and beat her, but, worst of all, he would sometimes lock her in the cellar beneath the pub.

To Kerry, the damp, black pit was sheer hell, for she was terrified of the dark. As a small child, a rat had bitten her leg, and to this day she would sit on the top stone step, knees hugged to her chest, shivering from head to toe in fear of being attacked again. The sounds of the nasty rodents scurrying about made her quake with horror.

Her mother begged her father not to put her there, but he seemed to take pleasure in doing so at the slightest provocation.

There had been a time when Kerry dared think a man might come along and ask her to marry him who would also be willing to take her mother to live with them. But that was long ago, before Meara's health began to fail. Kerry then had to do the chores for both of them to appease her father. He hated sick people, he said. Especially women. And when her mother took to her bed, he stood over her and screamed that she was useless and should be done away with like an old horse.

So marriage had passed Kerry by, and now, just past her nineteenth birthday, she was considered a spinster. But she did not mind, and if she was unable to take her mother with her she would not leave home, anyway.

Wistfully, she continued to watch the swaying daffodils, enjoying the moment, as well as the fresh air. Inside, the pub smelled of tobacco smoke and ale and men in their smelly work clothes. It was Friday, and the night would be busy. She would carry and serve trays of drinks till the wee hours, as well as wash dirty glasses and mop spills on the floor. If she slowed, her father would cuff her behind her ear or take her into the kitchen and force her to bend forward and lift her skirts so he could lay his paddling board across her buttocks.

She shuddered to think about it and tarried a bit longer to savor the last peace she would know for many, many hours.

"There you are, you lazy strumpet."

Sean O'Day burst out of the back door of the pub to clamp a beefy hand on her shoulder and spin her about.

"This is all you have to do on a Friday?" he roared, slapping her so hard she would have fallen had he not been holding her. "You've a floor to mop, but first you need a lesson in obedience. To the kitchen with you.

"Now!" He gave her a rough shove to send her stumbling forward. "I'll be along in a minute."

He went behind the cluster of trash barrels and began fumbling with the fly of his trousers.

Kerry smelled the whiskey on his breath and hated to know he had started drinking earlier than usual. By night's end he would be roaring drunk, and that could mean a trip to the cellar for her if she wasn't careful. So she went hurriedly, obediently, to the kitchen, knowing he would be right behind to wield the paddling board once he had relieved himself.

Her mother was standing at the sink, hot suds up to her elbow.

"What are you doing here?" Kerry whispered. "I told you I'd take care of your chores tonight." She did not like the way her mother had looked all day. Her skin was a pasty color, almost yellow. Her breathing seemed shallow, raspy, and she kept touching her thin fingers to her chest as if she were in pain but denied it when Kerry asked. She had never been the sort to complain, no matter how bad she felt.

Meara lifted a mug from the suds and put it in the rinsing basin. She managed a wan smile. "I'm fine, dear, really. And it's not right you should have to do my work, too."

"Mother, I don't mind." Kerry went to her and gently lifted her hands from the water and began drying them with a towel. She could not let her witness the paddling. It would upset her too much. "Now I want you to go upstairs. I'll be up in a little while and bring you a nice cup of tea. Please. I'll worry if you don't."

It was obvious to Kerry that her mother was feeling too poorly to argue.

"Well, if you insist . . ."

"I do. Now be off with you this minute."

Just then Sean walked into the kitchen and took the paddling board from where it hung on a peg next to the door. "I'm gonna give you an extra lick for not bein' ready to take your punishment. We got no time to waste with customers waiting."

Kerry was dismayed to see the stricken look on her mother's face and rushed to get it over with quickly. She went to a chair and bent over, lifting her skirt as she did so.

"What . . . what are you doing?" Meara cried. "No, you can't hit her, Sean. She hasn't done anything."

"Stay out of this," he warned, "or I'll give you a lick, too. I'm sick and tired of her dawdling. I'm also sick of her catering to you. It's time she took a husband."

Kerry felt a wave of foreboding.

"What are you talking about?" Meara demanded.

"I'm talking about her marrying Rooney Sluaghan."

Meara swayed. "He . . . he's as old as you are, Sean."

"That he is, and he's rich, too. He's offered a good price for her and says she can keep working here, but she'll be goin' home to his bed—not yours to wait on you," he added with a snicker.

He turned on Kerry. "Now you'll pay for shirkin' your work when my back's turned."

"I said you're not to hit her," Meara shouted.

Kerry knew he was not above striking her mother, though it had been years since he had. But now she was so weak Kerry could not risk him hurting her. "Go ahead, Papa, please," she begged. "Get it over with so I can go back to work for you."

Meara started towards them. "Sean, no . . ."

"Drawers, too," he roared. "Pull 'em down. I'll make

your cheeks so sore you'll be glad to stay on your feet workin' instead of sittin'."

With a rush of humiliation, Kerry reached for the waistband of her underdrawers. Seldom did he make her bare herself for him, and then only when he was drunk.

Meara screamed, "No, I'll not let you do it, Sean O'Day. I'll not have it, do you hear?"

Stunned by her mother's unfamiliar show of spirit, Kerry quickly straightened and spun about to see her father about to hit her with the paddle. Grabbing his arm, Kerry held tight. "Don't you dare. She's sick . . ."

But as she wrestled with him, mustering all the strength she possessed to hold on to him, Meara gave a little cry and crumpled to the floor, hands clutching her chest.

"Leave her be." Sean grabbed Kerry by the throat and twisted her back around and over the chair. "She's doin' it to make me stop, but it won't work. You're gonna take your licks . . ."

Holding Kerry down, he yanked her skirts back up, her drawers down, and then mercilessly brought the board down across her buttocks, again and again.

The red-hot pain of her flesh was nothing compared to the agony as Kerry managed to turn her head to watch her mother lying so still on the clay floor.

"Now then," Sean said, hitting her one last time. "Take her upstairs out of the way and then get back to work."

"No, I won't." Kerry fixed her clothes, then whirled on him, green eyes flashing with fire. A knife was lying on the table, and she snatched it up. "I'm sending for the doctor. I'm going to take care of her, and you can wash your own dishes and tend your own customers this night."

Sean backed away, face red with fury. When he was out of striking range, he shook a fist and roared, "You'll pay for this. I'll beat you till you're bloody and feed you to the rats in the cellar. You'll see . . ."

He turned on his heel and staggered out.

Kerry had no time to worry about his threats. She ran

into the pub and yelled to no one in particular, "Fetch Dr. Muldune, please. My mother is terribly ill."

She hurried back to drop to her knees and place her ear against her mother's chest. She could hear her heart beating, though faint. Then she began to rub her hands, which were terribly cold. "You're going to be all right, Mama. Dr. Muldune will be here soon."

Though it seemed to take forever, it was not long before he arrived.

Kerry stood back while he did a cursory examination.

The kitchen was becoming crowded with curious customers, and she was relieved when Dr. Muldune motioned to some of them to carry Meara upstairs.

As he and Kerry followed behind, he said, "I think it's her heart. She came to see me a few months ago and said she had been having a lot of pain."

"Dear God, I didn't know."

"She didn't want you to. She knew you would worry, and there was nothing you could do. I've known your mother a long time, Kerry, and she's always been a bit on the sickly side. I've suspected it was her heart, but"—he shrugged—"we doctors know so little. I feel so helpless."

Kerry felt alarm shoot to her toes. "Surely you can do something."

He patted her arm. "You know I will do my best."

She cut a glance at him as they entered the living quarters and was not encouraged by his expression.

"In there." Kerry pointed towards the corner room. The men carrying Meara exchanged curious glances as they walked by the open door leading to the spacious bedroom where her father slept.

It had been another reason for Kerry to despise her father when he made her mother move into the room with her several years ago. His reason—though he made it clear he did not need one, since it was, after all, *his* house—was that Meara's wheezing kept him awake.

Kerry had given her the bed and made a pallet for herself

on the floor. Now she kicked it aside to make room for
the men to maneuver her mother onto the mattress.

She shooed them out with a quick thank you, then closed
the door and turned on Dr. Muldune to implore, "Please.
You've got to do something. You can't let her die."

He placed his leather bag on the table next to the bed,
opened it, and took out a contraption Kerry had never
seen before. It had a silver bell-shaped object on the end.
Black hoses snaked out from each side, the tips of which
he put in his ears.

Seeing her curiosity over it, Dr. Muldune explained,
"It's called a stethoscope. It was invented by a French
doctor. It transmits her chest and heart sounds to my ears
and tells me how weak they are."

Kerry clenched her hands to her chin as he leaned over
her mother and put the silver bell to her chest. He listened
for a few moments, then began moving it around to different locations.

Finally, with a sigh and a slight shake of his head, he
straightened and removed the tips from his ears. "Her
heart is terribly weak, Kerry. I'm so sorry to have to tell
you this, but I'm afraid she won't last the night."

A cry tore from Kerry's throat, "But surely there's something. Please . . ."

He reached into his bag once more. "Nitrates will relieve
some of the pain she may be having. And she needs to
rest, so I'll leave some laudanum for you to give her when
she wakes up. It may make her dizzy and talk out of her
head, but don't worry. Just try to keep her quiet. I'll come
back in the morning.

"Unless something happens before then," he grimly
added.

Kerry was not surprised her father did not come upstairs.
He was probably too drunk to notice she wasn't around.

As for concern over her mother, that would be the last thing on his mind.

Time passed, and night came. Meara slept on, and Kerry kept constant vigil. And all the while she was thinking how, if her mother did live, she was going to take her and leave. Starving to death would be better than the misery they were forced to endure, especially now that her father had decided she should marry Rooney Sluaghan. But they would survive. Kerry reasoned she could find work at a pub in another village. After all, Galway was not the only place to live nor the only village with pubs.

Her mother had no family, her parents having passed away in only the past few years. She had few friends, because Sean did not allow her to go out except to church once in a while.

There was, however, one person who might be willing to help them escape. Sometimes her father would leave the care of the pub to Rooney Sluaghan while he disappeared for a few days. Kerry suspected he went to see a woman. Her mother had said as much. But neither minded, because it meant he was not around to abuse them. And that was when Edana O'Malley would slip in to visit. She was a kindly woman who seemed to adore Meara. But their times together were infrequent, and Kerry recalled one occasion when her father had returned early and gone into a rage to find Edana there. He had beaten her mother, and Kerry, going to her defense, had wound up locked in the cellar for several days. After that, Meara would sneak out to meet Edana in—of all places—the village cemetery.

Theirs was, Kerry acknowledged, a strange friendship, but she was thankful her mother had that much, at least.

Finally, Meara stirred, moaned softly, and opened her eyes.

Kerry was ready with the laudanum. Lifting her head

from the pillow so she could drink, Kerry noticed how warm she felt. Pressing her lips to her mother's brow, she winced to realize she was burning with fever. Dr. Muldune had not said anything about that but reasoned the laudanum would help.

"I . . . I'm so sorry," Meara said thinly as Kerry gently lowered her to the pillow once more. "I . . . couldn't stop him . . ."

"It's all right," Kerry assured, her bottom still smarting from the brutal licks of the paddle. "But I don't want you to talk. Dr. Muldune says you need to rest."

Meara groped for her hand. Kerry quickly laced fingers with her and squeezed. "Don't worry. I'm not going to leave you. Now try to sleep, please."

Meara's smile was bittersweet as she looked up at Kerry with rheumy eyes. "Soon I will sleep forever. For now, I want to be with you. Oh, Kerry, how I have loved you . . ."

"And I love you." Kerry was fighting tears. "Now stop talking nonsense. You're going to get well, and then we're leaving here. I can find work, and I'll take care of you. I will never let him hurt you again."

"He . . . he will make you marry Rooney when I'm gone."

"But you aren't going anywhere." Kerry tried to make her voice light, positive.

Again, the bittersweet smile. "It's my time, Kerry. I've heard the angels calling. I'm going to a better place, and so must you. Your father . . . he's waiting for you. He . . . he will take care of you."

Dr. Muldune had said the laudanum might make her talk out of her head, but never had Kerry thought she would be so delirious as to say she would be better off with her father. "Rest, please," she urged, pained to hear such nonsense.

"No . . . time . . ."

Meara lay very still, her breathing shallow.

Kerry tensed.

Meara's eyelashes fluttered. "No . . . time . . ." she repeated. "You have to know . . . about your father. What a good man he is . . . how much I love him . . . how much he loves you."

"Mama, please." Kerry could not bear it. Should she give her more laudanum? Enough to put her to sleep? She did not want to hurt her. Maybe if she tiptoed out her mother would fall asleep. "I'm going to make you some tea." She started to rise.

"No. Don't go."

The protest was spoken with such force that Kerry sank back to the chair, startled.

"Edana . . . Edana . . ."

"You want me to get her?" If she did, Kerry knew she would bring her no matter how mad it made her father.

"She . . . will help you."

"I don't need her help till you're better. Then we'll both go to her. We can hide there for a while, and—"

"No. You don't understand." Meara's eyes flashed open, bright with fever. Finding Kerry's hand once more, she squeezed with unbelievable strength. "You have to hear me out, Kerry. I told you—it's my time. And you have to know about your father. I wasn't going to tell you . . . afraid you would be so ashamed of me, but I can't let Sean make you marry Rooney Sluaghan.

"And with me gone"—she paused to take several deep, gulping breaths, her face contorting with pain from the effort—"you will be at his mercy. So you must go to your father. Edana will help you."

Kerry shook her head. "Mama, I know you're sick, but you aren't making any sense. Please just try to sleep. When you wake up, we'll talk."

"No. You have to listen." She tugged at Kerry's arm to pull her closer. "I swore I would take the secret to my grave, because I didn't want you to be ashamed of me. But when I heard Sean say tonight that he intends for you to marry Rooney Sluaghan, I knew I couldn't let that happen. And with me gone, you'll be at his mercy unless you go to your father."

Kerry blinked, still not understanding. "My father? But you just said—"

"Your real father."

Kerry sat straight up. "What are you saying, Mama?"

Meara's hands fluttered to her chest, fingers massaging ever so gently as though she were trying to rub away the pain that was wrapping about her heart. "His name is Flann . . . Flann Corrigan, and I have loved him with every breath I have drawn for over twenty years."

Above the roaring in her ears, Kerry told herself it was only the delirious ramblings of a sick woman, drugged with laudanum.

But, as her mother talked on, Kerry began to realize that she was not having delusions, that, God help her, the detailed story she was telling could only be true.

Flann Corrigan and Meara Shanahan had fallen in love in their teen years. Meara's father, however, did not approve of the match because the Corrigans and Shanahans had been feuding for so long no one remembered the reason anymore. But the tradition of hating each other was enough for Regan Shanahan to forbid the union.

Flann decided the only thing they could do was run away, but not merely from Galway. He knew that to stay in Ireland would only bring grief, because his family and Meara's would never give them peace. So he had left to make a new life for the two of them in America, promising to send for her as soon as he could. Neither of them were aware at that time that Meara was going to have a baby.

When Flann's letter finally came—sent to Edana, who was Flann's sister—along with the money for Meara's passage, over a year had passed. It had taken him a while to find work, he wrote, and even longer to save money. But he still loved her and wanted to marry her. Sadly, however, by then Meara's father, learning of her pregnancy, had quickly arranged for her to marry Sean O'Day in time to make everyone think he was Kerry's father.

"My heart ached to take you and go to America," Meara implored Kerry to understand. "But I couldn't shame my family, and Sean swore if I ever tried to run away, he would kill me . . . and you, as well. So I stayed, hoping for the best, but it never came. And all the while I prayed you would one day meet a man who would take you away from this hell we live in, but it was not to be."

Kerry's head was spinning. It was too much to absorb all at once, but for the moment she was concerned only with her mother. "I'm glad you told me, but we can talk about this later, when you're stronger."

Tears trickled from Meara's eyes. "There won't be a later for me, but for you, my beloved daughter, there is a bright, brilliant future in America with your father. Edana will see that you get there. She has been keeping all the money he sent through the years. As soon as I am gone, run to her. You must get away from Sean as fast as possible. Don't wait for my funeral. Promise me . . ."

"I promise," Kerry said to pacify, wincing as her mother's nails dug into her flesh. If her mother died, she would leave, of course, but not until after she made sure her mother had a proper funeral. Sean O'Day could certainly not be depended upon to see to it.

Kerry gently unwound her mother's fingers from her wrist. "I'm going to send someone for Dr. Muldune."

"Please tell me you don't hate me."

"Hate you? Oh, dear God, Mama, I feel nothing but jubilation, and I can't wait for you to tell me more about my real father. He has to be wonderful for you to have loved him all these years," she added with a caressing smile.

Meara whispered, "Stay with me a moment . . . till I fall asleep. Don't leave me alone."

Kerry pressed her lips to her mother's fevered cheek. "I won't," she promised fervently.

"Tell him . . ." Meara said, so low that Kerry had to strain to hear, ". . . that I loved him with my dying breath . . ."

And with one last, agonized gasp, she was gone.

Chapter 2

Kerry paused beside the coffin to straighten the lace border that draped down over the side.

She had been stunned when Sean left all the funeral arrangements to her. She was not, however, surprised that he played the role of grief-stricken widower to the hilt. It brought more customers to the pub, which he kept open, to spend money drinking as they offered their condolences.

When she had cried till there were no tears left, Kerry went to Muir Tiernan, the village undertaker, and chose the finest coffin he had in stock. Made of fine polished rosewood, it had flowers carved into the top, and the handles were fashioned of shining brass. She also bought an expensive satin and lace shroud for her mother to be buried in. It was, Kerry sadly reflected, probably the nicest thing she had ever had to wear in her life.

With the help of the ladies in the parish, the tiny living room of the upstairs quarters was rearranged for the wake. The coffin was placed against a wall, and it was there that her mother reposed for the three-day wake.

Sean stayed in the pub below, leaving Kerry to receive the many callers. A funeral was a social event in the village. It gave people a break in their normal routines, and they welcomed the chance for fellowship and food even under such bleak circumstances.

Kerry was grateful Sean kept his distance. He was angry that she had chosen to bring Meara's body home and refused to sleep in his own bed with a dead person in the next room. That had not been Kerry's intention—to drive him away—but she was glad she had. The less she was around him, the better, because it was so very hard to pretend she did not know the truth. She ached to let him know how thrilled she had been to discover that his mean-spirited blood did not flow in her veins. It was important, however, to go on as though nothing had happened, so she could flee as soon as the last clod of dirt covered her mother's grave, lest he try to stop her.

Feanna Galbreath, one of the ladies of the parish, walked to where Kerry was standing to quietly tell her, "The scones are out of the oven. Shall I start sprinkling them with sugar or would you rather do it? I know you're trying to stay busy to take your mind off your grief, dear, and I don't blame you."

"I'll take care of it." Kerry hurried into the kitchen, with Feanna right behind her.

"You should open a bakery," Feanna complimented as she helped herself to a warm scone. "You're a daughter to be proud of, for sure. Meara was blessed to have you to care for her in her final years when she fell so sickly."

"It was a privilege," Kerry said. "I loved her very much."

"As she loved you."

Kerry turned at the sound of a new voice in the kitchen. It was Edana. Kerry stepped into the circle of her arms and pressed her lips to her ear to whisper, *"Aunt* Edana . . ."

The other women were busy and not paying attention.

Edana smiled and hugged Kerry all the tighter. "So Meara told you. I prayed that she would."

They moved into the living room. It was still early. People had not yet begun to arrive for the evening.

"She's at peace now," Edana murmured as they stood beside the coffin gazing down at Meara. "Her suffering is over."

"Aunt Edana . . ." Kerry hesitated. It seemed so strange to call her that. "My mother did tell me everything just before she died. She might not have, though, if Sean hadn't told us that he plans to make me marry Rooney Sluaghan. She wanted me to go to you, because she said you'd help me get to where my father is."

"And that I shall. Don't worry." Edana pulled her black shawl tighter around her shoulders as she glanced about to make sure no one could hear. "I will make all the arrangements."

Kerry squeezed her hand in a rush of gratitude. "This means everything to me. Losing Mama breaks my heart, but at least I can look forward to being with my real father. And I can't wait for you to tell me what he's like. I want to know everything about him."

"He's a wonderful man," Edana said with a firm lift of her chin. "He was devastated when he heard what had happened, how Meara had been forced to marry someone else. Especially a hooligan like Sean O'Day. It tore the soul from him, to be sure, but there was nothing to be done. The families hated each other, you know."

"Mama told me. But what about you?" Kerry had to ask. "Were you in favor of your brother marrying a Shanahan?"

Edana confided, "Of course not. All I wanted was my brother's happiness. And after things happened as they did, I was only too glad to be their link to each other, futile though it was."

Still dazed by the wonder of it all, Kerry sought reassurance that it was not merely a dream. "And you will help me go to him?"

"Oh, yes. I only wish Lennon were here to help hurry things along."

Lennon was Edana's husband, and she went on to explain how he had gone away over a week earlier on a fishing trip. He was not expected back for a fortnight.

"But don't you worry," Edana assured. "I'll keep you hidden till he returns."

The question had been nagging at Kerry, and suddenly she had to ask, "Did my father ever marry anyone else? Does he have other children now? I don't want to cause trouble or be in his way."

"You won't be. And he has no wife that I know of."

"And when was the last time you heard from him?"

Kerry tensed to see how Edana's brow furrowed.

"Nearly three years."

"Three . . . years?" Kerry gasped. "Why, anything could have happened. How do you even know where he is after so long a time?"

"There has been a war in America. Between North and South. We heard it ended some time ago. Two years, I think. The North won."

Kerry was aware of that. She had learned long ago to eavesdrop on the men's conversations in the pub if she wanted to know what was going on in Ireland or anywhere else in the world.

Edana continued, "Flann was in that war. He fought for the South. As for knowing where he is, he sent me a map showing me his farm in North Carolina, and that is where you will go. He never gave up hoping for a miracle and that Meara would join him. That's why he always let me know where he was through the years. And he's most proud of his farm. I'm sure that's where you will find him."

"Mama said he also sent you money, that you were keeping it for her. I'm so glad, because if he hadn't I don't know what I'd do. I have nothing."

Edana began glancing around once more, and Kerry thought she seemed unduly nervous as she said, "I'd better leave now. Sean might come upstairs, and it wouldn't do for him to find me here and see us talking. He might wonder if Meara told you everything.''

Kerry assured her she did not have to worry. "He's far too busy turning drinks and pretending he's beside himself with grief.'' She told Edana how he had refused to sleep near Meara's body. "I don't think he's even seen her since she was brought here.''

"I'm not surprised. He never cared about her.''

Many questions had plagued Kerry since her mother's deathbed confession, and one of them had been why Sean O'Day married her when he obviously did not love her. She asked Edana, who did not mince words in response.

"Your grandfather paid him. He was desperate, and Sean knew it, so he took him for a tidy sum.''

"Then it was all for money,'' Kerry said with a shake of her head. "But that still doesn't explain why he mistreated her so terribly . . . why he seemed to hate me.''

Edana had an explanation for that as well. "As a young man, Sean fancied Meara, but she only had eyes for Flann, and that infuriated Sean. She told me once that she believed his abuse was his way of getting back at her, and that he hated you because you were living proof she loved another man.

"But enough of this,'' Edana said, leaning over the coffin to give Meara's cheek a soft pat of good-bye. "It's over. All of it. And you've a brand-new life before you. Have you a plan to run away?''

"Yes. I'm going to slip away after the funeral and hide somewhere till dark. Then I will come to your cottage.''

"Good. Just be careful. And don't give Sean any reason to suspect anything.''

"I won't,'' Kerry assured her, "but dear Lord, I'm counting the hours.''

People were starting to filter into the room.

"I must go,'' Edana said, and, with a swish of her black crepe skirts, hurried out.

* * *

It was nearly nine o'clock when the last of the callers left. An hour later, the ladies helping in the kitchen finished their cleaning and said their good-byes.

A few of them offered to stay and sit up with Meara, knowing there would be no one else to keep Kerry company. After all, the noise from the pub below was loud and boisterous. Sean O'Day was hosting the kind of Irish wake usually observed by men who had been frequent customers and would have expected such revelry. In this instance it was disrespectful but not surprising to anyone who knew him.

Kerry refused the ladies' offers. She welcomed sitting alone with her mother for the remainder of the night.

She would never return to visit her mother's grave, so it seemed important, somehow, to be with her now as long as possible.

"You do look at peace," she whispered as she stood next to the coffin. "I only wish you had found it with my father. But don't worry, Mama. I'll tell him what you said—how you loved him with your dying breath."

She heard the sound of clattering footsteps coming up the stairs. Backing away from the coffin, she cringed at the sight of Sean stumbling into the room.

"So they're all gone, are they?" He held on to the doorframe as he swayed from side to side. His eyes were bloodshot, his hair disheveled, and the front of his shirt was covered in drink and food stains.

Lurching, he went to the coffin.

Fear rising, Kerry moved to distance herself from him.

"They're a pain in the arse, they are," he said, hiccuping. "Nosy old crones. Two of 'em had the nerve to march right in the pub and say I wasn't showin' proper respect for the dead. None of their business, I say. They don't have to worry about making money to pay for *this.*"

He made a fist and slammed it against the coffin, setting it to rocking.

Kerry jumped and took a few more steps backwards to find herself pressed against the wall.

He moved towards her, his face red with anger. "Why did you choose something so fancy? A plain wood box would have been good enough for the likes of her. But you didn't care, did you? It's not your money that has to pay for it. And Muir was in the pub earlier and told me how much it cost, that and the shroud. I ought to beat it out of you, damn you."

Cowering, Kerry threw up her arms to fend him off.

He dug his fingers into her hair and gave it a hard yank that made her cry out.

"Shut up. I won't listen to your wailing. And I'll not be paying for your fancy coffin and shroud, either. It's just going to cost Rooney more money to wed you, that's all."

Kerry thought she knew why, through the years, Sean had never lost control and taunted her about her mother's shameful secret. He did not want anyone to know he had married a woman pregnant by another man. But she suspected he was hard-pressed to hold his tongue at times, like now, when he was obviously boiling with rage.

"The banns will be posted this week. Rooney wants the marriage to take place as soon as possible, and so do I."

Kerry hung her head and nodded, as if obediently submitting to anything he wanted.

Roughly he cupped her chin, forcing her to look at him. "You think like them do-gooders, don't you? That I'm being disrespectful again. Well, I don't care what you think. And neither does Rooney. He wants you in his bed, and I want the handsome price you're fetching. And he's agreed you'll keep on working here, too. So don't you do anything to make him change his mind, understand?"

He squeezed her face so hard she feared her jaws would break, and it was all she could do to nod once more.

He continued to hold tight. "He's downstairs. He wants

to come up here and cozy up with his little bride-to-be. And don't you do nothing to make him mad."

He released her with a shove that sent her head cracking against the wall.

"And close the damned coffin lid," he roared, crossing to slam it down. "Rooney don't want to be around no corpse any more than I do." He twisted the key to lock, then put it in his pocket.

As soon as he left the room, Kerry rushed to lay her head on the coffin. Her hands fluttered back and forth across the top as she quietly, softly, wept. She would miss her mother deeply, but soon the time for grieving would be over, and she could look to the future with her real father in America. It would be a whole new life, and she was deeply, deeply grateful.

"Ah, my pretty little bride is crying."

She lifted her head and shuddered at the sight of Rooney Sluaghan. He swaggered through the door and crossed the room to yank her into his arms. "You don't know how long I've wanted to do this," he said, covering her mouth with his.

She struggled against him, gagging at the taste of rye whiskey and how his wet, thick tongue was trying to pry her lips apart.

He laughed and let her go. "Too much for you at once, eh? Well, just you wait till you see what else will be too much . . ."

Repulsively, he reached down to squeeze his crotch, and Kerry cried, "No, please . . ."

He grabbed her, and though she struggled, he wrestled her to the sofa and threw her down. "I think I'll show you right now . . . maybe even let you have a little sample . . ." He began fumbling with his trousers.

The sacrilege of it all was too much for Kerry to bear. She leaped up, striking his chest with her open palms to send him staggering backwards. Before he could grab her again, she ran into her room, slammed the door, and locked it.

"All right, all right," Rooney yelled to concede. "Maybe it's not the proper time. I'll be patient, owing to your grief, but I warn you—set your mind to being an obedient wife or I'll beat you worse than your father ever did."

Relieved that he had given up, she busied herself packing her few belongings in her satchel. Then she dropped it out the window.

And for the remainder of the night she sat beside her mother's coffin, now and then murmuring her love . . . as well as her good-byes.

Kerry had not slept a wink.

As the first light of dawn crept through the window, she hurried downstairs and out the back door to hide the satchel behind the trash barrels where no one would see it.

But when she went back inside, her blood ran cold to find Sean standing in the kitchen.

He was bare chested, and his belly hung over his ankle-length drawers. He was scowling and reeked with the odor of sour whiskey and ale. "What are you doing skulking around at this hour?" he demanded, eyes hooded with suspicion.

Quickly, she fabricated an explanation. "I felt the need to walk. I'm afraid I'm not feeling well."

"And I'm afraid you upset Rooney last night, and if I didn't feel bad myself I'd give you a few lashes on your rump to wear to your worthless mother's funeral. Now get upstairs before I change my mind and do it."

She ran for the stairs.

He shouted after her to warn, "You best be feeling good enough tonight to be nice to your future husband or I'll peel you down and whip you good."

She kept on going, heart racing, hands squeezed into

tight fists at her sides. *Please, please, Lord,* she prayed, *make the time pass quickly . . .*

Kerry only had one decent dress. Pale blue and made of wool, it was a bit heavy for the unusually warm spring day. It was also worn and faded, but she would have worn it even if a leprechaun had suddenly appeared with one fashioned of the finest silk, because her mother had made it by hand.

Kerry felt fresh tears welling in her eyes as she fingered the delicate stitches. She had sat beside her mother near the kitchen stove as she worked each and every stitch with her nimble fingers and needle.

Finally it was time, and men from the church came to take the coffin downstairs and place it in a horse-drawn cart.

Kerry stepped in place behind to follow, head reverently bowed, her trembling hands folded beneath her bosom.

As always, she cringed at Sean's presence as he fell in step beside her.

"It's a long walk to the church," he groused, still smelling of all he had drunk the night before. "It's a good thing it's not raining, or I'd never do this."

She ached to call him what he was—a hypocrite. He only walked because they would pass through the village proper. People would be watching, and the men would again take pity on him and go to the pub later to extend grief and buy the drinks he was not about to give away, even in honor of his own wife.

"I'll be needing you to cook up some kidney pie later," he said under his breath, nodding to an old lady standing on a corner. "There wasn't enough food last night. And when there's no food, the customers don't drink as much. Be sure to use a lot of salt, too, so they'll be good and thirsty."

Kerry kept her head bent, teeth clamped tightly together.

A few more hours, she told herself over and over, and it would all be over. He could never hurt her again.

The church was small but filled with mourners. Kerry was touched. Though the times Meara had been allowed to leave home had been sparse and limited, people she encountered had adored her. Even Sean was stunned by the outpouring.

"Can't figure out why anybody cared about the old crone," he mumbled under his breath.

At that, Kerry bristled and dared hiss, "Don't speak of her that way. And if you had come upstairs the past few nights and received callers as would have been proper, you'd have seen how many friends she had."

He pressed back against the wooden pew to give her a sideways glare. "Hold your tongue," he whispered, "or I'll lock you in the cellar with the rats till your wedding day."

Kerry knew he was capable of doing just that and remained silent as he continued to make snide remarks about her mother. She was grateful that, at least, no one could overhear because she and Sean were seated away from the others, with a wood screen giving them privacy.

At last, the service was over. The coffin was carried out for burial.

They stepped from behind the screen, and the first person Kerry saw was Rooney Sluaghan. He walked right over to take Sean's hand and say, smirking, "I want the banns posted before dark. I spoke to the cleric before the service and told him what we agreed to claim—that it was her mother's dying wish that Kerry marry me as soon as possible. He reacted just like we thought he would, saying it would not be unfitting to honor it."

Sean wrapped a possessive hand around Kerry's arm. "I can go along with that, but first we've another matter to discuss."

Rooney's face darkened with suspicion. "And what might that be, Sean O'Day? We agreed on the price."

"That was before there were funeral expenses to be paid."

"And why is that my responsibility?"

Sean smiled. "One of the first things you will need to teach your new wife is not to be so foolhardy when it comes to money. I gave her free rein to bury her mother, and she gave her the very best. I can't afford to pay for it, but you can . . . and will, if you want to marry her."

Kerry was shaken to her toes with humiliation that they could talk about her as though she were a cow to be bought at market. No matter they were in a holy place to commit a soul to God.

She glanced about wildly, hopefully, wishing someone, anyone, would approach so they would have to stop talking about it. However, everyone was filing out the doors to the cemetery, no doubt anxious to finish the service and get back to their normal routines.

"How much are we talking about?" Rooney asked, flicking Kerry with a lusty gaze. "And she'd better be worth it."

"She will be."

Rooney petulantly reminded, "She was cold as her mother's corpse last night. I'll not be paying for a dead fish."

Sean gave Kerry a sharp jab with his elbow that made her gasp out loud and cover the pain with her hand.

"Tell him you are sorry. Tell him it will not happen again."

Kerry could not speak past the bile that had risen in her throat.

Sean jabbed her again. "Do it or be damned to the cellar. I swear it, and . . ." He froze, then flushed with anger to see Edana standing there. "What do you want? How dare you intrude on our grieving?"

Edana's lip curled with contempt but she managed to calmly say, "I apologize, but I was sent to tell you that they are waiting on you. It's time for the graveside prayers."

With a sympathetic glance at Kerry, she turned and hurried away.

"They could have sent someone else," Sean murmured. "I despise that woman. She's nothing but trouble."

Rooney laughed. "I thought it was only the Shanahans who hated the Corrigans."

"It doesn't matter. I want nothing to do with any of them." He gave Kerry a rough shove. "Let's get it over with. Then the three of us are going home to talk about this. I'll not have you troubling Rooney."

Rooney chuckled. "Oh, she will learn her place soon enough. I just want the banns posted so the waiting period will begin. My bed has been cold long enough."

Kerry was pained to think how Rooney had buried three wives, the last one less than a year ago. It was said he had worked them to death—in bed and out. His last was rumored to have taken poison to end her suffering, but no one knew so for a fact.

But in that anguished moment, if Kerry had not been secure in the knowledge that she would be spared the fate of his other wives, she might have been tempted to seek a similar end to what could only be hell on earth.

The words spoken by the minister and the prayers offered did not take long.

Finally the coffin was lowered into the ground.

The grave diggers stood back, waiting for Sean to toss clods of dirt as the minister intoned, "Ashes to ashes . . . dust to dust . . ."

But Sean stood there woodenly, not about to get any closer to the gaping hole in the ground than he already was.

Kerry quickly bent to take a handful of earth, then, tears streaming down her cheeks, dropped it into the grave where it landed on the coffin lid with a dull thud.

Immediately, she turned away to say to no one in particular, "I don't feel well. I may be sick to my stomach."

Lifting her skirt, she ran towards the church and around the side to where the outside toilets were.

No one came after her. Sean would think she was nauseated and wait for her return. By the time he realized she was not coming back, she would be far away.

She passed the outbuildings and ran down the sloping hill that led to the cobbled street below.

On and on she ran, all the way to the one-room school she had attended as a child. She hurried around to the back, where a wood hatch door opened to the cellar below.

This time she did not mind being in the dark with rats scurrying about. It was the only place she knew to hide . . . her only chance to escape. She could, she knew, endure anything for the moment to make it happen.

Night had fallen when Kerry finally crept out of the cellar. There was no moon. She could not see her hand before her face. But after a few moments, when her eyes became adjusted to the dark, she could make her way and hurried towards the pub.

It was very late. She had waited to make sure everyone would be in bed. Her stomach growled with hunger, and her throat was parched and dry. She took comfort in knowing Edana was expecting her and would have food and drink waiting.

Soon, so very soon, thank God, she would be safe.

As she rounded the corner, she was not surprised to see the glow of lights coming from the windows of the pub. As she drew closer, she could hear shouting, laughter, as the men drank and made merry. No doubt Sean's rage over her running away would have led him to also imbibe heavily. Probably he was biding his time, confident he would find her in the morning light. He would ask everyone to search, claiming she was crazed with grief and must be found. The entire village would hunt for her. And, of course, Edana would pretend to be as concerned as everyone else.

Groping her way along behind the pub, Kerry counted off the paces she had taken that morning. Knowing she would be fighting darkness when she returned that night, she had wanted to make sure of exactly where she had hidden the satchel.

The barrel was right on target. Without making a sound, she reached behind it . . . and found nothing.

Panic welling, she felt all around, then retraced her steps. It had to be the right barrel. But perhaps someone had moved them about for some strange reason. Frantic, she searched behind each and every one but found nothing.

So be it, she told herself, turning back towards the street. She had only what she was wearing, but with the money Edana had been keeping for her, she could buy new clothes. What she had put in the satchel had been only sentimental, everything made by her mother.

Reaching the street, she took a deep breath and was about to take off running right down the middle to distance herself as quickly as possible from the pub and the memory of all the tortured years.

But suddenly a hand closed about her throat, and she was lifted off her feet.

"Did you think I wouldn't see for myself what you were doing out so early this morning?" Sean squeezed, and she clawed at his fingers, fighting to breathe. "I found your satchel, little strumpet."

He let her go, and she fell sprawling to the ground. Gasping, coughing, when she could at last speak she furiously cried, "Do with me what you will, you . . . you evil bastard. I'll die before I marry Rooney, do you hear me? So go ahead and kill me."

He kicked her in her side, and she curled in a fetal position, clutching her stomach, again fighting to breathe as the wind was knocked from her lungs.

"You will beg to marry him by the time I'm done with you. I swear it."

Grabbing her by her hair, he dragged her into the pub's kitchen and across the floor to the storage room and the cellar door. Opening it, he threw her down the stairs.

Kerry rolled head over heels, her arms and legs cruelly bruised as she fell all the way to the bottom.

"I'll leave you to die with the rats unless you obey me," he yelled after her. "It's what I should've done when you were born instead of passing you off as my own."

The door slammed.

The lock clicked.

A rat scampered across Kerry's face as she lay on the floor.

But, by then, she had mercifully fainted.

Chapter 3

Kerry opened her eyes to total darkness.

She touched her forehead, felt something sticky, and knew she had a cut there.

She had no idea how long she had been unconscious.

Her stomach gave a hungry growl. She had not been able to eat much breakfast and hoped Sean would come soon . . . hoped he did not mean his threat to let her starve to death.

She tried to get up but fell back when her left ankle gave way. Her sides also stung with pain, and she feared she might have broken a few ribs.

Never had he thrown her so violently down the steps. She could have been killed, but he would not have cared.

And in the back of her mind she began to wonder if perhaps that might have been a blessing, for quick death would be better than slow. After all, she was trapped. No one knew where she was. Sean would say she had run away, crazed with grief over her mother's death. He would not be suspected of causing her death, which appeared inevitable if she did not agree to marry Rooney.

Hopelessness was a shroud, prematurely wrapping her for the grave.

From above, loud, raucous laughter filtered through the ceiling, along with the music of fiddles and dulcimers. It was either the same night or she had slept around the clock, and she doubted that. The blood was still sticky on her forehead, not hard and dry, and she would have been far hungrier.

Easing back to the floor, she decided it had only been a few hours. Maybe Sean would bring food after the pub closed.

She burst into tears and cursed herself for being so weak. It was important to keep her wits about her in readiness for any chance to escape, even though the possibility seemed unlikely when she could not even stand, and every breath she drew was agony.

It was damp and cold, and she tried to roll to her side and wrap her arms about herself for warmth, but it was too painful.

Sleep would not come. There was nothing to do but endure the misery.

Finally the noise above ceased. Kerry waited, prayed that Sean would come. Surely he would not leave her there into the day without so much as a sip of water.

She bolted upright at the sound of the cellar door opening, wincing from the pain in her sides.

A lantern's glow illuminated the stairs as Sean came stomping down.

Towering over her, he grunted with satisfaction to see how she looked. "Well, now that you've had a taste of how it's going to be, have you come to your senses?"

"I will not marry Rooney," she said quietly, firmly.

"You would rather die?" he asked, tone incredulous. "Because that's what will happen if you don't give in, girl. He's waiting upstairs now . . . says if you will go with him to his bed now he's willing to forgive your insolence and give you another chance."

Kerry well remembered Sean's words as he had thrown her down the steps—how he should have killed her when she was born rather than pass her off as his own. It was so tempting to gloat that she knew the truth. However, she felt it might be to her advantage to pretend not to have heard what he said and instead challenge, "How can a father treat a daughter this way? Surely you've some love for me in your heart. I can't believe you'll let me die . . . *Papa.*" She nearly choked on the word.

He hesitated before answering, obviously caught off guard and not sure how to respond. His voice was not slurred as it had been when he had thrown her down the steps. He had sobered and probably forgotten his parting words and now tried a ploy of his own. "How can a daughter refuse to help her father? Rooney is paying a handsome price for you, and I have gambling debts. If I don't pay them, I'll lose the pub and have nothing.

"Besides," he added tightly, angrily, "you are supposed to obey me, and obey me you shall."

He squatted beside her. "Rooney is a wealthy man. He will take good care of you, so be sensible. You can't expect me to support you."

"I'll find a job and take care of myself."

He sneered. "Doing what? Working in another pub? It's all you know how to do. It's not likely you'll find another husband."

"I can't marry Rooney. He puts his wives in early graves, and you know it. I might as well die here."

"Then die you shall," he roared, bolting to his feet, again giving her a sharp kick in the ribs.

Kerry screamed.

"A few days of no food and water, and I'll wager you'll change your mind. Ungrateful bitch," he muttered, starting back up the stairs. "Just like your mother. I saved her from shame, but she never appreciated it. So stay here and feed the rats. It's what you deserve."

The door slammed, and Kerry was once again swallowed by darkness.

Sometimes she slept but mostly the pain in her ankle and ribs kept her awake.

In an attempt to keep her sanity, she fantasized about her true father and what he was like. Did she favor him? she wondered. Even when she believed Sean was her father there had been no resemblance between them. His eyes were as black as his heart, while hers were green like her mother's. Yet, that was all that was similar. Kerry's hair was bright red, true Irish, unlike her mother's which was dark. Was hers the same color as her father's? She hoped so.

She envisioned his farm, probably typically Irish with a sod roof and fences made of stones. Perhaps he had even planted shamrocks to grow on the lawn. There would be sheep grazing, and a few goats for milk. Potatoes would be abundant, and she would help to dig them ... help him do any chores needed. A good life it would be, and maybe her father would know other Irish immigrants, even a kindly man in need of a wife. Kerry would like that—having a husband, a family. And if she loved the man she married, so much the better.

Only it was never to be.

Her stomach twisted into knots of anguish.

Dear God, she was so very hungry and wondered how much longer she could survive. Weakness kept her from getting up even if her injured ankle could support her. And her throat was parched, her lips cracked and bleeding.

The rats were venturing closer. She had to muster all her strength to slap them away when they tried to crawl on her. Soon, though, she feared she would be too weak.

Sean came and went. Always he asked the same question—was she ready to come to her senses? The past few times she had not bothered to answer.

"You're an ugly sight," he taunted during his last visit.

"Soon Rooney won't have you, and you'll lose your chance to keep from dying here, you little fool."

Kerry could only lie there, drifting in and out of consciousness.

There were moments when she tried to convince herself to surrender, to do whatever it took to survive. Yet, thoughts of what it would be like as Rooney's wife kept her from yielding.

Through the fog that had enveloped her, Kerry heard the cellar door opening.

She did not so much as lift her head. What difference did it make? He would jeer at her again. He might even kick her or hit her. But she could do nothing, for she was numb . . . with cold, with pain . . . and the resignation that sooner or later she was going to die.

"Kerry? Are you here?"

She tensed. It was the voice of an angel, come to take her. Would she go to heaven? She prayed that would be her destination. Surely that was where her mother had gone. They would be together, and—

"Kerry, answer me. Oh, please, please answer me. There isn't much time."

Kerry raised her head. She could see the tiny light of a candle, seeming to float down the stairs. Whoever was carrying it took hesitant, fearful steps.

"Kerry, please . . ."

She heard the voice crack, break, followed by an anguished sob.

"God, please don't let me be too late . . ."

Dizzily, Kerry rationalized that an angel would not be crying.

An angel would know where she was.

"I . . . I'm here." She did not recognize her own voice . . . rusty as an old nail . . . fragile as a spider's web in the breeze.

"Praise God."

Suddenly a figure loomed above her, then dropped beside her.

"Can you stand, Kerry? Can you help me get you out of here? We have to hurry."

She recognized Edana in the candlelight, her face twisted with anguish and fear.

"I prayed I'd find you here. I overheard Sean threaten you in the church that he'd lock you in the cellar. He's told everyone you ran away, but when you never came to me I knew he had somehow caught you. Now are you hurt?"

Kerry's throat was dry as dust, making it difficult to speak. "My ankle is hurt, and I may have broken ribs. How long have I been here?"

"Three nights. I've been here every one, waiting for a chance to get to you, but he's kept the back door locked. Tonight I was peeking in the kitchen window when I saw him take a whore upstairs. I waited to give him time to get her into bed, then broke the window. He wouldn't have heard it, but there's no telling when he'll come back down and see it. We have to hurry. Now let me help you up."

"Edana, I haven't eaten ... haven't had anything to drink. I'm so weak. I don't think I can do it."

"You have to." Edana carefully set the candle aside, then slipped her arms under Kerry's shoulder and helped her to sit. "You have to try," she urged. "No matter how bad it hurts. And you'll have water as soon as we get to the kitchen."

Mustering all her will, her strength, Kerry managed to stand but could not put her weight on her injured foot.

"Lean on me," Edana instructed. "And hop along. We'll make it. God will help us ... and the spirit of your sainted mother."

With that thought in mind, Kerry was able to climb the stairs. She bit back gasps and cries of pain, knowing it was her last chance to survive.

Edana unlocked the kitchen door, and after Kerry took

a few precious sips of water, they headed into the night, as fast as Kerry could manage . . . and to freedom.

"The man should be horsewhipped," Lennon O'Malley exploded when he returned from sea and heard what had happened. "He should be put in an old-fashioned block in the public square and his behind switched by everyone in the county."

"Aye, but there's no time for revenge," Edana said. "She's been here over a week, and I'm afraid Sean is getting suspicious. Rooney Sluaghan was here yesterday, knocking on the door, asking had I seen her. He would not have come if Sean hadn't said something to him. Maybe he even told him Kerry's not his true daughter."

"I'm sure he has," Kerry said from where she sat near the fireplace, sipping spiced tea. "He said as much to me when he was drunk, but I didn't remind him when he was sober. It stands to reason he would tell Rooney."

Her ankle was much better. She was able to walk a few steps. And Edana had bandaged her ribs, which weren't hurting as bad as before, so mercifully nothing had been broken. She was feeling stronger, definitely on the mend, and anxious to leave.

Edana had told Lennon what had happened the instant he walked in the door. He had not sat down but began pacing about, scratching his beard as he pondered what to do.

He asked Kerry, "Are you sure this is what you want to do—go to America to find your father?"

Kerry blinked, nodded, wondering why it was even a question. "Why, yes, of course. I have nowhere else to go."

Edana pointed out, "She can go by boat from Galway Bay to Cork and from there take a sailing ship, or maybe one of the new steamers to cross. I've made discreet inquiries but do not know the schedules. Surely with so many wanting to immigrate to America, there will not be a long wait."

"Longer than you might think," Lennon said quietly, thoughtfully. He went to his rocker by the fire to finally sit, then held a straw to the flames in the grate and lit his pipe.

Kerry and Edana exchanged anxious glances. He was being mysteriously reticent, when they had hoped he would be as anxious to hasten her departure from Ireland as they were. Kerry was, after all, still under Sean's charge, being she was an unmarried woman and believed to be his daughter. If he discovered her whereabouts, he could force her to return home. If that happened, there would not be another chance for her to escape. Sean would see to it.

Edana urged, "Lennon, my dear, I know you are tired after being away so long, but we have to move quickly. Each day that passes means danger to Kerry, and—"

"She cannot leave as vulnerable as she is now," he said, pointing a finger in warning. "She would not survive over there."

"I don't understand," Kerry said, slightly defensive. "Once I find my father I will be fine."

"And if you don't find him?" he challenged. "What then? You will be a woman alone in a strange land with no family, no friends. How will you live?"

"There's the money my father sent through the years. I will have that."

She looked to Edana for confirmation, but Edana seemed not to hear as she argued to her husband, "She must leave as soon as possible, I tell you. She is not safe here any longer."

"When is the last time you heard from Flann?" he asked.

"Three years, I think. He wrote that the war was almost over and how glad he was, even though the South was losing."

"What if he was killed in the war?"

Kerry gasped, her hand fluttering to her throat. Though it was a possibility, she could not let herself think it.

Edana had the same attitude. "We have to believe he's alive. I have the map of his farm. You know how he was always hoping Meara would go to him, and he sent specific directions how to find him in a place called North Carolina."

Lennon took a long, deep draw on his pipe before grumpily declaring, "The woman was a fool not to go. Why she lived in hell with Sean O'Day has always been a mystery to me."

"Well, not to me," Edana promptly said. "Her mother only passed away a few months ago. And her father not long before that. She'd never have dared shame them by leaving her lawful husband to go to another man, and she never wanted Kerry to know, anyway."

Kerry shook her head. "I wish she'd told me long ago. I would have been begging her to leave."

Edana patted her hand. "I know you would have, but Meara always feared you might hold it against her. Towards the end, though, she obviously realized she had no choice if you were to have a better life than the one Sean O'Day wants for you.

"That is why she has to go to America," Edana said emphatically, turning on her husband. "And you have to help her."

Lennon sighed. "I suppose you're right. But she can't go as she is now."

Kerry was quick to protest, "But I'm getting stronger every day. And how tedious can a voyage across the ocean be? I'll have nothing to do but rest, and—"

"And that is not what I'm talking about." Lennon fixed a serious gaze upon her. "You must be prepared to take care of yourself should you not find your father."

Edana was beside herself with impatience. "We don't

understand what you mean, Lennon, and this is all taking a toll on me. As much as I want to help her for Meara's sake, and for my brother's sake, the sooner she's out of this house, the better. I shudder to think of what Sean O'Day might do if he finds out we've helped her, and I'm sure he suspects. Who else would have broken the window and got her out of the cellar? He might think Meara confided in me, but he can't be sure, and he doesn't dare confront me without proof. Still, it's best to send Kerry on her way."

"And that we will," Lennon assured. "But after she spends a few weeks in Donegal with my brother, Timothy."

"Timothy? What on earth for?"

Kerry looked from one to the other, wondering what was going on and feeling an edge of panic to think her leaving would be delayed.

Calmly, Lennon explained, "Timothy will teach her what she needs to know so she won't be at the mercy of any man. He will teach her to ride a horse, shoot a gun, as well as milk a cow and tend sheep. Not only will she be able to protect herself, but she'll be a big help to Flann with his farm, as well."

Thinking that way, Edana seemed a little appeased but still worried how long it would be.

"It depends on how fast she learns." Lennon smiled at Kerry for the first time. "How fast do you learn, girl?"

"Very fast," she smiled back, heart filled to bursting with determination. "If it means saving me from the devil that's hounding me, I'm willing to do anything."

Timothy O'Malley was much larger and more rugged than his brother. He could outride and outshoot any man in Ireland. He was also smart enough to eke out a living on land considered unfit for farming, having cleared the fields of stone by hand to smooth the way for potatoes and other vegetables to feed his very large family.

For the next month, he took Kerry under his wing, and by the time she left Donegal, she felt she was fit not only in spirit, but in mind as well, for whatever the future held.

"You still need practice," Timothy said, giving her a gun of her own to keep hidden, as well as a knife to strap to her leg beneath her skirts. "But if you keep your head, you can stand up to any man. Just remember to always look over your shoulder, and never trust anyone who won't look you in the eye."

And on the day she left, he surprised her by saying, "My wife and I have been talking, Kerry, and we want you to know you don't have to go. You can stay and be a part of our family. We've come to love you like our own, even if it's only been for a short while."

Deeply touched, Kerry admitted the offer was tempting but explained, "I really want to go. I've only bad memories here, and I can't help but think that once I get to America they won't haunt me any longer."

"Then Godspeed," he said, hugging her so hard she was gasping for breath. "And remember everything I taught you."

Kerry had thought she would be returning to Galway and setting sail from there. Instead, Timothy took her southwest to Cobh, the port in Cork Harbor.

"It's not safe for you in Galway," he explained. "Lennon sent a message that Sean O'Day is relentless in his attempt to find you. He's been to see Edana and threatened her. And they've heard Rooney has hired men to watch each and every passenger board ships. The only thing to do was have you sail from Cobh."

Kerry did not mind but worriedly asked whether Lennon had also sent money for passage, shyly explaining, "There should be more than enough for my ticket. My mother told me my father had been sending money to Edana for years to keep for her, should she find a way to go to him.''

Timothy said Edana had sent a little package. "I imagine that's what it is. I'll give it to you just before you sail. No need for you to be bothered with it while we travel.''

Kerry desperately wanted it then and there, so she would know exactly how much money she had to survive on till she found her father. But, not wanting to appear concerned, she did not press Timothy to hand over the package.

They traveled by open wagon. Timothy gave her a turn with the reins to give her yet more experience with a team of horses.

The journey took several days through a part of Ireland Kerry had never seen ... but then she had never been outside Galway. There had never been opportunity, and Sean would never have allowed it, anyway.

Rocky headlands met the open Atlantic, where four great mountainous peninsulas parted the waves rushing up to the drowned valleys between them.

Killarney took her breath away with its lakes nestling at the foot of Macgillycuddy's Reeks. Scudding clouds and azure skies framed weathered stone crosses, round towers, and abandoned castles.

The beauty was splendorous, and she found herself wishing that there had been a chance in the past to know, and enjoy, her homeland.

At last they reached Cork, with its wide main streets and narrow alleys. It was situated well inland along the wooded valley of the River Lee, which flowed into the natural harbor of Cobh—and Kerry's point of departure.

They spent the last night in a stone and wood inn. Timothy treated her to a huge meal of lamb stew and hot, buttered soda bread. He even insisted she have a cold glass of ale. "You're a woman on your own. You need a drink now and then.''

Kerry had laughed at that, sure her mother would not

have approved. But the ale tasted good and also relaxed her a bit, for as the time approached, she could not help feelings of apprehension . . . and fear.

"You'll do fine," Timothy told her the next morning as they stood at the pier, waiting to board the ship. He handed over her satchel, as well as the small package from Edana. "I suppose everything you need is in there. She said for you not to worry, and promise to write."

Kerry said she would, and then it was time to say good-bye.

Standing at the ship's railing, she waved until Timothy was almost out of sight, then could wait no longer.

Hurrying to a spot off to herself, Kerry tore open the package. The detailed map was there, along with directions her father had written down. But, to her dismay, there was very little money. However, there was a little velvet pouch, and she opened it with trembling fingers, praying it would somehow hold more.

The morning sun was blazing down, and when it struck the huge stone of the emerald ring, Kerry had to blink against the brilliance. It was beautiful. But what was its meaning, she yearned to know, and where was all the money her father had sent through the years?

There was a letter, and her worst fears were answered as she read:

Dearest Kerry,

Please forgive me. I had not the courage to admit to your face that dire circumstances in the past caused me to spend your father's money. I also have to admit that after many years passed, I felt it would never be needed for the purpose it was intended.

I am giving you what little Lennon and I have managed to gather. I pray it will be enough to see you to your destination.

I also give to you the ring your father wanted you to

have. It belonged to our mother. I hope it will bring you joy.

Again, I beg your forgiveness and pray you have a safe journey.

> *With all my love,*
> *Aunt Edana*

Kerry tried to feel anger but knew that had it not been for Edana, she would doubtless have been dead by now. And she could understand her temptation to use the money when year after year passed and Meara continued to be afraid to leave.

Putting the ring on her finger, Kerry promised herself that somehow she would find a way to survive till she got to her father.

Timothy had done his best to see to it that she knew how to take care of herself, and she would not let him down . . . or her mother.

Because, Godspeed and bless her, she was on her way at last.

Chapter 4

Slade Dillon heard the loud pounding on the door through the sleepy fog that held him captive. He moaned, stirred, but the effort to lift his groggy head from the pillow was too great.

The pounding continued, and someone called his name.

"I think you better see who it is."

His eyes flashed open at the sound of a woman's voice right at his ear.

It all came flooding back—the poker game the night before when Lady Luck had smiled till the wee hours. Winning a lot of money, he had drunk more than usual, and somewhere along the way he had wound up with the yellow-haired woman who was now lying next to him.

She was also naked, he realized as he felt her breast against his arm.

"Don't you remember me, sugar?" she asked with a shrill giggle that set his head to hurting even worse. "My name's Doralee."

She giggled again and slid her fingers down his belly to gently caress him between his legs. "It was real good, honey, and if you'll get rid of the bastard banging on the door, we can do it again.''

Making love was the last thing on Slade's mind. He couldn't have felt worse if he had been thrown from his horse to land in a briar patch. Hell, it wasn't like him to get dog-assed drunk, but since the war, he had done a lot of things he'd never done before.

The door sounded as if it were about to splinter, because whoever was outside wielding their fist was not about to give up.

''Dillon, damn it, I know you're in there. Now open up, or so help me I'll break it down.''

Slade bolted upright and grabbed his gun from the holster hanging at the head of the bed. He cocked the hammer back and pointed it at the door. ''You're fixing to get blown away, stranger.''

The pounding abruptly stopped, and he heard a laugh, followed by, ''Stranger? We rolled in the pits of hell together for four years, and you've forgot me so soon? Damn you, Dillon, I should've let that Reb kill you in Gettysburg back in '63 instead of saving your worthless hide.''

Slade bolted to yank on his trousers, stumbling in his haste. Unbolting the door, he yanked it open and was immediately crushed in a bear hug by his old friend as he cried, ''Sam Pardee, you old goat. What are you doing here, and how'd you find me? I'm on leave. Have been for nearly two weeks.''

Sam stepped back to give him a playful cuff on his jaw. ''There aren't that many white officers at Fort Davis, *Captain* Dillon. I went there, and they said you'd probably be in Pecos, that you didn't usually wander far.''

''There's nowhere to go,'' Slade said dully. He sure as hell couldn't go back to his home in Tennessee unless he wanted a constant fight on his hands. Folks there hated him for siding with the North. His father had died when he was still a boy. His mother had passed on not long after the war after working as a nurse in a field hospital. Wanting to make a new life, Slade had accepted appointment as Captain of the Ninth U.S. Cavalry, a newly organized African-American regiment sent west to reopen Fort Davis in west Texas.

"So now you're a *Buffalo Soldier,* right? Isn't that what the Apaches are calling your regiment?"

Slade smiled. "Yeah, because they claim to see a resemblance between the black soldier's hair and the buffalo's shaggy coat. Actually, it's an honor, since the Indians consider the buffalo a sacred animal."

"And rightfully deserved, too, from what I hear. You and your men are doing a good job fighting the Apache."

Slade's smile faded. "Not good enough. There are still too many raids on settlers, too many attacks on wagon trains. We can't be everywhere at once." His eyes narrowed. "But you didn't come all the way out here to tell me I'm a good soldier."

"That's right. I didn't." Sam looked beyond him to the woman. She had pulled the sheet above her breasts and sat propped against the pillows, watching and listening with interest. He asked Slade, "Is this your room or hers?"

Slade had a vague recollection of having paid for it. "Mine."

"Then can we talk private?"

Slade went to the bed, took some money out of his pocket, and gave it to the woman. "Thanks for a nice night, but it's time you were leaving. We've got business."

She muttered an oath, threw back the sheet, and walked naked across the floor to where she had left her clothes. Sam watched her with interest while Slade went to sit on the side of the bed in hopes the throbbing in his temples would ease up.

Sam noted his suffering. "What you need is some of the hair of the dog that bit you." He reached inside his coat and brought out a flask.

Slade gratefully took a few swallows, then, wiping his

mouth with the back of his hand, agreed, "I think you're right."

Sam helped himself to a drink, then capped the flask and put it away. He was wearing a gray suit, white shirt, and silk vest. "It's hot as hell out here," he said, removing his coat. "I'd rather be back East where it's cooler."

Slade waited till Doralee left, angrily slamming the door behind her. "Well, get to the point of what you're doing here, and you can head on back."

The room was sparsely furnished. Besides the bed and a rickety nightstand, there was a chest of drawers and a wooden chair that sat precariously on three legs. Faded blue curtains fluttered at a window looking down on the main street. It was midmorning, the sun already high in the sky. A few cowboys were milling about in front of the saloon, waiting for it to open, while most everyone else stayed inside, seeking shade.

"Oh, I'll get to that directly," Sam said as he went to the window. He was thoughtfully silent for a moment, then said, "First, I want to say I'm real proud of you for accepting an assignment out here. Not many men would do it, especially commanding black regiments."

Slade lifted his shoulders in a careless shrug. "I've never had a problem with that."

"No, you've never been prejudiced against any man. And to be blunt, a lot of your fellow officers take offense at how you mingle with the lower ranks. Most hold themselves apart from enlisted men."

Slade gave a careless grin. "I guess that goes along with it."

Sam's expression had been amiable, pleased to see the man he had fought side by side with for so many cruel, bloody years. But suddenly his eyes turned grim, along with the lines of his mouth. "That's exactly why I'm here. I need a man who's not prejudiced for a very special assignment."

Slade laughed and threw up his hands as if to ward off

any notion Sam might have. "Whoa, there. I think we had this discussion back in '65 before Lee even surrendered at Appomattox."

Sam did not share his humor. "That's right. We did, when Congress passed an act setting up the Bureau of Refugees, Freedmen, and Abandoned Lands to supervise reconstruction in the South. It came to be known as the Freedmen's Bureau, and I was able to get both of us an appointment to be on it. You turned it down."

Slade nodded, wondering where this was all leading. He had not wanted to go back South where people he had known all his life hated his guts. And anyone else who found out he was Southern-born but fought for the North would feel the same. So he had decided to head west and make a new life fighting Indians instead.

"I'm glad I didn't turn it down," Sam continued. "It's all that kept me going after Martha died."

"It's good that you were able to make a new life for yourself." Slade knew the death of Sam's wife right after the war had left him devastated. No doubt the responsibilities and travel connected with his job had cushioned his grief a bit.

"And what about your life? What will you do once the Indians are under control?"

"Oh, I imagine I'll stake out a piece of land somewhere. Start a herd of cattle and become a rancher."

Sam gave him a sharp look. "You think about that real serious, do you?"

"Actually, I'm not serious about much of anything these days . . . except trying to stay alive."

"You didn't used to be that way. I remember in the early years of the war you talked about going home despite how your neighbors felt and taking back your farm, getting married, and settling down."

Slade winced to remember. That was before he went home on leave to find the girl he had loved with every breath he drew married to someone else and carrying his baby. Mary Beth Canady had promised to wait for him forever. But forever turned out to be less than a year. Like the other folks in the area where he had lived in Tennessee, she had decided she wanted nothing to do with a traitor. Only in Slade's mind, she was the traitor, because she had known where his loyalties were long before then.

"It's because of Mary Beth, isn't it?" Sam gently prodded. "She's the reason you live so reckless."

Slade frowned. Although it had been several years, the hurt was as fresh as the smell of hot biscuits wafting from the cafe across the street. "That's got nothing to do with it," he lied, not about to admit he never intended for a woman to get close enough to him again to break his heart. So when he had needs, he sought out someone like Doralee, who only cared about getting paid for a few hours of pleasure.

Sam's expression indicated he did not believe him.

Slade was losing his patience. His head wasn't hurting as bad as before, but he was hungry. He also wanted a bath and a shave. Still, he was glad to see his old friend and wanted to spend time with him—but not waste it with cat-and-mouse games. "Goddamn it, Sam, get to the point."

"All right." Sam spun around and carefully lowered himself into the rickety chair. "But hear me out . . . hear all I've got to say."

"Then get started."

"The Freedmen's Bureau has always suffered from not having enough money and men to do everything that needed doing. Primarily, we're supposed to distribute food and clothing to anybody in need but, most of all, to look after the freed slaves. They've got no homes, most of them, and they can't get jobs because of who they are—*what* they are. Worse, there's a lot of trouble in the South because of the Ku Klux Klan."

Slade had heard about the hooded vigilantes that had taken it upon themselves to keep what they considered uppity Negroes in line after the war. The Klan had been started, it was said, in his own hometown of Pulaski, Tennessee, sometime in late spring of '68 by six young Confederate officers. Knowing they would be arrested if their identity was discovered, they wore a disguise—white mask with holes for eyes and nose, a high conical cardboard hat which made the wearer seem taller, and a long, flowing robe.

"There have been killings, Slade. Lynchings, burnings, beatings. It's been real bad in middle Tennessee where, as you know, there are die-hard whites who consider themselves victims of oppression. They lost their money, slaves, control of their government. And the sight of free Negroes roaming around puts them in a rage. Things are so bad in Pulaski, especially at night, that no man is safe on the streets alone after dark."

Unable to keep silent any longer, Slade again threw up his hands. "If you're here to try and talk me into joining the Bureau and going to Pulaski to fight a war with a bunch of embittered rednecks, you're wasting your breath. I hear the stories, Sam, and it makes me mad as hell to know what's going on. I don't like it any better than you do. But I won't go back to Pulaski. That would be asking for trouble, and you know it. It wouldn't make any difference to the Klan if I was working for the Bureau. I'm considered a traitor. They wouldn't listen to a damn thing I said."

Sam's laugh was light, shaky, meant to ease the tension but it fell flat. Still, he pointed out, "We don't try to reason with the Klan. We go after the leaders, try to find out who they are in hopes the others will dwindle away without anyone to give orders. But I'm not asking you to go to Pulaski . . . or anywhere else in Tennessee, for that matter."

Slade lifted a curious brow. "Then what?"

"Like I said, hear me out."

"Well, hurry up. I'm getting awfully hungry and this conversation is a waste of time for both of us."

"It won't be when I'm done. Let me tell you a story." Sam shifted in the chair, careful to keep the three legs balanced. "In North Carolina there was a Negro the Klan suspected of thievery. They called him out of his house one night and hung him by the neck from a tree limb several times, raising him just enough so he had to stand on his tiptoes, trying to torture him into confessing. When it didn't work, they beat him bad and ordered him to leave within ten days. When he didn't and went to his former master to complain, his master told him to keep his mouth shut and said the men who had beaten him were ghosts, risen from the dead. The Negro didn't accept that, because there had been sixteen attackers, and he recognized two of them who weren't wearing masks. So he went to the county seat, made a formal complaint against those two, and had them arrested."

"And?" Slade prodded when Sam paused.

"For revenge the others hanged his wife and baby daughter. The Negro then said he made a mistake, and when the two were let go, he wound up beaten to death a few days later.

"What I am saying"—Sam leaned forward, hands gripping his knees—"is that things are getting real bad in North Carolina, and the Bureau doesn't have anybody to send down there. We need you, Slade."

The fierce rumbling in Slade's gut had nothing to do with hunger. He had not felt so sick with rage since the day, when he was only ten years old, that he had watched a slave cruelly beaten to death. The slave had run away, and when he was caught, his master decided to set an example for his other slaves should they be tempted to do the same. So he'd had them all gathered to watch.

Slade had been a witness by accident. He and one of the little Negro boys, the same age as him and one he called friend, had sneaked off to a nearby creek to fish.

Hearing the commotion, they had crept into a plum thicket to look on in horror.

And to make it even worse, the slave who was beaten to death had been his friend's father.

From that day on, Slade had hated slavery and anything to do with it. So when war broke out to abolish it, he had been the first to head North and enlist in the Union Army.

"Slade . . ."

He shook his head, plunged back to the present, but his eyes were still dark with fury, and perspiration dotted his forehead.

"Slade, you can join us and go undercover, and we both know you have a way to do it. I remember your mother—"

"I haven't thought about that in quite a while."

"But you said before your stepfather died—"

Slade cut him off again. "I never thought of him as my stepfather. Hell, I didn't even know they were married till she wrote me he had died. I figured it was something she did because she felt sorry for him and wanted to make his last days easier. She was that kind of woman. Good-hearted to a fault."

Sam gave a vigorous nod to agree. "I know. I know. You told me all about her, but there is a chance that you might still have a claim. Wasn't your"—he started to say stepfather again but checked himself—"the man she married, wasn't he from somewhere around Raleigh? I seem to recall you reading me that from her letter."

"Wayne County. It's about forty miles from Raleigh as the crow flies. I looked it up on a map once because I was curious."

"You think you would have moved there with your mother had she lived?"

"Maybe. But like I said—I put it out of my mind. The property was probably sold for taxes long ago."

"You could buy it back. Don't you see? It would be the perfect cover for you. You'd blend right in with everybody else, and I'll bet two shots of popskull that before long the Klan will be after you to join."

Slade sucked in his lower lip, then felt the sudden need for a smoke. He leaned to take his uniform shirt from where it had been carelessly tossed the night before. Taking out paper and tobacco pouch, he rolled, then lit.

Sam waited, and when long, tense moments passed, he said, "Would it make any difference if I told you General Howard sent me here on his behalf to personally ask you to join us?"

Slade turned sharp eyes upon him. "You know damn well it would." General Oliver Howard was a man he respected more than anyone he knew. In charge of the Union's Eleventh Corps, he had seen to it that Slade got promoted up the ranks, all the way to captain. He was smart, decisive under stress, and brave as they came. "Why didn't you tell me right off he sent you here?"

Sam's wrinkled face split with a wide grin. "I guess I wanted to see if you'd do it for me. I figure you owe me."

"And just how do you figure that?" Slade's eyes were twinkling. He knew what was coming.

"That Reb in Gettysburg—"

Slade cut him off. "I know. If not for you, that Reb at Gettysburg would have put me in my grave. I believe you mentioned that when you first got here."

With mock severity, Sam declared, "I reckon I have to remind you often, because you damn well seem to forget it."

"Not with you around."

"So will you do it? Will you join the Bureau and help us destroy the Klan?"

Slade knew his mind had been made up the instant he learned General Howard was behind it all. "I guess I have to either say yes or starve to death listening to you rub it in that you saved my life."

Sam, relieved, slapped his knees hard. The three-legged chair wobbled to one side, dumping him on the floor.

With both of them laughing, Slade helped him up, shook his hand to seal the agreement, then finished dressing. He knew he was wearing his Army uniform for the last time, and, with a twinge of concern, wondered if he was doing the right thing.

Something told him that fighting Apaches would be a hell of a lot easier than waging war on the Klan.

After all, when he faced Apaches, Slade could be sure of just who the enemy was.

Kerry stared dismally at the map.

She could not remember ever being so tired in her life. But it was not due to the voyage from Ireland. Though her accommodations in steerage had been bleak—only a hammock hanging in a corner of the women's dormitory— she had managed to rest, eat lots of fruit and vegetables, and make a few friends to pass the time with.

It was the trip from New York that had been exhausting. She had to go by crowded stagecoach to Philadelphia because railroad tracks were being repaired. Once there, she had to wait three days for a train that would take her on to North Carolina. With no money left after paying for her ticket, she could not afford a hotel room and had slept under steps or hidden in livery stables. Hunger had driven her to rummaging in trash barrels.

So now she stood outside a railroad station that looked as dilapidated and worn-out as she felt. The sign above the door read Goldsboro.

She knew the map by heart but studied it again just to make sure. As best she could figure, her father's farm was a few miles farther to the southwest.

She shifted her bag from right hand to left, shoulders aching. She would have to walk the rest of the way. It was midafternoon, and she probably could not get to her destination by dark but knew she had to try. Besides, a woman and a little girl were sitting on a bench nearby eating pieces of something brown and crispy that looked, and smelled, delicious. It was torture to watch.

She had only gone a few steps when the woman called out to her. "Miss? Oh, miss?"

Kerry turned, swaying at the smell of the food.

"Miss, would you like some of our fried chicken? I don't mean to embarrass you, but you look hungry."

Kerry licked her lips, too embarrassed to accept. "No, thank you. I'm fine, really."

"Please," the woman beckoned. "We have plenty. I'm waiting on my husband, but I know the train from Raleigh is always late so I made a little picnic to help pass the time. And goodness knows, I'm used to seeing hungry people, and I always share my food when I can."

She held up a drumstick, and Kerry could not resist. "Well, if you're sure you have enough . . ." She hurried to perch on the end of the bench. She took the chicken with quiet politeness, but once it was in her hand she could not help devouring it.

"My, you are hungry," the woman murmured. "I was right. And that's a strange accent you have. Where are you from?"

Kerry swallowed and said, "Ireland. I come from Ireland. I'm going to live with my father," she added proudly.

"Is he from around here?"

"Oh, yes, ma'am. According to my map"—she pointed with her free hand to where it lay in her lap—"it's not too terribly far from here. A few miles, perhaps, but I don't mind walking—not when I've already come so far." Her eyes were shining to think the long journey was almost over and her new, wonderful life about to begin. But, most of all, she was overcome with joy at the thought that soon she would come face to face with her real father. He would love her. She was sure of it. And she would love him, too, and—

"May I see it?" The woman gestured to the map. "I've

lived here all my life, and I know everyone. I may be able to help you."

"Oh, please," Kerry said quickly, handing it to her.

The woman went on to sadly lament how so much had changed since the war. "A lot of folks have lost their land for taxes." She wrinkled her nose and whispered to add, "Or the blasted Yankees confiscated it. My husband, Ethan, and I were lucky, though, because he's a doctor. When Sherman's army came through, and there was that terrible battle at Bentonville, he did what any good doctor would do and cared for wounded Yankee soldiers, as well. So we've been treated better than most by the occupational troops.

"I'm Abigail Ramsey, by the way," she added. "And this is my daughter, Belinda."

Kerry expressed her pleasure to meet them both, then said worriedly, "My father was a Confederate soldier. I hope the Yankees didn't take his land because of that."

She was about to help herself to another piece of chicken from the box Belinda held out to her but hesitated when she noticed that Abigail was looking at her with—what? Pity?

"Is this your father's name written by the X—Flann Corrigan?"

Suddenly Kerry was frightened and did not know why. A strange tingling was worming its way up her spine, and her knees began to knock together. "Yes. Why? What's wrong?"

Abigail shoved the map into Kerry's hands. "I think you should go to the courthouse and ask for better directions at the clerk's office. Your father's farm won't be as easy to find as you think. Things have changed since that map was drawn." She took the box of chicken from her daughter's hand and gave it to Kerry, then said, "Come along, Belinda. We need to find somewhere you can wash your face before your daddy's train gets here."

She walked away, calling over her shoulder, "Good luck to you, Miss Corrigan."

Kerry stared after her, the knot of foreboding that had tightened in her throat making it impossible to speak.

Something was wrong.

Terribly wrong.

Taking the rest of the chicken with her, because she knew she had to eat, regardless of what lay in store, she went to the dispatch window and asked directions to the courthouse.

"Two blocks that way," the man behind the wooden bars pointed without glancing up.

She would have run had her legs not been so weak with dread.

The streets were crowded. She cringed to see men wearing tattered gray trousers and shirts, hobbling along on crutches. Most people, she noted, were poorly dressed, but now and then she saw nattily dressed men. They wore white shirts with brocade vests and elegant waistcoats. Shiny leather boots peeked out from beneath tight-fitting trousers. And they all seemed to be carrying colorful bags that looked as though they were made of a carpet-like material.

Just as she reached the courthouse, she saw an old woman sitting on the steps. Her clothes were nothing but rags. She seemed to be in some kind of trance, her eyes staring vacantly from a face that mirrored sorrow and despair.

Kerry started by her, but just then one of the men carrying a colorful bag brusquely passed. Bumping her, he stumbled against the woman. The woman's head snapped up, and when she saw him, she screamed, "Dirty Yankee carpetbagger. Damn you to hell."

She spat at his feet.

The man gave her a glare of disgust and continued on his way.

The woman then focused on Kerry. "Vultures. That's

what they are. Feeding on the carrion that is the South. I wish them all to rot in hell."

A soldier, standing at the courthouse door, came stomping down the steps. "It's time for you to move on," he warned, towering over her, "or I'll have to arrest you for disturbing the peace."

"Wait till you have a really good reason," she said, glaring at him as she struggled to stand, "like me really losing my temper and putting my fist in some dirty carpetbagger's mouth."

Kerry reached to help her up, and the soldier shot her a look that told her she was interfering. She threw one right back to let him know she was not intimidated.

"Be off with you now," he said as the woman shuffled away. Then he turned to Kerry. "These old war widows can be a nuisance, miss. It's best you don't get involved."

"And it's best if you mind your own business," she said with an arrogant toss of her long red hair. "I'll help anyone I choose."

With a swish of her tattered skirt, she continued on inside the courthouse.

Inside, she found a door with a sign proclaiming Land Records. Entering, she handed her map to the man standing behind the counter and explained, "Someone said I should ask for directions to my father's farm, because this is an old map and roads and things have changed."

He looked at it and said, "I'll check on it. Your father's name is Flann Corrigan, like it's written here?"

"That's right."

"Sounds familiar. Wait here."

He went into another room. She heard the sound of drawers opening and closing, papers being shuffled. When he returned, his expression was the same as Abigail Ramsey's had been after she saw the map—one of sympathy and pity.

He cleared his throat and pushed it across the counter. "I'm real sorry to have to be the one to tell you this, miss, but your father was killed in the war. Now, about his land . . ."

Kerry, knees buckling as she fainted, heard nothing more.

Chapter 5

Kerry shook her head slowly from side to side. Something sharp, pungent, was being pressed to her nostrils, making her nose burn and her eyes sting.

She was wrapped in a velvet cocoon of oblivion and wanted to stay there. To return to consciousness would mean facing grief too great to bear.

From somewhere far away she heard an anxious voice. "Lady, wake up. Are you all right? Lady, please . . ."

A hand patted her face.

"Come on now. You've got to wake up."

A different voice spoke. "Here. This ought to do it."

When the cold water hit her face, Kerry jerked upright, coughing and gasping.

"See? I told you it would work."

"Well, I didn't want to get her all wet."

The second voice snickered. "Looks to me like she could use a bath."

Kerry sat up to wipe her face with the backs of her hands, then blinked at the two men towering over her. She was lying on a wooden bench in the room where she had fainted. Pieces of fried chicken from the box she had been holding were scattered about the floor.

"Are you all right now?"

It was the clerk who spoke, and he sounded as if he cared. The other man looked annoyed.

Kerry could not find her voice. It was buried somewhere in the anguish that was squeezing down, making it hard to breathe.

"Look, I'm real sorry. I know it was a shock, hearing about your pa, but you can't stay here. Is there anybody you want me to send for?"

She shook her head. "No. There's no one."

The other man snickered again, and, her eyes focusing at last, she recognized him as the one who had been so unkind to the old woman on the steps. *Carpetbagger*, the woman had called him.

"She's just another whiner," he said. "She had to have known he was dead by now. She just wants a handout. I saw her right before she came in here. She wheedled that fried chicken that's now all over the floor from Doc Ramsey's wife. You know how she is with these beggars."

Rage tore Kerry's voice free. "I resent your accusations, sir. I am not a beggar. And I did not know my father was dead, or I wouldn't have traveled across the ocean to find him. And I will thank you to stay out of my business. None of this concerns you, and I want nothing to do with your kind." She was on the verge of tears but refused to succumb to any sign of weakness. Because, amidst her sorrow, she was fighting mad at anyone and anything connected with the damnable war that had killed her father. And right then, her wrath was focused on the carpetbagger.

The man's face reddened as he sputtered, "Why . . . why, you little upstart. Who do you think you're talking to? I'll report you as a vagrant, and the soldiers will lock you up and—"

"Mr. Douglas, leave it be, please," the clerk cut him off. "She's not from around here. Don't you hear her accent?

It's Irish. I know, because my mother came from Ireland, and she sounds just like her. Now, why don't you go your way and let me handle this?''

Kerry glared at the carpetbagger. "I think that's a wonderful idea.''

She was amazed at her sudden show of spirit. In the past, she had accepted whatever life dealt her but knew that had been because of her mother. To have stood up to Sean O'Day would have brought his choler down on both of them. Now, things were different. She was in a strange land and fired with determination to survive. Though weak from hunger, and dazed by the shock to learn her father was dead, Kerry nonetheless knew she had no choice but to fight back.

And she also knew it was what her father would want her to do.

The carpetbagger, bristling, snapped, "I will leave when I have finished my business and not before." He demanded of the clerk, "I want the list for this week's auction.''

"It isn't ready yet. Come back tomorrow.''

"You had better damn well have it ready by then. And see to it you do something about this . . . this beggar.'' With a last venomous glare at Kerry, he turned on his heel and walked out.

The clerk sat down beside her. "I'm real sorry about that, miss. Mr. Douglas gets upset once in a while because of the way people treat him and others like him.''

"Carpetbaggers,'' Kerry said.

"Yes. Because of their satchels. They come from the North with lots of money and buy up land. We Southerners despise them, but there's nothing we can do about it.'' He leaned to look her full in the face. "Are you sure you're all right? You didn't get hurt when you hit the floor? I wish I'd been on the other side of the counter so I could've caught you and—''

"No, I'm all right, really. It was just a shock. I never thought . . .'' She shook her head. "I won't burden you with my problems. And I know now why Mrs. Ramsey told me to come here. She didn't want to be the one to tell me my father is dead. So if you'll draw in the new roads on the map, I'll be on my way.

"That is," she added warily, "if my father's land hasn't been sold."

"As a matter of fact, it's on the list Mr. Douglas was wanting to see. It's been up for sale a few times, but nobody has taken an interest in it, because it's not near town. The carpetbaggers want land they can build houses on, stores, things they can make money on. Farms bring very little."

"Did you know my father?"

"Only vaguely. I'd see him when he came in to pay his taxes. To tell you the truth, I hadn't thought about him in years till I looked up the deed. Then I remembered him being killed and how nobody has wanted the land. It just sits there. He listed a few slaves on his tax records. With nobody to run them off, they're probably still living there, though the Lord only knows how they get by."

Kerry was eyeing the chicken on the floor. It would be humiliating to pick it up, but hunger was pushing pride aside. Legs still wobbly, she got the box and knelt down.

The clerk was horrified. "Oh, please. Don't do that. I'll give you some money to buy food."

She continued until she had retrieved every piece, then said, "This will do nicely. I can brush away the dirt, though I don't see much." She smiled. "But thank you for your offer."

"Well, I just wish I could do something to help."

She could tell he was sincere and ventured to say, "You could leave my father's farm off the auction list this week and give me time to see what I can do about it."

"I'm sorry. I can't do that. It has to stay on every week till it sells. I'd get in trouble if I removed it. And as bad as I hate to say it, little lady, it will eventually sell, and there's nothing you can do unless you can pay the taxes."

"I have no money," she hated to admit. "But as long

as the land belongs to my father, it belongs to me, and I'll have a place to live . . . a roof over my head."

He was sympathetic but had to ask, "Do you even have proof you're Flann Corrigan's daughter? I mean, as it stands, you have no claim to the land."

"But I do," she was quick to inform him, reaching into her satchel to take out the bundle of letters from her father. "He wrote in several of these that he wanted me to have his land. Isn't that proof enough?"

"It is for me, so I tell you what I'm going to do. I'll stick my neck out and pull the farm off the list for this week, anyway, and get you a little time, though I don't know what good it will do you."

Her smile was thin. "You never know, sir. Sometimes miracles do happen."

His expression said he did not share her optimism.

Sure enough, Kerry needed the new markings on the map. A bridge her father had drawn had been burned out and rebuilt so far down the Neuse River that she would never have found her way.

As she walked slowly along, she was sickened by the remaining signs of conflict between North and South. It had been several years, but the terrain was still gutted and blackened by the fires of war. Few trees had dared to bud into new life, most standing stark against the sky, grim sentinels to remind of the tortured years of civil strife.

It was getting on into summer, and the heat was unbearable. Kerry wished for a bonnet, like the ones she saw some of the women wearing in fields just outside Goldsboro. Another hour of walking, however, and she saw little sign of life. Broken-down fences and barren fields as far as the eye could see. And never had she seen such flat land. No hills or mountains, just level ground.

The farther she walked, the heavier her heart. How was she going to eke out a living from the land? Despite all she'd been told, she knew little about farming and had no money to buy seeds for planting, anyway. As for the taxes owed on the land, all she could do was pray it would remain unwanted. She could then live on it, at least have a home and . . .

A sob rattled through her body, making her quake from head to toe. She stumbled and almost fell.

What difference did it make? she asked herself bitterly. She could not survive on her own. The thing to do was turn around and go back—but to where? Even if she wanted to return to Ireland, she had no means. Still, it seemed foolish to keep trudging on towards wasteland. In Goldsboro, she might find work. She had seen several saloons. When she told of her experience in the pub back home, she might be able to find a job.

Yet, with all the rationale spinning in her head, giving up was not what she wanted. All she had left of the father she had never known was his land, and she felt driven to save it. Not only to honor his memory, but her mother's as well. By living there, she would feel like a part of them . . . a part of something. And being alone in a foreign land, belonging seemed terribly important.

She did not feel well. She stumbled more frequently and had not passed water since the river and was terribly thirsty. The piece of chicken she had eaten did not stay in her stomach very long, and after it made her sick she threw the rest away.

The sun was sinking lower in the western sky. Soon it would be dark. She looked at the map but had no idea how long it would take to reach her destination . . . if she could even find it. Panic clawed to think she might be lost.

Her head began to pound, and she was having difficulty focusing her eyes. Everything seemed blurred. And, dear God, she was so hot, even though the sun was going down.

On she plodded, each step more difficult than the last.

From somewhere far away she heard a dog bark. That could mean people . . . or it might mean a dog was as lost and lonely as she was. Maybe they would meet. A dog would be nice, she thought dizzily. Then she would not be alone.

She laughed aloud to think how wonderful it would be to have a dog. Her father—no *stepfather*, she chided herself for not remembering—had hated all animals. As a child, she had begged for a puppy, and once he had even beaten her for pestering him about it.

She tried to walk faster. The dog was still barking and the sound seemed to be a little closer. She attempted to whistle, but her lips were too parched and dry. Pursing them brought pain and the taste of blood to her mouth.

"Here, boy," she called, but her rasping voice was barely audible.

She stumbled again. If only darkness would come she would be cool. If only trees had leaves she could . . .

Could what?

There was a giant roaring in her head, wiping out all reason. Frightened, she pressed her hands to her temples, swaying from side to side. The hunger, the heat, the weariness and thirst were taking their toll all at once.

She stumbled again.

And this time she did not get up.

"Who do you reckon she is, Bessie?"

"You're askin' me? How should I know?"

"She looks real poorly, don't she? You think she's gonna die?"

"Hush up, Luther. Don't be talkin' like that. She's down with the fever, that's all. I've packed bacon rinds around her neck, and I'm gonna spoon her some of my onion syrup. A few days, and she'll be fine."

Kerry heard the voices but did not open her eyes. As long as they thought she was still unconscious, they would continue talking about her, and she might learn who they were, where she was, and, most of all, if she was in any kind of danger.

So far, they seemed anxious to help. She could also tell by their dialect they were colored . . . Negroes, they were called. And, from all she had learned since arriving in the South, they were as bad off as she was. So perhaps their plight would bond her to them.

A gentle hand slipped behind her head to lift it, and she felt something being pressed against her lips.

"Come on, honey. Wake up and eat this. You got to get strong."

The voice, the words, were so compassionate that Kerry's eyes fluttered open so she could see who spoke them.

"Lordy, you're awake."

The woman was so startled that some of the foul-tasting syrup spilled on Kerry's face.

"Oh, I'm sorry. I didn't mean to do that. What's your name, child?"

Kerry saw that the woman was not too old, perhaps the age her mother had been. Her face was thin and gaunt, but her eyes were warm as sunshine. A faded bandana was wrapped about her head, concealing her hair.

The man standing behind her, anxiously staring over her shoulder, had hair the color of the cotton Kerry had seen struggling to grow in the parched fields. He, too, was on the lean side.

Kerry flashed cursory glances about the room. She was lying on a bed with rusting iron posters. The only other furniture was a small table with benches and some rickety-looking chairs. The floor was dirt.

"This is where we live," the woman said, knowing Kerry was wondering about her surroundings. "It ain't much. But when the master was alive, it was nicer. The Yankees took most of what we had.

"My name's Bessie, by the way," she added. "And this here is my man, Luther. Our boy, Adam, is out rootin' in the fields, diggin' for taters and anything else he can find."

"How . . . how long have I been here?" Kerry tried to lift her head but the effort was too great.

"Since yesterday. Adam found you in the road. He brought you here. But now don't you be doin' no talkin' till I get some of my syrup in you. Then you'll feel better. You got a touch of the fever, that's all. And I don't reckon you've had much to eat lately, either."

The onion concoction tasted terrible, but something told Kerry the woman meant her no harm. The bacon rinds wrapped around her neck were another matter, however, and when Bessie seemed satisfied she'd had enough of the syrup, Kerry said, "Get them off of me, please," and gestured to the greasy strips.

Bessie looked uncertain. Then, pressing a hand to Kerry's cheek, she said, "I reckon it'll be all right. You aren't hot like you were."

Luther brought a bowl of thin potato soup, and Kerry ate every drop.

When she had finished, Bessie asked, "You reckon you're ready to tell us your name now . . . and what you're doin' way out here by yourself? It's not safe for a lady alone, you know. And I can already tell by the way you talk you ain't from around here."

Luther gave a soft chuckle. "Almost sounds like the master, don't she?"

He had Kerry's attention. "What did you say?"

He glanced at Bessie worriedly, as though afraid he might have said something to offend.

Bessie spoke when he feared to. "He said you sounded like the master—the man we used to belong to."

Kerry's breath caught in her throat. "Might that be Flann Corrigan?"

Bessie's eyes went wide. "Praise be, yes, child. Did you know him?"

"He was my father."

Bessie murmured, "Dear Jesus," and swayed as if she were going to faint.

Luther looked at Kerry and said, "You . . . you must be Miss Kerry."

"You've heard of me?"

"Oh, child," Bessie gave an adoring chuckle. "Master Flann, he was all the time talkin' about you. Through the years when he'd get a letter from your mama from across the ocean, he'd tell us what she said—how big you was gettin', how pretty you were."

Luther ducked his head, unable to look at Kerry as he whispered, "I'm so sorry to tell you this, but your daddy died in the war, Miss Kerry."

"I know," she said. "I didn't find out till I arrived in Goldsboro."

Bessie sighed. "Such a long trip for nothin'. Now you gotta just turn around and go back, 'cause there's no reason for you to stay here unless you brought lots of money with you so's you can pay the taxes and keep from starvin' till you can get new crops goin'. All the horses and mules are gone. Cows, too."

Luther said Flann's house was still standing. "But the Yankees stripped it clean, too. It was such a pretty little house. He kept saying one day he was gonna bring you and your mama to live in it. But it's empty now, 'cept for a little bit of furniture the Yankees couldn't carry off 'cause their wagons were full."

Kerry saw their despair and knew life had to be terrible for them. "But how have you survived since my father went away?"

Luther explained that in the beginning there was plenty of food. "We had vegetables. We had chickens. And there was crops, too. Your pa was growin' cotton. And he had just started growin' tobacco. He said it was gonna be the crop to make North Carolina one of the best farmin' places in all of America.

"We took care of everything for him when he went off to the war," he proudly went on to declare. "And he'd come home once in a while and stay a few days and tell us how good we was doin'. He'd give us what money he could to keep things runnin'."

"And you didn't leave after the war, when you were set free?" Kerry asked with all innocence.

Bessie looked aghast. "Oh, missy, we was never slaves. Your pa, he gave us our papers after he bought us. He said he didn't hold to keepin' no man in bondage, but he needed workers. So he told us if we stayed and worked for him, he'd see to it we had a roof over our head and food in our stomachs. And bless him for the fine man he was, he kept his word as long as he could.

"But when he didn't come back," she added, her dark eyes brimming with tears, "we knowed he was dead. Adam, my oldest boy, he walked all the way into town to get somebody to read him the names off the list of the dead posted on the courthouse door. I think he must've cried all the way home from the way his eyes were swollen when he got back."

"We've been scrapin' by since the Yankees came through like a pack of vultures," Luther said, resentment thick in his voice.

Bessie rushed to say, "We loved your daddy, Miss Kerry. And we know we'd have loved you, too, for bein' part of him. It's sad you come all this way and now have to turn around and go right back where you came from."

Kerry managed to muster the strength from somewhere deep within to get up and walk slowly to the window and gaze out as she said, "I've nowhere to go back to, Bessie. My mother is dead. The only home I have is here, so this is where I'll stay."

Behind her back Bessie and Luther exchanged incredulous glances. Then Luther asked, "But how will you live, missy? We ain't got no money. And unless you do, this place is gonna be sold for taxes sooner or later. They keep comin' around, lookin' at the place, every month when they have the sale. Nobody's wanted it yet, but Adam said when he was in town a few days ago he heard a lot of men were comin' in on the train this week with bags of money anxious to buy up all the land they can get their hands on."

Ire rising, Kerry snapped, "This was my father's land, and now it's mine, and no one is going to take it away from me. Somehow, I'll find a way to keep it."

"You do, and we'll stay and help you," Luther assured.

She turned to look at them, hope surging. "You would? Even if I can't pay you? Even if I can only do as my father did—give you food and shelter?"

Luther saw Bessie's nod of assent but frowned to prod Kerry, "You never did answer her when she asked if you brought money, missy. We don't have nothin'."

Kerry hated to have to tell him, "I'm afraid I spent everything I had to get here."

Luther sighed and began to shuffle wearily towards the door. "Then there ain't no need in talkin', 'cause with no money you can't get no crops started or buy food or nothin'."

Turning from the window, she begged, "Give me a few days, please, to get my strength back. Then I'll think of something, I promise. But don't give up, please."

Luther kept on going, head bent.

Kerry looked to Bessie. "We'll manage somehow, Bessie. You have to believe me."

Bessie managed a wan smile. "I reckon we got no choice, missy." She went outside to sit on the porch step with Luther.

"I'll do it," Kerry vowed under her breath as she looked out the window once more at the land her father had loved . . . had wanted so desperately for her to have.

"I have to," she whispered, voice breaking. "Because it's all I have in this world."

Chapter 6

In the weeks that followed, Kerry quickly fell in love with the land.

Her father had built his house on the only place that had a slight rise, and it looked down on a gently flowing stream.

Beyond, she could imagine what a breathtaking sight it must have been when cotton dotted the fields in popcorn blossoms of white. Now, sadly, the stalks were gnarled and rotted.

The barn was in ruins. Luther's son Adam had told her how he and the other Negroes had tried their best to put out the fire after General Sherman's army came through. They had formed a bucket brigade to the stream but were unable to save it.

Kerry had sifted through the dirt and ashes to find only a halter, unscathed because it had fallen under a metal bucket that had partially melted but not burned completely. Lovingly she held it in her hands each evening as she sat on the porch steps, thinking about her father. No doubt he had sat there, as well, but instead of a harness had caressed her mother's letters, dreaming dreams of what might have been . . . and bemoaning what could not be.

Before leaving Ireland, she had sewn the emerald ring inside the hem of her skirt. Her fear was that some scalawag might put a knife to her throat and take it before she could whisk her own blade from where it was strapped to her ankle to defend herself. Now, however, she wore the ring on her finger.

It was midmorning as she sat once again on the steps, knees hugged to her chin as she gazed out into the hot summer day.

Things were not as bleak as when she had first arrived; at least there were not many nights when she went to bed hungry. She and Bessie had found some stray chickens and a rooster in the woods one day when they were picking blackberries. Now there were fresh eggs every day, and they had enjoyed a nice stew with a few of the fat hens. Three were also setting, so there would be baby chicks soon.

But the real thrill had come when Adam found a wandering cow and brought it home. They all shared the milk, along with the chore of milking. Kerry laughed out loud to think how they sometimes played and squirted each other while milking.

Then it dawned on her that the laughter was coming easier these days. She and her new friends truly enjoyed working together.

No one talked anymore about the dreaded taxes. Kerry dared think that because of the distance of the farm from town the carpetbaggers would continue not to be interested. Though it might prove to be foolish optimism, it was far better than worrying about it all the time.

Stretching her arms above her head in the sweltering heat, she decided she could not postpone the berry-picking any longer. If she waited for evening and cooler temperatures, the mosquitoes would eat her alive. The berry patch was also near where the stream entered the thick woods, and there was always the danger of a bear feeding or maybe even a boar hog. So she needed to pick in the heat and daylight.

No one was around to help. Bessie, Luther, and Adam had all gone to help some freed slaves who lived a few miles down the road dress a wild boar someone had killed. In exchange, they would be given a little meat, and they were all looking forward to a delicious supper. Kerry's contribution would be blackberry dumplings. Sugar and flour were in short supply, but Bessie had swapped a chicken for enough of both to last a while.

Kerry put on the bonnet Bessie had given her, saying it would help keep her from having sun sickness.

Then, with bucket in hand, she walked along the stream to the berry patch.

It was a nice day. Not a cloud in the sky. Kerry hummed as she picked the plump, juicy berries. Now and then she would pop a few in her mouth, delighting in the sweetness.

Life, she thought, was good. No matter that times were hard and it was a struggle to survive. It was far better than her existence would have been had she stayed in Ireland.

Lost in thought, she forgot to worry about bears or wild hogs or anything else.

Thus, she did not hear anyone approaching until he was right behind her.

"Ah, a wood nymph. I knew if I looked hard enough I would find something beautiful left around here."

She whirled about, dropping the bucket. The berries scattered on the bank, most rolling into the stream. "Who . . . who are you?" she asked irritably as she stooped to retrieve what she could. "You've no right sneaking up on me like that."

He sat atop a magnificent black horse, and he bent forward in the ornate saddle and tipped his hat to her. "Allow me to introduce myself. The name is Lorne Petrie.

And I apologize for frightening you. I would have thought you'd heard my horse."

"Well, I didn't." She was careful to keep her skirt about her ankles so he would not see the knife. He was well-dressed and did not look at all fearsome, but she would take no chances.

Raising her hand to shade her eyes against the sun, she looked him up and down. He wore fine clothes. His silk shirt was open at the throat. His riding breeches appeared to be made of suede, tucked into fine leather knee-high boots. Obviously, he was a man of means.

"So what do you want?" she asked bluntly, not liking his smug grin.

"I told you my name. Don't you think it would be the polite thing for you to tell me yours?"

"I haven't decided yet whether there is any reason for you to know it. You haven't told me what you're doing here."

He gave his head a reckless toss and chuckled, "Ah, so I am given to believe that it would be your business."

"I would say so," she retorted sharply, "being that this is my land, and you're trespassing. And if you aren't going to tell me what you want, then I'll be asking you to leave."

He snapped his fingers. "Irish. You're Irish, aren't you? I detect the brogue. I had an Irish nanny once. A sweet lady but not nearly as lovely as you, my little colleen."

Kerry was losing patience. Fast. Hands on her hips, she glared up at him. "I am not your little anything, sir, and I'll thank you to be on your way. You've caused me to lose almost all my berries, and I have to find more."

"First, I want you to tell me by what right you claim this land. I was told it had been abandoned."

She tensed. "It was my father's. It's mine now."

He lifted a brow. "And I suppose you have some sort of proof?"

He had black eyes that stared down at her beneath thick eyebrows. His facial features were hard, chiseled, and he had a deep cleft in his chin. There were flecks of gray in his dark hair, and his neatly clipped mustache gave him an aristocratic air. Yet there was something about him that made her take instant dislike. "I don't have to prove anything to you."

"Well, you are certainly going to have to prove something to someone." He reached behind him and took out several pieces of paper from his saddlebag. Glancing over them, he found what he was looking for and asked, "Would your name be Corrigan?"

Kerry felt a chill shoot up her spine. She gave a reluctant nod.

"I thought so. I'm good at following maps, and I didn't think I was lost. This land"—he shook the papers at her—"is up for sale for delinquent taxes. It's been in every list for weeks.

"And I am going to buy it," he added with an insolent wink. "So you will soon be trespassing on my land, Miss Corrigan."

"I . . . I think not, sir," she managed to say over the angry pounding in her temples. "Now go, please."

"Oh, I've lots of time," he said with an airy sniff. "There are two other farms being auctioned before this one. A friend of mine is interested in them, and I didn't want to bid against them, so I came here to look this one over." His eyes raked her with a heated gaze. "And so far, I like what I've seen just fine. Perhaps we can work something out for you to stay on after I buy it."

"There is nothing to be worked out," Kerry cried, fists clenched. "And you aren't buying it. This is my land, and as soon as I have the money, I intend to pay the taxes. What do you want it for, anyway? You can see it's in great disrepair—like all the South.

"And it's far from town," she quickly added, clinging to the desperate hope that the reason it had been saved from sale thus far would prevail. "You have no use for it way out here."

He wagged a finger. "Ah, but I do. You see, I might have no need just now, but in the future it will be worth something. Then I can sell it for a nice profit. The South will not always be on its knees, little colleen. It may take some years and a lot of hard work, but there will come a time when it prospers.

"Just look at the lay of this land," he said, sweeping an arm in gesture. "Perfect for tobacco as well as cotton. And with this stream, it's even more valuable. I do have a reason to buy it . . . which I intend to do when the auctioneer and soldiers get here."

"Why . . . why soldiers?" Fear made her voice a thin ribbon, barely audible.

"They always go to the auctions in case they are needed to evict those reluctant to leave—like you. Sometimes people do not like to admit when they're beaten, Miss Corrigan."

"I'm not beaten, Mr. Petrie. And believe me, they will have to drag me away. Now go. You're just another dirty, greedy carpetbagger." She snatched up the bucket and turned back to the berry patch. She would not be intimidated, would not let him frighten her.

"Don't call me names," he cried fiercely, leaping from the horse to come up behind her and grab her arms and squeeze tightly. "And don't be insolent with me."

She twisted in his grasp, but he held her tight, hands groping at her breasts, and with heated breath whispered in her ear, "It doesn't have to be this way, you little fool. I told you—we can work something out. Now stop fighting me."

But Kerry was not about to yield. She continued to struggle mightily, straining to get to her knife.

"I like your spirit. Already I find you pretty, and when you're cleaned up, with stylish clothes, you'll be a beauty. I'll be proud to have you for my mistress—"

"Your what?" Kerry yelped. "I'd rather die." She managed to sink her teeth into his arm.

With a cry, he let her go but shoved her roughly to the ground as he did so.

She went for the knife.

He saw in time and swiftly kicked her. The knife went flying into the brush, and she cried with pain and grabbed at her ankle.

Then he was upon her, pinning her down as he straddled her. "Now listen to me," he said harshly when she could no longer move and was struggling to breathe. "You don't look like a stupid girl. And you should realize there are very few options for desperate people like you. I'll let you live here. I'll even fix up the place and give you money. I can't have you in town. My wife might find out."

She bit out the words between anguished gasps for air, "I . . . would . . . rather . . . die."

He gave her such a shake her head bounced up and down on the ground. "Foolish little hellion. Do you know how many women would leap at such an offer? Look at you—your tattered dress of muslin and—" He was holding her wrists as she fought to break his grasp, and that was when he saw the ring she was wearing. "Now where would a ragamuffin like you get a jewel like this?"

He tried to pull it from her finger, but she squeezed her hands into tight fists. "You won't get it . . ."

"Oh, I'll take anything I want, and it's time you found that out."

He maneuvered to hold both her wrists in one hand and, with his other, plunged downwards to yank up her skirt. Thrusting a knee between her legs, he spread them apart.

She was vulnerable beneath him as he began to eagerly grope.

"I'll show you how good it can be," he said, running his tongue down her cheek as she screamed and twisted her head from side to side. "Then you'll be glad to be my mistress. You'll live like a queen. And when you get tired of this pigsty of a farm, maybe I'll move you to something more fitting in Raleigh. You won't have to grovel ever again, my sweet."

"I'll see you dead, you bastard." She fought to bring her knee up against him, but he roughly shoved it down.

"I don't want to be rough, but I will. Now stop fighting me. I'm going to have you, and you might as well enjoy it."

She thrashed beneath him, determined to fight to the death if need be.

"I want to see more of you," he taunted, taking his hand from between her legs to undo the buttons at the bodice of her dress. "I want to see you naked. And I'd prefer to have you in a bed. But you've made me crazy, and I can't wait, but I can still feast on everything that is going to be mine."

When her bodice was open, he scooped out her breasts. And as his mouth closed about a nipple, she arched her back, her throat, and screamed as loud as she could.

He raised his lips to murmur, "There is no one to hear you. I told you. The soldiers and the others are far away."

He bit down.

She cried in anguish rather than terror.

He let go. "Don't make me hurt you," he warned tightly, evenly. "And don't make me any angrier than I already am, or I'll make it so painful you'll beg me to kill you. I know how, you know. I've had experience with little whores like you. That's how you got that ring. I know it. Some man paid you with it to sleep with him, and here I'm offering you your damn worthless farm, and money to boot, and you still fight me."

Kerry could not breathe. He was pressing the very life from her as he mashed down on her with his body. The only chance she had to take a gulping breath was when he lifted his mouth to take turns between her breasts.

"Now . . ." he said huskily, fumbling with his trousers. "I'm going to take you now. And when I'm done, I'll carry you up to the house and have you again. And you'll do everything I want or you'll be sorry, I swear it.''

She felt something hot, hard, and probing, and from somewhere deep within her an inner strength burst forth. She was able to give one quick twist to the side and throw him off of her. It caught him off guard only for an instant, but it was enough for her to roll to her knees and scramble away. If she could make it to her feet, reach his horse, then she could get away . . .

His hand snaked out to close about her ankle. "Get back here, you little bitch. This time you're going to learn who's master around here . . ."

They heard it at the same time—horses splashing through the stream.

With an oath, he let her go.

Kerry scrambled to her feet, crying with relief to see the men in blue uniforms riding in. Stumbling towards them, she called, "Help me . . . please . . ."

A man in front—an officer, Kerry decided at once from the bars on his shoulders—held up a white-gloved hand in signal and the men behind him reined to a halt.

Kerry moved towards him, stepping into the stream and almost falling. With shaking hands she fumbled with the buttons of her dress. "You have to help me. That man . . . he tried to . . ." She could not say the ugly word.

The officer, registering no alarm or undue concern, looked from her to Lorne, who was coming up behind her. "What's going on here, Mr. Petrie?"

Lorne laughed. He had stuffed his shirt back in his pants, closed his fly, and looked not the least unruffled. "Oh, she got upset when she found out her farm is being auctioned off today. You know how some women get, Lieutenant."

"That . . . that's not true," Kerry sputtered, turning on him in a fury. "You lying bastard. That's not true. You attacked me when I said I wouldn't be your mistress."

A few of the soldiers chuckled but fell silent when their commander turned to glare.

Lorne snickered. "Now, does she look like the sort any man would want for a mistress?"

The lieutenant remained expressionless. "So what did happen, Mr. Petrie?"

"I told you—she got upset. I told her I was sorry, that land gets sold when people don't pay their taxes. Then she said if I'd give her a little more time, she would, you know . . ." He lifted his shoulders in a helpless shrug.

The lieutenant finished for him, "She offered herself to you."

Lorne smiled. "Exactly. So I did what any normal man would do. I accepted her offer. Then she started screaming I was trying to rape her and attacked me."

Kerry shouted, "You are lying, and you know it." She started towards him, rage taking over, but the lieutenant signaled to the soldier closest to her. Quickly dismounting, he grabbed her and held her back.

Lorne walked over to the bushes, searched about for a few seconds, then held up the knife. "See? She came at me with this. The little vixen was going to kill me and claim it was self-defense. She's a crafty one, all right. Better handle her with care. She might have something else hidden on her."

"Want me to search her?" the soldier restraining her eagerly asked.

The lieutenant shook his head, then asked of Lorne, "So what do you suggest we do with her?"

Kerry was beside herself. Lorne Petrie and the lieutenant were obviously well-acquainted, and the lieutenant was going to do whatever he was told. "Please," she begged him. "You have to believe me. I'm telling the truth."

The lieutenant frowned. "You did try to stab him."

"Yes. To keep him from having his way with me, don't you see?"

Lorne, she noted, had the audacity to actually yawn,

then patted his mouth with his hand and said, "I'm afraid I just don't have time for this. She's held me up enough as it is. I see the auctioneer coming." He pointed to a man riding up.

"Well, what do you want to do?" The lieutenant was impatient. "It's up to you. Want us to take her into town and put her in jail? She'll likely get a stiff sentence. The judge is tired of these Rebs causing trouble, especially when it has to do with losing their land for unpaid taxes. He says it's time they realized how things are and quit their whining."

Panic had Kerry's stomach tied in knots. She was in deep trouble and completely helpless. The soldiers did not believe her, and it sounded as though the judge would not either.

Lorne scratched his chin thoughtfully as he went to Kerry and walked around her, looking her up and down. "I don't know, Lieutenant. It seems a shame to send a young girl like this to prison. After all, she's desperate, and the war wasn't her fault."

"Well, make up your mind."

"Give us a minute," Lorne said. He nodded to the soldier. "Let her go. And you men ride back to the house and wait for me there."

The soldier was skeptical. "Are you sure, sir? Like you said, she could have another weapon hidden."

"I handled her before. I can do it again." He waved him away.

When they were alone, it was all Kerry could do to keep from raking her nails down his smug, lying face. "I hope you rot in hell."

His mouth tightened to a thin line, and his eyes became black holes in his reddening face. "You little fool. With the snap of my fingers I can have you thrown in jail till you rot. The guards will have you any time they want. You'll die a thousand deaths."

"I'm sure I will," she said calmly, matter-of-factly, "but

if you think I am going to throw myself at your feet and beg for mercy, you're insane."

"That's not what I want," he said grimly, casting a worried glance at the departing soldiers before continuing. "I'm not the evil-hearted monster you think me, Miss Corrigan. I'm just a businessman, out to get richer than I already am on the spoils of war. I found you lovely. I wanted you. I made a nice offer. You rejected me. I don't take rejection lightly. It's that simple. Therefore, you must pay for offending me."

Recklessly she declared, "Then let them take me to jail. Maybe someone else will believe I'm telling the truth."

"That won't happen. I'm a rich, powerful man, and you are nothing but white trash. You've got but one chance to save yourself from a living hell."

Her laugh was loud and bitter. The soldiers heard, glanced around, but kept on going. "You are a fool, Lorne Petrie. I will never bed you—"

"That's not what I want any longer."

His anxious gaze darted to the soldiers once more, and Kerry was puzzled by how nervous he seemed all of a sudden.

In frustrated anger he said, "I'd have to beat you to death to break your spirit. And I'd never know when I'd find a knife in my throat. You're too damned rebellious to make any man a good mistress."

"Then what do you want of me?" She was worried that Luther and the others might return early. If they tried to stop the soldiers from taking her, they would be arrested, too, and she could not let that happen. "I'm ready to go to jail. Anything to get away from you," she added, revulsion making her shudder.

He grabbed her wrist and held tight. "This ring." He shook her hand. "I want it. Give it to me."

She was horrified and tried to twist from his grasp as she again squeezed her hand closed. "No. I won't. It was given to me by my father, and it's all I have, now that you're taking his land."

"I want it for my wife, don't you see? Some of the soldiers in that patrol don't like me, and they will see to it that she hears about this little incident today. My story will be that it didn't happen at all like they say—that our meeting was quite pleasant—that I came and bought your land at auction, and afterwards you offered me this ring if I would let you keep it.

"Which I will do," he hastened to add, glancing once more at the soldiers to make sure none had turned back to see what was going on. "That is my proposition. The ring for your pitiful little dirt farm."

She did not trust him. "And why this ring? You can obviously afford to buy any kind of jewelry she wants."

"Emeralds are rare. Especially one of this color and clarity. I know gems, Miss Corrigan. This is a fine piece. She'll come nearer believing me when she sees that it's an exceptional piece, one I might not have easily found in a store. Where did you get it?"

He released his grip. She rubbed her wrist and glared up at him, thinking he was every bit as evil and contemptible as her stepfather. "It's none of your business."

He looked towards the house, where two of the soldiers had dropped back and were staring at them curiously. "Look, we don't have much time. I am willing to make you a nice deal here. I'll buy your land, deed it back over to you, and give you a little money to keep you going till things get better. All I want is the ring."

Kerry was starting to believe he was sincere. Boldly, she demanded to know, "And why is it so important to you that your wife believe you?"

"There . . . there have been a few indiscretions. Her father has a lot of money. There could be problems." He licked his lips nervously. "Look, Miss Corrigan, I really didn't intend for things to work out this way."

Amused, she retorted, "Oh, I believe that."

"The auction was supposed to take place at the court-house, but there were some new bidders in town who don't know the lay of the land, so the auctioneer agreed to do everything on site. Otherwise I would've bought it there, and you wouldn't have known till it was too late. But since the soldiers arrived early, things are working to your advantage." He pointed to the ring. "Do we have a bargain?"

Kerry realized she had no other option. She also knew that her father would not mind her parting with the ring to save the land. Minutes were ticking by. She turned with Lorne Petrie to see that the two soldiers had started coming towards them.

"What will it be?" he asked, perspiration dotting his forehead.

Confident she had the upper hand to a point, Kerry took a chance and said, "I will agree, on one condition."

His face clouded with suspicion. "I can't give you much money. And you have to agree to keep your mouth shut about all this.

"I can make you sorry if you don't," he added to warn.

Something told her he was capable of doing just that, and, so as not to provoke him further by prolonging his misery, explained, "I want your word that if I ever have the money to buy the ring back, you will sell it to me. You can tell your wife it was stolen. I don't care. I just want that promise. It means a lot to me."

His entire body seemed to relax as a grin took over his face. "Of course. You have my word."

She knew he gave it only because he believed she would never have the means to buy it back. But he was wrong. Some way, somehow, she would do it, no matter how long it took.

She took the ring off her finger and handed it over.

"It's extraordinary," he breathed in awe. "You must tell me where you got it."

At that point, she saw no reason not to. "According to one of his letters, my father found it when he joined others who heard there was gold to be discovered in a place called Stonypoint, somewhere here in North Carolina.''

"Yes, yes," he nodded briskly. "I've heard of it. It's in the mountains. Sometimes they do find nice gems there. Mostly rubies. I've never heard of an emerald being found, though. It makes it all the more valuable.

"Now listen." He caught her arm and held it as she tried to twist away. "I will talk to the lieutenant and tell him I've changed my mind about having you arrested. Then the auction will proceed. Afterwards, I'll see that you get the deed and the money."

"How much money?" she pressed coldly.

His face clouded once more. "Not a lot. You're getting your damned land. What more do you want?"

"Enough to buy food, seed, supplies."

He stared at her for a long, tense moment, then whispered—for the soldiers were drawing quite near—"Very well. But do not provoke me, Miss Corrigan. I have ways of dealing with people who do."

She told herself not to be afraid. She had won.

But still a shiver rippled over her as she watched Lorne Petrie walk away.

Chapter 7

Slade took the cigar General Howard offered. Inhaling as he slid it under his nose, he gave an approving nod. Howard knew his tobacco.

They were sitting in the general's office in Washington. Slade had been kept waiting and took the time to appreciate the furnishings. The desk was a rich burnished mahogany. The smell of the chairs and sofa assured they were made of the finest hand-worked leathers. There was a portrait of Lincoln, two walls filled with books, and a huge window offering a view of the city.

General Howard had breezed in, motioning Slade to stay seated as he shook his hand before settling behind his desk. He looked through a sheaf of papers on his desk, then at Slade to tersely say, "I'm counting on you to carry this off, Captain."

"I'll give it my best, sir."

"You always do. That's why I told Sam Pardee not to take no for an answer when I sent him to find you. His orders were to arrest you, if need be, to get you back here to accept this assignment."

Slade knew he was not joking. General Howard was not a man known for his humor. "I imagine he told you I wasn't hard to persuade once he mentioned your name."

General Howard looked pleased. "Yes. As a matter of fact, he did. I appreciate that. You're a good man, Dillon. Brave. Courageous. If anybody can infiltrate the Ku Klux Klan and expose the leaders so the government can prosecute, you can."

"I appreciate your faith in me. And I won't let you down," Slade added, hoping he wasn't making a reckless promise.

"I know that," the general smiled. "Now then," he continued, "you understand you were chosen to be our undercover agent in the Goldsboro and Wayne County area due to the fact you have a reason to go there."

"*Had* a reason, sir," Slade corrected.

General Howard dismissed his pessimism with a wave of his hand. "Doesn't matter. Even if circumstances have changed, you have reason to go there to find out. And if they have, it's up to you to find one to stay."

Risking impertinence, Slade inquired, "Well, why can't I just invent one for going in the first place?"

"You'll come nearer being accepted. After all"—he paused to flash a crafty smile—"you're going to present yourself as a former soldier for the Confederacy, and those rednecks down there will love you even more when they hear you're also the stepson of a *dead* Reb soldier."

Kerry did not tell Luther and his family the ugly side of her dealings with Lorne Petrie. She merely explained that she had sold him a family heirloom he took a fancy to when they met the day of the tax auction. They had seen the ring, admired it, and had no reason to question her story.

However, Kerry became alarmed when she went to the courthouse to pick up her new deed. Lorne had told her just before he left with the soldiers that he would leave it there, along with the money he had promised.

When Sim Higdon, the clerk who had befriended her before, handed it to her, she saw it was still in her father's name.

"I don't understand," she said, shaking her head. "Mr. Petrie bought it but said he'd have the deed changed to my name."

Sim promptly told her, "Just be glad the taxes are paid, Miss Corrigan, and don't argue about a little thing like the name on the deed."

"But it's not how it was supposed to be."

"I wouldn't know anything about your agreement with Mr. Petrie. As I understand it, there was no auction. He told Wally Tredham, the auctioneer, to just skip your place 'cause you sold him something—a ring, I think he said— in exchange for him paying the delinquent taxes. He came in the next day and did just that.

"Left you this, too," he said, reaching under the counter to bring out a thin envelope. "As for changing the name on the deed to yours, I'm afraid you'll have to petition the probate judge to do that. You'll need to show him proof Flann Corrigan was your pa, but you shouldn't have no trouble doing that."

No, she wouldn't. She had the letters and the map to prove he meant her to have it. "And how do I go about doing that?"

"See Paul Younger or one of the other lawyers in town. They'll take care of it."

She frowned. "And do you have any idea what it will cost?"

He shrugged. "Twenty dollars. Thirty, maybe."

She tore the envelope open and blinked in shock and disappointment. There were only a hundred dollars and a slip of paper indicating she had credit enough at the general store to buy seed and a little food.

It was, she supposed, all she could hope for. And what

could she do about it, anyway, if he had decided to give her nothing?

She supposed that if she was careful, she could survive the winter. The chickens were laying, and there were baby chicks coming along. But so was cold weather, and she needed shelter for them. Luther had said he thought there might be enough wood left from the barn to build a small one. He was not able to do it alone and counted on Adam to help him.

Kerry left the courthouse in fairly good spirits after convincing herself that things were not as bad as they could be. After all, she was not alone. She had Luther and Bessie and Adam. There was the cow, too. And she was healthy. Strong. She could survive. As for changing the deed, well, with the taxes paid it no longer seemed important.

As she descended the steps, she saw a trio of well-dressed women standing on the boardwalk below. They wore colorful dresses of calico and taffeta and twirled silk, ruffled parasols over their feathered hats. She felt so dowdy in her worn muslin dress that had once been blue but had faded to gray from so many washings.

They were chattering happily among themselves, oblivious to everyone else.

She moved by them quietly, careful not to brush against their fine clothing. That would surely elicit a scathing glare that would only make her feel worse.

But just as she was almost by them, she heard one of them say, "Oh, look, coming out of the bank across the street. It's Lorinda Petrie."

Kerry slowed to stare. The woman was plump, her purple dress making her look like a huge turnip.

Another of the trio said with a sniff of disdain, "It's disgusting how she wears all that jewelry. Even in the daytime. Such poor taste."

"Oh, I agree," the woman who had spotted Lorinda said. "Come. Let's go before she sees us. I'm sick of her showing off her latest bauble."

"I know, I know," chimed in another. "But it is a lovely ring, isn't it? Wherever did Lorne find an emerald like that? I'm so envious, but I'd never let her know it."

As they turned, one of them bumped into Kerry. With a gasp of disgust, she cried, "Oh, get out of my way." To the others she said as they breezed on by, "I do wish the soldiers would do something about the riffraff on the streets. It makes me angry that we moved down here with our husbands and have to be exposed to all kinds of low-life people."

Kerry stared after them, contempt smoldering. They were carpetbaggers' wives. The worst kind of snobs. Not about to be put down, she yelled after them, "At least we don't profit from the hardship of others."

They turned about, obviously astonished that anyone would dare reproach them. Then one gave a high, shrill laugh that cut to the marrow of Kerry's bones as she taunted, "At least we *profit,* you little gutter rat. We aren't wearing rags and starving."

Then, all of them tittering among themselves like school-girls, they continued on their way.

Kerry chided herself for having spoken to them at all as she turned back to watch Mrs. Petrie waddle along. She thought she saw the emerald glittering in the sun but could not be sure.

Men tipped their hats as Mrs. Petrie passed. Obviously, she was held in high esteem for her money if for no other reason.

Kerry walked on down the street to the store where Lorne had given her credit. Her feet were aching from the long trek into town. She had blisters and could feel them bleeding inside her shoes, the soles of which were worn almost through to the ground. By the time she got home they probably would be.

She was limping when she walked in the door. She saw a lady in the rear, her attention focused on a table where bolts of fabric were stacked. Kerry was glad no one else was around. After the way the carpetbaggers' wives had acted, she felt shabbier than ever.

"Can I help you?" the bespectacled man behind the counter asked. He was bald, had a pointed nose and a kind face. The sleeves of his white shirt were rolled up and held by thin black bands, and he wore a wide apron over his trousers.

"I have this," she said, almost apologetically, and showed him Lorne's note.

His pointed nose wrinkled. "Oh, yes. I know about this." He stared at her over his glasses.

Kerry tensed in anticipation that he was going to be as haughty as the women had been. But then he smiled, putting her at ease.

Leaning across the counter, he gave the paper back to her and whispered conspiratorially, "I think it should have been a lot more. Blasted carpetbaggers. They'd pick the pockets of the dead, if they thought they had any money in 'em. Thank God, I was able to keep my store. They can't touch it."

He straightened and, extending his hand, said, "And I'm pleased to meet you, Miss Corrigan. I knew your pa. A fine man, he was. And you're the spittin' image of him. The name's Horace, by the way. Horace Bedham."

She stammered to thank him, touched by his kind words.

"Now then," he straightened and rubbed his hands together. "What will it be?"

"Not much, I'm afraid. Only what I can carry."

He stiffened in surprise. "You're joking. You mean to tell me you walked all the way from your pa's place?"

Suddenly she felt self-conscious again. "I had to. I don't have any other means."

A vaguely familiar voice suddenly came from right behind her. "Then how does that colored woman deliver your eggs?"

Kerry whirled about and saw that the woman who had been looking at fabrics was the same one who had befriended her at the train station the day she arrived. So many weeks, but she would never forget that soft, kind voice. "You mean Bessie?"

"I don't know her name," Abigail Ramsey said. "But she did tell me that the eggs came from the Corrigan farm. I assumed that was you."

"Yes, yes, it's me," Kerry hastened to confirm. "Bessie walks to town with the eggs once a week."

Abigail patted her hand. "Well, they are wonderful eggs. I buy a dozen from her. I'd buy more, but she says the others are promised."

"Because she can't carry many. Maybe later on . . ."

"Maybe later on, she'll be too exhausted to come in at all—like you appear to be right now. My, my," Abigail made a tsking sound as she looked her up and down. "Are you going to look exhausted every time I see you?"

"I . . ." Kerry started to speak, but Abigail interrupted as she addressed Horace, "I hope you're going to give this young lady credit, Horace. After all, her father died for the Confederacy, and it's heartbreaking how she came all the way over here from Ireland only to be told he was—"

Horace held up a hand in surrender. "I know all that, Miz Ramsey. And she already has credit. Lorne Petrie came in and arranged everything. It's not much, but it will help till she gets a garden going. And I'll even be glad to take some of her eggs."

"If she can get them to you," Abigail said, lifting her chin and glaring at him as if it would be his fault if she were unable to.

Turning back to Kerry, she asked sharply, "Now why would you be having any dealings with a dreadful carpet-bagger like Lorne Petrie?"

"He was going to buy the farm for the delinquent taxes. Instead, he bought a ring from me and paid the taxes for me. This credit was part of our bargain."

"Oh, for heaven's sake," Abigail cried. "That must be the

beautiful emerald Lorinda Petrie is wearing. What a shame.'' She sighed. "But I know you had no choice. Still . . .

"Horace,'' she snapped so suddenly that he jumped. "I know the credit she had couldn't be much, but do you suppose you could let her have a mule?''

He scratched his chin. "I don't know.''

"Of course, you can. I happen to know you've got two. Give one of them to Kerry, and you can swap out the cost in eggs.''

His eyes went wide. "Miz Ramsey, do you know how many eggs it will take to pay off a mule?''

"Well, it couldn't take any longer than you're doing to pay my husband for delivering your last baby.''

Kerry put her hand to her lips to stifle a giggle, as Horace, face reddening, sputtered, "Well, I suppose I could work something out.''

Abigail was holding a folded parasol, and she tapped it on the counter and said, "See that you do. And I think if you look hard enough, you can find a nice little cart for her, too. Now I have to be running along.'' She gave Kerry's cheek a gentle pinch. "I'm going to be looking forward to having three dozen eggs a week from now on.''

"Oh, you'll have them, I promise,'' Kerry eagerly assured.

Abigail was almost to the door when she turned to say, pointing the parasol at Kerry's feet. "And another thing, Horace. See that this poor child has some new shoes. I can almost see her toes peeking out of those. And a new dress, as well.''

Kerry could tell by Horace's expression that he was not angry as he called after her to protest, "Your husband didn't deliver twins, you know.''

"Oh, I know,'' she paused to sweetly say, "but I am aware that Mrs. Bedham is in the family way again, so the bill just keeps getting bigger, Horace.'' Then she wagged a finger at Kerry. "When you get that new dress, and that mule and cart, I want you in town every Sunday to go to church. You need to meet people. And we're going to start having some socials, too. Dances and things. We're going to show those haughty carpetbagger-wives that we Southerners can have our own socials."

"What does she mean by that?" Kerry asked Horace after Abigail breezed on out the door.

"Oh, the carpetbaggers' wives are always having teas and socials and won't have anything to do with the women that have lived here all their life—like Miz Ramsey.

"Now then," he said, motioning Kerry to go with him. "Let's see about that dress."

Kerry stood rooted where she was. "Mr. Bedham, you don't have to do this. I don't want charity."

"Charity?" he echoed with a mock glower. "Who said anything about charity? You'd just better talk to them hens of yours and get them to laying eggs overtime, 'cause it's going to take you a long time to pay your bill here, young lady."

With a broad smile and a warm glow to think how fortunate she was to have made such good friends, Kerry hurried after him towards a rack of dresses.

It was late afternoon when Kerry got back to the farm. Her stomach was growling with anticipation to think of the supper Bessie would have prepared. One of Bessie's friends, a freed slave, worked for a farmer who was faring better than most. She had promised Bessie some turnips and fatback. Kerry had no idea what fatback was or what it would taste like, but, so far, everything Bessie had cooked had been delicious.

The house was a two-story, the front porch stretching across the front. The kitchen was in the back. It had a nice cook stove that had not been used since her father had left for the war. Since Kerry had arrived, however, Bessie, with Kerry's blessing, had started cooking there again for all of them.

Reining in the mule, Kerry was disappointed that no one came out to meet her. She was anxious for them to see both the mule and the cart, as well as the food she had brought. And she could not wait to show her new dress and shoes to Bessie.

She got down and tied the reins to the hitching post by the porch. She smiled to think that it was the first time she'd had reason to use the post. Things were, thank goodness, looking better all the time.

"Isn't anybody going to help me unload all this food?" she called brightly as she went around the side of the house.

There was no answer.

She went to the kitchen and found it empty, then looked all through the house on both floors, even though she knew she would not find anyone. Bessie and the others never went inside. They refused her invitations to eat with her, saying it wouldn't be proper. She told them that was nonsense but understood they adhered to the old ways and would for a long time to come.

It was getting dark. Kerry hurried to empty the cart, then unhitched the mule and walked him around back to tether him for the night.

The chickens, she noted, had all gone under the house as they did every night, seeking shelter. Maybe it would not be too long before Luther and Adam got the henhouse ready. They needed a roost, and proper laying boxes. Now she and Bessie had to search in the bushes to find eggs. With so many orders, and now having the means to deliver them, it was urgent that they get organized, because there was money to be made.

Worried that someone might be sick, she decided to follow the path to what had been the tiny row of slave cabins.

She corrected herself.

Her father had never owned slaves. He had bought them, freed them, then given them food and shelter in exchange for work. Bessie had confided that his neighbors hadn't liked that one little bit, but, being he was the kind of man that was not given to concern over what others thought, they soon learned to keep their opinions to themselves. After all, Bessie had told her, other than how he felt about slavery, Flann Corrigan had been considered a loyal Southerner.

To the death, Kerry thought grimly, sadly.

There was still enough light that she could see the six shacks, three on each side of the path. She thought it a miracle the Yankees hadn't burned them, along with the main house, when they had torched the barn. Bessie said they had threatened to, but then another patrol came along and said they had received word a big battle was taking place at Bentonville. So all the soldiers had taken off to join the fight.

The windows of the first shack, where Bessie and Luther lived—and where they had carried Kerry that day when she was found on the side of the road—were dark.

Kerry swallowed against the apprehension bubbling in her throat. There was probably a simple explanation, she told herself. Maybe another wild boar had been killed and Luther and Adam had gone to help clean it. Bessie said it was quite a chore.

"That's it. They're off helping someone." Saying it out loud made her feel better.

Nothing was wrong. And she was silly to worry.

She was about to turn back to the house but just then saw Adam coming out of the shack on the end where he lived.

Waving, she called, "Adam, I've been looking everywhere for you and your parents. Where is everybody?" She saw he was carrying a burlap bag . . . and also saw how he quickly ducked his head and would not look at her as though he were ashamed. "Adam, what is wrong? Where are you going?"

He still would not look at her, staring down at his bare

feet. "They've already gone, Miz Kerry. I came back for the last of my things. Didn't have much, but I wanted to get my blanket. It'll get cold soon and—"

"Adam, I don't care about your blanket." All patience was tossed aside. "What is going on here?"

Shifting the bag from one shoulder to another, he dug in the dirt with his toe. "Hate to tell you this, Miz Kerry, but Master Allison, he asked me and Mama and Papa to come to work for him. We all hate to leave you like this, but the Allisons, they got plenty of food. We won't be hungry no more. And Mama, she said you'd likely be movin' on sooner or later, anyhow, 'cause there ain't no way you can run this farm by yourself."

"Not when people I considered friends desert me," she snapped like the crack of a whip. "We were doing fine. We're doing even better now that I've a mule and a cart. Food, too. And seed. But I need help to work the fields, and—"

"And I got to be gettin' on."

He started by her, but she quickly moved to block his way. "How can you desert me this way?"

Misery was thick in his voice as he mumbled, so low she had to strain to hear, "We don't want to, Miz Kerry, but it ain't safe for freed slaves to live off by themselves like we been doin'."

She was completely bewildered. "Whatever are you talking about? What do you mean you're scared? What is there to be afraid of?"

He glanced about nervously, as though someone might be around to overhear, then whispered in terror, "The night riders, Miz Kerry. The Ku Klux Klan, they're called. They hate the freed slaves. And last night, they caught Ben Bodine down by the creek when he was hookin' catfish, and they strung him up and beat him. Said the creek warn't his, and he didn't have no right to be there. But that warn't the only reason they beat him. Ben talked uppity to a white man in town the other day that yelled at him to get off the walk and in the mud so his wife could walk by. Ben, he said he didn't have to walk in the mud for nobody no more.

"And he won't never have to, neither," he finished, voice cracking. " 'Cause Ben's dead. The Ku Klux Klan beat him to death."

Kerry reeled, sickened to the core. "Dear God, I'm so sorry. But, Adam, what does it have to do with you and your family? My father freed all of you before the war even started. You told me that. Why would those savages bother you?"

"There just ain't no telling what they might do. We're scared to be off by ourselves, but we'll be safe at Master Allison's. He's got lots of freed slaves working for him."

Anger boiling, Kerry exploded, "Yes, and he treats them like they're still slaves in bondage, too. Your mother told me she's heard he beats them. They're scared to death of him. Oh, Adam, how could you?"

He lifted his chin in a sudden show of defiance. "We're more scared of the Klan. At least Master Allison will protect us from them. They're bad, Miz Kerry. Real bad. And the best thing for you, anyway, is to move into town and get away from here. It just ain't safe no more."

He continued on his way, shoulders slumped by more than just the weight of the sack he carried. Despair echoed in every step he took, for the future was perhaps bleaker for him and his people than ever before.

Kerry could do nothing but watch him go, her heart aching, for she had not felt so alone since the night her mother had died.

Chapter 8

Kerry was exhausted but not about to give up, determined to build a shelter for the chickens herself.

Luther had pulled a few boards from the remains of the barn but not nearly enough. He had stacked them next to the burned-out hulk, and that was not where she wanted the henhouse. Instead, she planned to build it not too far from the main house so if a fox or raccoon came around, it would be easier for her to hear the ruckus.

She had found tools she needed that Luther had salvaged—a hammer that was not too badly rusted, nails that had not melted. Best of all, there was a prong-type instrument that kept her from having to use her hands to yank the boards loose. Still, she had blisters and wished for a pair of gloves.

It was Sunday morning. When she had delivered her eggs the day before, Abigail Ramsey had told her she was looking forward to seeing her in church.

Kerry tugged with all her might to pop another board free. She had been to church the past two Sundays and had enjoyed it. Abigail introduced her around, and she was looking forward to going back. But she wasn't sure she could go today. She had lost another hen last night, no doubt to a fox. She had to build a shelter. Otherwise, to keep from losing all of them she would have to put them to roosting in one of the slave shacks. She did not want to do that, because, foolish or not, she clung to the hope that Luther and his family might return, or some other freedmen might want to work in exchange for their keep.

Had the nails not been driven so far into the boards by the scorching heat of the fire, she would have been able to use the hammer's claw to pull them out. It would have been much easier—and less work.

As she struggled with one particularly difficult board, she thought of what she had overheard in Mr. Bedham's store when she had brought his eggs. Another freedman— as she had learned the former slaves were being called— had been beaten.

Abigail had told her that the soldiers were questioning everyone, even the women, to try and find some clue as to the men responsible. Abigail said neither she nor her husband approved of such horrid goings-on by the secret night riders known as the Ku Klux Klan. However, if they did know anything, they would never risk being involved. The Klan had killed white men in other counties for betraying them.

Kerry was glad she knew nothing. She might be tempted to go to the soldiers and tell them, and that could get her in serious trouble. Still, she wished there were some way she could bring peace so Luther and the others would come back. Then they could all get down to the business of living without having to worry about hooded cowards sneaking around in the dark attacking helpless people.

Abigail had said there was to be a social—a dance—at the church in a few weeks to celebrate the beginning of fall, but Kerry could not get excited about the cold weather sure to come.

Bessie had told her, "Sometimes it gets so cold your toenails will pop off if you aren't careful."

Kerry knew she had been teasing. Still, with no blankets and now facing the chore of having to cut her own firewood, she truly dreaded the months ahead. In addition, she had to keep the chickens warm somehow.

But she would go to the dance, if only for one last chance to have a little fun before winter's gloom set in. Abigail had promised to make her a new gown to wear, something bright and cheerful with lots of ruffles. Kerry knew Abigail was hoping Kerry would find a husband. Well, that was the least of her worries. She had no intention of ever marrying if it was only to have someone to take care of her—not after learning to do it herself.

Besides, the only men she had met so far were old, their wives having died. The young men, it seemed, had either been killed in the war or taken their families and fled elsewhere to escape the poverty left by the war.

There were times when Kerry wondered if she should do the same. In the large cities of the North she would be able to find a job in a pub—or saloon or tavern. Yet, even when she was exhausted, as she was at the moment, she felt a bonding with the land. It was all she had left of her father . . . her heritage, and she wanted so desperately to make his dream come alive again.

Frustrated, she gave the board a vicious yank. It was the most difficult yet, and the last one she would loosen before trying to make it to church on time. If not for the picnic being held on the grounds afterwards, she would have stayed on and worked despite being so tired. But the thought of all that food had her mouth watering.

The board came free, but with such force Kerry lost her balance. She fell backwards to land soundly on her bottom and cursed, "Hell and damnation!"

A man's voice, preceded by a soft chuckle, declared, "Well, that's no way for a lady to talk."

Kerry dove for the shotgun propped on a nearby stump

as her heart leaped to her throat. After the ugly scene with Lorne Petrie, when she had failed to get to her knife in time, she always kept a gun nearby.

"Not so fast."

The gun was yanked out of her reach as her hand was about to close around it.

"There's no call to shoot a fellow just because you're feeling foolish about falling on that pretty little derriere of yours."

"You . . . you've a nerve to speak to me this way, sir, and—" She had scrambled to her feet before actually looking at him. When she did, it came as a shock to instantly find him so attractive.

He was probably a head taller than she, with hair the color of a raven's wing, shimmery and blue it was so black. It fell just below the collar of his tan shirt. It was unbuttoned, open to reveal a muscular chest with hair trailing down to disappear into the trim waistline of very tight denim trousers.

A double-holster hung low on his hips, and something told her he knew how to use the guns it held.

"Where . . . where did you come from?" she asked when she could find her voice. She was careful to distance herself from him, wishing she had tied the knife to her ankle. Now she had no weapon at all—except the tool she had been using.

He followed her darting gaze and, with a sigh, reached over to pick up the tool from where she had dropped it and tossed it out of her reach. "Are you always given to violence? Don't you ever try to work out a peaceful solution to a problem?"

His grin, as well as how he was mocking her, sent her temper soaring. "I don't call it peaceful when you're trespassing, sir. Especially when you take my gun."

"I took your gun to keep you from doing something foolish. And I'm trespassing because I've been watching you from the road for some time now, and it appears you could use a hand. The name's Slade Dillon, by the way."

He held out his hand, then dropped it when she remained rooted where she stood.

"So you've been spying on me, as well."

"Oh, I wouldn't call it spying." Lazily he walked over to the pile of boards and put the shotgun down beside it, then faced her with arms folded across his chest. "I was waiting for you to look up so I could wave and ask if I might talk to you. But you kept on working, so I came on in. Sorry I scared you."

"I'm not scared," she said between clenched teeth. She was too mad to be frightened. And even if she were, she would never let him know it. Fear, Timothy O'Malley had told her over and over, made one weak in front of his enemy. And she was never, ever, to let any man think her weak.

He pushed back a lock of hair that had tumbled onto his forehead. "Well, you've no reason to be. I'm not going to hurt you. Neither am I going to let *you* hurt *me*," he added with a smile.

Kerry could not help noticing what beautiful eyes he had. They were a deep, dark blue, reminding her of the ocean. So many days she had spent at the ship's railing on the voyage from Ireland, watching the rolling waves and thinking how mysteriously lovely the color of the water was.

He had strong lines to his face, a good, firm jaw. But she noted scars here and there. Nothing big but enough to keep him from being flawless, and reminding her that beneath the gentle curve of his lips and the warmth of his eyes, there was a man to be reckoned with.

Curtly she said, "Well, we have nothing to talk about, so I'm asking you to leave."

"Not till I finish pulling the rest of those boards for you."

She was astonished. "And why would you want to do

that? You can look around and see how poor I am. I can't pay you anything."

Jovially, he challenged, "Why do you find it so hard to believe I'm only wanting to do a good deed because I don't like to see a woman work so hard?"

"My ... plight is not yours, sir. Do ... not concern yourself with me." She was stammering, her composure waning under the way he was looking at her, drawing her into the depths of those sea-blue eyes. His soft, drawling voice was gentle as a caress, stirring unfamiliar emotions that sent waves of heat soaring through her body.

"And I'll not be beholden to any man," she added. "So I bid you good day, sir."

Hating to leave the shotgun behind, she started towards the house. There was a chance he might steal it when he left, but it was far more important that she get to safety inside—and the pistol she kept there.

She had taken but a few steps when he pleasantly called, "I'm not leaving till I've finished pulling the boards out that aren't completely burned. And I can see you're as poor as everyone else around here. So I'm not asking to be paid. But I could sure use something to eat. I haven't had a meal in days. Just scraps here and there."

She paused. The memory of how her own belly had ached from hunger would likely never be forgotten. She could empathize with the stranger. She turned. "I don't have much. Eggs, of course, and some bacon and coffee."

"That would do nicely," he said quietly, humbly.

She cocked her head to one side in disbelief. "And you'll pull the rest of those boards for a meager meal like that?"

"And stack them, too. By the way, what are you planning to use them for?"

"A chicken house." She pointed to the rooster as he came strutting around the corner of the back porch, two hens clucking along behind him. "I'm losing too many to foxes and raccoons. The egg money is all I have to do me now, and ..." She trailed off into embarrassed silence.

He was a stranger, for heaven's sake. She knew absolutely nothing about him, and yet she was blathering like a fool. "It doesn't matter," she murmured.

"Well, to me it does."

"And why should you care?" Wariness was taking hold again.

"Because as long as you feed me, I'll work for you."

Her green eyes widened. "I . . . I'm not sure that would be proper," she said uneasily.

"Ma'am, please listen." He started towards her but froze when she began to back away. Spreading his hands in a pleading gesture, he said, "Look, I'm all alone in the world. I lost everything I had in the war. I've no family. No friends. No home. And no place to go. I'd like to stay here and help you, because I can see you're in desperate need. You've nothing to worry about."

"How do you know I've no one to help me?" she posed the question. "How do you know I don't have a husband who'll be home soon?"

"If you had a husband, he'd have already pulled the boards loose and built your chicken house. I can see they've been laying here awhile. A lot of what isn't burned is rotten. You're going to have to buy some lumber."

She had already thought about that but wanted to salvage as much from the barn as possible.

"Be that as it may," she said finally, "I am quite able to take care of everything myself. Now if you want to finish pulling those boards, fine, and I'll make you something to eat. Then I'm going into town to church, and I'll thank you to be gone when I return."

She turned towards the house again but then whirled about to hurry and retrieve the shotgun. He made no move to stop her and went to the task at hand.

Kerry told herself she had nothing to be afraid of. It was common for vagrants to work for food. She was grateful for the help. And the fact that he was ruggedly handsome was beside the point. She was lonely, and that was why he had affected her as he had. It was only natural. She was, after all, a woman. And maybe romance . . . love . . . had passed her by, but the pulses of desire still beat helplessly within. She would just stay away from him as much as possible till he left. Then it would all be over.

She vowed to be more careful in the future. She had been fortunate this time that the stranger meant her no harm. She would have to get herself a holster and wear her gun at all times. She couldn't take any chances, alone as she was.

She had gathered eggs earlier and cracked a half dozen in a bowl to scramble. She fried bacon and made a fresh pot of coffee. When everything was ready, she took a tray out to where he was diligently pulling boards free.

"Oh, that looks good," he grinned, wiping his brow with the back of his hand.

He had taken off his shirt, and Kerry kept her gaze averted lest he see how her cheeks had to be flushed from the warmth within. As she had walked from the house, his back was turned, and she had seen how his muscles rippled as he worked, flesh pulled taut across his shoulders. Her eyes had also been drawn to his well-molded buttocks.

He was truly a fine figure of a man, and she admonished herself for having such thoughts. To mask what she was feeling, she spoke curtly as she set the tray down on the stump. "Here. I've kept my end of the bargain. I expect you to keep yours and be on your way."

He immediately tossed his tool aside and sat down, legs crossed, and began to eat. Between bites, he said, without glancing up, "I'll leave when I finish, ma'am, and not before. I always keep my word."

"Well, you're almost done," she said crisply.

She was dressed for church in her one good dress that Abigail had arranged for her to have. It was fashioned of rich green taffeta with a lime-colored sash and a bow on the back. The neckline was high, with a lacy collar, and the sleeves templed at her wrists. The skirt was full and bouffant, thanks to the silk petticoats Mr. Bedham had also let her have.

Her red hair was pulled back from her face and tied with a ribbon to match her sash, and she felt pretty—even if she did wear the same dress week after week. No one cared, if they even noticed, because not many people had nice clothes, anyway. The important thing for church, the pastor had said, was to be there.

When she went to where she had left the mule tethered near the shacks, she was surprised to see that he was already hitched to the cart.

"You did this?" she whirled on the stranger to ask.

"I did." He took a gulp of coffee and complimented her on how good it was before explaining, "I figured you'd be all gussied up and didn't have any business fooling with an old mule."

"You didn't have to do that," she said, feeling ill at ease. "But thank you."

She scrambled up into the cart before he could get a notion to help her do that, as well. Popping the reins, she set the mule moving past him without further conversation.

She could feel his eyes on her until she was out of sight.

When she arrived at church, everyone was gathered on the lawn outside. The women were already setting up tables for the picnic afterwards.

Abigail saw her and waved her over. "I'm so glad you came, dear. There's a nice man I want you to meet—Thad Albritton. He's an old friend of my husband and me. He lives in Raleigh and sadly lost his wife a few months ago, the poor dear. She died in childbirth. So he's got this precious little bitty baby to raise by himself."

She droned on and on, but Kerry was not listening. The last thing she wanted was to be paired off with a man looking for a mother for his baby, and she knew that was what Abigail had in mind.

Grateful when the bells in the church tower began to ring, Kerry was careful to distance herself from Abigail and sit off by herself. But then she saw how the man four rows in front of her kept twisting around to stare, and she knew Abigail had pointed her out to him. That meant once the service was over, he would be after her like the flies on the food waiting outside.

Feeling naughty but not caring, Kerry slipped out of her pew as the choir stood to sing the last hymn. "Not feeling well," she whispered to a few ladies sitting on the ends of their rows who glanced at her reprovingly.

Once outside, she dashed across the lawn to the food-laden tables. Snatching up a linen napkin, she opened it to fill with as much as she could carry—fried chicken, slices of baked ham, and biscuits. She took that to the cart, then quickly returned to fill another napkin with slices of chocolate cake and blackberry muffins.

By the time the church bells pealed again, and the front doors swung open for everyone to spill outside, Kerry was on her way home.

As she neared the house, she could not help thinking how the stranger would have enjoyed the delicious food. She really did not feel bad about taking so much. It would hardly be noticed. Folks in town owning stores and having professions like doctors and lawyers had more than those who lived in the country, thanks to Yankee money.

But it was best the stranger had moved on. She had enough problems without him evoking strange feelings she could not understand. Why, she could never in her whole life remember staring at a man's bottom, for heaven's sake, and having a little rush go up her spine. And never, ever, had she felt all warm at the sight of a man's bare chest. What was wrong with her? Was living alone making her a crazy old woman? She had to get hold of herself and—

With a soft gasp, she pulled back on the reins.

He was still there, the afternoon sun making the skin on his bare back shimmer like gold.

And not only was he still there, he was working, and the

sight of the walls of what looked like a chicken house evoked another gasp . . . followed by a cry of delight.

"I . . . I don't believe it," she said when she had coaxed the old mule down the drive and scrambled down out of the cart. "You . . . you're unbelievable."

"I told you—I like doing good deeds for ladies."

He dazzled her with his smile, and despite how she had lectured herself all the way home, she was glad to find him still there . . . glad to see all the work he had done.

A frown creased his forehead. "You don't mind, do you? I mean, where I put the chicken house and all. I figured you'd want it near the back door so you can hear if something gets after them. Later on, when you can afford to buy wire for a pen, you can move it farther away."

"It's fine," she exulted. "Right where I wanted it. And look at the chickens." She pointed. "They're already trying to get in like they know it's theirs."

"Maybe they do. Who knows how a chicken thinks?"

They looked at each other and suddenly burst out laughing.

Then Kerry got hold of herself, feeling foolish all over again, and her laugh trailed to an awkward silence. Finally, she was able to say, "Well, thank you for all your help. I brought some more food. The church was having a picnic. After you eat, you'll be wanting to be on your way."

Their eyes met and held. "And what do you want?" he asked quietly.

She blinked and looked away. Meeting his gaze was much too unnerving. "I . . . I don't know what you mean."

"I mean that I would like to hang around awhile and finish the chicken house and do a few other things I've noticed need attention. I took the liberty of nosing around a bit, and I can bunk in one of those slave shacks in the back."

The heat wave was starting again, creeping upwards and heading straight for her face. "I don't know. I'm afraid it would be improper. I mean, a man and a woman, alone, and—"

"Hey," he cut her off, tone sharp. "In case you haven't noticed, lady, these are not proper times we are living in. Folks are having a rough time trying to survive in the aftermath of the hell known as war. So I imagine they've got a lot more important things to worry about than you having a handyman sleeping in one of your shacks and doing chores in exchange for food."

Tension hung between them for long moments as Kerry pondered his words and knew he was right. Finally, she gave a long sigh and said, "Very well. I suppose it would be all right if you don't come around the house.

"And only for a little while," she hastened to add as she saw how his expression relaxed and a smile began to curve his lips. "Just till you finish the chores. And you must remember that I don't have a lot of food. Eggs. Berries. Some biscuits when I have flour. You'll have to make do on what I have."

"Anything is better than nothing, Miss . . ." He paused, then cocked his head to one side. "If I'm going to be working for you, it'd be nice if I knew your name."

"Kerry Corrigan."

"Well, I'm pleased to meet you, Miss Kerry Corrigan." He held out his hand, and this time she took it, though shyly and briefly.

"I'll get the food from the cart," she said, anxious to get away from him, for her flesh tingled where his fingers had touched.

He watched her walk away, his brow creased in deep thought.

So she was his stepfather's daughter.

His lips curved ruefully to think she might be considered his stepsister.

She was beautiful.

Damned beautiful.

He had been struck by the flame brilliance of her shining hair tumbling luxuriously down her back. He had also been able to tell, even from a distance, that she was well formed, her body molded in all the right places.

He had stood by the road for a long time, observing as she doggedly attacked the ruins of the barn. And he had thought about what the clerk at the courthouse had told him about her when he had inquired as to whether Flann Corrigan's land had been sold for taxes.

Slade had managed to keep a poker face as the clerk went into detail about how she had managed to strike a deal with one of the most ruthless carpetbaggers around.

As to Slade's explanation for asking about the property, he'd had to think fast. The last thing he would have imagined was that Flann would have a daughter show up, all the way from Ireland, to claim his land. So Slade had hastily made up the story about having known Flann in the war, before he was killed. He had heard him talk about his farm and thought maybe he would take it over if it was still available.

The clerk had no reason not to believe him and said he was sorry Slade had wasted his time.

But Slade had noticed something when the clerk had pulled the deed to make sure they were talking about the same piece of property. It was still in Flann's name, and he found it odd the girl hadn't changed it.

The more he thought about the deed, the more the idea took hold that his claim of ownership might override hers. After all, he had a will, signed by Flann Corrigan, leaving his farm and anything else he owned to the woman he married shortly before he succumbed to his wounds.

And that woman had been Slade's mother.

So his intent when he went to the farm had been to inform Miss Corrigan that the farm was legally his. He planned to generously reimburse her for anything she had spent on the place; then she could be on her way.

But all that had changed when he saw her up close.

She had finely molded cheekbones, and her skin was creamy and glowing with health. Her lips were full, soft, but her most striking feature was her eyes. Beneath delicately arched brows, incredibly long, thick lashes fringed eyes that were the color of emeralds—vivid and startling in the intensity of shimmering green.

Although their meeting had been awkward, and he didn't like to think she might have actually shot him had she got her hands on the shotgun, he had been at once drawn to her. He liked her spirit, her peppery style, and her Irish brogue was delightful.

With a deep, harsh sigh, he took up the hammer and began working on the henhouse again.

He had got himself in a fine mess, all right. Instead of telling her she'd have to move on and settling in to do the job he'd been sent to do, he was now her hired hand. Working for food, for God's sake, when he had several thousand dollars in his saddlebag.

Slade cursed under his breath and wondered if he had lost his mind, then argued that it was the decent thing to do. He couldn't just walk in and tell her to leave. No matter that she was illegitimate. When his mother had written him to tell him about her marriage, she said it was the first time for Flann, which, if he was telling the truth, meant he had never been married to Kerry's mother. But that made no difference. She obviously had no other family, and she was near about destitute.

He would just have to let her down easy, a step at a time. Then he would give her some money to settle somewhere else, like in town, where a young lady belonged.

Meanwhile, he would just have to get a rein on the way she made him feel all hot and steamy inside with just a glance from those green, green eyes.

Chapter 9

"*I'm* supposed to be feeding *you*," Kerry laughed when she saw the deer Slade had killed and brought home. "Not *you* feeding *me*."

He pretended to think about that, then said, "You know, you're right. I guess I'll just have to eat all this fine venison by myself. Wouldn't want you to feel you weren't living up to your end of the bargain."

"Oh, you can't do that," she cried in mock horror. "I get tired of eating eggs all the time myself."

"Have you heard me complain? Although I have been afraid I'm going to start clucking like a chicken."

She slid easily into the playful banter. "You've got it wrong. You'd start crowing like a rooster. I'd be the one sounding like a hen."

"Is that so? Well, you'll have to overlook me. I'm just a poor, dumb country boy."

He might be poor, Kerry thought as she watched him clean the deer, but he was certainly not dumb. In the two weeks they had been together, she had learned so much about farming, and so many other things, as well.

He dug a pit, gathered firewood with Kerry helping, and, in no time at all, had a nice-sized chunk of meat roasting on the spit.

Kerry was also impressed over how he was able to do so many things, like building a chicken coop out of the little bit of wood from the barn that was useable. He had even painted it, saying he'd found some old paint in one of the shacks. And wire for a pen, as well, so shiny it looked new, but he said that was because it had been hidden under a mattress, also in one of the shacks.

The evening he returned from town with yet more lumber, this time to build a corral for the mule, cow, and his horse, Kerry demanded to know how he was able to buy it. She had long since used what credit Lorne Petrie had arranged for her at Mr. Bedham's store.

His explanation had been simple. He said he came upon a man whose wagon had overturned. A wheel was broken. He had fixed it for him, and in gratitude the man had given him part of his load, which happened to be lumber. Kerry was grateful and thought it a true blessing.

It was late afternoon before the venison was ready. Kerry had boiled some turnips she had found in the old garden. She had even managed to pick one last pan of berries from the dwindling blackberry bushes.

She no longer gave him his food on the back porch to eat alone. They now sat together in the cozy dining room, because, the more she was around him, she more she trusted him . . . and liked him. In all the time they had been together, he had been only polite and helpful. And she was secretly dreading the time when he decided to move on, knowing she would feel even lonelier.

Slade had managed to get a jug of peach cider by swapping eggs. It was delicious, but it had ripened, and Kerry was feeling a bit tipsy . . . and loose-tongued.

"I guess now that you've done all there is to do around here, you'll want to look for work elsewhere," she said, breaking her rule not to bring up the subject until he did.

"Oh, I don't think so," he said breezily. "I see lots that needs doing. Why? Are you ready for me to move on?"

"Oh, no, nothing like that." She fought to keep from sounding horrified at such a thought. "I just thought maybe you might want to be paid in money for a change."

"Don't worry. I'm happy with the way things are."

He had reached across the table to pat her arm as he spoke. The gesture was natural, kind, not meant to be forward or intimate. Yet Kerry was stirred by his touch.

Reluctantly, she reminded, "Well, I'm afraid with winter coming on, there won't be much to do."

"Which is all the more reason for me to stay. You're going to need firewood. You'll also need somebody to hunt and keep meat on the table."

He poured them both another cup of cider.

Absently twirling the cup in her hands, Kerry told herself it was probably not wise for him to stay, no matter how much she wanted him to. They were spending more and more time together when they weren't working, and winter would doubtless drive them indoors to be even closer.

Still, there was no denying she wanted him to stay, even though she knew so little about him. And suddenly it seemed important that she did. "You know, you never talk about yourself, Slade, but you're always asking me questions. I think it's only fair you share a little of yourself, as well."

He kept his head bent as he cut into the venison on his plate with a knife. "There's nothing to tell. I'm just an old soldier trying to stay alive, that's all."

"Where do you come from? Where were you raised?"

He met her intent stare. "I think I've always been a drifter, Kerry. I don't have roots anywhere."

"But you're from the South. You fought for the Confederacy. You told me that much. So you have to have a reason for having done that, and—"

He cut her off, almost sharply, his words firing like bullets. "Kerry, a man does what he has to at the time. He doesn't always have a reason. He just does it. And later, when he tries to figure out the *why* of it, he doesn't remember. And he no longer cares, because it's over and done with. That's how I feel about the war. All that matters is now."

There was a moment of awkward silence. The intensity with which he had spoken left her feeling guilty somehow, as though she had wrongly trod on troubled waters, stirring within him an eddy of bad memories. "I'm sorry," she said quietly. "I shouldn't pry."

"It's all right." His smile was tight, fleeting. "It's only natural to wonder about a man like me, I guess, but the fact is, there are thousands more who feel the same. They want to think about today and tomorrow, not look back on yesterdays they can't do anything about."

"Well, I can understand that." She bobbed her head up and down, then realized it probably made her look foolish and got very still. Yet, though she had apologized, she could not help feeling she had a right to know about the man she was drawn to more and more with each passing day. Only he did not know that was her reason, her motive, and she was not about to let on.

"I'm sorry," she repeated. "It's enough that you have been a blessing in my life."

He glanced away, but not before she saw the shadow cross his face. She wished she had kept silent. The last thing she wanted was to drive him away.

"I don't know what I would have done if you hadn't come along. When Luther and the others left because they were scared of what the Ku Klux Klan might do, I wondered how I'd get by. I was determined to try, though."

"This land means that much to you, doesn't it?"

There was an edge to his tone, as if maybe he did not approve of a woman feeling so strongly about land. And despite how she regretted the tension that had sprung up between them, it made her defensive. "Yes, it does. You see, I never knew my father, but he wanted me to have this land."

"But why did he leave you and your mother in Ireland? Why didn't he bring you both with him?"

The bluntness of his question caught her off guard. Though she had told him she had arrived in America to learn that her father had died in the war, she had not confided anything else.

"Kerry?" he prodded when she did not respond.

She set the cup of cider down and folded her hands in her lap. They had begun to tremble, and she did not want him to see. "He and my mother were never married. I never knew him . . . never knew about him till my mother lay dying. She married someone else before I was born, and I always thought he was my father."

She proceeded to tell him of the cruelty of her stepfather and how he tried to force her to marry someone so he would have money to pay his debts.

When she finished her story, Slade stood and began to pace about the room.

She could tell he had something on his mind. "Whatever it is, say it, please. I mean, if we're going to work together, there should be no tension between us."

He bit down on his lower lip thoughtfully, hands on his hips as he stared through the window and beyond.

Kerry waited.

Finally, with a gut-wrenching sigh, he posed the question, "Have you ever stopped to think maybe you don't have legal claim to this land . . . that maybe you're doing a lot of work for someone else to step in who does?"

She laughed—but nervously. The graveness of his voice was almost frightening. "I don't know what you mean. I told you how I worked out an agreement with that carpetbagger Lorne Petrie. I gave him my emerald ring in exchange for him paying the taxes and giving me a bit of credit at Mr. Bedham's store. Who else would dare claim it?"

"These are strange times we live in," he murmured.

"Yes, but I'm not worried about anyone trying to take the land away from me. Especially now that you're here. Even though you think it's fine to nose into my past without saying anything about your own, I can tell you know about farming, and . . ."

She trailed off to silence.

If she could have managed such a feat, Kerry would have given herself a sound kick for having such a big mouth. Things had been so pleasant. He was seemingly so understanding and sympathetic to her plight. Then she had to be sarcastic, and she'd not missed how his face darkened once more. No doubt he had a tragedy in his past that haunted him still, and every time she brought up anything other than the here and now, it took him back to all the pain.

"I'm sorry," she said, perhaps too loudly, as she bolted from her chair. "Forget I said that. I think I've had too much cider. I'll get the berries."

As she passed by him, he caught her wrist, his touch searing her flesh like a branding iron.

Their eyes met and held, tension crackling like hot logs in a fire.

Slowly, never taking his gaze from her, Slade stood. "Stop apologizing, Kerry," he whispered thickly as his hands slid up her arms to finally rest on her shoulders and hold tight. "I'm the one who owes you an apology, because I . . ."

She felt him shudder deep within, saw the way he slightly gave his head a shake, as though to fend away something too terrible to contemplate.

"Slade, what—"

His warm lips silenced her.

Kerry could only stand there, rocked in wonder. She had never known a man's kiss, never experienced sweet, tingling shudders that spread down to her belly and beyond . . . into her loins . . . making her tingle between her legs, hot . . . moist . . . wanting more, yet not understanding what her body demanded.

He held her for long, long moments. She sighed deep within as his tongue parted her lips to plunge inside her mouth. Dizzily, she realized her hands had moved as though with a will of their own to twine about his neck and cling tightly.

Lifting his mouth from hers, his lips trailed a hot path across her cheek to her ear as he whispered, "Kerry, I'm sorry. I shouldn't have let this happen, damn it. I should have kept on going . . . do what I'd planned . . . but when I looked into those damn green eyes of yours, something came over me. I've never felt this way about a woman before . . ."

"And I've never felt this way about a man," she said tremulously.

His tongue touched the lobe of her ear and began delicately probing each crevice, tracing each curve. Kerry moaned as waves of tension seemed to quake through every nerve in her body.

Feeling how she trembled, Slade boldly plunged his tongue into her ear as his hand sensually began to stroke her neck. Then, with maddening slowness, he began trailing burning kisses down her neck. "Tell me to stop," he huskily commanded. "Tell me you don't want this . . ."

She could sooner have made the sun cease to shine or the clouds disappear, for desire, raw and wild, was taking over her will . . . her body.

Arching her neck, as though offering her carotid like the weak wolf to the stronger, her response was a tiny echo of a tortured whisper. "I . . . I cannot. God help me, but I cannot . . ."

The sudden sharp calling of a woman's voice jolted them apart.

Slade moved towards the back door to distance himself from Kerry.

"Kerry, dear, where are you? I knocked, but you didn't

hear me, and . . ." Abigail Ramsey's voice trailed off to puzzled silence as she appeared in the doorway to stare from Kerry, who stood frozen, face ashen, to Slade. "I didn't know you had company."

Kerry had purposely not told Abigail about Slade, feeling she had begun to take too much of an interest in her private life. Abigail had soundly scolded her for leaving church early that day without meeting the man in town looking for a wife and mother for his newborn.

So Kerry had kept silent about her new situation, knowing Abigail would not approve and not wanting to listen to her harping.

"Well?" Abigail asked, suspicious eyes glued on Slade as Kerry struggled to frame her response.

"He's my hired hand," Kerry said, knowing it was the only logical answer but would doubtless elicit an astonished reaction from Abigail.

And she was right.

"Hired hand?" Abigail sputtered. "Why . . . why, how on earth can you afford a hired hand? You can hardly take care of yourself, much less anybody else. And who is he, anyway?"

"I can answer for myself, ma'am," Slade said coolly. He introduced himself, then went on to explain, "I'm just passing through, or I may decide to settle around here. I haven't made up my mind yet."

"He works for food." Kerry felt that needed to be understood after Abigail had helped her in so many ways. "And I don't know how I would have managed if he hadn't come along when he did. He's built me a chicken house, and a pen, and now I don't have to worry as much as I did about wild animals killing them."

"No, I suppose you don't." Abigail turned to Slade to ask, "So how long do you plan on working for Miss Corrigan?"

Kerry held her breath.

"I haven't given it much thought, ma'am. Till the work or food runs out, I guess."

Kerry breathed easier, then asked Abigail what brought her so far from town.

"My husband delivered Mrs. Annie Potts of a fine baby boy a short while ago. I came with him to help. We were with her since yesterday evening. She had a difficult time. We were on our way home, and I wanted to stop by and see how you are doing."

"Fine, just fine," Kerry said lamely, wondering why she felt so guilty. After all, she was a grown woman, and she had every right to hire someone to help on the farm.

Abigail shot a condemning glare at Slade, then motioned to Kerry and said, "Walk with me to the buggy. I told my husband I'd only be a minute."

Kerry turned to Slade, but he was already on his way out. "Wait for me," she called. "I want you to take the leftover venison with you in case you get hungry later."

Slade pretended not to hear and cursed himself all the way to the corral.

Quickly he saddled his horse and mounted.

Damn it, he was making a fine mess of things. He'd been sent to do a job and instead let his head get turned by a pair of incredibly green eyes that melted his heart with just a glance.

He had sworn to keep a rein on how he was feeling, because, by God, he'd wanted her on sight. Now he had crossed the line, reached the point of no return, and had no idea how to handle things from here on.

It was not the way it was supposed to be. His plan had been to show Kerry the papers proving that, as the legal stepson of Flann Corrigan, he was the rightful owner of the land. And she, as Flann's illegitimate daughter, had no claim. He would give her some money, out of the goodness of his heart, to help her get a start somewhere else. Then he could settle in, become a hardworking member of the community, and eventually the Klan would try to bring him into their fold.

And that was how it had to be. His plan . . . his assignment . . . had to be carried out.

Regardless of how he felt about Kerry.

He rode into the woods, cutting down by the Neuse River.

A few days earlier, when he was in town, he had stopped in a saloon for a beer. He had sat way at the end of the bar and given the impression of having nothing on his mind except sipping his brew and minding his own business. But he had taught himself to read lips and kept an eye on the mirror behind the bar. That was how he knew that the two men at the other end were talking about the Klan. They had heard there was to be a meeting at a place called John's Bend. They weren't going. They weren't Klan members. They heard things, and they talked, but they weren't involved, and from other things they said, Slade knew they did not want to be.

It had taken two more beers and an hour of appearing nonchalant before he managed to get the bartender to himself and make up the lie about wanting to do some fishing. John's Bend was a good place, he'd heard. Where might that be? He planned to go Sunday. The bartender was not in the least suspicious and gave directions.

So now Slade was on his way to start working on what he'd been sent to do. He would spy on the meeting and maybe find out exactly where the Klan planned to strike next. He might even see some faces, recognize somebody. Then again, he might not learn a damn thing, but at least he was trying. General Howard expected him to carry out his mission, and Slade demanded it of himself, as well.

As for Kerry, he was procrastinating, and, despite resolve, knew he would continue to do so as long as possible.

Because, no matter how hard he fought against it, he was thinking with his heart and not his head.

* * *

Kerry hurried after Abigail, intending to get rid of her as quickly as possible and return to Slade. She feared that what had just happened might make him think it best to leave, and she could not let that happen . . . not till she came to terms with what it all meant. It was as though she were in the throes of a spell cast by leprechauns, dazed and dizzy with the wonder of longing to be held by him . . . kissed by him . . . possessed by him.

As soon as they reached the front porch, Abigail turned on her, hands on her hips, face pinched in annoyance. "Oh, dear, dear Kerry, whatever are you thinking, inviting a hired hand to come into your house and eat at your table?"

Though grateful for everything Abigail had done for her, Kerry was not about to be made to feel ashamed for something she did not regret. "It seemed like the polite thing to do. And besides, I get lonely eating by myself all the time."

"Which is why you need a husband," Abigail said, gently patting her cheek. "Thad Albritton would have been perfect for you. And he went back to Raleigh quite disappointed not to have met you, I might add. We might still be able to do something about that. You and I could go for a visit. I've a cousin there. We could stay with her, and—"

"I don't think so," Kerry said, wanting to nip that idea in the bud. "I've got too much to do around here."

"Then I'll write him to come back to Goldsboro. There's a social in a few weeks, and it's going to be such fun. We have what's known as a pie dance. The ladies all bake their favorite pies, and they're cut into nine slices. Then they're auctioned off, one by one, to the gentlemen, who get a dance for each slice. The money goes to the needy, and neighbors get to meet neighbors, because the wives don't mind the husbands bidding on other women's pies, and the husbands don't mind their wives dancing with other men since it's all in fun and for a good cause. I'll invite Thad to come back for a visit, and you can get to know each other."

"I really don't think that would be a good idea."

Abigail's face darkened. "If you don't participate in the social, people will think you unfriendly, and that is not a wise thing, living off by yourself as you do. You never know when you might need someone's help.

"And your hired hand," she added with a sniff, "won't always be around when you need him."

Kerry bit back a groan. She did not want to make Abigail or anyone else mad. "It isn't that. Of course, I'll come. But I don't want Thad Albritton getting the wrong impression, because, as I have told you over and over, I am not looking for a husband."

Abigail smiled, undaunted. "Well, I'm going to write and invite him anyway. You might change your mind after you meet him. You'll love the baby, and—"

"Abigail, are you going to stay all night?" Dr. Ramsey called impatiently. "I'm tired and hungry." He tipped his hat to Kerry. "Good evening, Kerry."

"Good evening to you," she responded, then urged Abigail to run along. "We can talk about this later."

Finally, waving them out of sight, Kerry hurried back inside. "Slade, I'm so sorry about all that," she called, resisting the impulse to run through the house. Bad enough she had so brazenly welcomed his kiss.

She came to an abrupt halt to find the kitchen empty. Then a relieved wave swept over her to think that, of course, he would be on the back porch, probably sitting in the swing he'd repaired.

Pushing open the door, she was disappointed not to find him there.

It was getting dark, the sun slipping into the pines that rimmed the horizon. Everything was still. The chickens had already roosted for the night, and not a breeze was stirring. The quiet was almost spooky, and she shivered against it.

The path to the shacks had once been well worn, but there were weeds in places, and thorns grew at the edges. Slade had said he'd clear everything when he got around to it.

Her dress caught, snagged, and she had to stop and gingerly extricate it lest it tear.

Close enough that he should hear her, she called out, not really wanting to go any farther, "Slade, can you come here, please? I need you to help me get out of these thorns before I rip my dress to pieces."

There was no answer, and the stillness around her seemed to smother her.

Finally, she was free and hurried along, wanting to find him as quickly as possible and get back to the house before it got any darker.

Several more times she called but with no response, and at last she was in the clearing and feeling a bit embarrassed. After all, he might be taking care of personal needs.

But something told her that was not the case.

Just as another wave of foreboding warned she would not find him there at all.

Mustering all her nerve, she walked up on the porch of the shack he used for sleeping. There was enough light to see inside, and, sure enough, there was no sign of him.

From there, she made her way to the corral, where she was totally bewildered to see that his horse was not there.

Slade had left.

And, with a heavy heart, she could only pray he was coming back.

Chapter 10

Kerry was having a hard time convincing herself to get out of bed. Through the window she could see it was a gray, gloomy day, which matched her mood perfectly.

Rolling over, she pulled the sheet over her head. It was chilly, but despair was her blanket, wrapping tightly to suffocate and make her wonder what she was living for, anyway.

She felt so stupid now to think how she had been so excited when she had left Ireland to begin her new life in America. Had she known what awaited, she might have been tempted to just stay in her homeland and hide from her stepfather till he tired of searching. But it was too late for that now. There was nothing to be done but try to make the best of things as they were.

If only she had not been so drawn to Slade, she would not be feeling so heartsick now that he was gone. And why had he left so abruptly, anyway? Because they had kissed?

Touching her fingertips to her lips, she imagined she could still feel the lingering warmth of his mouth.

It had been sweet, wonderful . . . everything she had

ever dreamed a kiss might be. There was no reason it
should have made him run away . . . unless he had regretted
it and never wanted it to happen again.

But that was not likely. So it had to be something else. He
had mentioned she should be concerned about someone
trying to take her land away from her. Maybe he thought
that would eventually happen, so he might as well move
on to another job. Or perhaps Abigail had made him feel
it was improper for him to stay.

Kerry did not know and told herself not to care. She
had no business being so attracted to a man who could
only be considered—as Abigail had called him—a vagrant.

Throwing back the sheet, she sat up as a terrifying
thought struck. She had taken a stranger into her home
who could very well have killed her. Shuddering, other
horrifying images popped into her head—images of what
a man might do to a woman alone and helpless.

"But I'm not helpless," she muttered, throwing herself
back against the pillow. "I just have to learn to be quicker."
Lorne Petrie had caught her off quard. She had not
reached for her knife fast enough. And when Slade had
slipped up behind her, she'd not left her gun close enough.
She had to be more careful in the future, as well as alert.

She needed to make friends, too. With the mule and
cart, she was less than an hour's ride to town. She could
attend more church activities, meet more people, and if
Abigail pushed men at her looking for a wife, she would
just not encourage them.

Staring up at the ceiling with its rusty spots from rain
seeping beneath the tin roof, Kerry felt no gusto for life.
After all, she was still in a quandary trying to take care of
everything by herself. If only Luther and Bessie hadn't left,
she would have all the help she needed, plus companion-
ship. She had enjoyed being around them immensely. But
fear had driven them away, and she only wished she could
have done something to prevent it.

The rooster crowed. She felt like opening the window

and throwing something at him. He should be glad to stay in the cozy henhouse Slade had built, not strutting around in the pouring rain.

But, like the rooster, Kerry knew she had to get up and face the day's chores. Rain or not, there were several crates of eggs that had to be delivered. She could not take a chance on losing the money they would bring. Slade had said he would make the trip into town, but now it was up to her . . . like everything else.

"Well, what did you expect?" she challenged herself aloud and irritated. "That he would stay forever in exchange for food he had to go out and find himself?"

With a groan that sounded more like a growl, she forced herself to sit up and swing her legs to the side of the bed.

She felt a shiver when her feet touched the cold floor, and she quickly reached for her heavy boots. They were all she had besides her Sunday shoes, and she wasn't about to wear the dainty leather slippers around the house. Mr. Bedham offered a pair made for that purpose, though. Fashioned of thick lambskin with leather soles, they would be perfect to slip her feet into on a frosty morning instead of the hard, thick boots. She planned to buy them as soon as she had the money, though heaven only knew when that would be. What little she made on the eggs went to buy feed for the cow and the mule, as well as food for herself. And she found no comfort in thinking how that was how it would be from now on—just herself, and no one else.

Still shivering, she dressed quickly in her muslin dress and old ragged sweater. At the top of her chore list would be carrying in wood for the stove. Everything stacked on the back porch had been used. She also needed logs for the fireplace, because it appeared the weather was turning colder.

Opening the door into the kitchen, Kerry blinked and gave her head a shake.

Was she dreaming?

Firewood was neatly stacked next to the stove. And it was dry, too, which meant it had been taken from beneath the tarred canvas Slade had put over the woodpile. But who—?

She ran to the back door, opening it to look outside, but it was hard to see across the yard in the fog and rain. Then, glancing down, she saw wet footprints tracked all the way into the kitchen.

She did not dare to think it might have been Slade. If he could have left so easily after how he had kissed her, he would not be coming back. No, it could only be Luther. Or Adam, perhaps. But she had to know.

A gray poncho, one that Slade said he'd used in the war, hung on a peg inside the back door. At least he had not thought to take that with him. She threw it over her head and shoulders, then plunged down the porch steps and into the rain.

The wind had picked up. Kerry ducked her head and held on tightly to the poncho. It seemed she was blown back two steps for every one she took.

Maybe, she rationalized as she struggled along, Slade had just gone to the next farm down the road, which would be the Allison place. Luther or Adam might have seen him and known then that she would be alone. After all, word spread, even in such a vast area, and they had likely heard about him working for her. Perhaps they had taken pity and decided to chance coming back, and she prayed it was so.

Finally, she reached the row of shacks. Seeing the glow of a lantern through the window of the one Slade had used, she rushed up the steps and through the open door. "Luther? Adam? Let me in. Oh, I am so glad to see you. Thank God, you—"

Kerry was stunned to instead find Slade. And, with a cry of embarrassment to see he was naked, covered her face with her hands and began to back out the door. "Oh, I'm so sorry. I didn't know you were here."

Slade snatched up the wet shirt he had just taken off and held it in front of him. "Kerry, what in God's name are you doing busting in here like this? And you can take your hands down. I'm covered."

She peeked cautiously through her fingers. "You . . . you're all wet," was all she could think of to say as she felt her cheeks burning.

"Hell, yes, I'm all wet," he said with a nervous laugh. "I got this way by carrying your firewood. But it's my own fault. I should have done it yesterday. Now would you turn around while I get dressed?"

Spinning about on her heels, for a moment Kerry could not think of what to say or do, then, feeling the misery of her own soaked clothes, timorously asked, "Do you think it's wise to put your wet things back on? I mean, you could catch your death, as Mama used to say."

Oh, what must he take her for, she fretted, charging in as she had on his privacy? But amidst chagrin, Kerry continued to see in her mind the image of him naked. He was glorious with his firm, cupped buttocks and strong, muscular thighs. And, God forgive her if it was wrong for her to think so, but what she had seen between his legs made her burn and tingle between her own.

"I think I'd better go," she said nervously.

"Kerry, wait."

Her heart gave a hard bump. "I don't want you wearing wet things because of me."

"And I apologize," she said in a nervous rush, not turning around but not making a move to go, either. "I thought you'd gone, that it was Luther or Adam who stacked the wood, so I came to see. The door was open, and . . ." she shrugged, swallowed hard, and concluded, "I was just so happy to think they were back that I rushed right in."

With a teasing lilt to his voice, he said, "Well, I can't say it pleases me to know you'd be that happy to have them back. I thought you were getting used to having me around."

She started to turn in her haste to remind, "I thought you were gone," but caught herself in time.

"What made you think that? And you can turn around now."

She did so, relieved to see that he had snatched the saddle blanket he'd been using for cover to wrap around him. But the sight was still unnerving. The blanket hung low on his hips. Her gaze went to his rock-hard chest and the tantalizing mat of hair that trailed down to . . .

She glanced away.

She knew where the trail ended . . . could see a slight bulge beneath the blanket.

"I . . . I was here last evening," she stammered, still struggling for composure. But then she'd never seen a naked man before, and this one, in particular, seemed to have an effect on her like no other. "I came after Abigail left, to make sure your feelings weren't hurt by how she acted."

"Kerry, I don't think I've ever had my feelings hurt in my entire life."

She eased her gaze back to him and saw that he was grinning. "Well, anyway, when I saw your horse was also gone, I thought you'd decided to leave. I mean, why else wouldn't you be here at night?"

"Because I like to ride at night," he said simply.

"But it's not safe. I mean, there's the Ku Klux Klan, and—"

"And they aren't going to bother me, a white man, Kerry. I'm afraid you scare too easily, as well as worry too much. But rest assured that when I do decide to move on, I'll let you know. I won't just go and leave you stranded, all right?"

It seemed so natural, the way he came slowly towards her to rest his hands on her shoulders. But Kerry began to tremble, as always, at his touch.

He felt it and thought she was having a chill. "You're a

fine one to talk about anybody wearing wet clothes. You need to get home and change."

It was only then, when they stepped onto the little front porch, that they realized the skies had opened to unleash a pounding downpour.

She was standing in front of him. His hands had slipped from her shoulders a bit as he absently caressed her arms. "You can't go till it eases up."

"I . . . I'll be fine," she said uneasily, moving from his grasp to stand at the edge of the porch.

An awkward silence descended.

Kerry bit her lip, wishing to heaven she had stayed at home. She could hear him behind her, so close, his breathing heavy, ragged.

Finally, to break the tension she said, "I'm glad to know Abigail didn't offend you, Slade. I'm happy to have you work for me, and I don't care what people think, either."

He surprised her by saying, "Well, you should. You're a woman, and it's important that you be above reproach. Maybe it would be best if I did move on before long."

"No." Throwing pride to the wind that howled through the pines, Kerry spun about to cry, "No. I didn't realize till I thought you'd gone how lonely I would be without you. You're my friend, Slade, and I want you to stay, and . . ."

She fell silent, bemused to see that suddenly his expression was one of concern as well as anger.

"Slade, what's wrong? I mean, if you've got a notion to leave, I won't try to stop you."

"It's not that," he said.

"Then what?"

Suddenly he reached for her, drawing her against his chest as he pressed his lips to her forehead. "You didn't figure into my plans, green eyes," he whispered huskily.

Kerry swayed in his embrace as he continued to hold her tightly. "And what plans did you have?" she asked, voice quavering.

He took her chin between his thumb and forefinger,

forcing her to look at him. "When the time is right, I'll tell you. For now, I can't think of anything but you . . . and this . . ."

His lips covered hers to sear and possess, but only for an instant as he paused to whisper, "Tell me to stop, Kerry, because, God forgive me, I want you."

Held captive by his protective embrace and seduced by his seeking mouth and caressing hands, Kerry could only cling to him and answer his kiss. His tongue plunged boldly into her mouth, and she met it with her own, pressing against him as though she could not get close enough.

She was not thinking about the right or wrong of it. All she wanted, needed, was here and now in his arms.

As his lips seized hers in a kiss deep and hungry, Slade swiftly, deftly, stripped her of her wet clothing and rendered her naked.

Hotly, feverishly, his hands moved up and down her back, then slowly lowered to squeeze her buttocks tight and roughly pull her into the swelling of his desire.

Kerry felt it, and with a half-groan, half-laugh, she wondered how she would ever be able to take all of him within her.

Then she was being lifted and carried to the bed, where he gently laid her down.

She watched, wide-eyed, as he yanked the saddle blanket from around him and tossed it aside.

She looked at him—*there*, and again marveled at the hugeness.

He seemed to know what she was thinking. "Don't worry. I'll be gentle."

He lowered himself to lie beside her, pulling her into his arms. For long, long moments he kissed her, bruising her lips with the intensity of his longing. Then slowly, very slowly, he lifted his mouth, and his tongue began to trail downwards.

Kerry's breath caught in her throat, expecting the same divine sensation of the night before when he had so sweetly assaulted her throat. But he did not stop there. The raging trail of fire moved on, and then she cried out loud with the delighted feel of his tongue against her nipple.

Rolling it around and around, he teased and tantalized before drawing it into his mouth to suckle. She arched against him, offering all she had to give. And as his lips devoured one breast, his fingers delighted by plucking the nipple of the other as she had picked blackberries from the bush.

Their breaths came in mingled gasps as he tore from his assault. He rolled to his side, pulling her to face him.

She stared deeply into his eyes. His tanned face was hard and flushed with passion, sea-blue eyes smoldering. "In a few seconds, Kerry, I won't be able to stop myself. So you'd better tell me now . . . before it's too late."

Kerry, in her naiveté, was unaware of just how hard Slade was trying to keep his passion under control. All she could think of was how her nipples tingled and longed for him to touch them again. And the burning deep in her loins filled her with the strange desire to move against him . . . *down there,* to feel him inside her, consuming her. Wanton. Wicked. She was all these things and did not care, for she was too far lost down the path of raw, raging hunger that could only be fed by unbridled lust.

She raised her hand to trace the line of his finely chiseled mouth, was about to brazenly tell him she wanted him every bit as much as he wanted her, when he drew a hoarse breath and warned, "Don't look at me that way with those damned beautiful green eyes. You don't know what it does to me, and I may not be able to hold back."

"I don't want you to," she said suddenly, boldly kissing him. This time it was she who parted his lips with her tongue to plunge inside. She felt him shudder, and then he was pushing her on her back, almost roughly. He began kissing her with unleashed passion, teeth cutting into her lips as though he could not get enough of her. His hands went to her breasts, squeezing, then letting go, only to squeeze again.

She delighted in the feel, the gentle, savage pain of having him caress so boldly.

"Tell me if I hurt you," he raised his mouth long enough to say, kneading her tender flesh possessively all the while.

For answer, her hands twined about his neck to pull him closer.

Never had she known it could feel so good to have a man touch her breasts. But then she knew so little about sex . . . about coupling between a man and woman. Her mother had told her it was necessary for a man to plant his seed to make a baby but had said nothing about the splendor to be experienced while he did so.

He lifted his mouth from hers and smiled down at her briefly before lowering to again suckle each breast in turn.

Kerry wriggled deliciously, undulating her hips as she felt his hardness between her thighs, pressing . . . seeking . . .

"Don't . . . don't do that," he whispered, tongue flicking across a taut nipple. "Not yet. I don't want to rush you, sweetheart. I want you ready . . ."

"I am ready," she cried hoarsely, feeling as though her heart was going to leap out of her chest because it was beating so fiercely. She could almost feel her hot blood rushing through her veins, for longing had taken over all reason. She was now careening into a blossoming abyss of pleasure from which there was no turning back.

Spreading her knees, he bent them against her chest, then raised up on his own between her. "I have to ask you this, Kerry," he said thickly. "Is this your first time?"

She blinked, at first not understanding.

"Have you ever been with a man before?"

Her whispered "no" was barely audible.

"Then it will make it easier if I do this first . . ."

And before she knew what was happening, he had thrust a finger up and into her. She felt one sharp pain and cried out, but he quickly muffled the sound with a kiss.

Then, in one swift motion, he entered her.

Kerry was slammed back against the mattress. His mouth slipped from hers, and she cried out again but this time with pleasure, not pain.

"Am I hurting you?"

She swung her head from side to side, dimly aware that even if he had been he would not have been able to stop. Not now. They were hurtling towards the stars and nothing could hold them back.

His thrusts were hard, rhythmic, as he held her tightly by her waist.

Kerry's nails dug into the hard flesh of his shoulders as she held on, wanting to meet his every jab. Soon her hips caught the cadence, and not only did she lift upwards, but she began to unconsciously wriggle about, as well.

"Oh, God, Kerry, you're making me crazy," he gasped.

Kerry could not respond. She was lost in the sensual drive of needs she'd never dreamed she had . . . and pleasure she never thought possible.

Suddenly he slowed. Kerry's eyes had been half closed, so lost was she in ecstasy. Now they flashed open, as she wondered what was wrong.

"I won't pleasure myself before you," he vowed as his thumb and forefinger closed on the tiny nub above her opening.

He began to squeeze and rub, all the while continuing to push himself in and out of her.

Kerry arched her neck, pressing her head back into the pillow as he continued to stroke the nucleus of her sex, every nerve in her body aflame. Her breathing was labored, anguished almost, and her heart thundered against his sweat-slick chest.

From somewhere deep within she felt the shuddering and was at first frightened, wondering where it would all lead. Instinctively, she tightened her legs about Slade and squeezed. He felt her and took his hand away, his thrusts becoming faster, harder. His mouth closed over hers, and she drank of the sweetness of his tongue as it seemed to devour her.

The shuddering became a violent tremor . . . and the tremor an explosion.

Kerry bucked from the bed, tearing her mouth from his as she grabbed him with all her might to hug and squeeze him closer.

In that instant she felt driven to become a part of him so they would soar to ecstasy nonpareil as one. It felt as though he had touched the very heart of her as he shoved into her with all his might. And, uttering several pleasured moans, he was spent and still.

It seemed an eternity before he moved from on top of her.

Outside, the rain had slowed, but wind still rifled through the pines. All was quiet, and Kerry felt her heart slow to normal, her breathing become even once more.

"I hope I didn't hurt you," he said, anxiously searching her face for any symptom of distress.

She touched his cheek. "No. I'm all right. I just hope you"—she hesitated, unsure how to say it, then plunged ahead—"don't think ill of me, Slade. I don't know what came over me. I could not make myself push you away."

"And I'm glad you didn't." He reached for her fingertips and pressed them against his mouth.

"We have to be careful," she said, feeling a wave of guilt. "If anyone were to think we had done this . . ." She shivered to think.

Suddenly, despite what had just happened, she was swept with embarrassment to be lying next to him naked. Drawing her hand from his, she groped about for the saddle blanket, then covered herself.

She stared up at the ceiling, feeling terribly awkward and wondering what people did . . . *afterwards.*

"Maybe I should go," she said thinly. "Someone might come. A hunter, or—"

She turned to look at him, wondering why he was so quiet.

His eyes were closed, his breathing slow and even as he slept.

Slowly, so as not to awaken him, Kerry got out of bed. Quickly putting on her still-wet clothes, she slipped out of the shack and into the morning mist.

They would talk later, she smiled to think, for something so wonderful could only mean the beginning of something even better.

Slade had lain very still as she got up. He only pretended to sleep, though God knew how bad he wanted to. He had been up all night. The meeting had proved not to be a meeting after all, because only three men showed up. He couldn't see their faces. They were wearing Klan garb. And he could not get close enough to hear what they were saying but could tell they were annoyed about the others not being there.

Though no one else came, the trio hung around till all hours, sharing a bottle of whiskey. When they finally gave up and went home, Slade decided to trail one of them. If he learned where he lived, then he would know the identity of one Klansman, at least. The problem was, he did not know the woods yet and lost him in the darkness—and got lost himself. It had been near day before he finally found his way back to the farm.

But he would not let that happen again. He intended to go out during daylight, on the pretense of hunting, and learn every back road and hog path there was in the whole damn county.

He had a job to do, and he was going to do it. And even though Kerry had sidetracked him for a while, he had made up his mind what to do about that. He'd had a lot of time to think during the long night, and the answer was really quite simple.

He would marry her.

He would court her proper and then make her his wife.

It was the only right thing to do. After all, she needed a man to take care of her, and it would solve all his problems about having a reason to stay around so he could carry out his assignment.

He was not ready, however, to think about what would happen when he finished. Since leaving Tennessee he'd given little thought to being a farmer . . . and even less to taking a wife. And would he take her with him or stay there? He could not think that far ahead for the moment.

As for loving her, well, he could not be sure. Not yet, anyway. But one thing was for certain, she was always on his mind, no matter where he was or what he was doing. So maybe, in a way, he did.

He liked to think so, anyway . . . and found himself hoping she felt the same way.

If so, they were on the right track to happiness somewhere down the road.

But for the present, Slade told himself he had to focus on whatever it took to carry out his objective.

There would be time later to find out whether he had made yet another foolish mistake with a woman.

Chapter 11

Slade well knew how a man could get a lot of foolish notions when stricken with the fever of passion. So when he awoke sometime around noon, the first thing he thought of was his plan to court Kerry.

He told himself he would never have entertained such a notion if not for the heat of the moment. But maybe it wasn't such a bad idea. He supposed he still had a bit of the wanderlust. There were places he'd never seen. He wouldn't mind staying a spell in Mexico. Then there was California and on up to Oregon and all the trails being blazed there.

So he hadn't given much thought to marriage, and now that opportunity was staring him in the face, he was forced to really consider settling down.

Marrying Kerry would solve a lot of problems, but, beyond that, he cared for her. Deeply. True, they hadn't known each other long, but what time they were together had been a pleasure he'd not known in quite a while.

Since Mary Beth, the only time he got close to a woman was in bed. With Kerry it had been just the opposite. Sure, he had wanted her all along, but he also liked being around her. They were friends first and lovers second, and he'd never had that with a woman before.

Not even Mary Beth.

Prim and proper, she was a lady in every way, the epitome of virtue.

And he had bedded her the first time they were alone together. After that, they could not seem to get enough of each other. Now he could look back and see that maybe that was all they ever had—lust. With Kerry, there was friendship and caring, which was new to Slade . . . and he liked it.

But first things first, he reminded himself with a deep sigh as he forced himself to rise up and sit on the edge of the bed. Things were going well with Kerry. He didn't have to worry about her running him off now. And there was time enough to start courting her. Meanwhile, he needed to find out when the Klan would have a big meeting.

He was glad to see it had quit raining. He was supposed to take eggs into town, and he was running late. By the looks of the sun behind the clouds yet hovering, it was probably getting on close to one o'clock. He would have to hurry.

He shaved, then washed in the overflowing creek just up the path. He dressed in clean denim trousers and a white cotton shirt, then went to the house.

Kerry was sitting on the back porch, carefully washing each egg with a wet cloth before packing it in a basket. Glancing up, she first frowned at the sight of him, as though not knowing what to expect. But when he grinned and waved, so did she, and it was as if the sun had finally come out from behind the clouds.

Kerry had seen him approaching but had pretended not to. She felt so miserably awkward. After all, she'd never had to face a man after he had made love to her, and she was not sure how to act. "I thought you were going to sleep all day," was all she could think of to say, careful to keep her voice as nonchalant as possible.

He sat down beside her on the step and gave her knee a little pat. "Well, I just wasn't in a hurry to wake up, because I was dreaming about you."

"That ... that's nice," she floundered, wishing she could think of something clever to say and not sound like an embarrassed schoolgirl. She was a grown woman, for heaven's sake. And this man before her had made love to her only a few hours earlier, and she could not let herself go all to pieces lest he think her a fool.

Noticing how she had paled, he asked, "Kerry, how do you feel?"

About what? she bit her tongue to keep from screaming. *Physically? Or emotionally, because I'm wondering if you think me a whore?* Instead, she managed to breezily tell him, "I'm fine. I was just getting ready to take the eggs into town."

"But that's my job."

She wrinkled her nose, her smile impish. "You might want me to go ahead and do it. Abigail Ramsey told me she'd need six dozen this week instead of her usual order, and she wanted them delivered to her house instead of Mr. Bedham's store. She's baking pies for the church social for those who can't afford the fixings to make their own." She told him about the auction, concluding, "So I didn't think you'd want to be around her after yesterday."

He looked her straight in the eye. "I don't run from anybody, Kerry. If you want me to take the eggs to her, I will."

He seemed rather snappish, which Kerry found strange. Wasn't it supposed to be a tender time between them? It would seem so. "Well, when I thought you'd left for good, I planned to make the delivery myself."

She stood, and so did he. "Well, I'm still here, and I'd like to keep earning my keep if you'll let me."

He turned away, then paused to look at her with an

almost wretched expression. "Look, Kerry, I'm not real good with words, and I suppose there's something I should say to you after"—he hesitated—"what we did."

Kerry looked everywhere but at him. "I don't know what there is to say, Slade. I mean, it happened, and there's nothing we can do about it."

"Then you don't think I should just ride on out of your life?"

"Of course I don't," she was quick to assure. "After all, we made a deal, didn't we? But maybe we should watch ourselves in other matters." It was as close as she could come to saying she did not expect it to happen again. As much as she wanted him, she would not let herself become his whore.

He stared at her for long, tense moments, then murmured, "I'm sorry you feel that way. You didn't seem to this morning."

"I've had time to think about it."

He nodded, more to himself than to her. "Well, if that's what you want."

He went to hitch the mule to the cart, taking the basket with him. She supposed she should offer him lunch but decided it best to let him go. It was awkward being together for the time being, and she wanted to be alone with her thoughts a while longer.

She sank back down and hugged her knees to her chin, watching him as he took the mule from the shed and began to fasten his harness.

It had been wonderful.

No, it had been more than that.

It had been the most incredible experience in her whole life and one she would never, ever forget.

So why, then, did she wish it had never happened?

Sadly, she knew the answer.

Because it could never happen again, even though she wanted it to—over and over. If she could be in Slade Dillon's arms for the rest of her life, she would never ask for anything more. But it was useless to hope, as she reminded herself over and over that he was just a drifter and, having drifted into her life, would doubtless exit the same way.

And although she had fought against it, she knew he would take a piece of her heart when he did.

"Miz Kerry, Miz Kerry . . ."

Her head jerked up at the sound, and then she was leaping to her feet to see it was Luther, coming around the side of the house. His black face was almost white with terror, his eyes big and round and filled with tears.

She bounded down the steps to meet him. "Luther, what's wrong? What's happened?"

He was out of breath from running and had to gasp a time or two before he could speak. "It's Bessie. She's just gone all to pieces, Miz Kerry, on account of Adam."

Kerry was clutching his shoulders, giving him a gentle shake in hopes he would get hold of himself. "What happened to Adam?"

"He got burned savin' Toby. He's gonna be all right, but he brought Toby home with him, and he's hidin' him from Master Allison, and Bessie, she's afraid of what Master Allison is gonna do if he finds out. Only Toby, he can't leave 'cause he's burned worse than Adam."

Kerry's head was spinning. "I don't understand, Luther. Now slow down and tell me from the beginning what happened."

He sank down on the bottom step. She went into the house and came back with a cup of water. After he drank, he told her that Adam had come to them last night and said he'd just heard that smoke had been seen coming from the home of a friend of his—Toby.

Luther paused to explain to Kerry how Toby had come to own the little cabin down by the river. It had been abandoned after the owner was killed in the war, and Toby had paid the taxes owed and taken it over. Adam had warned Toby there might be trouble. White folks, Luther

said, did not like freedmen owning land, especially if it
had belonged to a Confederate soldier. To make for even
more resentment, Toby had earned the money to pay the
taxes by going North during the war and working in a
munitions factory.

Luther went on to say how he and Bessie tried to keep
Adam from getting involved, but he was bound and determined to go to his friend's aid. A few hours later he
returned, his hands and arms burned from trying to put
out the fire after the Klan left.

"Toby's wife was in the family way," Luther said, bowing
his head as though embarrassed to speak of it to Kerry.
"But she lost the baby right after Adam brought 'em to
our place."

Kerry's hand went to her throat as she swallowed back
tears. "Oh, I am so sorry, Luther. What can I do?"

"If you could come see to Bessie, I'd be real grateful,
Miz Kerry. She always thought so highly of you, and only
the good Lord knows how she hated havin' to leave you
like we did. And now we're afraid Master Allison will find
out Adam brought Toby and his wife home with him, and
Bessie is frettin' something awful. Maybe you can get her
to calm down. Maybe you can help with Adam's and Toby's
burns, too."

Kerry did not hesitate. "I'll do what I can, of course.
Just give me a minute to gather some things I'll need. I
found some aloe plants growing at the edge of the woods
the other day and made some syrup in case I ever got
burned. I'll get it and . . ."

She fell silent to see Luther beginning to back away from
her, looking terrified all over again.

Following his stricken gaze, she saw Slade coming
towards them in the cart which he had hitched to the
mule.

Kerry put a hand on Luther's trembling shoulder. "It's
all right. He's a friend of mine. My hired hand, actually.
His name is Slade Dillon, and—"

"And he ain't got no business knowin' about none o' this, Miz Kerry," Luther whispered in panic.

"I told you—it's all right. We can trust him."

Slade reined in the mule and got down off the cart. He saw how Luther was looking at him and asked Kerry, "What's wrong? What's going on here?"

Despite how Luther was twisting his straw hat in his shaking hands, his watery eyes mirroring a plea for her to keep silent, she repeated the story to Slade, then urged, "Promise me you won't tell anyone."

Slade drew a long, harsh breath. "Don't worry. I don't want to be involved in any of this, and I'd advise you to stay out of it, as well."

"Well, I'm afraid I have no choice. Somebody has to help them."

He drew her to one side and quietly reminded, "You don't owe them anything. They didn't mind leaving you to fend for yourself."

"They were scared," she defended. "And they are even more so now. But that's beside the point. I have to do whatever I can, so I'm going with Luther now. If I'm not here when you get back from town, you'll know where I am."

He frowned. "I can't stop you. Just be careful."

He loaded the cart with the rest of the eggs that were stacked on the porch. Then, without saying anything more, he got back in the cart, snapped the reins, and left as fast as the mule would go.

Kerry hurried inside to gather what she wanted to take with her. Luther followed Slade to stand in the road and watch till he was out of sight.

When she came back out, Luther was sitting on the steps again. His shoulders were slumped, and he was shaking from head to toe.

"Stop worrying, Luther," she said, patting his shoulder. "Everything will be all right. Now let's go."

"You don't understand, Miz Kerry," he said brokenly,

hands splayed across his face as he shook his head from side to side. "You shouldn't have tol' that man about this."

"Please stop fretting over that. I assure you he can be trusted."

"Miz Kerry," he said miserably, taking his hands from his face so he could look straight into hers, "how do you know he ain't one of 'em?"

Slade was mad enough to bite a nail in two.

Now he knew what had happened last night . . . why the meeting never took place. The nitwits he had overheard talking got their directions wrong. They were waiting at the wrong spot. And while they were waiting, the Klan had met elsewhere, then taken off to burn Toby's shack.

"Damn it, I could have been there," Slade spoke aloud between clenched teeth. And while he could not have stopped what ultimately happened, he might have managed to get some clue as to who was responsible . . . who some of the cowards were that hid behind their masks.

And now, on top of everything else, he had to worry about Kerry getting involved. He did a lot of listening when he was in town and had heard that Hank Allison was the sort of man who would be real upset if he found out his workers had taken in a man targeted by the Klan.

It was also said he still treated his black workers as if they were slaves and beat them sometimes. Slade did not want Kerry around should that happen.

As for Allison himself being in the Klan, Slade did not think so. He had already checked him out. Allison had publicly denounced the Klan and said they'd better leave his coloreds alone, promising to shoot any man who came on his land causing trouble. He was a bully through and through, but a very private bully, having nothing to do with anyone outside his family.

* * *

Slade made the delivery to Bedham's store, then headed for the Ramsey house. Despite giving Kerry the impression he didn't mind, he was dreading the encounter with Abigail and hoped he could just leave the eggs on her porch and go. She could pay Kerry the next time she saw her. Because the fact of the matter was he thought Abigail was a big snob, even if she had been nice to Kerry by seeing that she got clothes fit to wear to church and had cajoled Bedham into giving her the mule and cart.

The Ramsey house was one of the finest in Goldsboro. On Elm Street, jutting off from Center Street, it was two stories with a turret. The dining room came out from the main part, making the porch L-shaped—running across the front and down the side.

Slade knew better than to coax the stubborn old mule into going down the path by the side of the house to the rear. So he got out and tied the reins to a tree. Then he took the eggs out of the cart and walked the rest of the way.

He made it to the back porch without seeing anyone. Folks like Mrs. Ramsey had maids. They wore white dresses with blue aprons and matching bandanas around their heads. He wouldn't mind running into her maid, but it looked as though he would be lucky enough to get away without having to talk to anybody.

He set the eggs down in the shade and turned on his heel, thinking how good the cold beer at Lloyd Swenson's saloon was going to taste.

"Just you wait a minute, young man."

A door banged, and Slade swallowed a groan.

It was Abigail.

"Since when do you leave my order and not ask to be paid?"

He forced himself to turn around and politely tip his

felt hat. "Well, I was in kind of a hurry, Mrs. Ramsey, and I figured you could just pay Kerry when you see her in church."

Abigail sniffed. "I don't recall seeing you in church, Mr. Dillon."

"I'm afraid I haven't been much lately, ma'am." Actually, the last time he'd seen the inside of a church was when his mother took him when he was still in short pants.

He had politely returned to stand at the bottom of the porch steps.

Abigail stared down her pointed nose in scrutiny. "Then I suppose we should take this opportunity to get to know each other better."

In his usually blunt way, Slade cocked his head to one side to ask, "For what purpose, ma'am? All I do is deliver your eggs each week."

"To be quite frank, Mr. Dillon, I have grown very fond of Kerry. She's a stranger in our land and has no family. I've taken it upon myself to look after her, which is why I feel I have a right to know a few things about you since you're living on her farm."

Biting back the impulse to tell her to mind her own damn business, Slade managed to genially respond, "There's nothing to tell. I'm a hired hand. Nothing more. I have the utmost respect for Miss Corrigan. And since it upset you so much for me to break bread at her table, I can assure you it won't happen again."

"And just how long do you plan to hang around these parts?"

She was starting to really get under his skin. Bad enough was her prying, but he did not like the way she looked at him as if he were so much dirt to be swept off the steps. Still, he did not want to risk making an enemy, not when it was important to his mission to be accepted by the townsfolk as one of them—a loyal Southerner.

"I'll stay as long as she needs help, Mrs. Ramsey," he said pleasantly. "But if you think it's improper—and I can see you're a lady of refinement who would know about such things—I'll move on. I don't know what she'll do, what with winter coming on. Then there's the matter of her safety, living off alone.

"However," he finished with a helpless shrug, "if you think it's best, I'll leave." He knew he was taking a chance, because she might tell him to do just that, and he had no intention of going anywhere till he was good and ready. But he had always enjoyed bluffing in a poker game, so it came as second nature to try it on Abigail.

And it worked.

He saw pure pleasure mirrored on her face, and the smile she bestowed upon him was warm as sunshine after rain.

"Why, Mr. Dillon, that's comforting to hear. But I'm sure that, now that you understand the decorum that's expected of you, everything will be fine."

"Yes, ma'am." He tipped his hat again. "And it was nice talking to you. Good afternoon."

He had taken only a few steps when she called out to him again. He cringed but managed not to scowl as he wheeled about.

"One more thing. It would be a nice thing for you to come to church sometime. Not with Kerry, of course. People might get the wrong idea. But we all need to feed our spiritual souls, Mr. Dillon. So I'll be looking for you."

She went inside, and Slade wasted no time getting to the cart and on his way. He wasn't taking any chances on her thinking of something else to say.

He was proud of how he had handled the situation but needed a beer more than ever.

Lloyd Swenson's place was in the heart of town. Slade took his usual seat at the end of the bar where he could observe without being obvious about it. Lloyd was used to seeing him and knew without asking to draw him a tall brew from the keg behind the bar.

Lloyd, Slade had noticed, had accepted the fact that

Slade was a loner. Lloyd would set the beer down, make a grunting noise of greeting, then leave him alone. But this day he lingered, polishing glasses and darting a cursory glance at him now and then.

Slade did not acknowledge his presence, just stared straight ahead into the mirror, surreptitiously watching everything around him.

He sensed that Lloyd wanted to say something, but there were a few customers on the stools not far away. Finally, when they drifted away, Lloyd edged closer to Slade and said, "You've been coming in here for a few weeks now. You planning on staying in these parts?"

Slade had hoped that sooner or later Lloyd would initiate conversation. Being the proprietor of a saloon made him privy to things going on that others might not be aware of—like Klan activities.

Careful not to sound too eager to talk about himself, Slade drawled, "Well, that all depends on how long the work lasts."

"You working out at the Corrigan place, are you?"

"That's right. How'd you know?"

"Word gets around. The county ain't all that big, and we old-timers notice new faces . . . especially when they are dressed in damned Yankee blue." He watched Slade for his reaction.

And Slade gave him what he'd hoped for. "You won't catch me in a uniform or around any sonofabitch wearing one."

Lloyd guffawed at that and reached to draw him another beer. "It's on the house. One Reb to another. But I could tell you weren't a blue belly. Didn't have the right smell," he said with a conspiratorial grin.

Slade managed to match it. "Good thing you figured me for a Reb. I'd hate to have to fight a man in his own saloon."

They both laughed long and loud. Then Lloyd got himself a beer and leaned on the counter to make small talk.

He asked how things were going at the farm. Slade said pretty good and easily brought up the Klan by adding, "Of course, if it hadn't been for the coloreds being scared off by the Klan and moving over to the Allison place, there'd be no work for me to do."

Lloyd's eyes narrowed. "And how do you feel about that?"

Slade feigned ignorance. "About what? Her coloreds leaving? Hell, it's fine with me. It gave me a job."

"No. I mean about the Ku Klux Klan," he said quietly, glancing about to make sure no one else could hear. "Folks have mixed opinions."

Slade lifted his shoulders in an indifferent shrug. "I don't know. Haven't really thought about it. But I have to say I'm all for keeping the coloreds in their place. Just because the war is over and they got freed doesn't mean they can take over and act like they're as good as we are."

It was the right answer, because Lloyd gave a slight nod and grinned. But Slade also knew Lloyd was going to take it slow and easy. After all, he was still considered a stranger. There would be much scrutiny before he was ever taken into any kind of confidence, much less invited to join the Klan. All that would take time, and he had to be careful every step of the way.

Still, it was a beginning, and Slade decided to lay the groundwork for making Lloyd realize he might soon have real roots. "You know, I like it here," he said with gusto. "I like it a lot. And if you can keep a secret, the truth is I might be staying, after all."

"Is that a fact? So what kind of work are you going to be doing once you're finished up at the Corrigan place?"

"That's just it." Slade winked. "I might not finish. After all, Miss Corrigan is a comely young thing, and she's in need of a husband with all that land to look after. I lost everything back home in Tennessee during the war. So who knows? I may just settle right here."

Lloyd held out his hand and grinned. "Well, I wish you luck, Dillon."

Others came in, and Lloyd had to wait on them.

Slade downed the rest of his beer, slid off the stool, and went outside into the gathering dusk.

Soon it would be dark, and he needed to get back to the farm in hopes Kerry would be there.

If not, then he might just have to go after her, because something told him all hell might break loose once the Klan found out where Toby had taken refuge.

And Slade was damned if she was going to be a part of it.

Chapter 12

The shack where Luther and Bessie lived was pitiful. There were cracks in the logs wide enough to slip a hand through. And not only was there no glass in the windows but no shutters either. Kerry supposed they would board them up in the winter, but even then there was no stove for heat. They would have to huddle next to oil lanterns to try and find warmth and wrap themselves in blankets.

Bessie had calmed a bit after Kerry arrived, but part of that, no doubt, was owing to the turned cider she had brought, left over from the night before. Now Bessie sat in the dilapidated rocker by the window, eyes closed as she softly prayed for them all.

Adam's burns were bad but would heal. Toby was not as bad as Kerry had feared. And other than suffering from a broken heart, his wife would be all right in a day or two. Bruised and swollen, she had fallen when she ran out the back of the shack after it was set afire. That had led to her miscarriage, which had left her very weak from loss of blood.

It was late. Long ago Luther had reported seeing the

lights go out at the big house, as he called the Allison mansion. After that, other workers living nearby slipped quietly in to offer what they could—blankets for pallets on the floor, because there were only two rickety cots in the shack. Toby and his wife each had one, and Adam slept on the dirt floor.

They brought food, as well, because Bessie had been too upset to join them at the communal pot where all the former slaves gathered to cook supper together. Kerry had never had catfish stew before but was willing to try it, along with the fried corn pone, because she was so hungry. Then she found she liked it and would have taken a second portion had there been enough for everyone to do so.

She heard a gentle snoring and was relieved to see that Bessie had nodded off. She tucked a blanket around her, then settled back on the floor where she had been sitting.

Luther, lying at Bessie's feet, said, "Bless you, Miz Kerry. You've been such a help to us today. But I'm worried about you gettin' home. I'll walk you if you're bound to go, but I don't think it's safe for us to be out at night. If any of the Klan was to see me walkin' with a white woman at this hour . . ." He shuddered to think about it.

She told him not to worry. She had no intention of doing anything so foolish. Besides, Slade knew where she was and would likely come get her in the morning. She hoped he would not let anyone see him. It was important to keep Mr. Allison from finding out what was going on.

Adam was awake and staring at her in the mellow light. She regretted having to remind him, "We have to get them out of here tomorrow, before Mr. Allison finds out they're here."

"I know," he said drearily. "I've been layin' here tryin' to figure out where to take 'em. They're not safe anywhere now."

Kerry was jolted. "You mean the Klan would still attack them if they found them?"

He gave a wrenching sigh. "Yes'm. They'll kill 'em if

they can. That's what they meant to do. They told Toby that before they threw the torches on the roof. They gave him his choice—come out and be hanged or stay inside and burn to death. They didn't count on him bein' able to escape in all the smoke or me gettin' there in time to help him.''

Kerry was sickened to the pit of her stomach.

She was also mad.

Very mad.

That human beings could treat other human beings in such a way was beyond the realm of her imagination. She had thought her stepfather cruel and vicious, but he was nothing compared to these masked monsters who seemed spawned of the devil himself.

"Do you have any ideas where we can take them?"

Adam blinked. "Did you say *we?*"

"Yes, I'll help you. I've got the cart and mule, and—"

Sharply, angrily, he cut her off. "You've done all you're gonna do, Miz Kerry. You can't be gettin' involved in any of this. It's too dangerous. And if I had known Papa was goin' to get you, I wouldn't have let him go."

"Had to," Luther said grumpily. "Your mama needed help. I didn't dare ask none of the other women, not in broad daylight. Especially when every hand is needed in the fields to pick the last of the cotton. I had to come up with a good story for the overseer. I said we all had dysentery."

Kerry opined, "And it's not likely he'll believe that story again tomorrow. So, Luther, you and Bessie can go back to the fields, but you, Adam"—she looked at him and shook her head—"will have to leave with Toby and Ellie. Your hands are too burned to pick cotton, and if word gets back to the Klan that you were the one who helped them escape, they'll be after you, too."

"She's right," Luther said. "You gotta run, too."

"Is there anyone who will help you who lives far from here?" she asked Adam.

Adam did not have to think about it and excitedly told her they could go to Atlanta. "I got kin there, and I won't have any trouble finding work on account of all the rebuilding goin' on. I've wanted to go before now but couldn't talk Mama and Papa into goin' with me, and I didn't want to leave 'em behind."

"This be my home," Luther said with a stubborn lift of his chin. "I ain't leavin' till the Lord takes me up to His."

Kerry was not about to get involved in family disagreements. With a clap of her hands, she declared, "Then it's all settled. Bring Toby and Ellie and meet me at first light at the bridge up the road. You should be safe leaving at such an early hour, because no one will be up yet. You can be out of the county by the time people start heading for the fields. Besides, you can't travel at night, because the Klan"—the word was like bitter bile on her tongue—"might be out tormenting some other helpless soul."

Adam held up one of his pitifully burned hands in protest. "No, Miz Kerry. We can't take your cart and mule. That's all you got to use for deliverin' eggs."

"Don't worry. I'll walk if I have to, but we've got to get you all to safety as quick as possible."

"I could take 'em and bring the cart back," Luther offered.

Kerry squelched that idea. "You need to be here to tell Mr. Allison you don't know anything about Adam's disappearance. If you're not around for a few days he might get suspicious. Besides, you need to be here with Bessie."

Adam crawled across the floor to his father, who seemed about to cry. "Listen, I'll be back. I'm not gonna leave you and Mama for good. When my hands heal, and I can do a little work and save up some money, I'll be back. Then I'm gonna try to talk some sense into you and get you out of here."

His jaw tight and eyes angry, he looked at Kerry to say, "Master Allison and his overseer don't like Papa. They say he's too old to be any good in the fields. I've been afraid they'd take the lash to him, and then I'd have to kill somebody. I want him out of here."

Kerry promised him they would work together to convince Luther to take Bessie and move somewhere else. "But right now we need to try and get some rest. We have to be up very early."

They settled back, and it was not long before Kerry could tell that Adam and Luther were sleeping soundly. She wished she could nod off, as well, but thinking about Slade and what had happened that morning kept her awake.

It had all been wonderful, every precious moment. And even though it probably should not have happened, she could only be honest with herself in admitting she was not sorry it had. The only trouble was, she now found herself wondering if she might be in love with him. But that was silly, wasn't it? A woman did not fall in love so easily . . . but then she was not learned about such things. All she did know was that every time she saw him, her heart slammed into her chest, and just thinking about him made her warm all over.

Folding her arms across her bosom, she recalled how it had felt when he had held her so tight. Never had she felt so protected . . . so wanted . . . so cherished.

But was it merely a man's lust that educed such emotions? Would any woman Slade Dillon held in his arms feel the same?

And would she, Kerry, experience similar emotions in the caress of someone else?

Something told her she would not, and that was what fired the burning question: Did she love him? Or, perhaps even more unsettling was to ask herself—did she dare?

The sound of footsteps on the porch made her bolt upright. Her fear mounted to think how it was far too late for any other plantation workers to be coming around offering to help. And neither Mr. Allison nor his overseer would come sneaking around.

It was also too late for Slade . . . which meant it could only be the Klan.

Somehow they had found out where Toby and Ellie were hiding. But how?

And then she remembered Luther's agonized question pertaining to Slade, *"How do you know he ain't one of 'em?"*

Dear God.

She groped for, and found, the gun she had tucked in her basket of supplies. Then she quietly got to her feet and tiptoed to the window. If the Klan were out there, getting ready to throw torches on the roof of the shack as they had to Toby's, then she would make a few of them sorry, by damn. There was a half moon, enough light so they would make a good target, especially in their white robes sitting up on their horses.

But she saw nothing . . . heard nothing more.

Better to be ready, she thought, and pulled the gun's hammer back with an ominous click.

"Kerry, don't shoot."

Recognizing Slade's voice, she was not letting her guard down and warily asked, "What do you want?"

He was brusque and to the point. "I came to take you home. Get out here."

She felt a tremor within to think he might care enough to have done just that, but she was still not completely at ease. "Are you alone?"

His voice was an irritated hiss, "Now who the hell would I have with me? Now come on before somebody wakes up and finds me here. Bad enough you got involved in all this."

Kerry bit her lower lip and glanced around in the muted darkness. Everyone was still asleep. When Toby awoke to find her gone, he would think she had somehow made her way home in the dark to get ready to meet them at the bridge.

She picked up her basket, stepped over Luther and Adam, and quietly went out to the porch.

"Where did you leave the mule and cart?" Slade asked at once.

She told him they were hidden in the thick bushes behind the shack.

He wasted no time. "Let's go." He went and got the mule and tied it and the cart to the back of his horse. "You can ride with me," he told her. "You'll be safer."

It was only when they were on the horse and had ridden a ways that Slade spoke again. "Did anybody see you there?"

She was sitting in front of him, hotly aware of his thighs pressing against hers. His hand, holding the reins, was just under her bosom, his arm about her. She felt her breath quicken and reveled in the masculine scent of his closeness.

"No," she murmured. "Just some of the other Negroes who live on the plantation, but they won't say anything."

"Well, I want you to bow out now, Kerry. There could be big trouble."

Anger overrode the tenderness she had begun to feel as she snapped, "There already is trouble when masked men can run rampant through the countryside terrorizing people ... trying to kill them. Somebody has to help them."

"Stay out of it," he said evenly. "Or it might be your house the Klan burns next."

"Let them try. I'll be waiting with a shotgun and blow the head off the first bastard I see with a torch in his hand. I'm not scared of them, Slade. Believe it or not, I know how to use a gun."

Slade might have been amused to see her so feisty if he weren't concerned for her safety. "You'd be outnumbered. And I might not be around to lend a hand. Kerry, you've got to promise me you'll mind your own business."

"It *is* my business," she retorted stubbornly. "Because I know what it's like to have a friend when you need one. I've got a few I owe a lot to back in Ireland or I wouldn't be here today."

"And how many times do I have to remind you that the

ones you're sticking your neck out for are the same ones that left you to fend for yourself? Why do you feel any obligation to them?'' God, he hated to hear himself talk that way, because he sure as hell didn't mean it. He was as mad over what had happened as she was. And maybe it was best he hadn't stumbled on the right place the night before. He might have been witness to the raid and wasn't sure how he would have reacted. But he had to say, and do, anything to try and keep her out of it.

General Howard had said he would have a contact, but so far no one had come forward. If he did not receive some kind of word as to who he should report to by the time he was onto something—*someone*—he would have to go to the army himself, and he did not want to do that. He preferred to work only with others working undercover as he was.

Kerry had lapsed into a sullen silence. Impulsively, he pulled her tight against him. "I guess I'm going to have to keep a tight rein on you from now on, green eyes, to keep you out of mischief. I don't intend to let anything happen to you."

He felt her tremble, then, with a resolute sigh she melted against him, leaning her head on his shoulder. "Let's not talk about it, anymore. Tell me what happened in town today. Was Abigail nice to you?"

"Oh, very nice," he chuckled. "She invited me to church."

Kerry was surprised. "That's odd. I can't imagine her doing anything to encourage us to be around each other. Especially when she wants to pair me with a friend of their family from Raleigh—a widower with a new baby that needs a mother."

"A ready-made family," Slade said, as though he were giving it a lot of thought. "You know, you ought to think about that, Kerry. Does he have any money?"

She squirmed in his arms, but he laughed and continued

to hold her as she said, "How should I know? And it doesn't matter, because I'm not looking for a husband."

"So tell me about this social you said she's baking pies for."

"Oh, it's kind of silly, but it's a way of getting folks acquainted. A woman bakes a pie, and the slices are auctioned off for a dance."

"Are you going to bake one?"

"I'd thought about it, just to please Abigail. I've a recipe for a vinegar pie that's really unusual, and . . ." They were passing beneath some tall pines, and she twisted her face about to stare at him in the ribboned moonlight. "Why do you want to know?"

"Oh, I don't know," he said with a mysterious smile. "I thought I might go. And if I do, I might just try one of your slices and have myself a dance."

She looked aghast. "If you do that, and people find out you live on my farm, they're going to think . . ."

"Think what?" he prodded when she did not finish. "Come on now. What do you mean?"

She turned back around before saying, "They might think you're courting me."

"Would that be so bad?"

He felt her tremble, and it was all he could do to keep from reining in his horse, dismount, and take her with him so he could hold her and kiss her the way he longed to.

He was learning a different side to her, discovering she had grit, courage, and could be quite stubborn.

And he was also realizing that the more he was with her, the more he cared about her.

"You haven't answered me," he whispered, lifting a hand to brush her hair back from her face so he could nuzzle her ear.

"I . . . I don't know."

"Well, you think about it," he said, smiling as they finally reached the path to her house. "And you let me know before I waste my money on that pie."

When they got to the porch, Kerry could not get down off the horse fast enough. But she did not run inside like a scared rabbit as he had expected her to do. Instead, she stared up at him, her lovely face bathed in a silver sheen, her incredibly green eyes shining beneath moon-dusted lashes.

"Remember what I said this morning about what happened between us?"

He did not miss how the corners of her lips began to twitch as she tried to hold back a smile. "I do."

"Well, you're making it hard for me to keep the promise I made to myself about that."

"Good." He laughed and got down off the horse, looped the rein over the porch railing, and reached to lift her in his arms all in one fluid motion.

He kissed her till they were both breathless, then carried her up the steps and into the house, careful not to trip in the darkness.

He did not know his way around too well and set her down to let her take his hand and lead. In a few moments, he felt his knees pressed against a mattress.

"This is where I sleep," she said, searching for—and finding—the buttons on his shirt.

When she had removed his shirt, she boldly worked on the buckle of his holster. He had been standing, waiting and amused, but his erection was starting to ache in the tight denim pants. Gently shoving her hands aside, he opened his fly and pulled down his trousers.

"Feel me," he commanded huskily, wrapping her hands around him. "This is what you do to me, Kerry. You make me hurt with want."

He kissed her again, fingers deftly moving to strip off her clothes. She helped him, and in seconds they were both naked.

All shyness and reservation were gone. His hands cupped

her buttocks and pulled her to him, and she whispered throatily, "Yes, take me now, Slade. I want you so bad . . ."

He was also anxious to take her but wanted to please her in so many ways.

Pushing her back on the bed, he spread her legs, then burrowed his face between. Her fingers found his hair and twisted as she arched her back and moaned long and loud beneath the sweet assault.

"Oh, Slade. I never dreamed it could be like this."

He found the little nub again and took it between his teeth to nibble and lick in unison. Working his middle fingers up inside her, he delighted in her wetness and knew she was close to climax.

He took her to glory, and she screamed and burrowed her face in the pillow to muffle the sound. But before it ended, he was up on his knees and shoving hers to her chest as he plunged inside her, hard and deep.

She rocked against him, hips bouncing up and down on the bed, meeting his every thrust. Her nails dug into his shoulders, and he reveled in the slight pain, knowing it was evidence of her carnal pleasure.

He tried to hold back, wanting it to go on and on, but then he could not help himself. With several mighty jabs that slammed her into the mattress, he climaxed.

Afterwards, he could only slump against her, weak and spent.

"My God, woman," he said hoarsely when he could finally get his breath. "You drive me crazy. I can't get enough of you."

She clung to him, reluctantly letting him slide to one side.

Her face was cradled in his neck, and he felt its wetness and wondered if she was crying. He asked if he had hurt her.

"No . . ." she said in a tiny, shaky voice filled with tears. "It . . . it was beautiful, Slade."

"But you're crying—"

He tried to rise up, but she held on tightly and said, "Only because I'm so happy."

He laughed and pulled away from her so he could kiss away her tears. He wished he could see her, but it was pitch dark. The moon had either slipped behind a cloud or dropped below the horizon. He figured it had to be pretty late.

"I'm glad you're happy," he told her, gathering her close once more. "I've grown real fond of you these past weeks, Kerry. I hope you feel the same about me."

"I do," she said fervently.

"But I shouldn't stay here," he said. "All we need is for Abigail to come busting in the door some night after helping her husband deliver another baby."

Groping about for his clothes, he dressed quickly, then found her in the darkness for one last, searing kiss. "I'll see you in the morning. Horace Bedham got those tobacco seeds in you wanted, and we need to think about making beds to get them started in early spring."

"But when did you order them?" She was stunned. "I mean, we talked about planting tobacco, because in one of Papa's letters he said the soil in this part of North Carolina was right for it. Only I don't have money for seed."

"Well, we've been making good money on the eggs," he lied. He had ordered the expensive seed and paid for it himself, but she would never know it. "So we can start making plans."

One last kiss, and he left her.

He led his horse to the stall and put him down for what was left of the night, then wearily found his way down the path to his shack and to bed.

He fell asleep almost as soon as his head hit the pillow . . . but not before he warned himself one more time that he needed to tread lightly.

The mission he had been sent on had not included falling in love.

* * *

Kerry awoke with a start. Bolting out of bed, she ran to the window to look out. There was just the faintest light to the east, and she felt washed with relief. She had not overslept after all.

Dressing quickly, she hurried out into the damp night mist and hitched the mule to the cart. Then, being as quiet as possible, even though it was not likely Slade would hear since the shack was so far away, she set out to meet Adam and his friends.

Her prayers were more than answered that they would be on time, because they were already there.

"God bless you, Miz Kerry," Toby said, his wife beside him crying with gratitude.

"Just take care of yourselves," Kerry said, lightly hugging him so as not to aggravate his wounds.

"Can you take the reins with your burned hands?" she asked Adam worriedly.

"I'm gonna take 'em," Ellie said bravely, stepping forward to put her arms around Kerry. "And I say God bless you, too, ma'am."

When they were all in the cart and ready to go, Toby called down, "I can't take your mule and leave you with nothin'. Adam went back to what's left of my place and rounded up my horse. We managed to set him free before the Klan got him. He's tied over there behind that tree yonder, and he's all yours."

Kerry protested, "No. Take him instead of the mule, please . . ."

But Toby would not hear of it. "He's a fine horse, Miz Kerry. It would raise lots of eyebrows for folks to see a horse like him pullin' a mule cart. And the last thing we need between here and Atlanta is to have folks starin' at us.

"Besides," he said, grinning and waving as Ellie popped

the reins and set the mule to moving, "it's my way of sayin' thanks."

She watched them out of sight, then went to where Toby had said she would find the horse, gasping at the sight of him.

He was a fine animal, all right. Magnificent, in fact. A gleaming black stallion.

She was awed.

And also struck with wonder as to how she was going to explain him to Slade.

Chapter 13

Kerry was in a maelstrom of emotions. So many things were spinning in her mind that she could not sleep despite being exhausted.

She had ridden the horse home and quietly put him in the shed. "We'll have lots of time to get to know each other later," she had told him, patting his neck.

Again she was grateful for all the things Timothy O'Malley had taught her before she left Ireland. And even though she needed more experience on horseback, she had confidence in being able to handle the stallion . . . or at least make the stallion think she did.

Returning to the house, she had changed into her nightgown, then snuggled beneath the covers hoping for a few hours' sleep before facing Slade.

Slade.

She felt a thrilling rush to even think his name.

Falling in love had been the last thing on her mind when she had begun her new life. But now that she was head over heels, where would it all lead? Dear Lord, she

had no way of knowing and could only hope she would
not wind up with her heart broken.

He had hinted at courtship, but he might have only been
teasing. Then, too, such talk might have been brought on
by the sensual tension at the time.

But, whatever the reason, she hoped that sooner or later
he would be serious enough to think about sharing a future
with her.

Arms folded behind her head, she looked towards the
window and the brilliant dawn unfolding.

She was happy. Truly happy. For maybe the first time
in her whole life. The only thing that could have made
things better would be if her parents were there to share
it all with her.

But she felt a guilty sweep to remember that, even in
her happy glow, Adam and his friends were experiencing
a wretched time in their lives. It was not fair that Toby had
to abandon everything he had worked so hard for, all
because of the despicable Klan. Worse, he and his wife
had lost their baby.

She also knew that Luther and Bessie were not content
at the Allison plantation. She wanted them back with her
but knew they would not leave as long as they feared the
Klan. And Slade being around did not make them feel any
safer with her, because they did not trust him.

She thought back to the conversation she'd had with
Frank Kearney. He owned a farm south of hers, towards
a settlement called Mount Olive. He and his wife, Hortense,
had stopped by one afternoon, a few weeks before Slade
had happened along, to introduce themselves and say welcome. When Frank said he had known her father well,
Kerry had been all ears, eager to hear everything he could
tell her.

A talkative sort, he was only too glad to sit back in one
of the porch rockers and reminisce about the peaceful
days before the war. He also liked to brag about how he

had managed to keep the carpetbaggers from taking his land by paying the taxes with Yankee money.

"This is how it happened," he had grinned to confide, leaning closer as though someone besides Hortense might overhear. "It was in the last days of the war. Me and some others from around these parts were feeling about as low as a turtle in a dried-up creek bed. We knew the South was losing. It was just a matter of time. All we was concerned about was getting home and saving what we could of what we'd had to leave. So when we stumbled on a federal payroll wagon, we robbed it. And instead of turning the gold over, like we was supposed to, we divided it up and kept it. It wasn't all that much, really, but it paid the taxes."

Kerry supposed she could understand the men's reasoning for disobeying orders but still felt uncomfortable that he had told her about it. She would prefer not to know such things.

But once he was done bragging about his thievery, Frank had gone on to talk about his plans for his farm.

Kerry had hung on his every word as he talked about tobacco and why he thought one day it would surpass cotton as the most profitable crop to grow in North Carolina.

She was delighted when he went into detail, explaining how seedbeds were made in the spring, around March. When the soil was warm enough, the seedlings would be set in the ground. By July the plants would be several feet tall, with harvesting in September. He talked of anticipated prices, and Kerry's mouth began to water as she mentally calculated how many acres would be perfect for the crop and the ultimate money to be made. And ever since, she had yearned to have her own tobacco crop.

Now, she smiled to believe it was possible. Slade had said he had picked up the seed. To get a head start, she was going to make the seedbeds inside. She would do it in the kitchen, where it would stay warm because of the stove she intended to keep going all winter. And, as soon

as they sprouted, Slade had said he would make a place
for them outside.

In the spring, she would be ready to set them in the
fields. Meanwhile, as weather permitted, she would work
the soil and make it ready. After all, she was not afraid of
hard work. It was all she had ever known, thanks to her
stepfather. And how much more difficult could it be to
chop dirt with a hoe than to scrub a floor on her hands
and knees, raw and bleeding?

But something else Frank had told her stuck in her
mind, and that was how he worried over having enough
workers to harvest his crop. He had owned many slaves
before the war. As a result of their having been freed, he
was going to have to pay for field hands. That, of course,
would cut into his profit.

Hortense at that point had hesitantly pointed out that
he could always do as other farmers were forced to do—
adopt the sharecropping system.

Frank had been at once enraged and told her, red-faced
and shaking a fist in the air, that he'd sooner die than
share his land with coloreds. He had then bolted from the
rocker, saying he was going to look around and see how
Kerry was doing with the place.

When they were alone, Hortense, at Kerry's prodding,
explained the system that made so many farmers livid to
think about. Former slaves would be given land to work
as though it were their own. When the crops were harvested, they would give a certain percentage to the land-
owner, sometimes as much as eighty percent. But more
and more freedmen, as they became accustomed to their
independence, were demanding a larger portion. After all,
the white farmers needed them, for they could not work
their land alone.

Kerry had begun to think how it might be possible to
work something out to sharecrop with Luther, if she could
convince him that he and Bessie would be safe living with

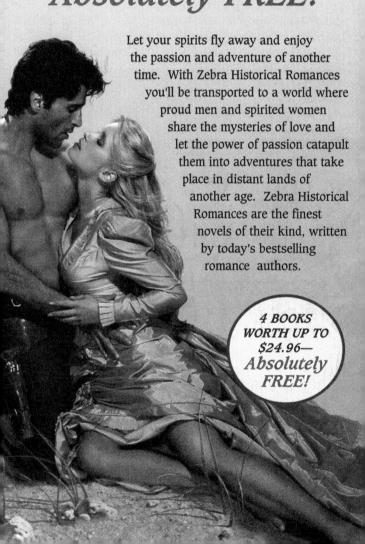

Take 4 FREE Books!

Zebra created its convenient Home Subscription Service so you'll be sure to get the hottest new romances delivered each month right to your doorstep — usually before they are available in book stores. Just to show you how convenient Zebra Home Subscription Service is, we would like to send you 4 Zebra Historical Romances as a FREE gift. You receive a gift worth up to $24.96 — absolutely FREE. There's no extra charge for shipping and handling. There's no obligation to buy anything - ever!

Save Even More with Free Home Delivery!

Accept your FREE gift and each month we'll deliver 4 brand new titles as soon as they are published. They'll be yours to examine FREE for 10 days. Then if you decide to keep the books, you'll pay the preferred subscriber's price of just $4.20 per title. That's $16.80 for all 4 books for a savings of up to 32% off the publisher's price! Just add $1.50 to offset the cost of shipping and handling. Remember, you are under no obligation to buy any of these books at any time! If you are not delighted with them, simply return them and owe nothing. But if you enjoy Zebra Historical Romances as much as we think you will, pay the special preferred subscriber rate of only $16.80 each month and save over $8.00 off the bookstore price!

We have 4 FREE BOOKS for you as your introduction to **KENSINGTON CHOICE!**

To get your FREE BOOKS,
worth up to $24.96, mail the card below.
or call TOLL-FREE 1-888-345-BOOK

Take 4 Zebra Historical Romances FREE!

MAIL TO: ZEBRA HOME SUBSCRIPTION SERVICE, INC.
120 BRIGHTON ROAD, P.O. BOX 5214,
CLIFTON, NEW JERSEY 07015-5214

❦ YES! Please send me my 4 FREE ZEBRA HISTORICAL ROMANCES (without obligation to purchase other books). Unless you hear from me after I receive my 4 FREE BOOKS, you may send me 4 new novels - as soon as they are published - to preview each month FREE for 10 days. If I am not satisfied, I may return them and owe nothing. Otherwise, I will pay the money-saving preferred subscriber's price of just $4.20 each... a total of $16.80 plus $1.50 for shipping and handling. That's a savings of over $8.00 each month. I may return any shipment within 10 days and owe nothing, and I may cancel any time I wish. In any case the 4 FREE books will be mine to keep.

Name _____

Address _____ Apt No _____

City _____ State _____ Zip _____

Telephone ( ) _____ Signature _____

(If under 18, parent or guardian must sign)

Terms, offer, and price subject to change. Orders subject to acceptance.
Offer valid in the U.S. only.

KN129A

her. Besides, she theorized, he would not be in any more danger than others who sharecropped, because the Klan was not going to like the system one little bit.

She had a pistol and had managed to persuade Mr. Bedham to sell her a shotgun at a good price. Perhaps she could buy more weapons and teach Luther, and anyone else who came to work for her, how to use them. Once, she would have been appalled to think of having to resort to such measures, but now it was a matter of survival . . . and hanging on to what was hers at all costs.

She wondered what Slade would think of what she was contemplating doing. The impression he had given thus far was that he wanted to avoid trouble at any cost. Well, she was not going to look for it, but if it came to her, she intended to stand her ground—not run away. Yet, in fairness to Slade, she reminded herself that he had no stake in the farm, and she could not expect him to stick his neck out. However, if things progressed between them, and he did court her, and they ultimately got married, things would be different. He would love the land as she did, and, accordingly, be willing to do anything to keep it and prosper.

Her eyelids were growing heavy, but she needed to get up and start her day. Slade had probably already begun his chores. He had said he wanted to cut a few trees for firewood so there would be time for the wood to dry a bit before using. Otherwise, the creosote would make for a lot of soot in the chimney, maybe even cause a fire.

She wanted to make his breakfast and lots of hot coffee to warm him for the task. It was a chilly morning. She had shivered the whole time she had been out in it. Slade would appreciate hot food and beverage.

Rolling on her side, she snuggled into the pillow. A few moments snoozing would make no difference, and she had not heard the sound of his ax.

And, at last, she slept.

* * *

"Kerry, wake up."

His voice came to her through a delicious, caressing fog. She was floating, dreaming of his strong arms about her, his warm lips on hers, tongue teasing. How wonderful it was to be held by a man ... but not just any man. Slade Dillon was special ... and he made *her* feel special ... and she wanted the moment to last forever.

"Kerry, we need to talk."

The sound was gruff. It did not belong in her dream. She burrowed deeper in the pillow and murmured a protest. "Go away. Leave me alone."

A hand clamped down on her shoulder to give her a rough shake that yanked her from the velvet cocoon.

"I'm not going anywhere, and you're going to wake up and tell me where that stallion came from, and also what you've done with the mule and cart."

Kerry was suddenly wide awake and rolling onto her back to find herself staring up into Slade's very angry face.

"Talk to me, Kerry," he ordered, lowering himself to sit on the edge of the bed. Leaning over, he braced an arm on either side of her. "There's a very fine black stallion in the shed. The mule and cart are nowhere to be found. Now, I've got an idea what all this means, but I want you to tell me."

She winced to see the fury in his eyes, the tiny red dots of rage. His nostrils were slightly flared, and she could see how his jaw tightened and feel the tension rippling through his arms pressed against her. Never had she seen him so upset, and, for an instant, she found it frightening. But then she felt resentment stirring. After all, even if she did fancy herself in love with him, it was still her farm ... her business. And who was he to demand explanation?

"I swapped the mule and cart for the horse," she said tightly. "I don't understand why that should upset you."

"Because I've got a feeling who that horse belonged to.

Just as I've got ideas who's riding in the cart making tracks to get out of Wayne County.''

She twisted beneath him till she was sitting up against the headboard. Folding her arms across her chest, she returned his insolent glare with one of her own and snapped, ''Like I said, I don't see why you're upset. The mule and cart were mine, you know. I could do anything I wanted to with them.''

He straightened to run agitated hands through his thick, dark hair, gave his head a shake, then, exasperated, said, ''Kerry, I told you to mind your own business, but now you've gone and gotten yourself right in the thick of things. Don't you realize people will recognize both the mule and the cart and know where those Negroes got them? It will spread like wildfire that you helped them.''

''And I don't give a damn.''

''Well, you'd better give a damn,'' he fired back, ''unless you want the Klan to come after you next. Jesus, Kerry, what could you have been thinking? How could you do something so stupid?''

''Somebody had to help Toby and his wife get away from here. Adam, too. And besides, by now they're probably so far down the road no one will recognize the mule.''

''And what about that stallion? There's probably not another horse as fine within fifty miles of here. And he's likely one of the reasons the Klan targeted Toby. They resented a Negro owning such a horse. I'm surprised he got away with him. But that's beside the point now. We've got to worry about what they're going to do when they find you have him.''

Kerry was close to tears—but not of regret or fright. Far from it.

She was mad.

Fighting mad, because she had, in the span of only a few months, dug her heels into the land and was not about to be intimidated by anybody. She was ready to do battle, if need be. ''If they dare step foot on my land, somebody is going to get shot, and it won't be me. You might not believe me, Slade Dillon, but I do know how to use a gun."

"Yeah, I'm beginning to think you're just cocky enough to think you can take on the Klan. Meanwhile, have you stopped to think how you're going to get the eggs to town without the cart?"

Kerry blinked, defiance yielding to bemusement. "I . . . I haven't really thought about that," she stammered to admit. "I suppose I can ride slow . . . tie the baskets on, and—"

"And break every egg you try to carry," he finished with a snicker, then took pity and sighed, "I'll see what I can work out for you. When I was in town yesterday I stopped by the saloon for a beer. A man asked me if I could do some odd jobs for him. It just so happens he has a livery stable. I think I can work out something to barter for another cart. Maybe a wagon this time."

Kerry fought against the sudden surge of hope. After all, seconds earlier she had been ready to angrily scream at him to stay out of her affairs. So she could not, with good conscience, allow him to come to her rescue. "That's kind of you, but I can't let you do it. This is my problem, Slade. Not yours."

He leaned closer. Tenderly brushing back a strand of her golden red hair that had tumbled onto her forehead, he looked into her eyes and murmured, "Haven't you realized by now that I care about your problems, Kerry? That I care about you? Your battles are mine."

"You shouldn't let them be," she said nervously, silently commanding her heart to stop pounding. Every time he came near . . . every time he touched her, she felt as though her heart would burst right out of her chest. And her pulses were racing, every nerve in her body raw with longing as he caressed her with his heated gaze.

"What I ought to do," he frowned to tease, "is turn you over my knee and give you a sound spanking for being so reckless. What I will do," he whispered huskily, "is this . . ."

His hands went to her shoulders, to tighten his grip and pull her close.

Bending his head, he claimed her mouth in a slow, compelling kiss, molding and shaping her lips sensuously to his. He held her for long, deep moments. Her arms twined about his neck to cling to him in surrender.

And then he abruptly let her go.

She fell back against the pillows to stare at him in wonder, for his expression was one of confusion, as well as annoyance. Perhaps he had realized he was becoming far more involved than he wanted to be ... that he had mistaken their passion for something else.

"Is something wrong?" she asked quietly, hesitantly.

He shook his head as though to clear it, and she could tell his smile was forced.

"Nothing. It's just that I have chores to do, and I need to get busy."

He stood.

Kerry scrambled from the bed and snatched up her robe. "I'll make breakfast."

"No, it's all right. I'm not hungry. I want to check out the stallion before I do anything else, make sure he's all right. I also have to go into town to see about that job. We can't get behind on the egg deliveries. You've got customers waiting.

"One more thing," he spun on his heel at the door to say. "When is that social at the church you were telling me about? The pie auction?"

"Tomorrow night." She was delighted to think everything was all right, after all. She had only imagined his sudden coldness. "I'll be going into town around noontime to help Abigail set things up.

"She expects me to stay the night with her," she added, wrinkling her nose in displeasure. "She says it's because it's not safe for me to travel after dark, but I think her house guest may have something to do with it."

"The man looking for a mother for his baby?"

She nodded, and from the tender look on his face she thought for an instant that he was going to step back into the room and sweep her in his arms and say to hell with his chores.

Instead, he touched her cheek and murmured, "Well, he can just keep on looking, because you might just be spoken for, green eyes."

I hope so, she thrilled to think as he continued on his way. *I dearly, dearly hope so.*

Slade told himself he was a lovesick fool.

He had no business to even remotely consider courting Kerry Corrigan. His involvement with her was getting in the way of what he had been sent to do, damn it.

General Howard and the Freedmen's Bureau were counting on him.

But, more importantly, and even though they did not know it, so were a lot of helpless people who would fall victim to the Ku Klux Klan if he did not find a way to expose the leaders and cause them to fall apart.

So why in hell was he thinking about getting married?

Because you love her, a little voice inside needled. *Like you've never loved a woman before. Even Mary Beth.*

He admitted he could not help himself, so instead of worrying about it, he would just try to deal with it.

One of the reasons he was drawn to Kerry was how she was so guileless. She wore her feelings, her heart, on her sleeve. And she was, beyond a doubt, one of the most honest and open women he had ever encountered. He was confident that once she committed to him it would be forever.

Besides, he wryly thought, she needed someone to look after her. She was getting way too bold in her involvement with the plight of the former slaves. That was his job. Not hers. And the sooner he took care of it, the better—and safer—they would both be.

He had pretended to get over it, but the fact was he was deeply upset over what she had done concerning the mule and cart. The story about him swapping work for a wagon had, of course, been a lie. He was going to have to pay for it himself. Otherwise, she would lose her egg business, and he couldn't let that happen. She had to keep thinking him indigent. He also knew it was important to her to feel she was making her own way.

Most of all, he did not intend for her to find out he was a federal agent. General Howard had taken care of his immediate appointment so he would be empowered to make arrests when the time came . . . as well as to shoot to kill without fear of prosecution by local authorities.

And he was still waiting to find out about his contact. He had been told to inquire at the post office on the first of every month whether there was any mail for him being held in general delivery. That was how he would learn who his contact was. Messages to the Bureau, and to the commander of the occupational troops, would be handled through him.

He had only been in town a couple of weeks when the first of the last month had rolled around. Checking, he was told there was no mail. He was not surprised. Now as the time neared once more, he hoped there would still not be a letter. He had nothing to report and was ashamed to admit it.

He knew he had to get busy, and the lie about swapping work for a wagon would actually work to his advantage. He needed to ride the countryside during the day to learn his way around. If he managed to learn of another Klan meeting, he would have an excuse for being out all night. Because it appeared that his original plan of being taken into the fold and asked to join was not going to happen. Had he been able to claim the land, as he had intended, it might have. But the locals were wary of strangers, especially drifters—which hired hands were considered to be. So all he could do was keep his eyes and ears open and work undercover.

He hurried and got the chores done so the afternoon would be free. He decided to go to the nearby town of Smithfield to buy the wagon. If he got it in Goldsboro, there was the risk Kerry might find out.

As he was saddling his horse, she came to the stall carrying a small sack. "You have to be hungry, so I sliced some of the venison and made biscuits. You can eat on the way."

"Rushing to get rid of me?" he teased, taking the food and kissing her cheek.

"Oh, no," she was quick to dispute. "I just want you to be on your way so you'll be home before dark."

He tied the sack to the saddle horn, then took her in his arms. "As bad as I want to get back to you, Kerry, it may be late. I don't know what kind of work the man I told you about has in mind for me. If it takes very long, I'll just spend the night."

She pressed her head against his chest as she hugged him in apology. "I'm sorry you're having to do this, Slade, but I did what I thought was right when I let them have the cart. And you don't have to, you know. I can manage somehow and—"

"I'll take care of it," he said, silencing any further protest with a kiss that left both of them shaken.

"Now I'd best be going," he said, finally releasing her and mounting his horse lest he be tempted to yield to the heated desire she so easily stirred. "You keep your guns handy and an eye out should any strangers come around. If I can get this man to barter work for a wagon, I'll also try to persuade him to let me go ahead and have it on good faith. I'd like for you to have it tomorrow when you go into town for the social."

Eyes twinkling with mischief, Kerry said, "Oh, I see. You want to make sure I get to Abigail's where a would-be suitor is waiting so you won't have to worry about me anymore."

He leaned down from the saddle to give her hair a playful tug, but he was quite serious as he told her, "After tomorrow night, everyone will know you're spoken for, Kerry. That is, if you want to be . . ." He trailed off on a questioning note.

Her eyes were misty as she whispered, "I do want it, Slade. I want it very much."

It was almost dusk when Slade reached Goldsboro after riding all the way to Smithfield. He was pleased with the wagon he had purchased. It was much nicer than the cart. Big and roomy with good, sturdy wheels. He figured the stallion could pull it for the time being. He could not take a chance on Kerry becoming suspicious if he tried to make her believe his new employer was willing to trust him for a pair of horses or mules, too. And if the stallion wasn't harness-broken, he could take care of that. He had trained a few horses in the past, like his own, which was now pulling the wagon.

He decided since he was in town to check at the post office for mail. If he could have another month without any, it should give him time to uncover a few clues, at least.

That hope, however, was short-lived.

"Yes, sir, Mr. Dillon. A letter come for you just yesterday." The clerk turned to scan the slots on the wall behind him, then drew out an envelope and handed it to Slade.

Slade waited till he was back on the street, then tore it open. As he unfolded the sheet of paper inside, a bright red feather fluttered to the ground. Puzzled, he retrieved it, then read the brief message: *"Lay the feather on the bar at Sadie's. I will find you."*

"Oh, that's just great," Slade muttered to himself as he ripped the letter to shreds. If it had been Sam's idea to arrange for him to meet his contact at a whorehouse bar, he was going to wring his neck the next time he saw him.

Sadie's was a saloon in the worst section of town. A

woman could be had cheap in one of the rooms upstairs. He knew about it, like every other man around, but he'd never been there and was annoyed it was to be the meeting place.

He supposed he should go ahead and get it over with. But it all seemed so stupid. What man in his right mind— especially one working undercover for the government— was going to frequent a whorehouse night after night waiting for somebody to contact him? If someone hanging around like that didn't raise a few eyebrows, then nothing would.

He had worked himself into an angry stew by the time he got to Sadie's. He was not looking forward to having to make excuses as to why he only wanted a cold beer and nothing else. And if whoever he was supposed to meet didn't happen to be around so early in the evening, it was a wasted trip, anyway.

The place was empty except for some women sitting on a pink sofa in the parlor. He decided to wait a bit anyway, and took a stool at the end of the bar.

The bored-looking bartender drily asked, "You want a glass or a bottle? You can take the bottle upstairs with you."

"A beer for now," Slade said.

Reaching into his pocket, he took out the feather and laid it on the counter near his elbow. When the bartender returned with his drink, Slade dropped his arm over it, then revealed it once more when he was alone.

He had only taken a few sips of his beer when he noticed one of the women watching him. She was pretty, in a coarse sort of way. And she had nice apple-shaped breasts that threatened to spill from the low bodice of her red velvet gown. A feathered boa was draped about her shoulders.

She started towards him, her purple-painted lids lowered in scrutiny.

He groaned under his breath. He would have to tell her he only stopped in for a beer and hoped she would go away and leave him alone. He did not need a whore hanging on to him, trying to get him upstairs, and . . .

And then she was beside him, to slide between him and the stool next to him, pressed tight as she whispered huskily, "Well, hello, handsome. I haven't seen you in here before."

"Just having a beer," he said, taking a long sip before adding, "And I'm not looking for company."

Her lower lip, bright red and shiny, dropped in a mock pout. "That's a shame, mister, especially when I think you've got something that belongs to me."

She picked up the feather at his elbow and drew it teasingly down his cheek, then pressed her lips to his ear to say, "My name is Rosalie, and I'm pleased to meet you, Slade Dillon."

He tossed down the rest of his beer in one swallow, then signaled to the bartender to bring a whiskey.

It was going to take something a bit stronger than beer to get him used to the idea that his contact was a prostitute.

"Let's get something straight right now, Dillon."

They had gone upstairs to Rosalie's room, where they could talk in private.

She seemed anxious to get right to the point, and that was fine with him. He'd never been one to waste time—till he met Kerry.

"I am a lady of the evening, doxy, harlot, whore, prostitute—whatever you want to call it. Don't matter to me. I'm not proud of it, but I sure as hell ain't ashamed of it, either. Want another?" she asked, pouring herself a drink from the bottle she had brought with her.

He shook his head. "No, thanks."

She sat down on the side of the bed and crossed her legs. "Now I know you're wondering why I'm your contact."

"The thought had occurred to me." He looked around the room. The bed dominated with its gaudy pink and red spread and tasseled canopy overhead. The lamps were also covered in pink, casting what was supposed to be a romantic glow, he supposed. Thick drapes at the windows shut out all light, no doubt so her customers wouldn't worry about what time of day it was.

She downed her drink in a few quick swallows and poured herself another.

He pulled up the only chair in the room, turned it around to straddle and wait to let her talk at her own pace.

"I was fifteen when the war broke out," she said, swirling the amber liquid in her glass and staring at it as if it were all there—every moment of the past that pained her to talk about. "We were living in Georgia. Me and my folks and my little sister, Edna. Pa didn't give a squat about the war. Hell, we didn't have any slaves, so why should he? He made a living on the little farm we had. We never went hungry. Life was good."

Slade was paying more attention to her expression than to what she was saying. It was hard to believe she was so young. He had taken her to be many, many years older.

Her voice suddenly became tight with bitterness. "But some of our neighbors had other ideas. They wanted everybody in our whole damn county to form a regiment and march off to kill Yankees. Pa told 'em to go to hell. So one night a bunch of 'em got drunk and came riding out to our place in the middle of the night. They shot Pa, and Ma and Edna died in the fire. I managed to get out of the house, but they made me wish I'd burned with the rest of 'em."

She turned up her glass and drank the rest of the whiskey in one gulp, then turned enraged eyes upon him. "I vowed I'd make 'em pay. Every goddamn Reb soldier and redneck that I could. I became a spy for the Union Army, and you can ask anybody in high command, and they'll tell you Rosalie Sauls was the best spy they had."

She laughed, a high-pitched laugh that Slade thought might border on hysteria.

"And it didn't mean a damn to me that I did it on my back, either. I got information out of every Reb I slept with. And now that the war between North and South is over, I'm ready to fight a different kind of battle—against the goddamn Ku Klux Klan, 'cause they're doing the same thing to the freedmen in the South now that those night riders did to my family back in 1861, and I'm willing to do everything I can to stop it.

"Are *you*?" she asked suddenly, sharply, leaning forward to look him straight in the eye, her hand gripping her empty glass.

It took but a second for Slade to respond, "Yeah. That's why I'm here."

She smiled. "Then let's talk a bit and figure out how we're going to go about it.

"And don't worry," she added with a laugh meant to put him at ease. "I never sleep with the good guys, so you can keep your money in your pocket and everything else in your pants."

Slade laughed with her and said yes, he believed he would have a drink with her.

And already he felt better about everything, because something told him they were going to get along just fine.

Chapter 14

It was very late when Slade got back to the farm. He had not meant to stay so long with Rosalie but found her to be an extremely fascinating woman, and he had lost all track of time.

Apparently, she had been invaluable to the Union as a spy during the war. Since then, she had dedicated herself to helping the plight of the freedmen. She said it was because she felt sorry for them, but Slade felt she was actually the one who deserved pity. To harbor so much bitterness that she would relegate herself to selling her body to do her job was a tragedy. But he told himself not to be judgmental. After all, he had no way of knowing how deep was her anguish over her family.

Their relationship would be, Slade knew, strictly business. She had made that clear, but it was not necessary. He might find her interesting but that was all. He felt no desire for her, and during the ride home wondered if he could feel anything for any woman other than Kerry.

It was a sobering thought.

He had not, of course, told Rosalie about his personal

involvement with Kerry, but she knew he was living at the farm. So, with her usual candor, Rosalie had accused him of not devoting himself fully to his assignment. He had finally admitted that perhaps his mind had been on other things but swore it would not be anymore.

She had then told him about overhearing a conversation that might suggest a meeting of the Klan that very night, and he had vowed to do his best to spy on it.

Having worried over how he would be able to slip away without Kerry knowing it, he was relieved to find the house dark. After putting the stallion away, he quietly went inside to make sure she was sleeping soundly. If she later asked why he did not come to her, or if she went to his shack and found him gone, he had a story ready. He would say he had gone out in the woods to be ready to hunt at first light.

Rosalie had heard the men mention an area known as Lawson's Pond. Afterwards, she had managed to discreetly learn that it was a swampy area southeast of town.

How easy it would be, she and Slade had agreed, if all they had to do was identify Klan members. But it was the leaders they were after, the ones who gave the orders. The ones following those orders were no more than drones, and with their leaders brought down, the organization would founder.

Slade saddled his own horse, then followed the well-worn trail down to the Neuse River that ran through Kerry's land. From there, he kept to the woods, which was not difficult. Seldom did underbrush grow under pines. And with the light of a half moon he could keep from bumping into any trees.

After a half hour or so, he could make out a huge glow ahead. He cut deeper into the woods, then dismounted to go the rest of the way on foot.

Reaching a clearing, he moved as close as he dared, then crouched down. He counted around twenty men, all carrying torches and wearing the ghostly white hoods and robes.

There was a makeshift platform, where three men stood, but these had different-colored hoods over their heads. He knew then they were the leaders and wished he could get closer to them but had stepped in wet marsh and feared the swamp might be deeper in that direction. He could not risk tripping, splashing, and being discovered. Neither was he anxious to go sneaking around in the brackish water with snakes and no telling what else.

He strained to listen as one of the leaders spoke.

"It is imperative that we remember the rules of our exalted order. Never speak of another Klan member by his given name. I am your Grand Cyclops." He gestured to the men standing beside him. "Your Grand Magi. Your Grand Turk. This is all you know of them . . . all you need to know."

Slade well knew the organization of the Klan. The identities of the leaders were protected at all costs. But he hoped it would be a simple matter to expose them, like following them home after the meeting. He nearly laughed out loud at his own absurd thought. The leaders were not that stupid. They feared betrayal among their followers—men jealous of their power. So they had trusted guards who would see they were not followed. But Slade knew that sooner or later they would make a slip. He would ultimately find out who they were. Meanwhile, he would try to discover when and where they would ride.

"There will be a new meeting place after tonight," the Grand Cyclops went on to announce. "We're going to have our own den, like our brethren in other counties. You all know where the Weston place is. It's deserted now, and there's an old tobacco-curing barn down by the river with perfect vantage points for our guards to keep watch while we're meeting."

Slade made a quick mental note to locate the new den, as well as a hiding place for spying.

The leader continued. "From now on, there will be no more verbal messages as to when we meet. It's too dangerous. So tonight we're giving out whistles, and you'll be told a code of signals."

Slade watched in the eerie glow of the torches as men moved about, handing out the whistles and instructing as to the codes.

He dropped to his belly and snaked forward. There were two Klansmen standing off to themselves, near some tall reeds of grass. He worked himself closer, trying not to think about how he was crawling in mud and slime. Something slithered across his outstretched hand. He told himself it was a frog, a lizard, anything but a water moccasin.

Finally, he was close enough to hear when the men were instructed in the code. One long whistle was to be given when there was a meeting to be held that night. Anyone hearing it was to pass it along. If there was to be a raid—someone to be beaten or burned out—it would be followed by two short whistles.

Once everyone had their whistles and codes, the leader made a speech about uppity niggers, greedy carpetbaggers, and disloyal whites who resisted joining the Klan.

The meeting droned on as the leaders urged recruitment of new members to strengthen their numbers.

At last things began to quiet down. Members began drifting away. And, as Slade had suspected, guards closed in when the leaders left to ensure they were not followed. Several even rode with them for added protection.

Slade waited a long time after everyone left to make sure it was completely safe. Then he returned to where he had left his horse. It was nearly dawn, and he was about to drop on his feet, he was so tired. He was also wet and dirty and couldn't wait to get a bath and into dry, clean clothes.

The sky was a rosy pink when he got back to his shack. He unsaddled the horse and rubbed him down, then hurried to strip and wade into the creek. He didn't mind the cold water, anxious to wash away the dirt and grime.

Afterwards, he wrapped in a blanket and lay down on his bed. He intended to take a short nap, because he was anxious to see Kerry. But he was more exhausted than he thought and quickly fell into a deep sleep.

Kerry balanced the tray of eggs and pancakes. She was careful not to spill the precious jar of blueberry syrup she had bartered for with a passing woman the day before. Two dozen fresh eggs for the delicious syrup, and she hoped Slade would be pleased with the treat.

She had been disappointed to awaken and not find him beside her.

She was also puzzled as to why he had been gone all day. Then, on her way to his shack, she saw the wagon and was delighted. It was much nicer than the cart. He was, she thought happily, a truly remarkable man. It was fortunate for her he wanted to stay and help, but she was, of course, hoping he did so for a reason—such as loving her as she loved him.

Life was truly good, she smiled to think as the row of shacks came into view, and it could only get better.

The door to the shack where Slade kept his things was open. She set the tray on the porch and went inside to make sure he was there. No doubt he had come in late and not wanted to wake her. He might even have gone hunting. They were out of fresh meat, and—

She froze to see him lying on the bed . . . naked.

For long, crystallized moments, Kerry could only stare, marveling at the glorious sight of him. Then a shiver rippled from head to toe at the thought of how wonderful it would be to stretch out beside him, to snuggle close and dance her fingers through the dark mat of hair on his chest and follow it downwards to . . .

Her heated gaze went to his manhood, which was nearly erect, lying across his flat belly.

Kerry could stand it no longer.

She wanted him.

As she took off her clothes, she marveled at her own audacity. Never had she dreamed she would one day be so bold.

But then never had she dreamed of meeting a man like Slade Dillon, who could set every nerve in her body afire with a mere glance.

Her knee pressed down on the thin pine straw mattress.

Slade's eyes flew open, his hand instinctively reaching for his holster on the floor next to him. Then he saw it was her and relaxed, his arm instead going about her.

"What a wonderful way to wake up," he murmured sleepily as he drew her against him.

She felt his full erection then, slipping between her thighs.

"I've got pancakes and blueberry syrup on the porch," she said, suddenly shy and wondering whether she should have been so bold.

His fingers sought and found her nipple and began to massage. "I've got everything I want right here," he said, dipping his mouth to suckle.

She arched against him and sighed, her hands moving to cradle his head to her breast.

He began to undulate his hips to and fro, sliding his hardness against her flesh.

It was more than she could bear, for she wanted him so deeply, so fiercely. And, reaching down, she maneuvered to pull him up and into her.

With a low, delighted growl, he quickly flipped her onto her back and drove himself in hard and deep.

Her nails raked his back, hugging him in tighter, lifting her hips to meet his every thrust.

Kerry felt it coming, the ultimate thrill of release. A moan escaped her as overwhelming shudders swept from deep within her belly.

He came with her, in quick, hard jabs that threatened to buckle the bed beneath them.

And afterwards, they held each other in quiet awe of
the deep, abiding passion that had captivated them so
quickly.

Kerry wanted to talk, to tell him how she truly felt about
him. But it was a tender moment, with his head on her
breasts, his arms still about her. It seemed too magical to
end with words, so she continued to hold him tight, waiting
for the proper time.

Then she heard his gentle breathing and knew he was
once again asleep.

She held him a while longer, then whispered, ''Slade?
Slade, we need to talk . . .''

He grunted something unintelligible and rolled away,
his back to her as he settled down to sleep once more.

Kerry smiled and ran loving fingers over his strong,
broad shoulders. He was so very tired. Perhaps the man
he had bargained with for the wagon had asked him to
begin paying him back in labor the day before, and it had
stretched on into the night. Surely that was how it was, for
why else would he be so weary?

She sighed to think how she would like nothing better
than to stay right there, cuddled close to him, and wait
for him to wake up. But she had to finish baking her
vinegar pie for the church social and get ready to leave
for Abigail's by noon.

Reluctantly, she got out of bed. Dressing quickly, she
brought the tray in and left it by his bed. If he awoke soon—
which she doubted—everything would not be spoiled. But
even if he didn't, he would at least see her efforts.

She bent to kiss his cheek, but he did not stir, and she
quietly left him.

Slade bolted upright and gave his head a vicious shake.

Leaping out of bed, he hurried out to the porch and
cursed to see the sun was dropping in the sky. Damn it,
he had slept most of the day away.

He went back inside and saw the tray on the floor. It came back to him then—Kerry there, naked in his arms. He'd thought it a dream, so tired was he, but even in his weariness it had been wonderful to hold her . . . make love to her.

Now he needed to go to her and apologize for having wasted the day. He also wanted to show her the wagon, get her reaction, and, of course, tell the lie he had ready about how he'd managed to get it for her.

He dressed quickly and started for the house but paused as he crossed the backyard to realize the wagon was not where he had left it. Then it dawned—tonight was the church social. Kerry had said she'd be leaving around noon, so she was already there by now.

"Damn it," he cursed, rushing to saddle his horse. He had planned to take her, but by now she would already be at Abigail's, and he wasn't about to go there.

Then he considered how he was dressed—which was not for a church social. He returned to the shack and dug down in his duffel bag to find his coat. It was wrinkled, but he smoothed it as best he could, then slipped his string tie under the collar of his blue muslin shirt. Not too bad, he decided, giving his boots a quick polish.

Maybe folks would not consider him just an aimless drifter, after all, and that was important since he intended to let it be known he was going to court Miss Kerry Corrigan.

It was almost dusk when he reached the church. The yard was filled with buggies and wagons. He spotted Kerry's near the front, but she was nowhere around.

He could hear music coming from inside—a banjo and guitar.

Moving to the side of the clapboard building, he peered inside a window, not wanting to just walk right in without knowing what was going on.

The church benches had been repositioned to line the walls, clearing the floor in the middle for dancing and socializing. Colorful bunting of red, white, and blue decorated the walls. Long tables covered in linen cloth had been set up in front, and he could see all kinds of pies on display.

Glancing about, he spotted Kerry, pretty as always in her one nice dress that she only wore to church. He intended to change that, though, anxious to buy her many fine clothes.

He frowned to see she was holding a baby in her arms. The man towering over her was beaming his approval. Slade knew it could only be Abigail's friend from Raleigh, the one in a hurry to find a wife and mother for the baby.

Slade was glad to see that Kerry looked anything but pleased. He could also hear her soft and polite protest, for it was a warm night and the windows were open.

"Mr. Albritton, I really need to help Abigail," she said, gently pushing the baby at him. "And the baby is starting to fret."

He held up his hands. "No, no. Abigail understands the need for us to get better acquainted. And call me Thad, please." He grinned down at the baby. "The two of you make quite a picture. She looks like she could be your very own."

The baby began to cry, and Slade was tempted to burst out laughing at the look of dismay on Kerry's face. She was clearly uncomfortable and even looked a little frightened.

"No, she isn't content at all, Mr. Albritton," Kerry said, again attempting to give him the squealing bundle. "She's as scared of me as I am of her. I don't know the first thing about babies. I've never even held one before, and—"

"And you will learn. You're a natural mother. I can tell. Just cuddle her and hold her tighter."

A woman walked by, and Kerry whirled on her in desperation. "Mrs. Talbot, will you take Mr. Albritton's baby? I can't make her stop crying."

The woman beamed, "Of course I will. As many children

as I've raised, I know a thing or two about crying babies, believe me."

Thad Albritton could only watch helplessly as Kerry handed over his daughter, then hurried away.

Slade hung around outside a while longer, wanting to give things inside a chance to get started. Finally, the preacher got up in front of everyone and said it was time to start the auction. For newcomers, he explained once more how it would work—for each slice of pie a man bought, he had a dance with the lady who had baked it.

Slade watched as Abigail held up the first pie and announced it had been made by Miss Kerry Corrigan. And when Thad Albritton stated his bid, all the other men politely did not raise it. Slade figured Albritton had let it be known he had designs on her, and they were not going to offer any competition. After all, finding a mother for his baby was a noble cause, they would say.

However, Slade had intentions of his own and was not about to share their compassion.

The rest of the first slices were auctioned off. Then the music started up, and couples took to the dance floor. He watched as Albritton swirled Kerry around, grinning down at her as if he owned her. Then it was time for another round of auctioning, and Slade made his move.

He walked in the back door of the church and took position against the wall, arms folded across his chest.

This time Kerry's pie was not the first offered.

He waited.

Then Abigail held it up once more and looked straight at Thad Albritton and coyly said, "Well, I wonder who's going to bid on Kerry's pie this time?"

Everyone looked at Thad, who smugly held up his hand and said, "Four bits."

It was the same bid he had made before.

And, as before, the other men just smiled among themselves and said nothing.

Abigail gave an approving nod. "Then I guess we know who has the next dance with you, Kerry."

"Ten dollars for the rest of the pie."

Everyone turned to stare at Slade, including Kerry who, as it turned out, was not very good at hiding her feelings. Her face broke into a wide grin of relief, as well as pleasure.

Abigail, recognizing Slade, frowned. "I beg your pardon. What did you say?"

Slade looked at Kerry, who was watching with wide eyes, cheeks slightly flushed with embarrassment. He smiled, winked, and she seemed to relax a bit. Then he told Abigail, "I just bid ten dollars for the rest of Miss Corrigan's pie."

"You . . . you want all the slices?" she sputtered in doubt.

"That's right."

Suddenly Thad Albritton stepped from the crowd and waved a fist in the air. "That's not the way it's supposed to be done."

Slade swept him with an insolent glare. "Saves time, sir. Care to bid against me?"

Thad flashed with anger. "Yes, I do. If this is the way it's to be, then I bid eleven dollars."

Slade nodded, pretended to think about it for a moment, then said, "I'm kind of hungry, sir, so I think I'll raise you to fifty."

Gasps rippled through the crowd. Kerry took a few steps backwards, mouth agape.

Thad Albritton sputtered, "This . . . this isn't a poker game, sir. This is a church social, meant to be only for a good time."

"And a good time it is," Slade said pleasantly, "especially when it's for charity. So I'm happy to spend the money. How about it? Do you wish to go higher?"

Thad turned on his heel and walked out, so mad he looked as if he could bite a nail in two.

Slade picked up the remainder of Kerry's pie and held out his hand to her, which she eagerly took.

"I can't believe you did that," she whispered as he led

her to a far corner where they could sit down. "Everyone is watching us."

"Then let's give them something to look at." He scooped out a wedge of pie and began to eat, then said, "This is quite good, Kerry. I'm pleased to find out you can cook something besides eggs."

She was paying no attention to what he was saying as she swung her head from side to side and murmured, "Fifty dollars. You paid fifty dollars." Suddenly she raised her eyes to look at him sharply. "That's a lot of money, Slade. Where did you get it?"

"I worked yesterday," he said uneasily, taking up another piece of pie he really didn't want.

She watched him for a moment in quiet study, then pointed out, "You also got a new wagon for me yesterday. What kind of work could you possibly have been doing that would reward you so handsomely with both wagon and money?"

"Kerry, I never said I didn't have any money at all."

"But you made me think you didn't."

"Well, I saved a bit of my pay in the war for an emergency." He managed to meet her suspicious gaze with what he hoped was a reassuring smile. "And I consider this an emergency. You didn't think I was going to let you have every dance with Albritton, did you?"

"You truly are a mystery, Slade Dillon." She gave her head a shake, sending her long red curls swinging about her face.

He thought again how beautiful she was and right then and there wanted to run his fingers through her hair, pull her close, and kiss her long and deep. "It's no mystery that I've grown real fond of you, Kerry. And I guess this is my way of letting you and everyone else know I'm real serious about courting you if you'll let me." Her hands were folded in her lap. He reached to cover them with one of his. "You know we could have a good life."

She bowed her head, and he tensed, awaiting her

response. They'd never had much serious conversation, but after the way she seemed to want him as much as he wanted her, he hadn't thought talk was all that necessary. But maybe he should have. Maybe she did not return his feelings as he had hoped.

"Kerry," he prodded, bending his head to try and see her face. "It is all right with you, isn't it? I mean, we've been very close, and I was pretty sure it meant something to you."

She looked at him then, and he saw the glimmer of tears. "Of course it meant something to me," she whispered shakily. "I've never felt like this about a man before. And . . . and"—she paused, swallowed, then said with a firm nod—"I'd be proud to have you court me, Slade."

The second auction had ended. The music had begun to play. Slade pushed the pie aside and stood, pulling her up with him and into his arms. "I paid a lot for the privilege of dancing with you, Miss Kerry Corrigan, and I aim to get my money's worth."

Slade had enjoyed going to the dances back in Tennessee before the war but could tell Kerry was nervous. "It's easy," he told her as he led her towards the lines forming to do the reel. "Just listen to the man calling out the steps and watch everybody else. You'll learn it in no time."

And she did. Within a short time, Kerry was laughing as she twirled and danced. But each time she flew back into Slade's arms, she gave his hands a squeeze to let him know she was happiest with him.

When the dance was over, they started back to their table, but suddenly Abigail appeared at Kerry's elbow to testily admonish, "Really, Kerry, it would have been a courtesy for you to let me know that you and"—she gave a curt nod to acknowledge Slade—"Mr. Dillon were more than friends."

Kerry gave her a quick hug, too exhilarated right then to have her spirits dampened. "I didn't know myself, Abigail, but be happy for us, won't you? We've so much in common. He loves my father's land as much as I do, and he wants to see the farm come alive again, and—"

"There's someone I think you should speak with," Abigail all but snapped to cut her off.

Slade, who stood nearby quietly listening to their conversation, saw a man approach in response to Abigail's signal. He seemed vaguely familiar, but Slade could not place him.

"Sim Higdon," Kerry said, taking the man's hand. "How are you?"

"I'm fine," he said curtly, then turned to Slade. "Do you remember me, sir?"

It was coming back to him fast. Sim Higdon was the clerk he had spoken with at the courthouse about Kerry's land when he had first arrived in town. And something told him this encounter was not meant to renew old acquaintances.

"Yes, I do," Slade said finally.

Sim's face was like granite. "Well, I find it quite interesting that you found your way to Flann Corrigan's land, after all. And it doesn't seem to have deterred your interest in it to find it wasn't available for you to take over, after all."

Kerry looked from Sim to Slade and asked, frowning, "What is he talking about?"

Sim did not give him a chance to respond, though Slade did not know what to say at that point, anyway.

"This man came to my office asking whether the taxes had been paid on your property. He said he had met your father just before he was killed in the war and came to see if his land was still available."

Kerry's hand flew to her throat as she recoiled in shock. "You . . . you knew my father?" she asked Slade. "And you didn't tell me? I don't understand."

"I think I can explain it to you, Kerry."

Thad Albritton stepped up to join the conversation. Placing a protective arm about Kerry's shoulder, he said, "This man is worse than a carpetbagger, my dear, because he's a sneak. He obviously came here hoping to pay the taxes and take over your father's farm. When he discovered they were not owed, and that you had already claimed the land for yourself, he decided to go about it in a different way— by pretending to be interested in you.''

Kerry's lips moved wordlessly for an instant, and then, eyes flashing, demanded of Slade, ''Is this true? But it has to be, doesn't it? It explains why you have money when I thought you were poor as me. The lumber, the food. Dear God, all you wanted was to get close to me to get the land.''

Slade knew what she was thinking . . . believing . . . that everything between them had been a farce, staged to fulfill his ultimate goal. And he also knew that nothing he could say was going to change her mind, especially with a crowd gathering.

He drew a deep breath and let it out slowly, then said, ''Kerry, we need to go somewhere and talk about this.''

He made to take her arm, but Thad Albritton yanked his hand away.

Slade turned on him then, eyes burning in the way that never failed to give a man a second thought about pushing further. ''Touch me again, Albritton,'' he warned through gritted teeth, ''and your daughter will also be needing a new daddy.''

Thad blanched and stepped back.

Slade focused on Kerry once more. ''I guess this isn't the time to talk.''

''No,'' she said frostily. ''And there never will be.''

She walked away, the others following after her.

Slade left quickly, not wanting trouble.

His interest in the land was just a ploy to give him reason for being there. The only thing he cared about was Kerry.

And now it looked as though he might have lost her.

Chapter 15

It had been three days since Kerry had learned the truth about Slade, and she was still livid.

To think that everything between them had been a well-thought-out plan for him to take control of her father's land made her blood boil.

Worse, she was furious with herself for having been so naive as to be taken in by him.

Dear God, what had she been thinking? She had given herself to him in wild abandon. She had fancied herself in love with him and wanted to marry him. And all the while he'd probably been laughing at her behind her back. Such a good deal it would be for him. The farm, she had learned, had some of the richest soil in the whole county. And had carpetbaggers realized that, the distance from town would not have mattered.

Kerry was so mad that it made absolutely no difference to her that Slade had, in fact, invested some of his own money in the property. Now she knew he had bought the tobacco seed, as well as the lumber for the chicken house, pen, and horse stall. But no matter. She had not asked him to do it, and since he'd lied about it, as well as had ulterior motives, she would not have reimbursed him even if she had the means to do so.

She had even, after stewing about it that night, changed her mind about giving him the wagon back, which at first she intended to do. After all, she grimly mused, in a way she had earned it. So the next morning she had taken it and gone home.

After the social, she had spent the night with Abigail, which had been utter misery. Abigail had herded her into a guest room, locked the door, and asked blunt, bold questions about her relationship with Slade.

Kerry had managed to make her believe there had never been any intimacy between them. Abigail had then apologized and said she should have known better than to probe but felt she had to since Kerry's virtue might now be questioned in the wake of the revelation about Slade. The local brethren had no use for carpetbaggers, and that was how they now regarded him.

But Kerry had responded in kind to Abigail's bluntness by asking her to refrain from encouraging Thad Albritton, or any other man, to pursue her. She wanted only to be left alone to make her farm prosper, and marriage was the last thing on her mind.

Abigail had indicated that she could well understand her feelings and promised not to interfere in her personal life ever again.

So now, as Kerry tended the tobacco seedbeds on a warm and sunny November day, she told herself not to look back. Nothing that happened yesterday mattered. She had today and tomorrow to look forward to . . . despite the ache in her heart.

She had loved him with all her heart and soul.

Now she willed herself to hate him instead so the pain would hopefully lessen.

"Damn him to hell," she muttered under her breath as

she yanked a weed from the ground with a vengeance. "May he rot there, and—"

"Kerry, it's not like you think."

A furious cry ripped from the core of her soul as she whirled about to reach for the shotgun that was no longer where she had left it.

Slade was holding it at his side, pointed towards the ground.

"How dare you sneak up on me?" she exploded. "But then you're good at doing sneaky things, aren't you?"

"Kerry, if you will only listen—"

"To what? More lies?" She tried to snatch the gun away from him, but he caught her arm and pinned it behind her back.

"I don't want to hurt you, but I'm not going to stand here and let you shoot me. Now be still and hear me out."

She tugged against him, and he let her go. She took a few steps backwards, her face twisted with rage. "I'm going to the house, Slade Dillon. I've a rifle there, and—"

Tossing the shotgun to the side, out of her reach, Slade grabbed her by her shoulders and lowered her swiftly to the ground. Then he dropped on top of her as she struggled against him to pin her down, holding her wrists at her sides.

"What are you going to do now? Rape me?" she hissed between clenched teeth.

"I didn't rape you before, Kerry," he said quietly. "Neither did I seduce you."

"No. You just lied to get what you wanted."

His lips quivered as he held back a smile to remind, "I seem to recall the last morning we were together that you crawled into bed with me."

Kerry felt her cheeks flush with shame, and she turned her face to the side so she would not have to look at him. "That was different. That's when I thought you loved me."

"I do love you."

"Liar."

He was straddling her to hold her down but not so tight as to make her uncomfortable. "If I didn't love you, I wouldn't have hung around as long as I did and spent my own money on this place."

"Don't throw that up to me. You did it because you planned to trick me into marrying you so could take it over. What did you plan to do then? Run me off?"

"If I had only wanted the land, I could have had it without marrying you, Kerry."

She laughed at his audacity. "That's absurd. The taxes are paid, so a vulture like you can't take it away from me. Carpetbagger," she spat the word. "I should have known."

"I'm not a carpetbagger, and I have a story to tell you. When I'm finished, I think you'll understand why everything happened like it did ... why I didn't just ride in here and run you off that very first day."

"Run me off," she echoed with a sneer. "Are you crazy? I told you then that the taxes were paid."

"Kerry, I'm staying right here till you listen to what I've got to tell you, no matter how long it takes."

She squirmed against him but to no avail. "So talk," she said, eyes sparkling with frustrated tears. "Then get the hell off my property. And if you expect me to pay you back for what you've spent, forget it. And I don't feel obligated to, anyway. I never asked you to do any of it, and you know it."

"True. You didn't. But maybe I wasn't doing it all for you, anyway, Kerry. Maybe I was doing it for us—and because the land is actually mine, anyway."

Her eyes went wide. "Are you mad?"

"No. You see, the fact is—Flann Corrigan was my stepfather."

Kerry was sure he was out of his mind and warned, "As soon as you let go of me, I'm riding into town and have the law arrest you, Slade Dillon. I'll not put up with your insane ramblings and your lies, and—"

"I can prove it."

She felt a shiver of foreboding. He looked dead serious.

"My mother was a nurse for the Union Army," he continued. "She met your father when he was wounded. She said it was love at first sight, and it wasn't long after that they were married at his bedside."

Kerry bit down on her lower lip and tasted blood. "I don't believe you. My father never stopped loving my mother. Not for a minute."

"I don't dispute that, Kerry. As a matter of fact, according to what my mother wrote me, he confided to her that there had been another love in his life . . . how she lived across the ocean, and he had been clinging to the hope for years that she would come join him. Only she hadn't. And he did not want to be alone any longer. Unfortunately, he didn't live long after they were married."

Kerry tightly closed her eyes as she tried to absorb it all. As much as she hated to admit it, she could understand why, as he lay mortally wounded, her father would have reached out for any hand to hold . . . made any promise. But it had nothing to do with her. She was still his daughter, and he would have wanted her to have the land, and she said as much to Slade.

He waited until she finished, then gently explained, "I can understand your thinking that way, but that's not how it is. You see, before he died, he wrote a will leaving everything he owned—which was this farm—to my mother. She continued working in the battlefield till the war ended, then went to a hospital in Washington to help take care of soldiers who needed a long time to heal. She wrote me that she wanted the two of us to eventually move down here and make our home on the farm, but she passed away before that could happen."

"Well, I'm sorry about your mother," Kerry said tartly, "but what makes you think you have a claim?"

"Because I am her heir, and her property passes on to me. I own the farm, Kerry. Not you."

"That . . . that is preposterous," she sputtered. Good

Lord, did he take her for the world's biggest fool? Did he actually think she was going to believe such a ridiculous lie?

"Like I told you—I can prove it."

"If that were true, you wouldn't have deceived me as you did."

"I didn't mean to. When I first arrived in town, I went to the courthouse, like Higdon said, to find out whether the farm had been sold for delinquent taxes. Then, when I heard that Flann Corrigan's daughter had showed up, I was curious. And I also didn't want to just throw a woman out, so I rode out to see what was going on."

She snickered. "And you made up your lies and moved right in."

"In a way, yes, but you make it all seem so devious. It wasn't. I liked you from the start, and I couldn't find it in me to just come right out and tell you that you had to leave. I thought if I hung around a while I'd find a gentle way of telling you. Only the more I was with you, the more I cared about you, and I kept putting it off."

"You mean you decided it would just be easier to court me, marry me, and then take over. And do you know why?" She lifted her head to make her glare even harsher. "Because you knew it was the only way you'd ever get your hands on this land."

He was silent for so long Kerry thought he was not going to answer, but when he did, his words were spoken with care, as though he had framed each and every one. "The fact of the matter is that I forgot all about wanting the land. I forgot about everything except the way I had come to feel about you."

"Well, that's just too damn bad," she retorted, "because you've lost both—me and the farm."

With a weary sigh, he rocked back on his heels, releasing her. As she scrambled to her feet, he said, "All right. I guess I have to accept that you hate me now. I suppose I can't blame you, because I can see how it must look to you. But I still care about you, and that's why I'm offering to buy you out—reimburse you for the taxes and give you enough money to get settled somewhere else. You ought to be living in town, anyway. It's not safe for a woman out here alone.''

"You go to hell. I'll never sell to you or anybody else.'' For a brief instant, she was tempted to snatch up the shot-gun but decided against it. All she wanted right then was for him to get out of her life and take his silver-tongued lies with him. "I think the best thing for you to do is leave before there is real trouble.''

"Don't you see that's what I'm trying to help you avoid?'' He stood to tower over her with beseeching eyes. "It would be easy for me to just ride on out of here and find land somewhere else. But if I did, you'd stay, and that stubborn streak of yours would have the Klan after you sooner or later.

"I should have got rid of that stallion,'' he railed on. "If any of them recognizes it as belonging to that Negro they were after, they're going to wonder if you had anything to do with him getting away. And the next thing you know, they'll be burning you out.''

With hands on her hips, she cocked her head to one side and mustered all her bravado to say, "Well, mister, just let them try it. Maybe you've caught me off guard twice now, but never again. From now on, I won't step foot outside the house without a gun strapped to me.''

He shook his head in frustration. "I want you to take my offer.''

"You're wasting your breath, carpetbagger.'' She walked over and picked up the shotgun. He made no move to stop her. Very calmly, she warned, "It's time for you to leave, and I'd better not see you around here again.''

She saw the dark look come over his face and tensed.

"Very well,'' he said with a curt nod. "I'll go, but you're forcing me to do something I don't want to do.''

She raised one eyebrow to warily ask, "Which is?''

"Have you thrown off my land," he said in a voice thick with pity. "I'll see you in court, Kerry."

He had left his horse out by the road. As he walked down the path, he could feel her eyes burning into his back and only hoped he wouldn't feel a bullet along with it.

No, he didn't want to force her off the land, but it was for her own good. Sooner or later she would cross swords with the Klan. She had that kind of fiery grit.

But he was also motivated by something else—he needed a reason for hanging around. Thanks to him letting his heart rule his head, he could forget about being asked to join the Klan. He could stand on a soapbox in front of the courthouse and scream lies all day about how he thought the niggers were uppity and needed to be put in their place, and it would do no good. He had now, thanks to his own stupidity and Sim Higdon's big mouth, been branded a carpetbagger. The Klan, and the local townspeople, wanted nothing to do with him. He could only turn to the carpetbaggers and did not relish the thought of that. Still, he needed contacts, because he yet had a job to do.

When he got back to town, Slade went straight to the courthouse.

When he walked into the clerk's office, Sim Higdon paled at the sight of him and nervously said, "Look, if you came in here to make trouble about the other night, I can yell out the window and the soldiers will come running, and—"

Slade cut him off. "I'm here on business, Higdon, so let's get down to it." He slapped the leather saddlebag on the counter, pulled the flap open, and drew out some papers. "I'm here to file a claim for the Corrigan farm."

Sim had edged towards the window, about to open it just in case he did need help. But at Slade's words, he stepped back to the counter, curiosity surging. "What the hell are you talking about? I told you the first day you were in here that the taxes had been paid."

"And I also noticed that the deed was still in Flann Corrigan's name."

"So?" Sim propped an elbow on the counter and smirked to ask, "What business is it of yours? Kerry will take care of that when she has the money to have a new one drawn up. There's no rush."

"And no need to waste the money," Slade said breezily as he unfolded the papers he had taken from the saddlebag. "You see, I am the legal heir to Flann's property. This is his will, properly witnessed, stating that he left everything to his wife, who happened to be my mother. With both of them dead, everything goes to me."

Sim shook his head and laughed, "This has got to be some kind of joke, Dillon. Kerry Corrigan is Flann's daughter."

"Not legally."

Sim's eyes narrowed. "I think you'd better watch your mouth. It's not proper saying something like that about a lady."

Slade hastened to assure, "I am not being disrespectful to her, believe me. But it just so happens that Flann was never married to her mother, which makes her illegitimate. I am legally his stepson, which makes me the rightful heir. Now how do I go about processing my claim?"

Sim was plainly dumbfounded. He quickly read through the papers, then said, "I've never had this happen before. I don't know what to tell you, but it seems to me that Kerry would have more of a right than you, being she was here first, and—"

"And that doesn't mean anything when it comes to the law." Slade took the papers from him and put them back in the bag. "So what you're telling me is that you don't know what I'm supposed to do."

"About what?"

The man dressed in gray waistcoat, white shirt, black cravat, and pinstriped trousers had entered the office while they were talking. Slade had been aware of his presence. No one ever slipped up on him.

The man stepped up to the counter, interest piqued, but faltered as Slade gave him an irritated glance.

"Sorry," he said. "I didn't mean to butt in. I'm a lawyer and thought I might be able to help."

"This here's Calvin Morehead," Sim grudgingly said to Slade.

Calvin removed his top hat and gave a slight bow. "I could not help overhearing a bit of your conversation, and I think you could use my services."

"Well, thanks for the offer," Slade said, "but all I want to do is file a claim for some land that's rightfully mine. Higdon, here, pretends not to know how to go about it."

Calvin smiled. "He doesn't. But I do. And it's not as simple as filing a claim, Mr. . . . ?" he quirked a brow.

"Dillon. Slade Dillon."

"Ah, yes, I've heard all about you and the little tiff you've had with the Corrigan woman. It wouldn't be her land you're trying to claim, would it?"

"My land. Not hers. And I know a judge will have to declare me the owner. All I need to know is how to go about getting a hearing."

Calvin gave his shoulder a friendly pat. "Just leave it to me, but first I need to know what kind of proof you have for making such a claim."

Fed up with how Sim was taking in every word and knowing it would be spread all over town within minutes of the courthouse closing, Slade motioned Calvin out into the hall. Then he showed him the will and explained the situation.

When he finished talking, Calvin was almost shaking

with eagerness. "You have a solid case, Mr. Dillon. Just leave everything to me. The circuit judge will be through here day after tomorrow. The docket is very light, and I am sure I can squeeze in your case if you want me to handle it."

It was sooner than Slade had dared hope. He held out his hand. "Do it," he said tersely. "I want it over with."

When he was finished with the lawyer, Slade headed straight for Sadie's and ordered a double whiskey. He had only taken the first swallow when Rosalie appeared at his side.

Running teasing fingers up and down his arm, she went through her routine of setting things up for a rollicking night upstairs.

Slade played his part, dickering over the price as the bartender listened. Finally, downing the rest of his drink, he followed her up the stairs to her room.

The minute the door closed behind them, Rosalie cried, "I heard what happened at the church. Slade, I'm sorry. Where does that leave you now?"

He told her he was going to court to claim the land. "It will give me justification for staying around here. And I'll keep on doing as I have been—spying whenever I can. And even that might get easier now that the Klan is going to have a den where they meet regular." He told her about the location, as well as the new method of signaling with whistles.

"Very well," she said with an approving nod. "But I want you to know I'm sorry things didn't work out the way you wanted."

"They seldom do," he murmured then: "I guess I'd better be getting along so you can get to work."

At that, she hooted, "Are you crazy? I am working—or at least I'm supposed to be. And you're going to have to hang around here for a while or questions will be asked."

He tensed, eyes narrowing.

She could tell what he was thinking and laughed, "Oh, don't worry. With you, it's another kind of business, although I have to say if I weren't already promised to somebody else I might be tempted to do otherwise."

Relieved, Slade sat down in a chair and gratefully accepted the drink she poured. She was a damn fine-looking woman, despite how her face mirrored the hard life she had lived. And he liked her personality, as well. She was fun and easy to talk to. He enjoyed being around her for friendship if nothing else.

Curious as to her private life, however, he could not resist asking, "This somebody you're promised to—does he know you're working undercover for the Freedmen's Bureau?"

"He should," she laughed, eyes sparkling. "He hired me."

Slade was confused but not for long as Rosalie delighted to inform him, "He hired you, too, Slade—your old friend Sam Pardee."

The instant Kerry heard the sound of hoofbeats, she snatched up her shotgun with one hand and her pistol with the other.

She had been sitting in the gathering dusk, miserably wondering just what Slade would do next . . . just how low he would stoop to try and steal her land.

She had also been thinking how, despite everything, she could not make herself stop caring about him. Dear Lord, it was so very hard to come face to face with the reality that everything between them had been a farce, staged to suit his purposes.

But regardless of how she might be fool enough to still love him, if he thought he was going to come riding up any time he pleased to aggravate and annoy, he was dead wrong. She did not aim to kill him, but he would take home a seat full of buckshot, for sure.

Standing inside the front door, hidden by the dark shadows, Kerry was relieved to see Sim Higdon and not Slade. She stepped onto the porch to call in greeting, "Whatever brings you out here so late, Sim?"

He dismounted quickly and bounded up the steps.

She could see by the scant light remaining that he was upset, but before she had a chance to ask, the words rattled from his mouth like marbles from a can.

"Slade Dillon is taking you to court. The circuit judge will be here day after tomorrow. He hired himself a lawyer who's got him on the docket. I got here as quick as I could to let you know so you can get a lawyer and fight him."

Kerry was momentarily shaken but managed to lift her chin and tersely declare, "I don't need a lawyer. I've got all the proof I need—letters from my father to my mother saying he bought the land to make a home for all of us. And a map, as well."

"I don't know, Miss Kerry." Sim was twisting his hat around and around in his hands, shoulders hunched in doubt. "He showed me a will. It was all signed and witnessed proper."

"That doesn't matter. A judge is not going to pay any attention to a will signed by a dying man who was no doubt crazed with pain at the time."

Sim started to say something, then shook his head to silence.

Kerry felt a chill move up her spine. "What is it, Mr. Higdon? What were you about to say?"

"Well . . ." he drawled, then said in a rush, "if it was any other judge, I might agree with you, but it's Judge Bailey Grissom that's scheduled to come."

Kerry licked her dry lips and sucked in a deep breath before fearfully asking, "What difference does that make?"

Sim's voice shook with sympathy. "Because he's a Yankee, Miss Kerry . . . and Slade Dillon is a carpetbagger. He's sure to lean towards him."

Kerry managed to swallow despite the lump in her throat, then mustered the spirit to say, "Well, I guess I've got a fight on my hands, Mr. Higdon. Thank you for letting me know."

"Oh, it's my duty as court clerk to tell you, and I didn't want to waste a minute getting out here."

She thanked him again, offered him coffee which he declined, and then he left her to her misery.

Kerry continued to sit in the dark, wondering just how she could win the judge to her side.

But despite her worries, one bright thought shone through the gloominess.

It was suddenly becoming easy to despise Slade Dillon.

Chapter 16

Kerry was wearing her Sunday dress, wanting to look as nice as possible for her day in court. She had braided her hair about her head hoping it would make her look older. It was important that Judge Grissom not think she was too young to run her own farm.

The day was clear and cold. Her only wrap was her father's shabby coat, and it did more than keep her warm. It made her feel as though he were with her somehow, his arms wrapped about her to give her confidence and hope that she could ultimately defeat Slade's quest to rob her of her inheritance.

Slade.

Where once it had thrilled, she now shuddered to think his name.

He was the epitome of greed, and she was prepared to prove it by telling how he had lied up and down, around and around, trying to get on her good side. Once wed, he would have taken everything, and, oh, what a charmer he had been. It would have worked, too, if not for Sim Higdon recognizing him. She was just relieved that it had happened before it was too late.

She was going to offer to return the wagon, having decided she would rather be inconvenienced. She would find a way to deliver the eggs. As for everything else, that was different. He had made her think egg money had paid for it or given some other devious explanation. So she felt no guilt whatsoever in that respect.

The stallion, she noted, did not like pulling the wagon, anyway. He was much too spirited to do the work of a mule or pull horse. But he probably would not mind having baskets across his rump. As smooth-gaited as he was, the eggs would not break if they went slowly.

Everything was going to work out just fine, she told herself for maybe the hundredth time. True, her heart still ached, and she continued to feel humiliated by it all, but she had learned a valuable lesson. Never again would she be so gullible.

She was on the outskirts of town when she saw a group of Negroes walking on the side of the road. Delighted to recognize Luther and Bessie among them, she reined in the stallion and happily called, "Get in. All of you. Luther, you and Bessie sit up here with me.

"Now tell me why you're all headed into town," she said when they were settled beside her.

Luther seemed surprised she had to ask. "Why, we heard about you having to go to court, Miss Kerry, and how that carpetbagger fellow is trying to take your land. We've been worried, and we wanted to be there to let you know we care."

Kerry was touched but asked, "Why didn't you stop by the house instead of passing on by? You knew I'd be going in myself and could give you a ride. Look how far you've walked."

"Yes'm, we knew that," Luther said, "but we didn't want to get you in no trouble. So we'll be gettin' down off the wagon in a little ways. Won't do for you to ride into town with all of us.''

"Nonsense. I don't want to hear such talk. What I do is my business. But how is it you were able to get away from Mr. Allison's today?''

"He said we could have the day off 'cause there's nothin' much to do anyhow, and him and his overseers are goin' to court, too.''

She thought it odd that there was so much interest, but was more concerned about whether they had heard anything from Adam.

Luther said they had not and did not expect to. Then, his face twisted with fear, he told her how Mr. Allison had asked where Adam had gone. "He was plenty mad. Said he had a beatin' waitin' on him when he comes back. I felt like tellin' him he'd be the one waitin' for a long, long time, 'cause Adam, he won't never come back.''

Kerry flashed with anger. "Has Mr. Allison beaten any of you, Luther?''

"Not me and Bessie. He whipped Edgar back there last week." He nodded to the wagon bed. "But he's all right now.''

"It is not right," Kerry said tightly, fiercely. "He should be reported to the occupation troops. They'd put a stop to it, and—''

"And then what?" Luther interrupted to ask, eyes round with terror.

Kerry saw how Bessie was also terrified and clutching his arm, tears spilling from her eyes.

"Where do we go?" Luther continued, voice thick with bitterness and despair. "The Klan would come after us if we tried to leave. We know that.''

"Do you think Mr. Allison is a member of the Klan?''

"Don't know. Don't want to know. Wouldn't make any difference. They'd still get after us. He asked us questions about Toby, too. Said he'd heard he'd been burnt out for bein' uppity and wanted to know if we knew where he'd gone. 'Course we said we didn't know nothin', but Bessie's afraid he thinks Adam had something to do with it.''

"That's right," Bessie whispered, trembling. "So I don't want him to come back. If they think he helped Toby get away, there's no tellin' what they'd do to him.''

Kerry was shaking, herself—but not with fear. Instead she quaked from head to toe with indignant rage to think such atrocities could go on. The law was not doing enough. The Ku Klux Klan was running roughshod over everybody, and something had to be done.

"Listen to me," she said tightly, evenly, then raised her voice and turned her head so the others could hear, as well. "All of you, listen. If you ever want to leave Mr. Allison's plantation, you can come to me, understand? I won't let the Klan harm you. I have guns. I know how to use them. I'll teach you, as well. So remember, you have a home if you need one, all right?"

No one spoke, their heads hanging down.

Kerry reached to pat Luther's hands, which were folded in his lap. "Remember what I say, Luther. You and the others are always welcome."

"We know that, Miss Kerry. And we also know it's gonna be real hard on you now that your hired hand turned out to be a no-good carpetbagger. We've talked about it, and we're thinkin' maybe we can sneak over sometimes at night and help you out.''

"No," she sharply disputed. "Don't do anything like that while you're working for Mr. Allison. If you got caught, you'd be beaten. I'll get by. I can set the tobacco seedlings out myself. It will take some time, but I'll manage. And I know about the suckering—how I have to pick the yellow flowers off the top when they bloom. As for harvest time, well, I'll worry about that later. Maybe I can get a loan at the bank to hire workers for that.

"I've a feeling it's going to be a good year," she exclaimed, wanting to fill herself with confidence before walking into the courthouse. "Everything is going to work out just fine. I'll make my father proud. Just wait and see."

"Yes, ma'am. I know you will."

Kerry could tell he did not believe it but was determined to keep her spirits up.

A mile on down the road, they rounded the last bend and the town came into view.

"Better let us off here," Luther said.

Kerry kept on going, ignoring his worried sigh and the fearful grumblings coming from those riding in the wagon bed.

"Miss Kerry," Luther said, exchanging glances with the others. "If you don't stop and let us off, we're gonna jump."

She had no choice but to rein in the stallion so they could get down.

"Don't forget my promise," she called to them, but they pretended not to hear as they moved to the other side of the road to continue walking as a group.

Kerry was astonished to see so many people in town. Surely they weren't all there to go to court, but, as she neared the courthouse, the number milling about increased.

She saw Abigail waving frantically from the steps. Then Horace Bedham appeared out of nowhere to tell her he would take her horse and wagon so she would not have to worry about it. One glance around made her glad to accept his offer, because there was no room at any of the hitching posts.

"I wish you had come into town last night and stayed with me," Abigail whispered the minute she reached her side. "I would have tried to talk you out of this, although I know I'd have been wasting my breath."

Kerry assured her that was true. "By now, Abigail, you should know how much that farm means to me."

"I certainly do—and so does everybody else in town. And they're here to show the judge they support you."

"Do they support *me*," Kerry could not resist the cynicism to ask, "or do they merely oppose a *carpetbagger?*"

"Probably a little bit of both," Abigail said airily, motioning people aside as she led Kerry on up the steps. "He hasn't arrived yet, by the way. Maybe he's lost his nerve."

"That will never happen," Kerry managed to laugh despite her rising nervousness. "You don't know how brazen he can be."

"And I hope I never do. Now take off that shabby coat. You want to look your best."

Reluctantly, Kerry removed her father's coat and folded it to carry under her arm for good luck.

They entered the courthouse lobby. It was small and narrow and extremely crowded. Everyone was staring, which made Kerry even more nervous. She had not expected such a turnout, hoping it would all be quiet and quickly over with.

"Where is your lawyer, dear?"

"I don't have one."

Abigail rolled her eyes in disbelief. "Pray tell me you are teasing, child."

"No. I can't afford one, and I don't need one, anyway. I have all the proof I need right here." She patted the worn bag she had brought all the way from Ireland. Her father's letters were tucked inside along with the map.

Abigail drew a lace handkerchief from the cuff of her sleeve and began to fan herself with it. "Oh, dear, dear God. I wish you had told me. I would have loaned you the money. I just never dreamed you would be so naive as to think you didn't need one. Mr. Dillon hired a Yankee lawyer to represent him. Sim told me. I guess he assumed you'd have sense enough to do the same."

Kerry was beginning to resent Abigail's fault-finding. "I told you—I have all the proof I need. I don't need to pay someone to present it for me. If Mr. Dillon wants to waste his money, that's his privilege."

Abigail clutched her arm and leaned to whisper, "But

the judge is a Yankee, too, Kerry. You need all the help you can get to stand up to him."

As they moved towards the doors marked Court Room many people called out words of encouragement to Kerry. She kept a smile pasted on her lips but stared straight ahead, praying it would soon be over.

Inside, there were twelve benches on each side of a narrow aisle. It appeared that all seats were taken, and Kerry politely said to Abigail that she was sorry she had missed getting a seat due to waiting out front for her.

"Oh, I'm sitting with you," Abigail said, leading the way down the aisle and through a short swinging wood gate to the open area beyond. Pointing to a table and chairs to the left, she said, "I believe this is where the defendant always sits."

Kerry quickly glanced to the right. The table there was empty.

The judge's bench, as it was called, stood in the center at the front. On the wall beyond hung a portrait of President Andrew Johnson with an American flag displayed on each side.

Nearby was a framed sign proclaiming: In God We Trust.

Kerry hoped it was so, because she was having a difficult time believing in anyone else these days.

They sat down. Kerry smoothed her skirt, patted her braids, and took a deep breath and told herself to calm down. There was nothing to worry about. Even if the judge was a Yankee, with so many people watching, waiting, and apparently in her favor, there was just no way he could rule against her, and—

Gasps and murmurs suddenly rippled through the crowd.

"There he is," Abigail whispered in her ear.

Kerry turned and swallowed an exclamation of her own as Slade took his place at the other table.

Dear Lord, despite everything, she was still moved by

the sight of him, and he made it worse when he looked
at her with a sad, apologetic smile.

"How dare he?" Abigail hissed. "Oh, don't look at him,
Kerry."

Kerry had already dropped her gaze to her folded hands,
afraid her feelings might show on her heated face. It was
all so tragic, and she only wished she had been smart
enough, wise enough, not to fall under his spell . . . and
into his trap.

"I'll give him dirty looks for the two of us," Abigail said,
continuing to glare in Slade's direction. "But he's not
looking this way now. He's busy talking to that scalawag
lawyer of his, Calvin Morehead. He's from New York, you
know. Came down here to make his fortune helping those
vulturous carpetbaggers get around the law at every
chance. Nobody decent has a thing to do with him."

Kerry wished she would just be quiet despite being grateful for her company. Had she been sitting alone, she would
have felt like even more of a spectacle.

Abigail turned to see who all was in the courtroom. "Oh,
dear." She began to fan herself even harder. "Look who
I see. The nerve of her. I guess she came to gloat over you
losing your land after all."

Kerry bristled, "For heaven's sake, Abigail. I haven't lost
my land yet, and I'm not going to, anyway. But whoever
are you talking about?" She was not about to turn and see
for herself, wanting to avoid having to look in Slade's
direction.

"Lorinda Petrie. Why, she's even wearing that ring her
scalawag husband made you give him. She's holding up
her hand and flashing it for all to see, and she's looking
right here at you and grinning. No doubt she's going to
stand up and cheer when the judge rules in Mr. Dillon's
favor, and I hope Lorne is around to tell her off good for
acting like a fool."

"Abigail," Kerry said, struggling for patience. "Why
would Lorinda Petrie even care?"

"Oh, didn't I tell you? She told some of the ladies that you put too high a value on the ring, that she has much nicer jewelry but supposed Lorne thought it was unique and she would want it for that reason alone."

Kerry clenched her hands into tight fists. "That ring was worth much more than the taxes Lorne paid. He knows it, and so does she. It's just her way of glossing over the fact that he was heartless enough to make me give up something that meant the world to me."

"Shush," Abigail said with a gentle nudge of her elbow. "I think Mr. Dillon can hear you."

Kerry dared glance from the corner of her eye and saw that he was, indeed, looking their way and frowning as though he had heard every word. He had not liked it one little bit when she had told him about having to give up the ring, but now she found his apparent show of concern further mockery. He could think it an injustice for her to surrender a *ring*, while he was trying to rob her of her *land*.

Kerry turned her attention as a man walked to the front of the courtroom to loudly command, "All rise."

A door to the side opened, and a hush went through the crowd as a tall, imposing man entered. He had silver hair that hung to his shoulders and hawk-like eyes beneath bushy brows. He walked up the few stairs to his bench, head high, black robe flowing about his ankles. Then he sat down to look at his audience through round spectacles perched on the end of his pointed nose.

He looked, Kerry decided, anything but friendly. She only hoped he would be fair.

Lifting the gavel, he banged it down once and said, "Be seated." Then, without pause, he nodded to the bailiff. "Let's get on with it. Somebody stuck this case at the top of the docket. I'm anxious to see why."

"Your honor." Calvin Morehead stood, fingertips pressed against the edge of the table. His smile oozed with confidence and charm. "I requested this case be heard first, because I knew it was going to bring a lot of onlookers who need to get back to their busy lives."

Judge Bailey Grissom reached to twirl his mustache, looking quite amused as he said, "Calvin, I don't care about people's busy lives. It's the law that comes first. But now that you've pushed your client in front of everyone else, get to the point."

Calvin did not appear in the least ruffled by the judge's censure and went right into his smooth spiel. "Your honor, I represent the plaintiff, Mr. Slade Dillon, who is the stepson and legal heir of Mr. Flann Corrigan, by virtue of Mr. Corrigan having married his mother. At the time Mr. Corrigan married Mr. Dillon's mother, he made out a will which was properly signed before witnesses. I offer it to you now for your inspection."

Calvin went to the bench and handed up a sheaf of papers, then continued, "As you will see, in that will Mr. Corrigan bequeathed his farm here in Wayne County to his wife. She died not long after he did, which, of course, passed the property along to Mr. Dillon."

The judge nodded, and Abigail dug her nails into Kerry's arm. Kerry winced and pushed her hand away, refusing to get upset. It was only natural Slade's lawyer would sound quite convincing, but she had her side to present, too, by God.

Calvin then went on to describe how Slade had learned upon his arrival in Wayne County that a woman had claimed the farm by saying she was Flann Corrigan's daughter. He told how Slade had felt sorry for her, not wanting to run her off and render her homeless. So he had not told her who he was, instead trying to help her in hopes they could come to some kind of agreement.

With a condemning glance at Kerry, Calvin continued, "Then he discovered that the woman in question was, in fact, the bastard daughter of Flann Corrigan and therefore not entitled to a claim for the land at all."

Kerry felt like screaming out that she was not the bastard

in the courtroom this day. Slade Dillon, the lying hypocrite, held that honor all by himself.

"Therefore we beseech the court," Calvin humbly concluded, "to declare Mr. Dillon owner of the land. And he is, by the way, willing to reimburse Miss Corrigan for the taxes that were paid; however, we point out that he has much more invested in the farm—not only in physical labor but monetarily as well."

The judge leaned back in his chair, continuing to tweak his mustache as he considered what he had just heard. Then he nodded to Calvin to sit down and swung about to direct himself to Kerry. "On what do you base your claim, little lady? Do you even have proof that Flann Corrigan was your father?"

"I do, your honor." Kerry rose, glad no one could see how her knees were knocking together and only hoped they could not be heard. "I have letters that my father wrote to my mother in Ireland, stating that he bought the farm for all of us, and how his greatest wish was that she would bring me and come here to live."

He held out his hand. "Give me whatever you have there, Miss Corrigan."

She prayed not to trip in her nervousness as she hurried from behind the table and crossed to the bench. Standing on tiptoe, she handed him the envelopes as she said, "There's a map, too. You can see he wrote down all the directions to the farm. If he hadn't intended for me and my mother to have it, then why would he have gone to so much trouble?"

His thick brows wiggled like gray caterpillars over dark, chastising eyes. "I'll ask the questions, if you don't mind."

"Sorry," she murmured. "But can I say one thing more on my behalf since I couldn't afford a lawyer to do it for me?"

For an instant she thought he was going to deny her, but a little ripple went through the crowd, as though people were grumbling among themselves, thinking he was being impatient with her. He did not fail to notice and gave a curt nod of assent.

Kerry cleared her throat and folded her hands behind her back. She tried to stand as tall as possible and held her head up so she could look him straight in the eye. "I want you to know that Mr. Dillon lied to me. He pretended not to have any money, and I felt sorry for him and let him work for his food. True, he's got some investment in my place, but here again, because of his lies I didn't know it. He said he swapped some of the eggs for supplies . . . things like that. And he pretended to salvage more wood from my father's burned-out barn than he really did, and—"

"But, miss," Judge Grissom interrupted to ask, "why do you think he did all that?"

Kerry bit down on her lip. Lord, she hated telling something so personal in front of all the people listening, but if she wanted to keep her farm, she knew she had no choice. "I believe, your honor, it was because Mr. Dillon wanted the farm at any cost. He knew how rich the soil is, how there's going to be a lot of money made on tobacco. And when he found out about me—how it all belonged to me—he decided the only way he'd ever get control of it was to marry me. That's why he bought all the slices of my pie at the auction, because he was going to court me, and then . . ." She trailed to silence to see how the judge was looking at her as though she were daft. There were also a few titters behind her in the crowd that set her cheeks aflame.

"That's how it was," she muttered helplessly. "I never asked him to spend any money on the place. He did it because he wanted to. But it's my land, and I don't see how the court can see it any other way."

He glowered at her, the caterpillar brows wriggling once more. "Thank you, Miss Corrigan, but the court will decide how it sees things."

He banged the gavel again, harder than before, making Kerry jump.

"Court is recessed for an hour while I go over all these documents and make my decision."

Everyone stood while he walked out. Then Kerry went back to her chair and all but collapsed.

Abigail patted her shoulder. "You did fine, dear. Now why don't we run to my house and have some tea while we wait?"

Kerry blinked back tears. "No. I don't want to go out in that mob. I'll just sit here. But tell me—is Slade leaving? I pray he is . . ."

Abigail made a face. "Oh, yes. He took off like a scalded dog, him and that detestable Calvin Morehead."

Kerry could hear people moving about. "Is anyone else leaving?"

"Not many. No one wants to lose their seats."

Kerry folded her arms on the table, then bent her head and closed her eyes. "I'm not moving," she said dully. "And if Judge Grissom rules in favor of Slade, I think I'll just stay and die here."

"Oh, you'll do nothing of the kind. You'll come and live with me till you find a place of your own."

Abigail talked on, about how Kerry should not worry. She was young and attractive, and other men besides Thad Albritton had expressed an interest in courting her. In no time at all, she would have herself a fine husband to look after her.

Kerry was not listening. She was too busy praying. If she lost the farm, she had no idea what to do. There was a little money, saved because her egg business was doing so well. More and more orders came in. So many, in fact, that she had decided to keep raising hens instead of selling them off. The income would tide her over till she could harvest her first tobacco crop. Things were looking so bright, and it just wasn't fair to lose it all now because of Slade.

She tried not to think about sweeter times, when he had held her in his arms and made her glory in being a woman.

But it was not just the memories of blazing passion that she treasured. There were other moments as well, when they had worked together, laughed together, and, yes, dreamed together.

Abigail was absently patting her on the back, saying something about how she needed to get her a new coat. The weather would be turning colder, and she should not go about in such a threadbare garment.

Horace Bedham appeared at Kerry's side to say he wanted to ask her something.

She raised her head and saw that he looked upset. "What's wrong?"

He chewed on the inside of his jaw for a minute, as if he hated to continue, then finally asked, "Where'd you get that stallion you got hitched to your wagon, Miss Kerry?"

She had an answer ready, having known that sooner or later someone would ask. "A man came by the farm one day and said he needed a cart and mule more than he needed the horse, so I traded him."

Horace's eyes narrowed. "Was that man a Negro?"

"Yes, he was." She was not about to lie, knowing it would only make matters worse if anyone recognized the stallion as being Toby's.

He dropped down on one knee, leaning close so no one could overhear. "Now you listen to me, Miss Kerry. You didn't know any better, but the fact is, you shouldn't have done that. You shouldn't be having anything to do with the Negroes—or freedmen as they call themselves," he added with a sneer.

"And how did you know the horse belonged to a Negro?" she coolly challenged.

"It figures. The Ku Klux Klan got after a Negro by the name of Toby who had got too uppity. He had a nice stallion like that. I saw him riding him one day, and I figured it had to be his. Now if any of the Klan finds out, they aren't going to like it one bit, but they'll see it like I did—that you didn't know no better. Just be careful next time."

"Mr. Bedham, I don't care what the Klan likes," Kerry said, fighting to keep from shouting, she was so riled. "And I don't need you or anyone else to tell me what to do."

Abigail grabbed her arm and squeezed. "Kerry, please. You're a lady. You have no business even discussing something like this. Just heed what Mr. Bedham is saying and learn from your mistake."

"But I—"

And that was all she had time to say before the bailiff came in to tell everyone to rise again.

Mr. Bedham quickly went back to his seat, and Kerry nervously settled into hers. But as she did so, she happened to glance in Slade's direction. Their eye contact was brief but it was long enough for Kerry to see that he still managed to keep a sympathetic look on his face.

Such a hypocrite, she fumed, squirming in her chair and wishing she could shout it to the world. Oh, who did he think he was? And why did he have to pick on her? He could have bought land anywhere, and—

Judge Grissom brought the gavel down, again making her jump.

He cleared his throat, then looked at her and began. "Miss Corrigan, I have read through most of the letters your father wrote to your mother, and it is clear that he did, in fact, intend for you and your mother to one day join him here."

Kerry was grateful the judge had discreetly not mentioned the fact that her mother was married to another man when those letters were written. Everyone was aware, of course, that she was illegitimate, but there was no need to make it seem her mother was unfaithful after her marriage.

She also took heart that the judge's tone was compassionate and dared think he might be in her favor.

"I can understand," he continued, "why you felt you had the right to claim the land."

Under the table, Abigail was squeezing her knee, and Kerry smiled, truly believing at that point that she had won.

But the smile quickly faded when Judge Grissom then turned his attention to Slade.

"I have also read Flann Corrigan's Last Will and Testament. Everything is in order. He did bequeath the farm to your mother, and, upon her death, it passed to you as her sole heir."

With sinking heart, Kerry shot a glance at Slade. His expression was impassive, no sign of gloating.

His lawyer, however, was grinning from ear to ear, but that was short-lived at the judge's next words.

"This is a very complicated situation, because I find that both of you have a legal claim." He looked to his audience for justification. "Think about it. Would Flann Corrigan have married Slade Dillon's mother had he known his flesh-and-blood daughter was coming to America to join him? Perhaps. But it's doubtful he would have signed away what security she would have upon her arrival. Yet, the court must acknowledge Mr. Corrigan's will."

He shook his head and sighed, then said, "I feel the fair thing to do is divide the property between both parties."

Kerry gulped, swallowed. She'd not thought of that possibility. Cut the farm in half? But which half would be hers? The part with the house? If not, what then? Where would she live?

But she did not have to wonder long, and any fears she might have had over division seemed small compared to worries birthed by Judge Grissom's ultimate verdict.

"The land will be shared, not divided, with each party receiving half of any profit, as well as being responsible for half of all chores and expenses. It is further stipulated that neither may sell their share to anyone except the other, and if one decides to leave, to abandon the land, title will then pass to the one remaining."

With one final slam of his gavel, it was over.

"Court recessed for fifteen minutes before the next case begins."

Kerry bowed her head, unable to look at Slade or anyone else.

It had been the last thing she would have expected.

Abigail began to pat her shoulder again. "Don't you fret, dear. You just go ahead and let him buy you out, because there is no way in heaven you could live under such conditions."

Kerry's laugh was sharp, bitter. "You're right," she agreed. "There is no way in heaven."

She turned to glare at Slade and continued, loud enough for him to hear.

"But there is a way in *hell*—and he's going to find out what it's like."

Chapter 17

Kerry had declined Abigail's plea to stay with her a few days and think things over, but she could not get out of town fast enough. She had pushed her way through the crowd, found her wagon, and left without a word to anyone.

She would think things over all right—but all she wanted just then was to return to the farm and prepare for battle.

She had expected Slade to show up that very afternoon, ready to move in. When he did not, she was surprised—but relieved.

The next morning, she gathered the eggs from the henhouse, washed them, and packed them in baskets. She did not relish going back to town so soon. Neither did she like the idea of Slade arriving while she was gone. But deliveries had to be made, and she needed the money. And, she decided, if she met him on the road heading for the farm, she would tell him then and there how it was going to be.

However, she did not see him on the road and only hoped she would not miss him while making the deliveries.

Hurrying every chance she got, anxious to get back, Kerry was in no mood for chitchat. But everywhere she went, people wanted to convey their sympathies as to how things turned out. Some were quite vocal in denouncing Slade, while a few of the women bluntly criticized her for not allowing him to just buy her out.

She knew they were probably echoing Abigail, who thought the arrangement was not exactly proper. But they did not have to worry, because if Slade thought he was going to move in the house and sleep under the same roof with her, he was dead wrong. She said as much to the disapproving women, and they allowed that it might be all right if he slept in one of the old slave shacks. After all, in these desperate times, they commiserated, people did whatever it took to survive.

As per their arrangement, Kerry took what eggs were left over to Horace Bedham. He only paid her half of what she got from the houses she delivered to, but it was better than nothing.

There was only one basket left. She could easily carry it in by herself, which was just as well. The store was empty of customers, and she could hear Horace busy in the back.

She set the basket on the counter, then tapped the bell. He came at once and was delighted that she had so many eggs to sell.

"You're really doing well with those hens of yours, Miss Kerry."

"That I am," she boasted. "The hens I found living in the wild gave me a nice start, and the first pullets are now starting to lay. I'm not going to sell them for fryers, either. I can make more on the eggs."

"A wise decision," he said, then narrowed his eyes to add, "A shame you don't make another one and let that carpetbagger buy you out."

"Well, that's not going to happen, Mr. Bedham. Now if you'll just pay me for the eggs, I'll be on my way."

He leaned on the counter, obviously in no hurry. "Listen, I hope you aren't mad at me about what I said to you in the courtroom yesterday."

"I was annoyed at the time, but I realize you're just concerned about me, and I thank you."

"I'm more than concerned. I'm worried. There's a rumor going around that you might have helped that Negro get out of town on purpose. And it doesn't help the situation any for you to have been seen giving some other Negroes a ride into town yesterday."

Kerry had run out of patience. All she had ever wanted to do was come to America, find her father, and live in peace forevermore. Instead, she had encountered a would-be rapist who had forced her to give up her most precious memento of her parents, given *herself* to a man who only wanted to steal her land, and now, because she chose to help a man escape to keep from getting killed and gave weary people a ride, she was being criticized.

"You know, Mr. Bedham," she said evenly, biting back her temper, "there's a fine line between being concerned about someone and just plain meddling. Now if you keep on, I'm going to think *you* are meddling, and then I will be mad."

She held out her hand. "Please. May I have my money? I have chores waiting at home."

She could tell he was annoyed, and when he paid her he warned, "These are terrible times we're living in, Miss Kerry. Folks got to tread lightly. You'd be wise not to be so stubborn."

She made no comment, wanting to escape further confrontation.

She gave the stallion the reins on the way home, not caring how fast he went. And he was a beauty. She loved watching him cantor, trot, and gallop at will. He held his head to the wind, his glorious mane flowing from his fine, strong neck.

"I'm going to buy a mule as soon as I can," she told him. "You're too magnificent to pull a wagon. And then we're going to ride—you and I—across my land forever and always, because no carpetbagger or hooded coward is going to run me off."

Tears ran down her cheeks, but to Kerry they were good tears, washing away all her frustrations to make room for the spirit needed to face the trying days ahead.

Finally she was home, and when she rounded the back of the house, she cringed to see Slade's horse tied to a post near the shelter.

She reined in the stallion and braced herself. He must have come out while she was making her deliveries or else taken a back road she didn't know about.

She got down out of the wagon and began unloading the empty baskets.

"Need a hand?"

It infuriated her how he always seemed to creep up on her without making a sound. "No, I don't," she snapped. "And as soon as I finish, we're going to have a talk."

"Good," he said pleasantly. "I guess there are some things we need to discuss."

Her annoyance intensified to see him walk right up on the porch and sit down in a rocker as if he owned the place. But then, in a way he did, she dismally reminded herself. Half of it, anyway. And that was what she intended to settle then and there.

Forgetting about unloading the baskets, unharnessing the stallion, or anything else that needed doing, Kerry marched up on the porch to join him. Only she did not sit down. Instead she towered over him, trying not to shake with the rage soaring through her so he would not mistake it for fear. "I know you think you won, but you didn't."

Rocking back, he propped his feet on the porch railing. With arms folded across his chest, he coolly informed her, "No, Kerry. I didn't win. If I had, you'd be packing right now."

"And you'd love that, wouldn't you? It's what you intended all along—to throw me out."

"No. You're wrong. I wanted you. I still do."

She leaned close, wanting him to feel the intensity of her ire, which surely had to be emanating from every pore in her body. "Well, you will never have me, you lying scalawag, understand? You try to come into my bed and I will blow you away, so help me."

He laughed. "And I always thought it was just a fable about redheaded Irish people having a bad temper."

"Don't provoke me, Slade," she warned. "And I'm going to tell you exactly how it's going to be. I sleep in the house. You sleep in one of the shacks out back. You don't come in the house for anything, and you stay out of my way."

He frowned as though he were really considering what she'd said, finally responding, "It isn't your place to set the rules. Besides, you heard the judge. Half the farm is mine. He did not say you could decide *which* half. Now as for me sleeping out back, don't worry. I've never forced my way into a lady's bed and don't intend to start now.

"Anyway," he added with a wink, "It's probably best I don't stay in the house. How do I know *you* wouldn't be trying to get into *my* bed? It's happened before, you know."

She itched to slap the smug grin off his face.

"As for staying out of your way," he continued, "if you'll recall, I paid for the tobacco seed, so I intend to have a lot to do with the crop. I've got money invested here, and I don't intend for you to make me lose it."

"Then we'll just divide the seedbed. You plant half the crop. I'll plant the other."

"No. That's not what the judge said. We're to divide the profits. That means we have to work together."

Suddenly he straightened, putting his feet on the floor. He tried to take her hand and pull her down to sit beside him, but she yanked away. "Come on, Kerry. Be reasonable. We've got a situation here neither of us can do anything about, so we might as well make the best of it."

She knew he was making sense but was still too mad, too humiliated, to admit it. "I have a few other rules."

"Then let's hear them."

"We don't eat together."

"Fine. You don't seem to know how to cook anything, anyway, except eggs. But you bake a tasty vinegar pie," he added to goad. "Now what other rules did you have in mind?"

"Just stay out of my way," she muttered, then went back to the wagon to finish unloading the baskets.

Slade got up and went to give the stallion a pat on his rump, then began taking off his harness. "How does he like pulling the wagon?"

"He hasn't said," she cracked.

"Funny, Kerry. Real funny. I can see we're going to have a wonderful life together."

She snorted. "You make it sound like this is a permanent arrangement."

"It is for me," he lied. Better, he figured, to let her think so. As much as he loved her, it would be best to move on once he accomplished what he had been sent to do. Seeing the hatred in the green eyes he adored was too much to bear. Now he wished he had gone about things in a different way but could not think of any way he could have. Confiding in her would have been a big mistake. As riled as she got over the treatment of the freedmen, she'd have wanted to ride with him to try and expose the Klan leaders. Besides, the way he figured, the less she knew, the safer she was.

However, he had wondered, after everyone had turned on him, just how safe she would be with him around. Then he decided he was worrying for nothing. The Klan left carpetbaggers—which he was now considered—alone. They focused on former slaves and any white person who dared side with them. So they wouldn't come after him, because he intended to give the appearance of minding his own business. Prowling around for information would have to be done under the cloak of darkness, and now, at least, he did not have to worry about Kerry wondering where he went at night. Hating him as she did, she probably wouldn't go anywhere near the shack.

Kerry had been glaring at him since his last remark.

He gave a helpless shrug. "It's my home now, Kerry. And the offer to buy you out is still good."

"I'd rather die than sell to you," she said with finality. Stomping up the steps, she paused before going inside to warn, "Remember, I want you to stay out of my way, Slade. I don't want any more to do with you than absolutely necessary."

"Then don't work the seedbeds tomorrow. And don't gather the eggs. Because I'll be doing both."

"The hens are mine, and you know it. Bessie and I found the ones that started me in the egg business, and you've no right to horn in on it."

"Anything on this farm is half mine. Regardless of when and how it got here."

With a final glare, she went in the house and slammed the door behind her.

Slade led the stallion to the shelter and rubbed him down, then filled a bucket with oats and left him to eat.

It was early yet, too early to do anything except think about what to have for supper.

He took his rifle and went in the woods. A half hour later, he returned with a rabbit and a squirrel. He cleaned them, then put them on a spit to roast over a fire in front of the shack.

He had bought himself a bottle of whiskey, knowing he would need it to ease the painful times—like now, when he thought about how much he loved Kerry . . . *and how much she hated him.*

It didn't help the situation any for him to make remarks like he had made about the chickens. But he could not tell her of his true intentions to do everything he could to make the farm prosper so she would be in good shape when it was time for him to leave. So let her think he was getting his hands in everything out of greed, if that was what it took.

The sun began to sink behind a stand of pines to the west. It was a chilly night, and the fire felt good. He only wished he could stay beside it but instead needed to ride out before dark. He had to find the new meeting place for the Klan. Their den, as they called it. If he could find a way to sneak inside and hide, he could observe everything that went on up close.

Rosalie had, in her discreet and cunning way, found out from one of her customers exactly where the Weston place was. She had pretended someone was looking for some land that adjoined it and had only vague directions.

Fortunately, it was not too far—perhaps a half hour's ride by road but longer through the woods, which is how he would have to approach it. Probably some of the Klan members would also have a private path, not wanting to all be seen riding down the main road around the same time.

He had told Rosalie there appeared to be three leaders of the Klan. Their identity was closely guarded, but if he could find out who they were, he was pretty sure the rest of the Klan would fall apart. By and large, the followers were all weaklings, rising to strength only when led to do so. Individually, or without strong leadership, they were like a herd of mindless sheep. Still, it was his plan to send as many of them to jail as possible as retribution for their malevolence.

He took a long sip of whiskey. It warmed him, and the warmth made him think again of Kerry. Damn it, what a fool he had been to let himself fall so deep. He should have backed off that very first day. Now there was nothing he could do to make things right between them, and he only wished it were not necessary for him to hang around. It hurt. Much more than Mary Beth ever had.

The only thing to do was get busy, finish his business, and ride on.

But he knew he would leave a piece of his heart behind.

Kerry sat at the kitchen table, aimlessly stirring her bowl of scrambled eggs with her fork. She had planned to buy food in town, but after Horace had made her so mad she had forgotten everything in her haste to get out of there. So there was nothing to eat besides eggs, and she was sick to death of them.

Well, at least she could take solace that Slade wasn't faring any better. He probably had some of those awful hard, saltless biscuits called hardtack she heard men kept in their saddlebags. But maybe he had a side of bacon and some beans, as well.

She got up and threw the rest of the eggs in the trash, suddenly resentful. He had money. She knew that now. So he had probably stocked up on groceries in anticipation of her refusing to cook for the two of them. He might be having himself a real fine feast, and she suddenly wanted to find out. If he hadn't thought to buy food, it would give her pure satisfaction to know he was as hungry as she was.

It was still good daylight when she stepped out the back door and into the biting wind after pulling on her father's old coat.

She walked carefully, quietly, not wanting Slade to hear her. It would not do for him to catch her spying on him, and she swore to yield to the temptation only this once. She had to get her mind set to ignore him and not care what he did. Otherwise, she was going to make herself more miserable than she already was.

Bad enough she was stewing over the future, wondering what it held, because if he did stay, what then? The situation could not go on and on, not amidst so much friction between them. And what if he met another woman and married her and brought her to the farm to live? The thought stabbed like an icicle to the heart. Even though she was trying with all her might to despise him, she could not bear the thought of another woman in his arms.

She was halfway across the yard when she slowed to sniff the air. Was it her imagination or did she actually smell something wonderful cooking . . . and was it coming from the direction of the shacks? But, of course, it had to be.

Quickening her pace but still careful not to give herself away, Kerry moved on down the path.

The smell was stronger, and without realizing it she hungrily ran her tongue across her lips.

It could only be a rabbit or squirrel roasting. Slade had cooked them for her before. He knew just how long to keep them on the spit, too, so the meat would be tender and pull right from the bone.

Drawing closer, she stepped behind a tree, then slowly peeked around it to confirm her suspicions.

She could see him casually lying on his side next to a little campfire in front of his shack. He was sipping from a bottle of whiskey, now and then rising up to turn the spit a little bit so as not to burn the meat.

Her stomach gave a big growl, and she drew back behind the tree, afraid he might have heard. Then, a few seconds later, she dared to look again, and it appeared he was unaware of her presence.

She could not tear herself away, staring in longing as he eventually took the meat from the fire and began to eat. She could almost taste the juicy morsels and cursed herself for having been so stubborn as to refuse to share. But no matter. Tomorrow she would just go hunting herself. He wasn't the only one who knew how to find food in the woods.

Finally she could stand it no more. It was starting to get

dark, and she did not want to risk stumbling due to not being able to see her way.

She crept back to the house but did not light any lanterns. Instead, she went to the front porch to stare out into the stygian darkness in her hunger and misery.

It was not fair, she thought with hands clenching the arms of the rocker. All along, she had been open and honest in all her dealings with Slade. And when she had given herself to him, it had been solely because she wanted him so badly she could not help herself.

Yes, she admitted to loving him from the start, though at the time she would not let herself believe it. As for guilt, she had tossed such ruminations to the wind, for how could she feel remorse believing they gave themselves to each other for no other reason than mutual desire? It was only when she discovered the truth that she regretted every kiss, every caress.

She gave her head a wild, vicious shake.

No. That was not true, for, despite everything, she would carry the memory of what they had together to her grave.

She had given with her heart . . . felt with her heart . . . and she would not, could not, lament the deep and abiding emotions she had felt in his strong, yet gentle arms.

Leaning her head against the back of the chair, she rocked slowly to and fro, pondering her situation. If the tobacco crop did well when it was harvested in the summer, her share of the profit, along with what she would have saved from selling eggs, might be enough so she could buy him out. Surely by then he would give up on her being the one to surrender.

The thing to do, she decided then and there, was to see that he worked hard until then . . . *very* hard. She would also be as unpleasant as possible to be around. *That* should not require much effort, she smiled bitterly to think. By summer's end he would despise her as much as she did him. He would be glad to take his money and go.

Yes, she decided with a sigh of satisfaction, that would

be her plan. Keep him working and make him as miserable as possible.

The wind was picking up as the temperature dropped. There was a damp sweetness in the air that Luther once told her meant snow. She had asked Abigail about that, who said it did not happen often, certainly not every winter.

Kerry hoped this would not be one of those winters.

She needed to put more wood in the fireplace but had forgotten to bring any in from the woodpile.

That provoked another thought.

Slade would feel no obligation to keep wood chopped for her. She would just have to do it herself.

Suddenly she heard something inside the house and angrily bolted to her feet. It had sounded like the back door opening and closing. If so, that meant Slade had come inside, and if he had, he was going to find out it was no fable about redheaded Irish people having a bad temper . . . in her case, anyway.

Inside the door was a table with a lantern and matches. She lit the wick, and the hallway was bathed in a mellow glow.

She went into the parlor and was instantly aware of how cozy and warm it was. When she had gone outside, the fire was almost down to embers, but now it was high and roaring hot.

Then she saw the neatly stacked pile of wood beside the hearth.

"I didn't ask for this," she grumbled, knowing he was trying to get on her good side. Well, it was not going to work. Her mind was made up. They would be bitter enemies to the end no matter what he did.

But then she went out back to the kitchen, and the first thing she saw was the leftovers from the meat he had roasted.

Hunger won out over the mad impulse to open the door and throw the food out into the yard.

She sat down and began to eat ravenously.

If he wanted to waste his time trying to win her over, let him.

Meanwhile, she would stay warm and fill her tummy.

After the way he had deceived her, Kerry figured she deserved it.

Chapter 18

Kerry awoke to the sound of sleet hitting the bedroom window. Leaping out of bed, she wrapped a blanket around her before padding across the cold, hard floor to look out at the wintry nightmare.

The clock on the wall said nine, but it was almost as dark as night. Thick, grayish-black clouds hovered like a giant hand, unleashing a steady torrent of freezing rain. Pine tree needles were encased in ice, the shorter trees bent nearly double to the ground.

She thought about the seedbed and began dressing in a panic. Slade had stretched tarpaulins across it, but all the trays would have to be brought inside. The fragile seedlings could not stand such frigid weather. She should have carried them inside the night before but never dreamed a storm was coming.

Three weeks had passed since Slade had moved back.

He did whatever she asked and took the initiative to do things on his own. All repairs had been made. He kept plenty of firewood chopped . . . for which she had coolly thanked him, of course. He had even fixed a way to safely burn a lantern inside the henhouse so the chickens would not freeze and die when the temperature plummeted.

He went about his work silently, ignoring her as much as possible. Once in a while he would leave meat on the kitchen table, but for the most part he avoided her.

Kerry told herself it was best that he did. The less they were together, the better. She tried to be as nasty as possible so he would not want to be around her, and evidently it had worked. Still, despite everything, she wished it did not have to be that way. The truth was, she still cared and knew she always would.

She had not seen him the day before. The hens weren't laying like they did when the weather was not so cold, so there were no egg deliveries to be made. All the chores were done, so Kerry assumed he had gone into town to spend some time.

She wondered what he did there . . . who he was with . . . but reminded herself it was none of her business.

With some of the egg money, she had bought overalls, a flannel shirt, heavy boots, and leather gloves. Not very feminine, but the clothes kept her warm. She could not have worked outside on such a day in just her muslin dress and worn-out coat.

The fire had gone out, but she did not take time to worry about it. She had probably lost some of the plants already and could not lose another minute.

It annoyed her that Slade was nowhere around. Moving the heavy trays was something he should have done, but evidently he had decided to wait out the storm in town.

The fact that he appeared to be less diligent and losing interest should have pleased her, but the truth was she needed his help . . . needed somebody's, at least. If Luther were still around . . .

"If, if, if," she fumed out loud as she tugged on her boots. "If frogs could fly, they wouldn't bump their bottoms on lily pads." She could see her breath in the chilly room.

Dressed at last, she braced herself before opening the door but was still blown back a few steps by the brutal wind.

Ducking her head, she clung to the railing as she carefully picked her way down the icy steps.

The seedbed was close to the house, thank goodness, but she was dismayed to see that part of the tarpaulin had blown off. A fourth of the plants were lost, she estimated, and quickly got to work moving the others into the house.

It took several hours. Kerry had to stop and get the fire going during that time. It would do no good to move the tender plants inside unless there was warmth. And if the storm passed on, and the sun came out by the next day, she could take them back out with no harm done.

Her shoulders were aching, and her arms burned with the strain of all the lifting. It was good that Slade did not suddenly appear, or she would have really thrown a tantrum. He could make merry in town, probably with one of those painted-up hussies Abigail said every wife wanted to run out of town, while she was freezing to death doing all the work.

She only wished the judge could know. Then he might realize he'd made a big mistake in his ruling. If Slade was to receive half the profits, then he should be responsible for half the work, and she was going to let him know that, by damn, the next time she saw him.

At last all the trays were inside, close enough to the fireplace to keep warm but not so near as to be damaged.

She was hungry and longed to heat some of the delicious turtle soup she had made the day before.

To spite Slade after what he'd said about her not knowing how to cook anything besides eggs and vinegar pie, she had started making Irish dishes when she could find the ingredients.

She could not resist leaving samples on the porch for Slade. He ate but made no comment except to mumble a thanks the next time she saw him.

But first things first, she told her growling stomach. The stallion, as well as the mule she had finally bought, would need feed and fresh water in their shed.

Hardly pausing to take a breath once the last tray was brought in, Kerry headed back outdoors. The sleet was still coming down, and it was hard to walk in the icy slush.

She was relieved to see that the stall door had not blown open. Pushing it open, she squinted against the darkness. The stallion and mule were, surprisingly, standing close together for warmth.

Then, her eyes adjusting to the dimness, Kerry was stunned to see that Slade's horse was also there. That meant he was not in town, as she had thought. And if he was in his shack, then why hadn't he taken care of moving the seedbeds—or at least shown up to help?

"Probably piled in his bed with a bottle of whiskey," she grumbled out loud. Well, she was going to tell him a thing or two, by God. If he thought he was going to snuggle down and not get out in the cold to do his share, he had another thought coming.

Snatching up the empty bucket, she struggled to keep from slipping as she went to the well to draw water. When that was done, she gave the animals their feed, then closed the shed door and made sure the latch was secure.

Then she headed for Slade's shack.

The first thing she noted was that no smoke was coming out of the chimney. Probably he had passed out drunk and the fire was dead. She thought about letting him just keep on sleeping and wake up freezing, but knew she would not relax till she spoke her piece.

She made lots of noise going up what steps there were, stamping her feet loudly. Then she banged on the door with her fist.

When there was no response, she yelled his name.

Still, there was nothing.

She went to the window and with her gloved hand wiped away the sleet that was like a curtain against the glass.

Peeking inside, she saw he was there, all right, lying naked on the bed. The blankets were on the floor.

She thought he had to be out of his mind. It would be as cold inside as it was out, and he could freeze to death.

"Slade, are you crazy? Wake up." She banged on the glass but could not see him moving, and, with apprehension mounting, knew something had to be wrong.

She opened the door and went inside, pausing to call out to him again. He lay very still, so still that a gasp tore from her throat and she rushed to his side, afraid he might be dead.

Pressing her head to his chest as she had to her mother's the night she died, Kerry could hear his heart beating and knew he was alive. But he was so hot, the heat emanating from his body almost searing to the touch. He was burning up with fever.

Picking up the blankets, she tucked them around him but knew he needed more. She would have to run back to the house and get some of her own, as well as bring firewood, for a quick look around told her that he had neglected to chop any for himself while keeping her well supplied.

"Oh, Slade, what a fool you are," she whispered, heart heavy with the love she had never been able to cast aside.

It seemed to take forever, but she made it through the storm with blankets, keeping them dry by wrapping them in the tarpaulin that had covered the seedbeds. She did the same with the firewood, which took several trips to bring enough.

When the fire was roaring hot, and Slade was covered, she returned to the house one more time to get the pot of turtle soup. She hung it from the hook in the fireplace, so it would be nice and warm when he woke up.

After that, she was unsure what to do. Somehow, it did not seem right to leave him, and it was hard to think about being mad when he was so sick.

Settling back in a rickety chair, she decided to wait a

little while, at least. There was nothing else that could be done, anyway, due to the storm—at least that was the excuse she gave herself for not leaving.

Wretched with fever, he would now and then throw back the covers. Kerry would hasten to pull them over him again and decided that that alone was reason for her to stay. But she had to admit she wanted to, because she was worried . . . and because she cared.

It was midafternoon when he finally awoke. Kerry had dozed off, head slumped forward, arms dangling off the chair.

"What are you doing here?" he asked thickly, pushing back the blankets.

Kerry was instantly alert and covered him as she scolded, "To keep you from doing this. Do you want to die from fever? You have to stay warm."

His eyes were glassy, and she saw how, when he rose up to glance around the room, his head bobbed dizzily as he fought to stay awake.

"It's . . . it's hot enough to spit-bake a deer," he said, falling back in his weakness. "Too hot . . . much too hot."

"It's your fever. Believe me, it's cold. And you should see outside—the world is frozen. There's ice all over everything, and . . ." She fell silent, because he had fallen back to sleep.

An hour passed, she estimated, maybe two.

Every so often she would go to the window to look out. It was hard to tell what time it was due to the thickly overcast skies. The sleet was still coming down. Once in a while she would hear a cracking sound, followed by a crash, and knew that another branch, or tree, had been unable to stand against the heavy ice.

The next time he woke up, she managed to get him to drink a little water and have a few spoonfuls of soup. He protested, saying he didn't feel like eating, but she kept at him until he did.

"You shouldn't be here," he said, a bit stronger than

before but still burning with fever. "You might catch whatever I've got."

"I doubt it," she said primly. "Unlike you, I know how to take care of myself. When did you get sick, anyway?"

He shook his head. "Don't know. Woke up this way. Sore throat, then the fever. I feel like hell."

"Well, it will pass soon enough," she said, careful not to sound too concerned. "You're strong. You'll survive."

"Much to your disappointment," he said thinly, attempting to smile but the effort falling flat.

Kerry flared, "Now that's a fine thing for you to say after I've been here the better part of the day taking care of you. And I dare say it's more than you'd have done for me."

"No, it isn't. I'd do the same, and you know it." He held out his hand to her, but she did not take it. He sighed. "You're going to keep on hating me, aren't you? No matter what I say or do, you'll keep believing the worst."

With an exaggerated sigh, she coolly said, "Do we have to talk about this? I'm only here to help you as I would anybody else. What happened between us doesn't matter."

"No, I don't guess it does. Not to you, anyway. And I'm a damn fool to let it matter to me."

She felt a rush and cursed herself for it. "You shouldn't tell lies when you're sick, Slade. If you die, you'll go straight to hell."

He laughed, then was seized with a fit of coughing. She held a cup of water to his parched lips, and he drank until she had to tell him he'd had enough.

"The seedbeds," he said, suddenly remembering.

"I took them inside the house. The fire has probably gone out by now, but the embers will keep the room warm enough that the seedlings shouldn't freeze."

"You . . . you took them in by yourself?" he asked in wonder.

With a haughty cock of her head, she boasted, "That I

did. And it goes to show I don't need your help or anybody else's. I can keep the farm going by myself.''

"Maybe," he allowed, eyelids growing heavy. "But you shouldn't have to. What about the animals?"

"I took care of them. The chickens, too. I think the storm is passing. The last time I was outside to get wood, I thought I saw some stars through the clouds. If the sun comes out tomorrow, everything will be fine.''

". . . got to get better," he whispered, as though speaking only to himself. "Job to do . . . been too long . . . have to take care of it . . .''

"There's nothing to be done," she said, puzzled as to what seemed to have him so concerned. "I told you—I took care of everything.''

He drifted away, and she was glad, because he kept mumbling incoherently. Nothing he said made sense.

She was kept busy making sure he stayed covered, for the fever continued to rage. But after a while, he seemed to settle down. Wanting fresh air even if it was freezing outside, she went out on the porch to gaze in wonder at the crystal world surrounding her. And, as the moon peeked out from behind a scampering cloud, the ice began to glitter like thousands of diamonds in the hallowed light. It was truly glorious, and she had never seen anything so lovely.

Finally, despite wanting to enjoy it forever, the bitter cold drove her back inside.

She was prepared to have to pick up blankets off the floor, sure that Slade would have thrown them off during her absence. Instead, she was startled to see that he was in the throes of a deep chill, his teeth chattering and body shivering violently.

She put more wood on the fire. There were no more blankets, and even if there were any back at the house, it would be too dangerous to try and get them. If she slipped on the ice in the dark and broke a leg or something, she could freeze to death by the time anyone found her.

Slade's tremors seemed to worsen. Kerry tried to get him to eat more soup, thinking it would help, but he was sleeping too deeply and she could not rouse him.

She was starting to get scared. People died from fevers, and the thought of losing him was more than she could bear. No matter what he had done—or had tried to do—she knew she loved him and would do anything to save him. When he was well, she could go back to the pretense of not caring, but for now all that was tossed aside.

Before she had time to think about it and change her mind, she drew back the covers and slipped into bed beside him. Snuggling close, she offered him the heat of her own body. Her mother had told her a story about a family she had known as a child. There was a terrible storm, and they had no heat, so the family had huddled together, naked, to save each other.

But why did they have to take their clothes off? Kerry had asked. Her mother had explained that what people wore was not warm on the outside. Heat came from the flesh.

Kerry hated to do it, but, remembering the part about the people being naked, she got back out of bed and, moving fast lest she lose her nerve, stripped and crawled in beside him again.

It would be all right. His fever was breaking. That was why he was having chills. He was exhausted and sleeping deeply and would be unaware she was lying next to him. She would stay there till the chills subsided, then get up and put her clothes back on. He would never know . . . she hoped. And at first light she would go home. The sun would be out. The ice would melt. Slade would be on the way to recovery, and things would go on as they had been.

She was relieved to feel his trembling lessen, but felt herself shivering on the inside. The feel of his body against hers was more than she could bear.

She turned on her side, away from him, then backed against him. Thankfully, he was still not aware of her presence, and in a few more minutes it would probably be all right to leave him. Her idea had obviously helped; her body heat was all the extra warmth he needed to make him stop shivering.

Still, it felt so good to be with him that way that Kerry told herself a little while longer would not matter. Besides, the wonderful emotions spinning through her just then would have to last a lifetime. Never again would she be pressed against him, melded as though they were one flesh.

He was breathing easier. He did not feel as hot. The fever was definitely on the way down, so the worst appeared to be over—for him, anyway.

Kerry was the one left with searing pain to think of what might have been . . . if only he had loved her.

Dreamily, she closed her eyes. If they were married, it would be like this every night of their lives—falling asleep together, arms about each other, as close as two humans can be.

It was so easy to pretend . . .

And so easy to drift off . . .

At first, Slade thought he must be still crazed with fever. It was the only possible reason he could imagine why he could feel Kerry's naked body lying next to him.

He decided to enjoy the illusion and pulled her tighter against him, desire starting to beat in his veins.

Her back was to him, and he slipped his arms around her to cup her breasts, then slide his fingers to her nipples and feel them harden at his touch.

He slid one hand down her flat belly, then felt the thick mat of hair between her legs and slowly twined it about his fingers.

He could feel the soft swell beneath and parted the gentle folds to dip into the moist velvet cocoon within.

She moaned, and he smiled. So damned real, this fevered dream. It made up for all the nights he had lain awake and ached to hold her. Maybe he should get sick more often if he could count on this happening.

He was hard and had been from the first instant he had imagined her firm, rounded bottom pressed against him. And all he had to do was lift her leg and slide himself between and up into her. She gave a little moan and wriggled back against him.

Clutching her sides, he began to rock to and fro, pulling her tight against him. His heart was hammering like an anvil, and lust was roaring through him like wind in a canyon.

He wanted more. He wanted her mouth, her breasts . . . every damn inch of her body.

He withdrew and rolled her over on her back, there in the darkness of his delirious fantasy. Straddling her, he feasted first upon her breasts, like succulent fruit, taking each in turn and licking her nipples before drawing them into his hot, hungry mouth.

Rising to his knees, he trailed his hardness between the thrusting globes, then teased beneath her chin before offering himself to her lips.

She touched him shyly at first, then opened her mouth to receive him. Her tongue rolled over him curiously, hesitantly; then she lifted her head from the pillow to take as much of him as she could.

Slade could stand the magic no longer. With a groan birthed from the core of his soul, he pulled away and lowered to plunge inside her.

She wriggled beneath him, clutching his shoulders. He felt her teeth bite into his flesh, but the pain was only pleasure to know she wanted him as much as he wanted her.

He found her lips and kissed her with a wild savagery he could not control. Bruising, burning, hungry, and eager, she yielded to him, touching her tongue to his in her own desperate passion.

She gave a cry at the same time he felt her squeeze about him as he rammed into her.

Then his own zenith came, and he pushed as deep and far as he could, wanting to bury himself inside her and stay there forever . . . in hopes the dream would never end.

"Oh, God . . ."

Her mournful cry jolted Slade to wonder if perhaps the magic could continue . . . if the fantasy really would last the night, anyway. If so, he wanted her again, and—

"Oh, God, I can't believe I let you do this!" Kerry burst into tears as she shoved him away from her. "Damn you, Slade Dillon, for the conniving hooligan you are. How dare you take advantage of me?"

It was as if someone had stabbed him with an icicle. It was no dream. He was not delirious. It was real. *She* was real. But what the hell was she doing naked in his bed? "Kerry, I didn't know," he said helplessly and jolted to full awareness. "I thought it was the fever, I swear."

"A likely story," she cried, trying to get out of bed, but he held her back.

"You aren't going anywhere till you tell me what's going on here."

Kerry was so overwrought that her words came out in a nearly incoherent stream. "You had chills. I couldn't think of anything to do except to warm you with my body, and I didn't plan for you to know. Only I fell asleep, and then I thought I was dreaming, and when I realized I wasn't, it was too late. You had already . . ." She shook her head in misery, unable to go on.

Though she continued to struggle, Slade was not about to let her go. Finally she crumpled against him, and he cradled her to his shoulder. Stroking her hair, he whispered huskily, "Both of us were dreaming, Kerry, don't you see? Because this is what we both want. There's no harm done, and there's no need for you to cry."

She raised her head to glare at him in the glow of the dying embers of the fire. "And you think this is how it is going to be? That I'll be your whore any time you want? Well, I promise you it will not be. It can never happen again."

"And why not?" Smiling, he began to kiss each and every tear sparkling on her lovely cheeks. "There's no harm in two people wanting each other."

"There is when one of them wants the other for the wrong reason."

"Listen, I know we got off to a bad start. I should have told you who I was, and someday maybe I can make you understand why I didn't. But till then, you've got to believe me when I say I care about you."

He searched the eyes he adored for some sign she was relenting, for he had felt the scorching glare of her hatred so many times in the past weeks.

"Kerry, you have nothing to fear," he said. "We both own this place. I can't take it away from you. I don't want to. So why can't we be happy together and see how things work out?" He could not ask her to marry him, was not even going to bring up the subject of courting her again. He still had a job to do, and until it was finished he was not free to give all of himself to her. But he could love her and take care of her, by God.

When she still said nothing, he let her go and rolled over on his back. Making love to her had left him weak and spent. Damn it, he could not remember the last time he had been so sick.

The night before, he had spied on a Klan meeting and found out where their next raid would be. A Negro named Spencer Wilcox, according to a Klansman, was getting too uppity and needed to be taught a lesson. Saturday night— which was only a few days away—they were going to drag him out of his house and hang him. Slade needed to get word to Rosalie to alert the soldiers. If the soldiers were waiting for them when they got there, the Klan would panic. He figured that would be his chance to follow one of the leaders home and find out who he was, because the guards would be trying to save their own hides.

So he needed to rest, to get his strength back so he would be ready.

"If you regret what happened," he said finally, feebly, "then I apologize."

He expected her to eventually lambast him and slam out of the shack. She had got out of bed when he released her and was putting on her clothes.

His head was hurting, from hunger, he figured. When was the last time he had eaten? He could not remember.

As though she could read his mind, Kerry softly asked, "Would you like some turtle soup? It's still warm. You had a few spoonfuls when you were dizzy with fever, but not enough to do you any good. You need to eat to get your strength back. Some whiskey might help, too. There's a bottle on the table."

He turned his head sharply in disbelief. Was he getting delirious again? Dreaming again? But no, she was there, living and breathing, not scowling, not angry, but with a very pleasant, albeit skeptical, look on her face.

He held out a hand to her. "I meant what I said, Kerry. Let's try to get along."

She almost fell in her haste to drop beside him on the bed. Fresh tears brimmed as she warned, "Never lie to me again, Slade. If you do, that's it. Whatever is in my heart for you will turn to hate. I swear it."

He knew she meant it, just as he knew he would have to take the chance he could keep his word as he said, "I won't. I promise."

"All right," she said finally . . . and wearily. "Now let's see about getting you something to eat."

He caught her wrist and held it. "You do that," he grinned. "Because you've just given me a reason to want to get well real fast, green eyes."

She brought him the soup. He ate his fill. Then he drank

a glass of whiskey, which burned his sore throat going down but warmed his belly as nothing else could.

Then he settled down to sleep through the rest of the freezing cold night.

And this time, when Kerry snuggled into his arms to doze with him, he knew, thankfully, that it was no illusion.

Chapter 19

As Kerry had hoped, the sun came out the day following the storm, and the ice began to melt.

Slade was still a bit weak but refused to stay in bed. He insisted on taking the seedbeds back outdoors, saying too much heat in the house would cause them to wilt. Kerry helped, though he told her he could manage by himself. She pretended it was only because she wanted to do her share, but secretly she just wanted to be with him.

She might as well have had a fever herself, because since they had made peace, she had experienced a warm glow within. But she did not let on to him just how happy she was, not wanting to appear too eager ... or give the impression she expected anything except the moment at hand.

She could not, would not, let go of her heart again ... at least not until she could be sure he meant everything he had said. Though she did not want to think about it, for she had resolved to forget and forgive the past, there was still the fear that he might be wanting all the land for himself and using her to get it.

Carrying out one of the trays, she thought she was being ridiculous. She was putting too much emphasis on Slade wanting the farm for himself. Why should he? He would be better off having a wife to help.

Besides, he had no real nostalgia for the place as she did.

That morning they had lingered in bed, wanting to give the sun time to warm things up before venturing outside. Lying close, arms about each other, Slade had talked about his mother and how she had tried to talk Flann out of leaving her the land. But he had insisted, saying she could sell it or do whatever she wanted to with it. He just did not want to die knowing it would be abandoned, which, till Kerry arrived, it had been.

"What made you want to come here?" Kerry asked as she set down the last tray of seedlings.

Slade was busy stretching the tarpaulin. "Oh, I don't know. I guess I just wanted a fresh start after the war."

"Well, I was wrong to call you a carpetbagger. After all, you're from the South."

"That wouldn't matter if I were a carpetbagger. Lots of Southerners went North during the war and came back to reap the spoils."

He took his hammer and nailed pegs in each corner of the tarpaulin to draw it high and tight above the tender plants.

"You never talk about the war," Kerry remarked as she watched.

"Well, I don't like to think about it."

Kerry pressed on, feeling the need to learn as much as possible about the man she had fallen in love with. "Do you have other family? Brothers? Sisters?"

"No. Just me."

"What about"—she hesitated—"a woman? Is there— was there—anyone?"

He gave the last peg one final tap, then turned to face

her. "I'm a loner, Kerry . . . till now. But why all the questions?"

She shrugged. "I guess I just want to know more about you."

He walked over to put his hands on her shoulders and look straight into her eyes. "I think it's best if neither one of us dwells on the past, all right?

"Now then," he said, changing the subject, "What about the eggs? Did you check this morning to see if the hens are still laying despite the cold weather?"

"Not as much as usual but enough so I can make the deliveries this afternoon."

He let her go and said, "I'll do it. You don't have any business being on the road. Some of the ice might not have melted, and where it has there'll be mud."

"I don't mind. Besides, I wanted you to do something else while I'm gone."

"Such as?"

"Move into the house."

He had been going in the direction of the horse shed but whirled about. "What did you say?"

Her smile was shy but certain. "I want you to move into the house."

He laughed uneasily. "Kerry, I can't do that. What if somebody found out, like Abigail Ramsey? Your name would be sullied, and we can't let that happen."

She lifted her chin in defiance. "Well, Judge Grissom certainly didn't care about that when he ordered us to share this place, now did he? I imagine people are already talking."

"I doubt it. After court, they figure we hate each other. But Abigail is a different matter. I've lost count of how many times she's been by here since I moved back, and she always has a different excuse."

"Well, it's not like she comes in the middle of the night. "Besides," she boldly pushed on, "I don't like your sleeping out in the shack. It's much more comfortable inside.

And if it really bothers you, you can always slip out before dawn.''

"I know, but . . ." He trailed off uncertainly, "I still think it would be best if I didn't stay the night inside with you."

Kerry figured that in light of what was between them she could speak her mind. "I don't understand. What difference does it make whether you leave early or stay all night? No one will know."

"I'd just rather sleep in the shack," he said and walked away, calling over his shoulder, "Please get the eggs washed if you haven't already. I need to get started."

Kerry did not see the need for such a hurry. He could make the deliveries and still be home before dark. Besides, he did need to rest.

"I'll go with you," she called. "To take over the reins in case you get to feeling bad."

He gave no indication of having heard her.

Kerry busied herself washing the eggs and drying them, which was time-consuming. But at last she had them all neatly packed, the baskets lined up in a row on the back porch for him to put in the wagon.

He brought the mule up, harnessed and ready to go.

"I've got some of that soup heating," Kerry said. "We can leave as soon as we eat."

"I'm not hungry. I want to get on the road." He began to fuss with the mule's traces.

She went back inside and changed into the blue wool dress she had bought for trips into town. It was not fancy, just a high collar, straight sleeves, and she wore no petticoats under the skirt. She thought it more fitting than overalls when she was calling on her customers. Besides, she smiled to think, she had another reason to want to look nice—she was going to be with Slade.

She planned to surprise him by suggesting that they have supper at the hotel. It would be nice to eat a good, hot meal prepared by someone else. She also had a bit of shopping to do, wanting to buy a pretty nightgown. One

way or another, she smiled impishly to think, Slade was
going to be sleeping in her bed every night. And soon, if
things went the way she wanted, he would want to make
things proper and legal . . . which meant marriage.

It was, she promised herself, just a matter of time, even
though a part of her warned not to be in such a hurry.
There were still many things that needed to be discussed,
and she had to be able to wholly and completely trust him.
But they were on the right path, and that was what truly
mattered.

The aroma of the soup heating on the stove was making
her even more hungry. She hoped Slade could smell it
and would change his mind about eating.

She filled two bowls and put them on the table, then
set out the platter of leftover scones she had warmed. He
would have enjoyed them the night before with a dollop
of honey, but she had forgotten to take them with her.

There was fresh milk, and she poured them both a glass.

When everything was ready, she went to the door to call
him . . . and promptly blinked in wide-eyed disbelief.

The wagon and mule were gone.

And so was Slade.

He had gone without her.

Slade hated doing it. Not only did he not like hurting
Kerry's feelings, but he also wanted more of the soup. He
still didn't feel completely well but could not risk taking
her with him. It would be real hard to find a plausible
excuse to get away from her long enough to pay Rosalie
a visit.

Once, he had come right out and asked Rosalie how
Sam was able to put up with her being a prostitute. She
had laughed and said he must not know Sam as well as
he thought—or her either—because both of them were
willing to do anything for the cause. And one day, she had
dreamily predicted, when their jobs were done, they were

going to get married and head west, going all the way to California to make a new life together and forget all about the trials and tribulations of the past.

Slade hoped it would work out for them.

And he also hoped the same could be said for himself and Kerry, at least the part about making a new life together. And it was fine with him for her to want to stay right there on the farm. He had come to love it, too. It was where he wanted to raise his children, in peace and plenty, and just as soon as he blew the Klan apart in Wayne County, that was it. He was quitting the bureau and hoped Kerry never knew he had been involved. He was going to ask her to marry him, and then life would be better than he had ever thought possible.

But he had to go easy, had to make sure she loved him and wasn't just clinging to him out of desperation because there was no one else.

Still, he was relieved that things were finally going in the right direction for the two of them. And if he could just get his job done, he could get on with his life . . . *their life* . . . together.

It was late afternoon by the time all the deliveries were made. Abigail had delayed him by asking all kinds of questions as to how Kerry was getting along. Lots of sickness going around, she said.

Finally he left the mule tied on Center Street and walked the rest of the way to Sadie's.

It was Thursday night, and luck seemed to be with him. Maybe he wasn't feeling like himself but at least he could ride, and with the Klan raid planned for the next night, there was no time to waste. He only hoped he could find Rosalie right away so he could head home.

Entering Sadie's, however, Slade feared that his luck had run out. Rosalie was nowhere around, so he went to the bar and took a stool.

Ebner, the bartender, brought him a glass of beer without being asked and tonelessly said, "I think this'll be the first of many unless you're willing to take somebody upstairs besides Rosalie."

"And why is that?"

"A man came in this afternoon and said he wanted some company for a while and was willing to pay. You know what that means." He winked.

Slade frowned. "Afraid I don't."

Ebner guffawed. "Means he can't cut the mustard. He'll be needing some extra time, so it'll be a while." He nodded to a yellow-haired girl who had sauntered up to the other end of the bar and was staring in their direction with interest. "What about Lola down there? She's new, but from what I hear, the gents really like her."

"No, thanks. I'll just wait for Rosalie."

Ebner shrugged. "Fine with me, but maybe one of these days you'll let me in on what's so special about her." He winked again. "I just might want to try her myself."

Slade bit back the impulse to tell him to go to hell. He downed his beer and slammed the glass on the counter so hard Ebner jumped. "I just need another beer. Not conversation."

"Hey, have it your way." Ebner hurried to refill his glass, and instead of bringing it to him gave it a vicious shove down the bar.

Slade caught it before it went crashing off the end, giving Ebner a glance of warning that made him keep his distance after that.

He noted that the place was clean but gaudy, with pink satin drapes at the windows and sofas and chairs covered in red velvet. There were mahogany tables and beaded lamps. The carpet was a bright purple with a yellow peacock design. An upright piano stood against one wall, and at night a man came to play it.

Slade alternated between watching the stairs and the big wall clock above the marble fireplace. He needed to be heading back but would not leave until he saw Rosalie. And then it had to look as if he were there for the reason every other man was. That meant even more time. A half hour at least, which she had told him, was the least amount he could spend without folks wondering.

The yellow-haired girl finally came up and boldly asked him if he'd like to go upstairs. When he said he was waiting for Rosalie, she responded as crudely as Ebner had.

"Would you mind telling me what's so special about her? I'm new here and it might help my business."

"Sorry, but that's a private matter, don't you think?"

"Well, excuse me," she cried shrilly, one hand on her hip as she swished away.

He was glad to be rid of her.

He had another beer, then switched to whiskey to try and quell the rising annoyance. If he didn't hurry up and get back, Kerry was going to wonder what the hell was going on.

Finally he saw a man coming down the steps. Actually he was running, as though he could not wait to get out of the place. Slade hated to have to speak to Ebner again but called him over to ask, just as the man rushed out the front door, "Is that him? The one who went upstairs with Rosalie?"

"Yeah," Ebner grunted, and, scowling, went back to the glasses he had been polishing.

Slade could not wait any longer. He got off the stool and started towards the stairs.

Halfway across the room, a big, burly man appeared out of nowhere to block his path and snarl, "Where do you think you're goin', mister?"

Slade drew himself up. "Since I'm headed for the stairs, it's obvious that's where I'm going."

"Not without one of Sadie's girls takin' you, it ain't. We don't let anybody wander around up there. So just go back and take a seat."

"I'm going to see Rosalie. She's expecting me."

"She didn't say nothin' to me about it."

Slade looked him straight in the eye, at the same time

resting the heel of his hand on the butt of his holstered gun. "Now look, friend," he said calmly, evenly. "There's no need for trouble. I told you who I'm going to see."

The man obviously decided the rules were not worth having a gunfight over. "Go ahead," he snarled again. "But I'm comin' up there in a minute, and I better not see you wanderin' around peekin' in keyholes."

Slade chuckled. "I'll leave that to you."

He hoped Rosalie had not changed rooms and was relieved when she answered his knock.

"Yeah, who is it?"

"Dillon. Have to see you now."

She went right into her act in case anyone could hear. They had agreed that he was to seem like a regular customer. "Well, aren't you the anxious one, honey? I wasn't expecting you for a while yet, but come on in."

She flung the door open. The instant he was inside, she closed and locked it. "I can tell you've got news by the look on your face. What's going on?"

"I've been downstairs for hours."

"Sorry. I had an unusual guest."

"Spare me the details and listen carefully." He told her of the planned raid for the next night and how he wanted her to get in touch with her contact in the army and have the soldiers waiting to ambush the Klan.

"Well, of course," she said, "but is that it? I mean, you still don't have any clue as to the leaders? Slade, I know you're trying, but this could go on forever if you don't bring them down."

"I think I can follow one of them tomorrow night. When all hell breaks loose, the guards are going to try to escape like everybody else. As soon as I find out where my man lives, I'll get back to you so you can tell the law. All they have to do then is search his house, and they'll find all the evidence they need—robe, hood, and whistle. Maybe even some records.

"I feel real good about this," he continued. "I think it's my first real chance to get one of them."

"Oh, God, Slade, I hope so," she said wearily.

He looked at her then, *really* looked at her, and could see she was worn out with it all. He patted her shoulder. "It won't be long. I want it over as much as you do."

She laughed, "Oh, no, you don't. It's not possible.

"Care for a drink," she asked with eyes twinkling, "to help pass the time while you're supposedly getting your money's worth?"

"If I have anything else I'll drown. What do you think I was doing all the time I was waiting on you?" He went to the window and pulled the curtain back just far enough so he could look out. He would stay the usual time, then leave. He could tell Kerry he'd had to fix a wheel on the wagon or something.

Rosalie was wearing a yellow satin robe, trimmed in the feathers she loved. She poured herself a glass of wine from a bottle on her dressing table, then propped herself in bed on a pile of lacy pillows. "So how are things going at the farm? Still scared you'll wake up with your throat cut?"

"We've got a treaty now," he said, not willing to elaborate.

"Is that a fact?" She smiled knowingly. "So does this mean you won't be riding on when this is over?"

"I don't know yet."

Suddenly her smile faded, and she took a sharp tone to warn, "You've let that little filly turn your head enough, Slade. Keep your mind on why you're here."

"I will. But I've been laid up sick for a day or two. But don't worry. Everything will go smooth from here on out."

"I hope so. And I also hope you don't mess up and let her find out what this is all about. It'd be dangerous for you both."

"I know that," he said, a touch irritated.

"Sorry. I don't mean to get you riled. It's just that I hear things, you know? And I've heard that little gal of yours upset some folks when she helped those Negroes get away that the Klan was after.''

Slade whipped about from the window, alarm shooting up his spine. "What have you heard?"

Rosalie blinked in surprise at his quick, harsh reaction. "It's being said she gave them her mule and cart in exchange for that stallion she rides."

Slade held back his anger. It would not do for Rosalie to know how upset he was over what she had just told him. Instead, he flippantly said, "So what if she did? She's got a right to horse trade, doesn't she? Hell, she probably didn't even know they were on the run."

"Be that as it may," Rosalie said quietly, evenly. "But if I were you, I'd keep a tight rein on her and watch everything you say. If she's sympathetic to the freedmen . . . if it's found out she helps them, then you could have the Klan on your back, Slade, and you don't want that. You ruined your first cover, you know. Don't ruin your second. You've got to lay low so you won't be suspect."

"Any more advice?" he asked sarcastically. He liked Rosalie. A lot. And she was to be commended for what she was doing. Not many women would. But then few women were spurred by the same lust for revenge against bigotry. Still, it irked him when she took it on herself to tell him how to run his personal life.

"No. Nothing else," she said finally, still staring at him with a worried look on her face.

Suddenly he wanted out of there. "Look, I'm going. I should have been back at the farm a long time ago."

Rosalie sat up to protest, "You haven't been here long enough."

He paused at the door to wink and say, "If anybody makes anything of it, just say you had two strange customers this afternoon. One couldn't cut the mustard and the other was extra randy."

She laughed and threw a pillow at him. He ducked and went on out, glad the tension between them was eased.

Hell, he didn't need to be worried about anything except what was going to happen Friday night.

It was, after all, his first chance to prove to General Howard and everyone else that he really was the right man for the job.

Kerry was ready to give up and go home. She had been waiting beside the mule and cart near Horace Bedham's store for over an hour. Still there was no sign of Slade.

She had been up and down the street, peering into every shop. She had even gone to the saloon but did not see him.

It was as if he had dropped out of sight, and she was starting to worry.

She was beginning to regret riding out after him, but when he had left without her, she decided maybe he hadn't heard her when she said she wanted to go, too. Disappointed because she had been looking forward to the outing, she decided to saddle Thunder, as she had named the stallion, and meet him in town. She wanted to take some of the egg money he had collected and finally buy herself a nice, warm coat. Afterwards, they would have that delicious dinner at the hotel she'd promised herself.

Only she could not find him and knew she would soon have to be heading home if she wanted to get there before dark set in.

Just then Abigail came along to cry in delight, "Why, Kerry, I didn't expect to see you in town with the weather so cold." She frowned. "If you needed supplies, why didn't you have Mr. Dillon get them? He was by earlier with the eggs."

"I, uh . . ." Kerry stammered, unsure of what to say. If she told Abigail she was looking for him, that would raise eyebrows. She thought quickly and said, "I decided to ride in to buy a new coat."

"Well, thank goodness. Where is it? Let me see."

"I haven't picked it out yet. I just got here."

Abigail tugged at her arm. "Well, let's just go in Horace's store right now, and I'll help you." She leaned to confide, "I'll also see to it he gives you a good price. He's way behind in his payments to my husband."

Kerry saw no other way but to let her pull her along, but, just as they were walking in the door of Mr. Bedham's store, she took one more glance over her shoulder and saw Slade coming around the corner at the far end of the street.

Not wanting Abigail to witness his surprise when he found out she had followed him, Kerry hurried on inside.

Mr. Bedham was not as friendly as in the past, but he was polite.

Kerry tried to see out the window, watching for Slade, but Abigail kept her busy trying on one coat after another. Finally, impatient to be done with it, Kerry picked one without regard to price or color. She told Mr. Bedham she would pay for it later, then hurried outside.

Abigail was right behind her. "What is your rush, dear? He had several others."

The cart and mule were gone.

Kerry felt like crying. Not only were her plans ruined for a nice supper, but she had to ride home alone unless she could catch up with him—which appeared would not happen, because Abigail was not about to let her get away.

"Come along. We're going to the hotel for tea and cake to warm you before you start back."

"Abigail, I really need to go now."

"Nonsense. I happen to know they have lemon cake on Thursday, and it's delicious. Besides, Ethan said something about having to go out your way this evening to see somebody ailing. You can ride beside him, because you've no business being out alone late in the day."

Kerry swallowed a groan.

She was trapped.

But as they went into the hotel, she glanced again in the direction she'd seen Slade walking from.

Abigail saw and asked, "What is it, dear? What are you staring at?"

Kerry pointed. "What's around that corner? I've never been there."

With a sniff of disdain, Abigail said, "I should hope not. That's the riffraff section of town. Nothing there but falling-down shacks and Sadie's place."

"What is Sadie's place?" Kerry asked innocently.

Abigail looked all about, making sure no one would hear as she whispered in disgust, "It's a whorehouse." She gave her arm a yank. "Now come along. We've no business discussing such things."

Kerry told herself it had to be a mistake. Slade would not go to a whorehouse. Why should he when they had just . . .

She gave her head a vicious shake.

A mistake.

That's all it could be.

Otherwise, she knew she had a big, big problem.

Chapter 20

Kerry did not tell Slade that she had gone into town to meet him. Instead, when she arrived at the farm shortly after he got there, she said she had just been out riding.

His quick flash of anger surprised her.

"Damn it, I wish you wouldn't keep riding the stallion. If the wrong people see you, it's not going to set well. You keep taking foolish chances, and sooner or later you're going to find yourself in a peck of trouble. How many times have I got to tell you these are dangerous times we're living in?"

Kerry had tried to talk herself out of her own pique during the ride home, but his attitude brought it all rushing back. "And how many times do I have to tell you I'm not afraid of the Klan? That *is* what you're talking about, isn't it?"

He was taking the empty egg baskets out of the wagon. His movements were quick, jerky. "I've heard talk," he said tightly.

"About me?" She was getting madder by the minute and hating it, because they had shared such splendor not so long ago. Now tension was an invisible curtain, dropping to tear them apart.

"Yes, about you and that damned stallion. There are those who think you deliberately helped Toby get away."

"I certainly did, and I've reached the point I don't care who knows it. And I should think you'd feel the same way. My God, Slade, I do believe you're afraid of the Klan, yourself."

He whirled on her, eyes blazing. "I'm not scared of anybody or anything, Kerry, but I don't go looking for trouble, either. The Klan is a power to be reckoned with in these parts. They've killed people, you little fool. So you'd be smart not to do anything to get them riled."

"But didn't you say you'd take care of me?" she goaded, provoked to wonder whether he had been to the whorehouse after all. But why would he? she asked herself. They had just made love. He had no need of a woman— unless there was more to it than that . . . unless he cared about that woman and felt the need to be with her.

"Kerry, I can't always be here." He reached to take out the last of the baskets, slamming them down on the porch in a vengeance.

"No, I guess you can't," she said tightly. "So there's no need for me to get used to having you around, is there?"

"And what is that supposed to mean?"

She ignored him to abruptly ask, "Why were you so late getting back from town, anyway?"

"A wheel broke on the wagon. I had to take it to the livery station and have it fixed. It took all afternoon."

He was not looking at her as he spoke, and Kerry knew why. He feared she would read the lie on his face—the lie she knew he was telling because she had seen the wagon on the street, nowhere near a livery stable.

"A broken wheel," she echoed, numb to the core.

"That's right."

She had dismounted and began to lead Thunder towards the pen. It was getting close to dark, and she was cold.

The coat she had bought was still in the package tied to the saddle. She could have put it on against the chill, but her anger was warmth enough.

Once again she felt like a fool. Only this time it was of her own doing. After all, she had gone to his bed. He had not come to hers. She was also the one who had asked him to move into her bedroom and now knew why he had hedged.

He had someone else.

And making love to her had meant nothing to him. After all, he was a man, and he had done what came naturally to find a woman lying next to him naked.

As for the tender plea that they should try to get along, things had been very unpleasant between them. Naturally he would like to change that. And what did he have to lose, anyway?

"I'll take care of your horse," Slade said, catching up with her and reaching for the reins.

She jerked away. "No. You might take him off and shoot him, since you seem to hate him so much."

"Don't be childish. I just think you ought to let me take him over to Smithfield and trade him for another horse. That way the sight of you riding him won't antagonize the Klan."

"To hell with the Klan."

He stopped walking. "You're making things real difficult. Why do you have to be so stubborn? Do you like causing trouble? Do you like fighting all the time? We were getting along real good there for a while."

She too paused, spinning about to point a finger and cry, "Yes, we were. Thanks to me. I took care of you when you were sick, kept you covered when you'd have frozen to death from tossing off your covers, and then I climbed in bed to keep you warm with my body. And how do you show your appreciation? By raising hell with me about a horse that I happen to love—all because you're scared.

"Well, I'm not, I tell you," she rushed to continue. "And I don't need you to take care of me, either."

"Then we're right back where we were before, aren't we?" he murmured, exasperated.

"I guess we are."

He dared attempt to ease the tension by flashing a crooked grin to ask, "Does this mean you don't want me to move in with you?"

His audacity was the last straw. "Go to hell," she snapped. "And stay out of my way."

"Kerry, what is wrong with you?" he called after her as she stalked away, pulling the stallion with her. "I've never seen you like this. We need to talk . . ."

"Leave me alone," she yelled. "I'm warning you."

How sorry and common could he be? she fumed as she unsaddled Thunder and gave him a quick rubdown. To go to a whorehouse only hours after they had lain together so tenderly. It had to be a particular woman, one he was very fond of. She could not be sure but would find out, by God.

Then she asked herself what difference it made. He only wanted her for a tumble in bed when he had a yen, anyway. And probably he was thinking that sooner or later she'd give up and leave and he would have everything to himself.

When she finished brushing Thunder, she gave him a bucket of oats, then took the package with the coat and went back to the house. This time, it was cold inside, because Slade had not started the fire. Neither had he carried in wood. So be it. She would do it herself. She would do everything herself, because she was damned if she'd ever ask him for anything again. Let him have his whore. He would surely not be having *her* again.

She continued to grouse as she got the stove going to heat up the last of the turtle stew. He could get sick and stay sick. Let his woman come tend to him. Probably he would be bold enough to move her into the shack with him, anyway, once he found out there would be no new beginnings for the two of them.

When the soup was warm she poured it into a bowl and tried not to think about the nice dinner she had so foolishly hoped to share with Slade at the Goldsboro hotel. No wonder he had pretended not to hear her when she said she wanted to go with him. It was now obvious why he hadn't wanted her around.

She took one bite and shoved the bowl away. She was sick of turtle soup. Sick of everything. And, giving way to the tears she had been fighting, Kerry put her head down on the table and wept.

She couldn't help it.

She loved him.

And it hurt deeply to know he did not love her.

Slade awoke the next morning with a grinding headache. He had finished the bottle of whiskey the night before. A stupid thing to do, but it was the only way he could deal with his misery over what had happened with Kerry.

What the hell was wrong with her? When she was in his arms, she acted as if she loved him to death. Then there was the way she had nursed him when he was sick. He had dared think she cared, after all.

It also puzzled him to muse over the way she had crawled in bed with him to warm him with her body. And the lovemaking later had left him shaken, it was so intense and satisfying. So how could she be so passionate in his arms and then turn against him merely because he mentioned she was playing with fire by provoking the Klan?

It didn't make sense.

He was starting to think that anything to do with women would never make sense.

So he had sipped the whiskey and brooded on into the night. And somewhere in the wee hours it had dawned that Kerry might just be using him as she had accused him of using her. After all, he had been doing some of her chores as well as his own. And once she got over her shyness, she was as randy as he was in bed. So everything had gone her way, and she had a nice arrangement going.

But no more. He was sick of trying to cope with her and the miserable mess he had made of things, thanks to their involvement with each other. By now, General Howard was probably regretting having given him the assignment. Likewise, Sam would be disgusted when he heard.

So the more he drank, the more determined he became, and that morning, despite the throbbing in his temples, he resolved to let nothing else stand in his way.

He dressed and went straight to his work. Kerry did not come outside. Good. It was early. Maybe she was still asleep. He didn't care. Let her haul her own wood and do all the other things he'd been doing to make her life easier. If she wanted to snap and snarl and act like a fool where the Klan was concerned—where *he* was concerned—then so be it.

He was hungry when he finished, and there was nothing in the shack to eat. Not about to go anywhere near the house or the kitchen, he saddled his horse and headed for town.

It had been a while since he'd had a regular meal, and he decided to go to the hotel. The food in the dining room was usually good, and they served big helpings.

The dish of the day was roast chicken, and he ate his fill. He did not recognize anyone around him and was relieved to have his privacy. He had too much on his mind for idle chitchat.

Kerry kept coming to mind, no matter how hard he tried to concentrate on the night ahead.

He knew the misery had to end. And if he could just finish his assignment, the best thing would be for him to ride on. Maybe then he could get her out of his blood . . . as well as his heart. Besides, they could still get some bad weather before spring, and he didn't want to risk being isolated with her in a storm again.

A man walking by Slade's table stopped to give him a second glance. The woman beside him, elegantly dressed but quite plump, tugged at his arm and said, "Lorne, come along. We have to hurry."

"In a minute," he said irritably.

Slade glanced up. He did not recall having seen him before.

The man smiled to inquire, "Aren't you Slade Dillon— the man who was recently awarded half the Corrigan farm in court? Someone pointed you out to me the other day."

Slade politely got to his feet in deference to the woman. "That's right."

"Well, I'm pleased to make your acquaintance, sir. I'm Lorne Petrie." He pumped Slade's hand with gusto. "And this is Mrs. Petrie."

Slade nodded to his wife.

Lorne gave her a gentle shove to stand to one side, then chattered on. "I just want to say I admire you for being able to contend with that Corrigan woman. She's certainly headstrong, isn't she? Thinks she knows everything. I can assure you I had a most difficult time dealing with her. She acted as though she expected me to pay the delinquent taxes and then give her the farm scot-free. Can you imagine? I'm just glad to hear she got her comeuppance. And sooner or later, she'll get enough of all the hard work if you don't humor her."

"That's possible," Slade said, not about to enter into a debate. He just wanted to be polite and get rid of him.

"Then you'll have the place all to yourself. A fine piece of land it is, too."

Kerry had told Slade everything that had happened between her and Petrie the day he came to buy the land at auction. Now, face to face, Slade itched to slam his fist into his smirking mouth. Instead, he conceded as though he really didn't care, "Yeah, I guess it is."

"Well, how are the two of you getting along?" Lorne persisted, eyes shining. "I'll bet she was real mad about the judge's ruling and is being a real little bitch about it, isn't she?"

"There's no problem. If there is, I can handle it."

"Oh, I'll bet you can. You seem to be the kind of man who can deal with a stubborn little tart. But you should have won your claim, Mr. Dillon. I heard all about it, and you are the rightful owner. But I suppose the judge took pity because she's a woman.

"But tell me," he nosily pressed on. "Are you planning to grow tobacco? I thought the soil would be fine for that."

"Yes, we've got seedbeds going already." His gaze had riveted on the emerald ring Mrs. Petrie was wearing. She had not yet put on her gloves before going outside, and the ring glittered in the light of the chandelier. He knew it had to be Kerry's.

Lorne saw him staring and said, "Well, I see you have good taste, sir. It is an exquisite ring, isn't it? I don't know exactly what it's worth. Enough, I hope, to compensate for my paying Miss Corrigan's taxes. I assume she told you about the little deal we made?"

Slade was fast losing his patience. "I'd like to get back to my supper, if you don't mind."

"Oh, of course, of course. I'm sorry. Good day to you, sir, and good look with that wretched woman."

"Thank you," Slade muttered, sitting back down and watching as Petrie took his wife's arm and walked on out. He might present himself as charming and cordial, but Slade knew what he was—cunning and unscrupulous to the bone.

But seeing the ring had made Slade feel sorry for Kerry all over again. It was beautiful, and it had to have broken her heart to part with it. So maybe she deserved to have the farm to herself. Hell, he had never wanted it, anyway.

He had only wanted her.

When he finished eating, he went to Sadie's to see Rosalie and make sure everything was ready for the night ahead. With gritted teeth, he managed to ignore Ebner's snide remark about how it would be cheaper if he just went ahead and bought the cow so he could get the milk for free.

Rosalie said she had taken care of everything. An army patrol would be in position and waiting for the Klan to strike. She said the army's intention was to gun them all down, if possible, so he might not have to worry about tracking any of the leaders. Slade said he hoped that was the way it turned out but doubted they would be so lucky.

He knew who her contact was—a captain who pretended to be a regular customer of hers, although Slade suspected he actually was. Well, if Rosalie didn't mind, why should he? It was her life.

He had made sure to find out exactly where the targeted Negro lived. It was a few miles north of town, and his name was Spencer Wilcox. Like Toby, he had gone North during the war to work in the munitions factories and made a little money. He had returned afterwards and bought a small farm and was said to be doing quite well. But he had made a big mistake. He had crossed a member of the Klan without knowing it. The Klansman had wanted to buy a mule Spencer was trying to sell, but he had offered such a ridiculous price that Spencer asked him if he was crazy. The Klansman took offense—not only to have his offer turned down, but that a Negro had dared scoff at a white man. It could not go unpunished.

Slade had heard the orders given at the Klan meeting when he was hiding up in the rafters of the tobacco barn. All of Spencer's livestock would be stolen and transported elsewhere so nothing could be traced locally. Then his house and barn would be burned. Spencer would then be hanged as an example to other Negroes tempted to be so insolent.

The army's orders had been for the patrol to hide in the woods nearby. They were to wait until the Klan approached the house and ordered Spencer outside; then the soldiers would surround them. Slade would have his eye on the leader he was after, and the second all hell broke loose, he would be right on him to follow him and learn his identity.

When it was almost dark, Slade left town as if heading for home. A little ways out, he left the road to take the way he had explored and found earlier.

Spencer's little cabin was smack dab in the middle of a corn field, which was barren for the winter. It was not a good place for an ambush. The closest the soldiers would be able to get and still hide till the right moment was a copse some distance away. They would have to ride like hell once they decided to take on the Klan and hope they got there before the Klansmen could get away.

As for Slade, he found a thicket just big enough to conceal him, closer to the house.

It was just past sundown, the earth still shimmering with shades of daylight. Slade saw movement within the copse, something shiny like the brass button on a uniform coat, and was relieved to know the patrol was in place.

The Klan would, he figured, ride straight in from the road. The river was a short ways on the other side. They would ride along the bank, then charge in to take Spencer and his family by surprise.

The windows of the cabin glowed with candlelight. Slade could make out a man and woman seated at a table with two small children. He wished there had been a way to warn them so they could get the little ones out, but it might have given everything away. Besides, the Klan would not have time to harm anybody before the patrol got there.

He did not dismount. When it happened, he wanted to be ready to ride.

Time dragged by, and the night wore on. He figured

the Klansmen were waiting for Spencer and his family to bed down so they would be too groggy from sleep to react very fast.

Finally, around midnight, as best he could figure, he saw lights flickering towards the river. A few moments later, he could make out men on horseback carrying torches as they came up from the riverbank.

They rode slowly, stealthily, across the empty corn field.

Slade strained to see the one he was looking for—the Grand Turk, as he was called, with the red hood. He was riding in front with the other two leaders.

Drawing close to the cabin, they fanned out. Slade guessed there were maybe eighteen or twenty of them.

It was an eerie sight, torches flickering within the half-moon formation of ghostly figures on horseback.

Someone shouted Spencer's name and told him to come outside or they'd kill his whole family.

"Get out here, boy, and take what's comin' to you," another cried.

Slade tensed, getting ready to ride. From the copse he could hear the faint sound of hooves crunching. He knew the soldiers would quietly draw as close as possible before charging in.

He kneed his horse to move on through the thicket, going slowly to keep down the noise.

And then it happened.

One of the Klansmen heard the soldiers and yelled, "Somebody's coming. I hear horses. It's a trap. Get the hell out of here . . ."

Panic struck as they made to flee, bumping into each other in their wild haste. The soldiers came in fast, but the Klansmen had a head start for the river.

Keeping his eye on the man in the red hood, Slade gave his horse a sharp kick in the flanks and took off after him. As expected, the guards also scattered. Each man was on his own.

Slade decided that the Grand Turk, whoever he was,

had to be either stupid or confident that he could outride the soldiers, because he did not throw down his torch. It afforded Slade a trail to follow him by.

The Klansman cut down to the riverbank, unaware that Slade was not far behind him. Crossing at a narrow bend, he slowed his pace once he got to the other side. Slade was far enough back to not be heard. All he had to do was follow the lighted beacon the man provided with his flaming torch.

They rode through a swampy area. Slade feared his horse might stumble in the bog and give him away. But the stallion was sure-footed, and they made it through.

Slade breathed a sigh of relief when they finally emerged from the swamp. He was surprised to find they were on the main road into town. So his man was not a farmer living in the country, after all.

Slade's heart was racing with excitement. He was about to take the first step to busting up the Klan in Wayne County. The other Klansmen were going to believe that one of their own had betrayed them; otherwise the army would never have known about the raid. Distrust and suspicion would then begin to erode their ranks like riverbanks after a flood.

The man threw down his torch, but Slade no longer needed to follow it. All he had to do was follow the road.

Once in town, the man turned down an alley off Center Street.

Slade dismounted to follow on foot, almost losing him when he did. By the time he sighted him again, he had left his horse somewhere and was going up a flight of stairs outside a building.

But which one? Slade cursed to wonder. He could not lose him now. And it was hard to see. There were a few lights on Main Street, but that wasn't helping him get his bearings in the alley.

A door opened and closed at the top of the stairs.

Slade uttered an oath and began counting buildings as

he hurried to the end of the alley. Then, cautiously keeping to the shadows, he counted the ones in front till he found where the man had gone.

Below was Lloyd Swenson's saloon.

And above, Lloyd Swenson lived.

Slade grinned in triumph.

He had identified the Grand Turk of the Ku Klux Klan.

Kerry had been tossing and turning in bed for hours. It was, she had discovered, hard to fall asleep with a broken heart.

She knew she had to learn the truth as to whether Slade was actually in love with someone else or go crazy. Because if it were so, then they might be scheming together to take the farm away from her. Perhaps he was even hoping the Klan would attack and frighten her so bad she would leave, which meant the farm would all be his then.

She bit down on her fist to keep from crying.

It hurt.

Oh, dear God, it hurt so bad.

Because she loved him so much.

Still, there was the chance she was overreacting. Maybe he hadn't gone to Sadie's place to be with a woman after all. There might be gambling there, and he had merely been playing poker. Thinking she would be angry about it, he had made up the lie about the broken wagon wheel. And the fight they wound up having probably would not have gotten out of hand if she had not been seething to think the worst as to how he had spent his afternoon.

Snuggling down under the blankets, Kerry was glad it was dark, cold, and blustery out. Otherwise she might have been tempted to find her way to Slade's shack and tell him she was sorry she had blown up at him like she had. And she would be damned if she would do something so impulsive and foolish, especially when she did not have all the answers.

But she was not going to lose him over a silly card game, if that was, in fact, what he had been doing. And the only way to find out was to go to Sadie's and see what it was like.

Having decided to do something besides feel sorry for herself, Kerry finally began to feel drowsy. It was so terribly late. Then she corrected herself. Actually it was early. Through the window she could see the first light of dawn and scowled to think how she had been awake almost all night worrying. But there was still time for a few hours' sleep, especially if she got up to put more wood on the fire.

Wrapping a blanket around her, she padded through the house to the parlor and the fireplace, only to realize she had neglected to bring wood in the night before. With a sigh, she headed for the back porch where it was stacked. There wasn't much left, but it would do till she either made up with Slade or chopped some herself.

She paused to hear a banging sound and turned to see that the gate to the horse shed had come open. That was strange, because she distinctly remembered latching it when she had put Thunder away for the night. Slade kept saying he needed to fix it, because sometimes it did not hold unless it was slammed good and tight.

She knew she had to close it. If one of the horses came out, it might jump the corral fence and take off.

There was enough light to see her way. She was about to throw the latch when she decided to make sure the horses had not escaped.

She peered inside and saw Thunder and the mule, but, with a groan, realized Slade's horse was not there. That meant she would have to go out to the shack and wake him up to go look for it before it got too far away.

But then she noticed something else in the dim light filtering in.

There was only one saddle on the railing where there should have been two.

And hers was not the one missing.

That meant Slade had gone back to town either to see a woman or to gamble.

And it was time Kerry found out which.

Chapter 21

When Kerry awoke after a few hours of fitful sleep, she immediately went to see if Slade's horse was in the stall.

She was disappointed not to find it but would not let herself believe the worst.

But one thing was certain, before the day was over, she intended to find out exactly what he was up to.

Besides, she grumbled as she did all the chores herself, he was responsible for half the work. So if he were gambling—and she hoped against hope that's what he was doing—then he was just going to have to put that aside and do his share.

At midday, she hitched the mule to the wagon, loaded all the baskets, and set out for town.

Before she even turned onto Center Street, she could sense excitement in the air. When she saw the throngs of people milling about, talking animatedly, she knew that something big had happened.

Abigail was coming out of Horace Bedham's store and waved to call her over and exclaim, "Have you heard?

They've arrested a leader of the Klan—Lloyd Swenson. He owns that saloon down the street.''

"Oh, that's wonderful," Kerry cried. "How did it happen?" She quickly got down out of the wagon to listen.

Abigail proceeded to tell her how soldiers had surprised the Klan the night before as they were about to burn a Negro out of his house. "All the Klansmen got away, though they think one was shot. Then somehow the soldiers found out about Mr. Swenson. They went to his living quarters over the saloon first thing this morning and found his costume. Ethan said the hood they found hidden under the bed was red instead of white. That's how they knew he was one of the leaders. Some of the Negroes that have been attacked had told about the different colored hoods three of the Klansmen wear.

"He's refused to tell who any of the others are," Abigail continued. "But that's to be expected. He's in jail. Now everyone is wondering about the one that got shot, and the soldiers are really watching Ethan's office in case he shows up there. But I'm not worried. He wouldn't be that stupid."

"No, I don't suppose so," Kerry agreed, a tiny worm of apprehension beginning to inch its way up her spine.

"Of course, there are mixed emotions about it all. Some people say the Klan is needed to keep the freed slaves in their place. Others think they're evil. Ethan tells me to keep my mouth shut and not say anything, so I don't."

Kerry wondered how Abigail truly felt but was afraid to ask. If she admitted to being a Klan sympathizer, she knew she could never have anything to do with her again.

But she was not afraid to state her own view. "Well, I think they're a bunch of murdering cowards, and I hope they catch every single one of them."

Abigail paled and gave a little gasp. "Kerry, you shouldn't speak that way. It isn't proper for a lady, and you never know who might be listening."

"I don't care," Kerry said . . . and meant it.

Abigail glanced around, frowning to see that a group of men nearby had apparently overheard what Kerry had said. They were staring and looking angry as they murmured among themselves.

Abigail pleaded with Kerry, "Oh, please lower your voice, or you'll force me to walk away and leave you standing here. It will look as though I'm agreeing with you if I don't."

Kerry gave a deep sigh of disgust. "Well, I wouldn't want that, so you just run along, Abigail. I have to deliver these eggs, anyway. Do you want your usual order?"

"I suppose. And I'll take them now to save you the trouble of coming by the house."

Kerry wondered if Abigail actually did not want anyone to see her there. She handed her a basket of eggs. "I'll get the basket next time I come by."

"Fine, dear. But let me pay you now." She reached into her purse and counted the correct amount. "And please do watch yourself, Kerry. Especially today. Everyone is all stirred up, as you can see. And don't tarry in town too long. Be sure to get off the road by dark."

Kerry nodded, not really paying attention. She was more interested in getting away from her. Abigail could be so worrisome. She reminded Kerry of one of her hens, clucking annoyingly after her baby chicks.

Next she went to Horace Bedham's store. There was a crowd blocking the door, and she had to push through them but listened to what they were saying as she did so.

"I think the army had a hell of a lot of nerve busting down Lloyd's door like they did."

"Yeah, and how can they prove that red hood belonged to him, anyway? It's the reason the war got started in the first place—Yankees interfering with a man's personal life."

"You got that right. I say the Klan is a good thing. If not for them, the freed slaves would take over and we'd be their slaves."

"Yeah, and now we got to worry that they're going to suspect everybody that ever went in Lloyd's saloon as being a Klan member, too."

Kerry was riled but was not about to get involved in their conversation. But if they had asked her opinion, she would not have minced words, for she felt so strong in her opposition to anything to do with the Klan.

Horace was polite but not friendly as in the past. She knew it was because she had put him in his place over his meddling in her business, which, she felt, was justified.

"So how many you got to sell me today?" he asked without so much as a hello.

"Three dozen."

He opened the cash register, paid her, then turned away in cold dismissal.

On her way out, she groaned to see Lorne Petrie breezing in and heading straight towards her.

"Miss Corrigan, my, my, it's nice to see you. How have you been?"

He held out his hand but let it drop to his side when she merely glared at him.

"Well," he said, undaunted, "I guess it's to be expected you'd be in a bad mood after that unfortunate court ruling. And I suppose you've found yourself wishing over and over that you had just let me take it over so you wouldn't have had such a terrible time."

"No," she said firmly, crisply. "I don't. Actually, things are going quite well . . . much to your disappointment, I am sure."

"Is that so?" He feigned confusion. "Well, that's not what your partner told me only a short while ago. He seemed quite disgruntled with the situation."

Kerry told herself to stay calm, not let him see how riled she was. How dare Slade even speak to the arrogant scalawag? Oh, she was going to have plenty to lambast him about when she finally saw him.

"I've no idea what Mr. Dillon told you, Mr. Petrie, but

you must have misunderstood if you thought he said anything to the contrary."

Lorne pretended to think about that carefully, then shook his head and said, "No. No, I understood him perfectly. We talked last evening when he was having dinner at the hotel. I distinctly remember everything he said."

Kerry was getting madder by the minute. "And what exactly was that, since you seem so anxious to tell me?"

He grinned. "That you are a stubborn little tart and could be a veritable bitch when you wanted to be. So it's obvious he's not happy with the way things are."

Bristling, Kerry knew that if he kept talking she was going to explode. The store was crowded, and she did not want to make a scene.

She attempted to brush by him. "Excuse me. I have things to do."

He stood aside and bowed with a flourish. "Of course, and I am sorry to find you having such a terrible time, my dear."

She had not gone two steps when he added to taunt, "By the way, you'll be glad to know Mrs. Petrie is really enjoying her ring. Everyone gushes over it."

That did it. Kerry spun about, not caring who heard as she cried, "Well, you just tell Mrs. Petrie to enjoy it while she can, because one of these days I'm going to make you keep your promise to sell it back to me."

"Oh, I doubt she'll have to worry about that for a long time." His smirk widened to add, "If ever."

It was not turning out to be a good day, Kerry thought as she hurried to finish making her deliveries. It was enough that she had let Lorne Petrie get under her skin, but everywhere she went, people were talking about the Klan, and she hated how they seemed so in awe.

Worse, in the back of her mind, she kept thinking about the wounded Klansman and how Slade had not shown up that morning. Whether he was with a woman, or playing poker, it was unlike him not to be there to do his chores.

He certainly would not want her to be able to say he was not doing his part.

She hated to even consider the possibility that he might be one of them, but she had never been able to get Luther's words out of her mind.

"How do you know he ain't one of 'em?"

She did not know. And now she wondered as to his true motive in his angry concern over her having helped Adam and Toby and his wife. Was it because he feared that his fellow Klansmen would hold him responsible for what she did?

He could even be the one that had been wounded last night and this very moment be lying in the woods somewhere bleeding to death.

But right then it was difficult for her to care about anything except that he had dared say such things about her to Lorne Petrie. He knew how she despised the man, and if Slade really felt that way, why didn't he just get out of her life?

She laughed out loud at the answer to that—it was because he was just as bad as Lorne Petrie—greedy to the bone. No wonder the two of them had enjoyed talking to each other.

She was relieved when all the deliveries were made, because she had no intention of going home until she found out the truth about where Slade had been all night. And if he were a Klansman, she would move heaven and earth to see that he was exposed. Because then the judge would declare her owner of the farm, and Slade would go to jail—where he belonged, like all the other Klan scum.

She took the wagon to Center Street and left it at the opposite end from Sadie's place. Then she set out on foot.

The boardwalks were crowded with people still gathering to talk about what had happened. She overheard snatches of conversation as they wondered whether Lloyd Swenson's arrest would stop Klan activities, for a while at least. And, of course, there was speculation as to who the others might be and whether the law had any clues to their identity.

"I think the Klan better clean up within itself," a man who was obviously drunk said as Kerry stepped around him. "It had to have been one of their own who tipped off the law."

"Hmph, that's not good to hear," another man grunted. "If the Klan can't trust its own, then it'll fall apart for sure."

Once more Kerry bit her tongue to keep from applauding that idea. She might not be afraid, but she had sense enough not to go out of her way to goad. And she would not be surprised if the two were actually members, anyway.

No one paid any attention to her as she reached the end of the street.

Rounding the corner was like stepping into another world. There were no manicured lawns and picket fences surrounding houses rebuilt after the war by those with the means to do so. Kerry saw dilapidated shacks and lean-tos on lots covered by weeds and trash.

But as she hurried along, anxious to pass such eyesores, she was surprised to see a fairly decent looking house farther down. It was painted bright blue, two stories, with a porch across the front.

Horses were tied to hitching posts at the street, but she was relieved not to see Slade's among them. She would not have had nerve enough to go inside if she had, and all she wanted to do was find out if there were gambling tables, anyway. True, that wouldn't prove he had not been with a woman, but it would give him the benefit of the doubt—as well as ease her mind—till she could get to the bottom of things.

She went up the steps cautiously, hoping she could just see through the windows and not have to enter. However, the drapes were tightly closed, so she was forced to knock on the door.

It was opened almost at once, and a woman with hair much redder than her own stared down at her with interest. She had purple eyelids, orange cheeks, red lips, and was wearing a bright yellow satin robe with most of her breasts hanging out.

"Well, well," she greeted Kerry with a pleased smile. "Just what I need. A new girl. But I have to say you look a bit green, honey. You ever do this kind of work before? Come on in. I'm Sadie, and I own this place."

She clamped a hand on Kerry's shoulder to draw her inside before she could change her mind.

Kerry glanced around wildly, taking in the gaudy furnishings and praying to see men gathered at tables playing poker. But there were no tables, just sofas and chairs and lewd paintings on the walls. And the only men she saw were on their way upstairs with women dressed like Sadie clinging to their arms.

"So what's your name, honey? You want a drink?" She was leading her towards the bar tucked in a corner, the arched doorway framed by strands of colorful beads. The beads clattered loudly as Sadie pushed through them. "It might calm you down. You're shaking like a newborn colt."

Sadie signaled to the bartender. "Ebner, get this little gal a glass of wine. She don't look like the whiskey type.

"Now then," she pushed Kerry towards a stool. "Tell me all about yourself."

"I'm not looking for work," Kerry rushed to make clear.

Sadie's face twisted with angry suspicion. "Then what are you doing here? If you're looking for your man, you'd best get out of here right now. I don't put up with jealous wives and girlfriends coming in here making trouble. I run a clean place."

Kerry was quick to explain, "It's not like that. I just thought maybe you had gambling here. I . . . I like to gamble." It was a feeble lie, even to her own ears.

Waving Ebner away as he was about to serve Kerry wine, Sadie snapped, "Never mind. She's leaving."

Kerry did not argue. Sadly, she had her answer. There was no gambling, so if this was, indeed, where Slade had been when she saw him, there was only one reason for his visit.

"I'm sorry I bothered you," she mumbled and slid off the stool, anxious to escape before Sadie got any madder.

Outside, Kerry was momentarily turned around in her haste, as well as her heartache. She went the wrong way but had not gone far before realizing she had to turn around. And when she did, she saw Slade's horse tied in back of the house.

She ran all the way to Center Street, not wanting him to happen out just then and see her. She had no intention of letting him know she was aware of what he was doing. Not yet, anyway.

And in that moment of despair to once again feel like the world's biggest fool, Kerry promised herself that this time she was through with him.

There would be no second chances ... regardless of how she loved him above and beyond reason.

This was the proverbial last straw.

Returning to where she had left the wagon, she was pleasantly surprised to recognize Luther and Bessie among a group of Negroes. They were standing outside the office of the commander of the occupation forces.

Despite her misery, she was laughing with delight as she hurried across the street to where they were.

But the laughter faded when she saw the face of one of the men she had given a ride to the day she went to court. Edgar, she recalled was his name. One of his eyes was swollen shut, and it looked as though his lip had been split open.

Giving Bessie and Luther quick hugs, she fixed her gaze on Edgar. "Who did this to you?" she asked, feeling a hot rush of anger, because she was sure she already knew.

"Master Allison's overseer, Mr. Buck," he confirmed.

It was hard to understand his words due to his injured mouth.

"And you came to report him? That's wonderful, Edgar. I'm proud of you."

Luther spoke up, and Kerry was thrilled to hear courage and fire in his voice. "We ain't takin' no more. If we stay there, sooner or later somebody is gonna get killed. So we all packed up and left in the night."

Bessie chimed in with uncharacteristic defiance. "We're tired of how he treats us. So we came to town to tell the soldiers and ask them if they'll help us get to Atlanta, in case Master Allison comes after us. We're gonna try to find Adam."

Luther put his arm around her. "And find him we will, Bessie, but you can stop hopin' for any help from the soldiers. They ain't got time to mess with us, but they sure do need to know how Master Allison lets his overseers beat us. And we're gonna tell how *he* beats us sometimes, too."

He explained to Kerry, "Some of 'em are still too scared to leave, so we want to see if anything can be done about him mistreatin' 'em."

The plan was churning in Kerry's mind like fresh cream to butter. "You're doing the right thing. And maybe the army will even see that he's punished. But you aren't going to Atlanta. You're coming home with me to live."

Exchanging worried glances with the others, Luther said, "Now, Miss Kerry, you know we can't do that."

"I don't see why not, and don't tell me you're scared of the Klan. You should have realized by now that the only freedmen they're attacking are the ones who live off by themselves. You left me because Mr. Allison put fear in you, and now that fear is not justified. All he wanted was for you to work for free."

Luther allowed as how that was so and how perhaps they had acted too quickly. "But you can't afford us, Miss Kerry. We'd be a lot of mouths to feed."

"I can't afford to pay you," she clarified, "but then *you*

can't afford to refuse the offer I'm prepared to make." Taking a deep breath, she plunged ahead. "I want you all to be sharecroppers. You know what that means, don't you? You'll have your own piece of land to work as though it's your own. Then when your crop is in, you'll share the profits with me. Meanwhile, we'll all work together to have food. You men can hunt, and we women will have a garden. The shacks out back might need a little repair work, but nothing really big, and—"

"Oh, hold on there, missy," Luther held up a hand and laughed softly to remind, "Ain't you forgettin' somethin'? It ain't all your land no more. The judge, he gave half to Mr. Dillon."

"That's right. But I can do anything I choose with my half, and I choose to share it with all of you."

Bessie caught her husband's arm and squeezed. "It might be all right, Luther. There's certainly no harm in trying, is there? What else can we do? If the soldiers won't help us get to Atlanta, then I'll be afraid for us to set out by ourselves."

"And I don't think we have to worry about the Klan," Edgar said bravely. "After all, the army done caught one of the leaders. That should scare the rest into quietin' down. And we won't do nothin' to stir 'em up, neither. We'll mind our own business, work hard, and I think they'll leave us alone."

Mumblings to agree went through their friends, who were watching and listening intently.

Luther scratched his head, looked at each in turn to make sure no one was opposed, then, with a gut-wrenching sigh, told Kerry, "I reckon if you're willin' to take a chance, so are we."

Kerry hugged each and every one of them and then even herself. It was the best thing that could happen, because she would no longer need Slade. She would have all the help she needed, and they would all profit.

"Let's hurry and get this over with," she told Edgar as

a soldier opened the door to motion him inside. "I can't wait to get you all home and settled in."

Kerry was beginning to think maybe things were going to be brighter, after all. It would certainly help to have Luther and the others living at the farm. For help as well as company. She certainly did not intend to depend on Slade any longer for either one.

But her contentment was short-lived when she saw Thad Albritton coming her way.

"Kerry, I'm so glad I found you," he cried, taking her hands in his. "Abigail said you might still be in town, and I've been looking all over for you."

"How nice," she said dully. "What brings you all the way from Raleigh?"

"I had some business here, and—" He looked at the Negroes with annoyance and promptly drew her away from them to quickly admonish. "Whatever are you doing standing with them like that, Kerry? What can you be thinking?"

"They used to work for my father," she said, "and I don't care to discuss it with you."

"I see," he said stiffly. "Well, I know it's probably taking you a long time to get used to our ways, but you should not have anything to do with them. Now let's go have a cup of tea at the hotel. I've so much to tell you."

"Oh, I'm not dressed for that," she protested. "I'm not even wearing a hat."

"Nonsense. You're so beautiful no one cares what you wear. Now come along. I insist."

With an apologetic glance to Luther and the others, Kerry let Thad lead her away. Edgar would probably be inside for a while, anyway, and she felt it was best to get Thad away from there.

Once they were seated at a cozy round table in a corner, orders placed for tea and lemon cake, Thad took her hands. "I've been so worried about you since that night in church. And Abigail wrote to me about that scalawag having the nerve to take you to court. He ought to be horsewhipped."

"Things are working out," she said, trying to pull her hands from his, but he held tight. "Mr. Dillon stays out of my way, and I stay out of his."

"Good. But there's no need for you to endure any of this." He took a deep breath and plunged ahead to admit, "Actually, you're the reason I came to town today, Kerry. I wanted to find out from Abigail how you're getting along.

"She's keeping the baby, by the way," he added with a smile, then continued, "Look, I am not going to mince words. I want to court you, Kerry. I want you to marry me."

It was the last thing she had expected to hear that day and certainly something she did not want to have to deal with in the wake of everything else going on in her life just then.

With a determined yank, she freed her hands and folded them in her lap so he couldn't grab them again.

"Mr. Albritton—"

"Thad," he corrected.

"Very well—*Thad*. I am quite flattered, but the truth is, I don't want to get married right now."

He laughed, "Oh, don't worry. I'm not talking about rushing into anything. I just want the two of us to get to know each other ... spend time together. And I know you'll want to be with the baby, too ... get her used to being around you. So the least you can do is agree to that. I mean, what is the harm? I will take you out to dinner, buy you pretty things. I'll treat you like the princess that you are."

"Thad, again I assure you I am flattered, but I am ready for neither marriage nor motherhood."

"How can you be sure until we're better acquainted?"

She was relieved the waiter brought their tea just then.

She busied herself adding honey and lemon and then began stirring furiously, anything to pass the time.

"Kerry."

He reached to put his thumb and forefinger under her chin, forcing her to look at him.

"Say you will let me call on you."

She was sitting facing the window and could see Edgar coming out of the army office. He and the others began glancing about, no doubt searching for her. She knew if she did not get out there immediately, they might change their minds and start heading to Atlanta.

Twisting her head to escape his touch, Kerry murmured to get rid of him, "Very well. One of these days, you may."

"Wonderful," he exclaimed. "And it won't be *one of these days,* either. It will be quite soon. I will let Abigail know, and she can tell you when you deliver her eggs when to expect me.

"And later," he rushed on, filled with enthusiasm, "when the weather turns warmer, the two of you can come to Raleigh and visit me. I have a nice house, and with Abigail along, it will all be quite proper. You'll love Raleigh, my dear, and—"

"I'm sure I will." She managed a broad smile as she stood. "But I really have to be going now. I just remembered I have to call on some new customers to take their orders," she lied. *Anything to get away from him.*

Reluctantly, he also rose. "Well, if you must . . ."

"I do. Really. Thank you for the tea."

"And I can call on you soon?" he asked again, desperate for reassurance that she meant it.

"Yes, yes," she said, anxious to get away from him.

Slade was still weary from the night before but knew he needed to get back to the farm. Kerry was going to be furious he hadn't been there to help with the chores. But after giving Rosalie the information about Lloyd Swenson, he had fallen asleep on her bed. She had not awakened him till a short while ago, saying she figured he needed the rest.

So now he was in a hurry . . . and also anxious to hear the news that had stirred up the whole town.

He went into Bedham's store to buy some bacon and beans. He had an idea Kerry would not be cooking for him any longer—at least not till he got things smoothed over.

Likely it would be okay for her to keep the stallion for a little while. The Klan would probably lie low in the wake of Swenson's arrest. Meanwhile, Slade intended to keep trying to persuade her to not be so reckless.

"How are things out at the farm?" Horace asked as he put Slade's purchases in a burlap bag.

"Fine. Just fine." Slade did not want to get into a conversation with Bedham or anybody else. He knew the local men now hated his guts and did not want to give them fodder for their gossip.

"Is she still riding that Negro's horse?"

Slade sucked in his breath, managing to keep his composure as he answered, "I've no idea what you're talking about."

"Sure you do," Horace grinned. "That stallion she's got belonged to the Negro the Klan was after."

"And how would you be knowing that?"

"In this store I hear everything that goes on, Mr. Dillon. And I hate to see Miss Kerry doing anything foolish. You know what I mean?"

Slade innocently said, "I'm afraid I don't."

Horace frowned. "Well, I've tried to talk to her, and she won't listen to me. I figure it's some of your business since you own half the farm now. These are sad times we live in, Mr. Dillon, and folks have to be careful who they make mad."

"Yes, I guess they do." Slade took the bag and threw it over his shoulder. "And what you're saying is you think I should convince her to get rid of that stallion so certain folks won't be upset.''

"Let's just say it's a reminder she got involved in something she shouldn't have.''

Slade nodded. "I appreciate your concern.''

So, he thought as he walked out, it might be a good idea to keep an eye on Horace Bedham, because he might just have a robe and hood hidden under his bed, too.

He was also concerned as to the boldness of Bedham's gentle warning. That could mean the Klan was not going to back down in the wake of their Grand Turk's arrest.

Outside on the street, the crowds were dwindling as the day came to an end.

Slade was about to mount when someone called, "Mr. Dillon, how are you?''

He turned and recognized Thad Albritton and wondered what the hell he wanted. Brusquely, he replied, "Fine, thanks, but I'm in a hurry.''

"Of course. I won't keep you. I just thought I'd let you know I'll be coming out to the farm soon so you won't be surprised when you see me.''

"Oh? And for what reason?''

Thad thrust his chest out as he proudly announced, "I'm going to be calling on Miss Kerry—courting her, actually.''

Slade was tempted to bust out laughing. "Have you told her about this?''

"Oh, yes,'' Thad exuded. "We had tea at the hotel this afternoon, and she is looking forward to it. So I thought since you live out at the farm—in one of the shacks, I understand,'' he added, wrinkling his nose in distaste, "that you'd be interested to know I'll be a frequent visitor from now on.''

Slade felt as if he'd been kicked in the gut.

He knew Kerry was angry with him—real angry—but surely she would not go so far as to agree to Thad Albritton courting her just for spite.

Still, alarm was creeping inside him to think maybe she thought it would run him off if Albritton started coming around.

And if that were the case, she might be right.

Because Slade was not sure just how much more he could take.

Chapter 22

Having few belongings, Luther, Bessie, and their friends were settled into their little shacks in no time.

The first one was left for Slade, of course, though Kerry doubted he would stay there much longer. She had thought everything over carefully and had decided how things had to be from now on. Anger and disgust to believe he was a part of the Klan overshadowed everything else she might feel for him.

And the fact that he could be a part of something so dastardly was even worse than discovering he was involved with another woman.

So now she no longer cared what his motives were as to the farm. Whether he wanted it for himself or the other woman made no difference, because there was no way he would ever get it.

She was proud of herself for having thought of the plan to sharecrop. The judge had said she and Slade were to divide expenses and profits. Well, she gloated to think, there would be expenses, all right—seed, fertilizer, feed for the animals, and so on. But when it came to profits, there would not be any for her to divide with him, thanks to the sharecroppers. Not for a long, long time, anyway, and she was sure that once he realized how things were going to be, he would move on.

But Kerry had no intention of having him around till then.

Because she intended to prove he was in the Klan, by God.

She was sitting on the back porch, wearing her new coat against the approaching chill of evening, when Bessie and Luther came down the path from the cabins. Luther was carrying a sack, and from the way they were both grinning, Kerry knew something was going on.

"Guess what we got?" Bessie called.

Kerry laughed, "I've no idea, but it must be something wonderful."

"It is, Miss Kerry, it is."

He put the sack down on the ground in front of her and opened it.

Her eyes widened to see a large smoked ham. "Luther, tell me you didn't take this from Mr. Allison's smoke-house."

His expression reminded her of a mischievous little boy.

"No, ma'am, I didn't take it."

"But it did come from there, didn't it?" Kerry could not imagine any other way he could have got it. None of them had anything hardly beyond the clothes on their backs.

"Yes, ma'am, I reckon it did. You see"—he exchanged a happy smile with Bessie—"Edgar said when he was gettin' his stuff together he needed a sack to carry everything in. He knows Mr. Allison always has some at the smokehouse for the hams, so he took one."

"He took a sack."

"Yes, ma'am."

"But he also stole a ham."

"No, ma'am. He took a sack. He just didn't notice there was a ham in it."

Luther and Bessie broke out laughing, but Kerry did not think it was a bit funny.

When they saw the grim way she was looking at them, they fell silent, and then Luther worriedly asked, "What is it, Miss Kerry? You ain't mad, are you?"

"I'm not mad, Luther, but he shouldn't have done it."

Luther tried to cajole, "But I told you, he didn't know the ham was in the sack, and . . ." Again he faded beneath her scolding glare.

"It's not funny, Luther. Mr. Allison is going to be mad enough when he finds out you've all left—especially when he hears how Edgar went to the soldiers. When he finds out a ham was stolen, he's going to be even madder."

With uncharacteristic rebellion, Luther fiercely said, "Well, I don't care. He ain't fed us no better than pig slop all the time we been there. We figure we had at least a ham comin' to us for all the hard work we did for nothin'."

"That's right," Bessie said with a curt nod.

Kerry looked at her and thought how it was one of the few times she had ever seen her show any spirit. Usually, Bessie was quiet as a mouse and about as unthreatening. Now, however, her chocolate eyes were spitting fire as she said, "But since you're worried about it, Miss Kerry, the best thing to do is slice up this ham and fry it for supper. Once it's gone, nobody can say we took it."

Kerry was too hungry to argue. Besides, she reasoned that if Mr. Allison was mad enough over the theft to ask her about it once he learned where the Negroes had gone, she could handle it.

Bessie remembered where the big iron skillet was kept in the kitchen cupboard. She got that out, while Kerry got busy firing up the stove. Meanwhile, Luther sharpened a butcher knife and went to work on the ham.

"It's a shame to throw away the shank," he said when

all the meat had been pared from the bone. "Sure would be good for soup."

Kerry could almost taste the ham broth with chunks of stewed potatoes. "All right. But pack salt around it and hide it in my father's old smokehouse."

When Luther went to take care of it, Bessie looked worried for the first time when she said, "I was just jokin' about eatin' all the ham so nobody can prove it was taken, Miss Kerry, but you don't really think Master Allison would come ridin' over here and look for it, do you?"

Kerry assured her that she would never allow Hank Allison or his bullying overseers to search for anything on her property. What she did not want to admit, however, was that her true reason for hiding the ham bone was to keep Slade from knowing about it so he wouldn't be expecting to share the soup. If she had anything to do with it, he would never put another bite of food in his mouth that she had anything to do with. Let him pay to eat at the hotel like he had done before. And he could also take his woman with him, so everyone could see he preferred the company of a prostitute.

There was enough ham for everyone to eat their fill. One of the women also surprised her by having a bag of grits to add to the wonderful supper. Kerry did not ask her where she got it. She did not want to know. All she wanted was to feast on the succulent ham, creamy grits swimming in red-eye gravy, and Bessie's hot, flaky biscuits that seemed to float on air from platter to plate.

They ate on the porch, oblivious to the cold wind, and not a morsel was left when they finished.

Kerry leaned back in a rocker and enjoyed having a full belly even if her heart was still aching over the day's painful revelations about Slade.

Then, out of the blue, Luther wanted to know, "How are we supposed to get by till spring, Miss Kerry?"

She told him there was nothing to worry about. "I make

good money off the eggs. We'll do just fine. You won't go hungry, and you won't have to steal food to keep from it.''

Edgar chuckled, still proud of his defense as to thievery. "Now it's like I said, Miss Kerry. All I did was take a sack. I didn't know there was no ham in it.''

She allowed them all to laugh over Edgar's foolishness. After all, the deed was done, and the ham had been a rare and wonderful treat. But they all knew she did not approve, so she wasn't worried that it would ever happen again.

"Hey, Luther, did you remember to take your banjo?'' someone asked.

Bessie pretended disgust. "That's like askin' if he remembered to put his clothes on this mornin'. He don't go nowhere without that banjo.''

Luther produced it as if by magic and began to play. The others sang along. Kerry did not know the words but clapped her hands in rhythm, trying to lose herself in the merry-making.

Her life was changing, she told herself, for the better.

And it did not include Slade Dillon.

After a while, Bessie brought out dessert—hoecakes she had made on the hot surface of the stove. Flour and water and a bit of sugar had been baked into a sweet delicacy, and everyone gathered around to have their share.

"Ain't much,'' Bessie humbly responded when Kerry gushed over the delicious little cakes. "But it'll do till we can grow sweet potatoes for pies. Maybe even some pumpkins, too.''

"And apples,'' Annie Potts, Edgar's wife, joined in. "We got to have apples.''

That began a discussion of all the foods that everyone had missed since the war. Kerry had not heard of some of them but assured she would be in favor of trying to grow anything they wanted.

"And we're gonna sharecrop,'' Annie said in wonder. "You know, I'd heard of some folks doin' that, but I never thought we'd be one of 'em. You're a blessin' from above, Miss Kerry."

"Oh, no," Kerry laughed. "It's all of you who are the blessing. Without you I wouldn't be able to survive. This way, all of us will profit, as well as have a home."

At that, Luther exchanged concerned glances with some of the others before hesitantly reminding, "Ain't you forgettin' about Mr. Dillon?"

Perhaps a bit too sharply, Kerry replied, "And aren't you forgetting that we're talking about *my* half and not his?"

Bessie gave Luther a jab with her elbow. "Will you stop worryin' Miss Kerry about that? She's done tol' all of us how it's gonna be."

They went back to their music, but Kerry no longer tried to keep up. Settling back in the rocker, she was content to just listen. But a few moments later Edgar eased away from the others to take the chair next to hers.

"Miss Kerry, there's somethin' I should tell you."

"Go on," she urged, noting he looked worried.

"It's about them night riders—the Ku Klux Klan."

"There's nothing to be concerned about. Tomorrow I'm going to show those of you who don't already know, how to use a gun. We aren't going to live in fear of those monsters, Edgar, believe me."

"But I think there's somethin' you need to know. It's about Master Buck, Master Allison's overseer, and—"

Kerry held up a hand. "Edgar, you've no reason to call them *master*, anymore. You have no master. You are a free man now."

"Yes'm. But it didn't seem that way when I was livin' over there. Anyway, I think Buck is one of 'em."

"One of the Klan? What makes you say that?"

"I heard him blow his whistle one night."

Kerry was dumbfounded. "You heard him whistling and that makes you think he's a member of the Klan?"

"No, that ain't it. He wasn't whistlin' himself. He *blew*

a whistle. It was late one night when I heard him, and he didn't know I did. I was out lookin' for a cow that got out of the pen, hopin' to find him before Buck found out he was gone, 'cause it was my job to make sure they didn't get out, and I knew he'd beat me bad.

"Anyway," he hurried to make her understand, "when I heard a whistle blowin', I got real scared, and I hid to see what it meant. Then he lit up a torch, and I saw it was him—Buck. I hid and watched, and a little while later another man rode up to him, and he had a torch, too. And I heard 'em talkin' about the whistlin', how the next man to hear it would blow, and the next, and the next, and when they all heard it, they'd know there was a meetin'."

"Signals," Kerry said in wonder. "Of course. And did you tell the soldiers about it?"

"No, ma'am. I thought about it, wonderin' if I should, but I was afraid I'd already made enough trouble for him by tellin' about the beatin's. The way I see it, if I'd told about him and the Klan, then I'd have all them mad at me instead of just Buck. But I felt like I had to tell you in case you hear some whistles around here one night. That might mean they're comin' after us."

Kerry knew that would not be the case, that the whistles were just for signaling, and she again told Edgar not to worry.

"Maybe if you tell the soldiers," he nervously suggested, "you could get 'em to promise not to say it was you that told, and then they'd go out in the woods and listen and know when there was a meetin'."

"Let me think about it, Edgar," she said, patting his shoulder. "And I'll let you know what I decide, all right?"

He sighed, relieved to let someone else worry about what should be done. "That'll be fine, Miss Kerry. Just fine."

It most certainly would be, she thought with an excited wave, because now she would be able to tell when the Klan was gathering. All she had to do was venture into the woods and listen for the whistles. Then she could follow the sound as it passed along, eventually leading her right to the Klan meeting . . . and Slade.

She noticed that Edgar had gotten awfully quiet and again looked worried.

"Will you relax?" she urged. "You've nothing to worry about. You're safe here."

"I hope so," he murmured, " 'cause I heard the whistles tonight, Miss Kerry."

She sat up straight and leaned close to him, not wanting the others to hear and be scared. "When did you hear them, Edgar? You should have told me before."

"It was on the way out here from town. I heard one right after we left, then two more the closer we got here; then they passed on in the distance, and I didn't hear nothin' else."

She told him to go back to the others and not say anything, that it probably meant nothing.

But if the Klan were meeting, she pondered after he left, it would likely be to try and lift their spirits after having their last attack thwarted and one of their leaders arrested.

But next time, she promised herself, she would do her best to be close by and listening.

Slade was in his hiding place, braced between the top rafters of the old tobacco-curing barn. He was probably fifty feet up and so swallowed in darkness that even if any of the Klan members below glanced up, they would not see him.

He was hungry and bone tired, and the last thing he wanted to do was spy on a meeting. But when he had heard the signal as he was leaving town, he knew he had to eavesdrop in case something important was going on.

It turned out to be exactly what he had expected—a meeting for Klansmen to tell each other that what had happened would not destroy them. The Grand Cyclops got up and made a spirited speech about how they still had two powerful leaders—himself and the Grand Magi, who stood to his right with arms folded across his chest.

"But we have to ask ourselves," the Grand Cyclops said, anger ringing in his voice, "who among us is the traitor? The army could not have known about our plans if someone hadn't told them."

A murmur rippled through the crowd, and a few men even stepped aside from those standing beside them, as though afraid to trust anyone.

Slade was pleased to see that his scheme to plant the seed of doubt was working.

"We aren't going to let this happen," the leader ranted on. "We are going to find out who the traitor is, and when we do, he will hang."

"Then let's find him now," somebody angrily shouted. "Before he does any more damage. How can we carry on our business if somebody is listening and waiting to run straight to the soldiers and tell them? We might as well forget about meeting for a while and stay home."

The leader screamed, "Fool. That's what they want us to do, and we aren't going to let it happen."

"Don't see how you can stop it," someone else irritably pointed out. "I mean, who do you trust?"

"I trust your Grand Magi," he yelled back. "And our guards. We will meet with them and decide what to do until we find the traitor. Till then, all of you listen and see what you can find out, and if you suspect anyone, let me or the Grand Magi know."

They talked on, griping and complaining. For Slade, it was a waste of time. He knew he wasn't going to hear anything important. They would likely not be planning to attack anybody any time soon. And there was no need in trying to follow either the Grand Cyclops or the Grand Magi to wherever they lived. They would have their guards with them.

He wanted desperately to climb down and go home. And to hell with waking Kerry when he got there. If she had food in the kitchen, it was half his. He had no intention of going to bed hungry.

He thought, too, of how he needed to have a talk with her first thing in the morning. Things were tensing up again, especially with Thad Albritton's announcement he would be coming around.

Finally, after what seemed forever, the meeting began to break up. The leaders left first, accompanied by their guards.

He wondered how many of the Klan actually knew the leaders' identities. Probably most, only they would never let on. After all, a man's voice could become familiar in day-to-day dealings. He could also be known by his horse. Even his boots. The problem was, Slade was not that acquainted with many men in the county. After all, he had talked with Lloyd Swenson before but never linked him to the voice he had heard at the meetings. So he never suspected him of being a leader.

Slade's assignment was, unfortunately, harder than he had imagined it would be. But, sooner or later, things would fall into place. Then he could try to figure out what to do about Kerry . . . whether there was anything between them—on her part, anyway—to make him hang around. Because, after all, if what Thad Albritton had said was true, then it was all over.

It was well after midnight when Slade decided it was safe to climb down and find his way deep into the woods where his horse was hidden. A light mist was falling, and he hoped the temperature wasn't going to drop any lower. The last thing he wanted was another ice storm to complicate things.

He decided that when he got back to the farm, he would forgo looking for food in the kitchen. In a few hours it would be daylight, and then he could ride into town and eat. Despite his rumbling stomach, he was too tired for any kind of confrontation with Kerry, which was how it would be if she woke up and saw him.

When he was far enough away from the tobacco barn, Slade lit his torch so he could see his way. No one would notice the light, for everyone had been gone quite a spell.

He rode along the riverbank, taking the back path to avoid going anywhere near the house . . . and Kerry.

He was having trouble staying awake, his head nodding. So at first he did not notice anything. Then, as he rode down the middle of the cabins, he began to realize something was amiss.

A mop was hanging over a railing.

A jacket had been carelessly dropped on a porch.

And a mule was tied to a post.

"What the hell . . . ?" he said aloud, reining to a stop and dismounting, drawing his gun as he did so while keeping hold of the torch with his other hand.

"Who's in there?" he roared. "Damn poachers. Get out here."

There were frightened cries, the sounds of people clamoring out of bed and rushing to the windows to look out.

Slade blinked in disbelief at the sight of all the terrified faces. "Who are you people?" he yelled. "Get out here right now."

"Don't shoot, Mr. Dillon. It's me—Luther. Remember? I used to live here."

Slade watched as the old man came out on the porch of the cabin beside his. He was holding his trembling arms over his head.

"Don't shoot me, neither," a man Slade did not know begged as he came out of the cabin on the other side. "We don't mean no harm. We just bedded down like Miss Kerry told us to. We didn't know we'd scare you, but you wasn't here, and—"

"She told you to bed down here?"

"Yessir," Luther rushed to explain. "We're gonna live here and be sharecroppers. She moved us in today."

That was all Slade needed to hear.

And to hell with worrying about waking her up.

"Go back to bed," he yelled at them; then, throwing down the torch, because he well knew the way, Slade took off for the house.

The back door was locked, but one swift kick took care of that. It bounced off the wall at the same time he shouted into the darkness, "Have you taken all leave of your senses, woman?"

Kerry appeared a few seconds later, holding a lantern in one hand, her shotgun in the other. "What do you mean breaking in here like this?"

"And what do you mean moving those people in here and telling them they could be sharecroppers? Are you crazy?"

Slade watched as she, with calmness that maddened, very slowly walked to the table and set down the lantern. Then, in its mellow glow, her expression as tight and cold as her voice, she said, "What I do with my half of the farm is none of your business, Slade."

"I'd say it is, being the judge didn't divide it up that way."

"Well, I guess we'll have to go to court again . . . which I am prepared to do, if need be." She lifted her chin in a gesture of defiance and challenge. "And I dare say he would not rule against my helping freedmen make a new life for themselves. It's an ideal solution—for my purposes, anyway. They get a home and a way to provide for themselves, and I have help that I desperately need because I can't count on you.

"More than that," she frostily added, eyes sharp and angry, "I don't *want* to count on you, Slade Dillon. Not for a damn thing."

Yanking a chair from the table, he threw himself into it to glare at her as fury raged. "Do you realize what you've done?"

"I most certainly do—helped a lot of desperate people."

"That's not what I'm talking about, Kerry. I'm talking

about sharecropping. It's something new . . . something that hasn't been started in Wayne County.''

"Then it's time it did, isn't it?'' she asked quietly, coolly. "I'm proud to be the first.''

"You're proud to be about the most stubborn filly I've ever met," he snapped, reaching to grab her arm and give her a shake. "Kerry, don't do this. I can't always be here to protect you.''

"Who says I want you to be?'' she flung back at him. "When are you going to get it through that thick skull of yours, Slade Dillon, that I don't need you, and I sure as hell don't want you?

"And keep your hands off of me,'' she said, jerking free. "If you continue behaving this way, I'll go to the judge, so help me. I'm sure he didn't mean for his ruling to include your bullying me.''

"No, I'm sure he didn't,'' he all but growled, adding, "And I guess you don't need me or want me, Kerry, not when Thad Albritton is going to start calling. What did you do—work out an agreement to marry him if he'd finance your stake in the farm?''

For an instant, he thought she was going to slap him. Her hand trembled at her side; then she took a few steps backwards as though fighting the temptation.

"Thad Albritton is a gentleman—something your kind would never understand. He's kind and honest and would never lie to me or betray me. As for him financing my *stake*—as you call it—I'm sure he'd be glad to if I asked, but I would never do that. Besides, I don't have a mere stake. All of this land is rightfully mine, and you know it. I don't care what my father's will said, because he had no idea I would ever come here. If he had, he probably wouldn't have married your mother, much less given her all he had to give.''

"Kerry, that may be true, but—''

"Hear me out,'' she raised her voice above his. "And hear me well, because after this day I want nothing more to do with you. We'll settle up once a year as to expenses and profits—if there are any—but other than that I swear I will not speak one word to you, and I'd be pleased not to have you talk to me, as well."

Slade looked deep into the emerald eyes he had adored and sadly knew, beyond all doubt, that it was over.

She loathed and despised him, and he was wasting his time and his breath. Let her have the farm, damn it. He never wanted it for anything beyond a cover, anyway, and soon he wouldn't need even that. He could hang around and be a hired hand, a drifter . . . whatever it took to get by without suspicion till he got his job done. He would listen to the night whistles, spy on the meetings, take care of business, and ride on. He did not, by God, have to waste another minute with an arrogant little brat who loved her land so much there was no room left over for a man.

He stood and saw how Kerry braced herself, a tiny shadow of fear in her eyes.

"You don't have to worry about ever hearing my voice again, Kerry," he said gravely. "It's all yours."

"What do you mean?" she asked, suddenly uneasy.

"I mean that I'm sick of warring with you, Kerry, sick of trying to keep you out of danger due to your own foolishness. You're on your own, now. And believe me when I say I wish you well."

He went to the door. His throat was tight, his heart pounding, and he knew if he didn't get out right then he might do something stupid—like take her in his arms and tell her the truth about who he was and why he was there. And he didn't dare. One word from her to the wrong person could cost them both their lives.

She was right behind him. "You heard the judge. If one of us leaves, the other gets their share. So you needn't think you can walk out like this and come back when the crops are harvested and hold out your hand."

He turned on his heel. "The way you're going, there won't be any crops. Or a house or anything else. You'll keep right on, doing everything you can to annoy the wrong people, and sooner or later you're going to be sorry.''

But not if I could help it, he fiercely vowed. And suddenly it was more important than ever that he bust up the Klan. Only then could he ride out of her life, because he had to know they would not be around to harm her.

She pointed to the door. "Get out of my house, Slade Dillon. And never come back.''

"Don't worry,'' he yelled over his shoulder. "And give Thad Albritton my sympathies. He has no idea what troubles he's going to have with a headstrong woman like you.

"As for me,'' he added, turning his head so she could see that he was smirking, "I'm going to town, get drunk, and try to forget I ever met you.''

He walked out, slamming the door so hard the whole house shook.

Kerry was shaking right along with it—but with rage, not fear.

He had threatened her by saying she would be sorry.

But she was no more afraid of him than the rest of his cowardly friends and was more determined than ever to see they were caught and punished.

And all she had to do was listen for the whistles.

Chapter 23

It sounded like thunder as they rode in, the very ground shaking.

Kerry fell out of bed in her startled haste to find out what was going on.

Snatching up her coat to wrap around her flannel nightgown, she tore from the bedroom, grabbing the shotgun as she went.

Flinging open the back door, she saw five men on horseback, framed by the rising sun.

They were red-faced and furious, but she was relieved to see they weren't wearing robes and hoods.

No one had drawn a gun, and she leveled hers but kept her finger close to the trigger. "Who are you and what do you want?" she demanded, chin high and eyes cold with challenge. She felt no fear. Not for the moment, anyway. She was too damn mad.

"Hank Allison's the name."

Her gaze swept him in quick scrutiny. He looked as she had imagined he would—big and mean. He had arms like ham shanks, and his portly belly was hanging over his gun belt. His eyes were dark and unfriendly, and the wrinkles on his face no doubt came from his constant scowl rather than age.

She gave him a mock sweet smile. "And might this be a neighborly visit, Mr. Allison?"

Rising up in the stirrups to appear all the more fierce, he snapped, "You know damn well why we're here, you little upstart. You stole my workers."

Very calmly, Kerry said, "That's not true, and you know it. And if you've come to make trouble, I'll be thanking you to leave."

She raised the shotgun a few inches.

Hank sank back in the saddle. "Nobody wants any trouble, Miss Corrigan. And quite frankly, I don't give a damn if you did talk them into moving over here with you. That's not why I'm here."

"Then what?"

"I want what's mine."

She laughed, "But you just said you didn't care, and I should remind you that they aren't yours, anyway, Mr. Allison. They don't belong to anybody anymore. In case you haven't heard—the war is over. The South lost. There are no more slaves."

"That's not what I'm talking about."

"Then please get to the point."

"They stole from me when they left."

Kerry hoped she looked as oblivious of the situation as she tried to sound. "I'm afraid I have no idea what you're talking about."

"A ham is missing from my smokehouse. And a sack of grits from the pantry. My wife noticed it this morning. I want it all back."

Kerry shook her head. "You'll not find any of those things here."

"Then you won't mind my boys looking around, will you? Those people are crafty. You never know what they might have hidden around here."

"As a matter of fact, I do mind, Mr. Allison." Her grip tightened on the gun. "I'll not have anyone nosing around my property. I said the things you're looking for aren't here, and that will have to be good enough for you."

Suddenly the man next to Hank yelled out, "And I say you're lying, 'cause if you weren't, you wouldn't care if we took a look."

Hank reached to put a hand on his arm. "Buck, there's no need for this to get ugly."

"So *you're* Buck," Kerry said in a voice ringing with contempt. "You're the big, bad overseer who beats defenseless old men." Her voice rose. "Why, if I were a man I'd show you a thing or two. I'd whip you with my bare hands, I would."

At that, the men burst into laughter, including Hank Allison.

Kerry did not like their scoffing and felt her face grow hot with indignity. She slowly raised the gun, and their laughter immediately faded to a tense silence.

"Now hold it, little gal," Hank said, having lost his bluster. "There's no need for you to get all riled. Believe me, I don't want a fuss over this, so let's settle it nice and peaceful."

"I've no need to settle anything," she said tightly. "I didn't start anything."

"That's right. You didn't. But the coloreds did. They came begging to you, and you being the good-hearted soul your pa was, took them in.

"And I knew your pa," he rushed to add, noting how her expression had softened at his mention. "He was a good man. A fine man. And we got along good. Oh, we had our differences over the slave issue, to be sure, but I respected him for his opinion, and we never had no trouble. So I figure you and me can get along, too. And I've been meaning to pay you a visit, I surely have. Me and the missus, we talked about it, but there never seems to be enough time."

Kerry was not impressed by his sudden show of friendship. "Well, back to your purpose in being here today, Mr. Allison, it appears you're wasting some of that time you never have enough of."

His pleasant expression faded. "Well, I think as a show of good faith that you ought to let my men look around."

She gave her head an adamant swing from side to side. "You have no business nosing around, and I'm asking you for the last time to leave."

"And what are you gonna do if we don't?" Buck yelped. He started to dismount, but Hank's hand snaked out to grab his arm and hold him back.

"That's enough. If Miss Corrigan wants to treat her neighbors this way, so be it." He turned back to her. "But let me tell you something, little gal. One of these days you might want some help, and when you do, don't come running to me. You'll not get it. Not after this."

He motioned to his men. "Let's go."

Buck was beside himself with rage. "Damn it, boss, I can't believe you're letting her get away with this. You know as good as I do they stole that ham. And there's no telling what else will turn up missing when your wife has a chance to look around the house. Thievin' bastards, that's what they are. I say we search all around, and when we get the evidence we'll make 'em pay. Hell, we'll lynch 'em here and now."

"Are you crazy?" Hank stared at him. "You talk about lynching? Hell, man, you'd be hung yourself for something like that. We got the army running things now, remember? Now you calm down and shut up that kind of talk. We're going to let the law handle this. I'm riding into town and report the theft, and they can take it up with Miss Corrigan."

When Buck made no move to leave, Kerry raised the shotgun and pointed it at him. "You heard Mr. Allison. Now I suggest you do as he says."

Hank gruffly said, "Let's go, Buck."

"Hey, look what I found!"

They all whipped about as a man Kerry had not seen before emerged from the smokehouse.

"Jeremy, what are you doing nosing around in there?" Hank demanded before Kerry had a chance to do so herself.

The man quickly explained, "Buck told me to ride in ahead of y'all and start looking around. He figured she'd refuse to let us do it. And be glad I did, 'cause look what I found hid in the smokehouse."

Kerry winced as he held up the ham bone for everyone to see.

"Found the sack, too." He showed it to Hank. "It's the kind you use, all right."

Hank turned back to Kerry and smirked. "Now what have you got to say? You still want to defend your thieving friends?"

"That doesn't prove anything," Kerry said, her insides churning as she tried to sound sure of herself. "Neither has your name on it, and I'm tired of arguing about it. Now get out of here."

Pointing the gun skyward, she pulled the trigger, the explosion sending the horses into a nervous frenzy as the men pulled back on the reins trying to control them.

"The next time I shoot I'll be aiming at somebody," she warned.

Hank shook his fist at her. "You haven't heard the last of this. I'm going to the law."

"Do that," she said, undaunted. "They'll probably laugh in your face for making so much over a silly ham bone, Mr. Allison."

When they were finally out of sight, Kerry sank to the porch steps in near collapse to have the tension end.

But she was not alone for long. Luther and the others came running, having heard the gunfire.

"It's all right," she told them. "It's over. Nothing to worry about."

Edgar was shaking all over in apology. "Oh, Lordy, Miss Kerry. It was on account of that ham, warn't it? I'm so sorry. I never thought it'd bring so much trouble . . . just one little old ham."

Wearily, she told all of them, "It wasn't just the ham. They think you stole other things, too."

"Just a sack of grits," Annie Potts spoke up. "And they're all gone."

"And so are Mr. Allison and his men," Kerry said, getting to her feet, determined not to let the incident spoil her day. "So let's get to work. We've a lot to do. There's vegetable gardens to be plowed, and some of your cabins need repairs. We don't have time to sit around and stew over what's done."

The day passed slowly, but Kerry worked hard to try and keep from thinking about the morning's incident, as well as her other problems.

She was not truly worried about Hank Allison doing anything else. Oh, he might tell the soldiers, and they might ride out and ask questions, but she doubted it. They had too many other things to do without having to investigate the theft of a ham.

That had not been Hank's real motive, anyway, and the soldiers would figure that out. But when he learned that Edgar had reported Buck to the army for his mistreatment, he'd be madder still. No doubt there would be an investigation, and Hank might be forbidden to have any freedmen work for him till he fired Buck. Kerry had heard that happened sometimes, when the charges were serious enough. That was why she had been so elated that Edgar had gone to the soldiers.

Bessie commented she'd never seen Kerry work so hard and wanted to know, "How come you're pushin' yourself this way, child? You're gonna wear yourself out."

That was exactly what Kerry wanted to do, so that when she finally did crawl into bed she would fall sound asleep as soon as her head hit the pillow. Because no matter how much she might loathe Slade by day, her nights were haunted by how she had loved him.

Edgar and Luther caught some catfish for supper. Bessie and Annie cleaned them, then dropped them in an iron pot filled with lard to fry.

Afterwards, it was all Kerry could do to help clean up. By the time she got to bed she was almost asleep on her feet.

And, mercifully, she had accomplished her goal—she sank into a slumber so deep she was oblivious to everything else.

That, however, proved to be her undoing, for she did not hear the riders coming in . . . was unaware of anything till the shouts came demanding that she come outside.

Instantly she was wide awake, not bothering with her robe as she grabbed up shotgun and pistol. Her room, she noted in horror as she ran out, was bathed in a red glow coming from the outside, which could mean only one thing—fire.

Terror washed like cold rain when she saw them—perhaps a half dozen men wearing white hoods and robes, all carrying flaming torches as they stood in a semicircle around the back porch. And, despite panic, she was relieved to see the light had come from the torches. Nothing had been set aflame . . . yet.

"Come outside, Kerry Corrigan," someone gruffly ordered. "Leave your guns inside and you won't get hurt . . . your house won't be burned to the ground. All we want is to talk to you."

Kerry stood inside the back door trying to decide what to do. If she went outside without her guns, they might shoot her dead then and there. But if she tried to fight back, they would burn her out.

She could hear the sound of her own heart beating, and then another voice rang out in the stillness. "We promise you won't be hurt. All we want is to talk to you. Lay down your gun."

Kerry realized she had no choice. Even if she did walk outside with her guns, she would not have a chance. She might get a couple of them, but they would ultimately kill her. Better, she decided nervously, to take a chance they might be telling the truth.

She put her weapons aside and stepped onto the porch.

"Hold out your hands so we can see you ain't got a gun."

She did so.

"All right, come on out."

It appeared that the man doing the talking was wearing a black hood instead of white. Figuring he was the leader, she mustered all her courage to ask, "So have you cowards taken to terrorizing helpless women now?"

"Just shut your mouth," he yelled. "And listen to what I've got to say unless you want to see this place burned down. We're here to tell you to get out of Wayne County. You're nothing but a troublemaker, stirring up the freed slaves against the whites. We don't need your kind. So we're giving you a week to clear out. If you're not gone by then, we'll burn you out.

"And don't even think about going to the law," he further warned as the others gave the torches they were holding aloft a threatening shake. "We'll show no mercy then, and we will get you, Kerry Corrigan. Have no doubt about that. We will find you no matter how long it takes and make you wish you'd stayed on the other side of the ocean."

"A week," someone else shouted. "Or else." He threw his torch down on the porch; then, amidst shouting and taunts of laughter, they rode away at a fast gallop.

Kerry ran inside and snatched the cloth from the table to beat out the flames before they could do much damage. Then she grabbed her guns and ran around the side of the house, knowing as she did that it was too late. They were gone, swallowed by the night.

The Negroes had heard the commotion and come running. The women were hysterical. The men were wringing their hands in frustration and fear, not knowing what to do or say.

Kerry could only tell them not to worry, but it was hollow advice, even to her own ears.

Finally, she managed to calm them by saying she would go to the soldiers and ask for protection. Her friends had not heard the Klansman's threat as to what would happen if she did. They were appeased, if only for the moment, and that was all she wanted, as she needed time to think.

They drifted away, but she knew they would not sleep the rest of the night.

And neither would she.

She was too damn mad.

No, she was beyond mad.

She was livid to the point of near hysteria, because she knew that one of those bastards wearing a hood had to have been Slade. It was his way of getting revenge on her for taking in the Negroes and making them sharecroppers.

It was also his way of planning to eventually take over the farm. With her gone, it would be his.

And now she knew, beyond doubt, that she had to expose him and had only a week to do it. But she would succeed, by God, no matter what it took.

This time, he had gone too far.

Slade tried to get comfortable, but it was impossible with only a thin blanket between him and the floor of Rosalie's room.

She watched him from where she lay in bed, sipping a whiskey. "I told you this is a big bed. You could sleep on the other side."

He was taking no chances on sharing a mattress with his best friend's woman even if she was a prostitute. "No, thanks. This will do fine."

"Well, I can't help thinking of what it's costing you to

sleep on the damn floor, Slade. You've got to pay up like you've been loving me all night so's I can turn the money over to Sadie. Otherwise, she'll ask questions.

"And I don't come cheap, you know," she added with a wink.

"Yeah, I know," he murmured, not caring. He was too ripped up over Kerry to give a damn about money. Besides, he figured that once things were over and done with, the Bureau would pay him back for all he'd had to spend.

Rosalie tried to lift his spirits. "Maybe tomorrow you can find work as a hired hand. It'll not only give you credence for hanging around since things blew up between you and that Corrigan gal, but you'll have a place to stay besides here."

"Actually, I don't plan on hanging around that long. I'm ready to bring things to a head."

"You've still got two leaders to expose. That may take a while."

He shook his head. "I'm sick of fooling around with this, Rosalie. I'm going to finish it up."

She sat up to stare at him, alarm flashing. "What are you talking about? You know the orders were—"

"To hell with the orders," he snapped. "I know the Bureau thinks the best way to bust up the Klan is to get the leaders, because if all I do is find out where they're meeting and send the army to raid and arrest, some of them might get away, and the leaders might be among them. But things are dragging too slow to suit me. I say let's get it over with. Next meeting, I want you to alert the army to show up."

"Can't do it, Slade," she said firmly. "I'd have to ask permission from headquarters, and they'd never give it. Because if all they wanted was to attack the Klan at one of their meetings, they'd have already done it. Hell, I've heard of some times and places before, myself. I could have tipped 'em off. But they wanted to do it the other way . . . destroy from inside. That's why you were called in."

"And it's not working," he said wearily, getting up from the floor to go and stand at the window and stare out into the night. "Oh, they ranted and raved when they met after Swenson was arrested, because they believed a traitor was responsible, just like we planned. So now we sit and wait for something to happen, and I'm tired of sitting and waiting." He jammed his fist against the wall in frustration.

Rosalie held up the whiskey bottle. "You need a drink."

"What I need," he snapped, "is to get this over with."

He sat down and reached for his boots.

"Where are you going at this hour?" Rosalie asked nervously.

"I don't know. At least my leaving will cut down on what I owe you. And don't worry. You can get back to business as usual tonight. I won't be here."

"And what will you be doing?"

He gave her a look that made her tremble despite knowing she had nothing to fear. Then, quietly, coldly, he said, "I'll be listening for a whistle, Rosalie . . . and praying to hear one."

Chapter 24

Slade heard the whistle around eleven o'clock. He had stationed himself near the tobacco barn, figuring if there was to be a meeting he needed to be nearby so he could get in position before the Klansmen began to arrive.

The sound came, as best he could estimate, from over a mile away. It meant it was probably the last one. Those who had heard first were already en route, so he had no time to waste.

He left his horse tied in a copse near the river. It was a cloudless night, and a full moon filtered enough light through the pines overhead that he could have seen his way even if he had not known it so well.

The barn loomed ahead, like a sentinel protecting the evildoers plotting within.

Slade hoped the army would burn the barn when all this was over. He did not want it to stand like some kind of shrine to the hooded bastards.

It had been raining earlier in the day, and the inside of the barn smelled damp and musty.

He began climbing up the beams that stretched from

side to side all the way to the top. They were positioned close together for hanging the poles of tied tobacco for curing above the smoke from fires below.

When he reached the point, halfway to the top, where he usually settled down to wait and watch, he kept on going.

Things were going to be different this night. He was not going to merely eavesdrop, trying to find out what meanness they planned next.

He was, by damn, going to follow one of the leaders all the way home.

There was an opening on the side at the top. Probably meant for air to circulate among the tobacco leaves while the curing was going on. For Slade, however, it was to be his quick exit once the meeting began to wind down. He had brought a rope, which he fastened to a beam just inside the opening. When the time was right, he would let the rope drop to the ground, then shimmy down so he could hurry to his horse. At the last meeting, he had managed to see which way the leader in the black hood went. It was Slade's plan to go in that direction and get in position to follow when the leader passed by with his guards.

The Bureau's plan was just taking too long to suit him. Hell, he could give the army the location of the Klan's den and even tell them when they would be there. All they had to do was surround it and arrest everybody at one time, as he'd told Rosalie. But, as she had argued, there was too great a chance that important people would get away to start things all over again with a new group.

But Slade did not, could not, wait any longer. He would give them one more leader, and then the Bureau would be on their own. He could not—would not—continue to hang around Wayne County . . . and Kerry. As bad as he feared for her safety, the cold, harsh truth was that she no longer needed him. She had Thad Albritton. And Slade would not be a bit surprised if she upped and married him before spring. After all, the damn farm meant more to her than anything else.

It had sure as hell meant more to her than *he* ever had.

That morning, after leaving Rosalie, he had ridden back to the farm, careful not to be seen. And he had watched Kerry without her knowing it . . . had seen how hard she worked, how she laughed with her friends, the sharecroppers.

She didn't need him . . . didn't need anybody. Just her damn land.

But despite his anger and disappointment over how he'd never meant a damn thing to her, Slade could not help remembering the good times they had shared. She was— or so he had thought—everything he ever wanted in a woman. Only it was not meant to be, and he had to get over her, blast it, because if he didn't, the memories would eat him alive, and—

They were coming, drifting into the barn like ghosts from the grave, their white robes billowing out behind them.

Then he saw the two leaders, flanked by a guard on each side. They walked to the makeshift podium and stood with their backs to the wall, whispering between themselves as they waited for everyone to arrive.

When he was satisfied they were all there, the Grand Cyclops waved his arms for silence, then began with the opening rituals. He droned on and on about how white superiority must be maintained at all costs, then preached about loyalty. Finally, with fire in his voice, he began to rant about how the traitors had to be found and dealt with before they destroyed their brotherhood.

Slade decided he was going after the Grand Cyclops, himself. With him out of the way, it would be just a matter of time till things fell apart. The army could take over, or the Freedmen's Bureau could send somebody else. He was through with all of it.

And his misery, he told himself, was his own fault. He

should have known better than to fall in love. And what a fool he had been to start thinking how it would be to marry her and have a home . . . a family.

The big leader talked about how they would not be attacking anybody for a while. They needed to wait for things to calm down after what had happened to Lloyd Swenson. Most of all, it was imperative that they lie low till they found out who had betrayed them. Too much danger, he said, of someone leaking the information to the army and having a repeat of the foiled attack on Spencer Wilcox.

Suddenly one of the men shouted, "What about the Corrigan woman? She needs her comeuppance."

Hearing Kerry's name, Slade nearly lost his balance and tightened his hold on the beam where he was perched.

"What about her?" the leader fired back.

"Didn't you know? She stole Hank Allison's workers away. Made 'em sharecroppers. If we let her get away with it, other farmers might have the same idea, and then it will spread all over. We can't have that in Wayne County."

Others grumbled to agree.

"That's right."

"Gotta stop it now."

"She needs to be dealt with before it goes any further."

"And it don't matter if she is a woman. She ain't got no business on that farm livin' with that Dillon fellow. What do we know about him, anyway?"

The Grand Cyclops waved his arms for silence. "Hush up now. I told you—we got to lay low for a while."

A Klansman standing at the rear suddenly cried out in triumph, "Hey, there ain't no need for nobody to worry about her. She's been dealt with."

Again, Slade had to struggle to keep from falling as he cursed to think something must have happened since he left the farm. But that was only a few hours ago, and all was fine then, and—

"What are you talking about?" the leader demanded.

"Me and some of the boys paid her a visit last night and told her she's got a week to clear out."

"Damn it, you had no right," the Cyclops roared. "She'll go straight to the army."

"No, she won't," the Klansman smugly responded. "We told her we'd kill her if she did.

"It's nothing to worry about," he went on as those around him glared through the slits in their hoods. "She's probably packing right this minute."

Slade shook his head. He had observed her almost all day. She behaved as though nothing had happened. But that would be her way, stubborn filly that she was.

And, swallowing a disgusted sigh of resolve, Slade knew he was not going to be able to leave after tonight like he planned.

Maybe he was determined to get over her, but the reality was that he hadn't yet.

And he could try to convince himself otherwise, talk to himself till he was blue in the face, but there was just no way he was going anywhere till he could be sure she was safe.

Kerry had followed the sounds of the whistles.

She had ridden the stallion along the river, the moonlight glinting off the water to light the way.

It had come as no surprise to hear a whistle from the vicinity of Hank Allison's farm, remembering what Edgar had told her about Buck being a member of the Klan.

The haunting sounds echoed in the night stillness, eerie and frightening, because she knew what it meant.

The devils were gathering.

She had her shotgun and her pistol.

Dressed in overalls and an old straw hat, she was also wearing her father's worn coat—but not to ward off the night chill. She needed to feel close to him, now more than ever, because this night she faced perhaps the most formidable task of her life.

When she had left the riverbank, she felt momentary panic. Ahead perhaps only fifty feet, she saw a ghostly figure on horseback. Had she appeared a few seconds earlier, he would have seen her.

But at least she now knew she was going the right way and followed behind him, keeping her distance. Under normal circumstances, she might have lost him, even in the moonlight, but the stark white costume stood out against the darkness.

When she saw the barn, Kerry drew back, knowing it had to be their meeting place. Dismounting, she led the stallion from the well-worn path and looped his reins about a tree back in the shadows. She gave him a pat on the rump, then went the rest of the way on foot.

The Klansman she had followed had apparently been the last to arrive. Through the open door of the barn she could see more white robes and hoods. She could not, however, hear what they were saying and crept closer.

She also wanted to move among the horses tied outside, anxious to spot Slade's, although he might be riding a different one as he had apparently done that morning. No doubt he was smart enough to switch mounts so he'd not be recognized. But she needed no proof, anyway. There were too many signs pointing to his involvement.

Kerry could not deny being more frightened than ever in her life. Not even the rats scurrying in the basement beneath the pub had filled her with such terror. The men inside would kill her if they found her, without batting an eye. They would likely throw her body in the river, and—

She stumbled into a bucket, the sound exploding in the stillness of the night. To keep from falling, she grabbed out for anything to steady her and wound up with her hands clutching a horse's tail. He whinnied, stomped backwards, then kicked his hind legs.

Kerry jumped just in time to keep from being struck, then dove behind a tree and held her breath.

"What was that?" came a shout from inside.

It was followed by another. "It came from out there. Somebody's nosing around. Let's get 'em."

Slade had scrambled towards the opening in the wall of the barn as soon as he heard the noise. And it was all he could do to keep from cursing out loud to see Kerry, bathed in a silver sheen from the moonlight, as she lunged for cover.

What the hell is she doing here? he fiercely wondered as he groped about for the rope he'd tied earlier. There was no time to lose. When the Klansmen spilled outside, they would spread out and search till they found her, and he didn't want to think about what would happen next.

Without hesitation . . . without a thought to the consequences, Slade took hold of the rope with one hand, drew his gun with the other, and leaped from the opening.

"Hands up, all of you," he cried as his feet hit the ground.

But then he lost his balance, pitching forward, and before he could right himself, they were on top of him.

"Hey, it's that stranger—Dillon," one of the men yelled. "He's been spying on us."

"And he'll die for it," the Grand Cyclops shouted as he stormed out of the barn behind the others.

Slade was yanked to his feet, a man on each side holding his arms.

The Cyclops screamed in his face. "It was you all along, wasn't it? You been spying on us. And somehow you found out about Lloyd and turned him in to the law. Now he'll go to jail, maybe even hang on account of you."

"Well, he ain't gonna send nobody else to jail." A man suddenly lunged from the pack to slam his fist into Slade's face. "But he's damn well gonna find out what it's like to have his neck stretched.

"And I want him to know who's responsible, 'cause it don't matter no more what he finds out." He yanked off his hood.

Slade, blood dripping from his mouth, tried to focus his bleary eyes to recognize Hank Allison's foreman, Buck.

"Hang him," Buck ordered. "Then we'll tie rocks around him and throw him in the river. Nobody will know what happened to him. And we won't meet here again, in case he's workin' with somebody."

The leaders hastily murmured among themselves, then the Grand Cyclops worriedly said, "Hurry up and do it so we can get the hell out of here."

Kerry peered from behind the tree, unnoticed but fearing they would hear her heart hammering in her chest as her brain dizzily tried to sort out the nightmare that had unfolded before her disbelieving eyes.

Slade was not one of them.

And, like her, he had obviously been spying. For what reason she did not know, but above all that was the soul-wrenching reality that he had been willing to die for her. He had known they were about to catch her but had diverted attention to himself.

And now he would pay with his life . . .

. . . unless she did something.

She watched as they bound his wrists behind his back.

"Somebody get a horse," Buck commanded. "Somebody make a noose and throw the end over the branch of that tree yonder."

Kerry chewed her lip and tasted blood.

There were so many of them. She quickly counted sixteen. And she was only one person. There was no way she could take them all.

Slade was roughly hoisted on the back of a horse, a hastily constructed noose dropped over his head.

Kerry had drawn her pistol and held it tightly in her sweat-slick hand.

There was one chance she could save him and then hope the Klansmen would be so stunned they'd think of nothing except saving themselves and scatter. They would not know whether there was one person shooting or an army patrol.

Timothy O'Malley had shown her how to shoot and said she was a natural. By the time she left Ireland, she could hit a target a hundred feet away. But that was what she had been shooting—a target.

Not a rope tied around a man's neck.

"We oughta leave him for the buzzards," a man angrily shouted. "As a lesson for anybody else who thinks they can spy on us."

"Don't be stupid," Buck growled at him. "The Cyclops is right. We can't let anybody know we had anything to do with him disappearin'."

Torches were hastily lit, illuminating the grisly scene.

Kerry stepped, unseen, from behind the tree. Their backs were turned, all of them facing Slade sitting atop the horse, about to hang. And just as Buck raised his hand to slap the horse's rump to set him running and drop Slade to break his neck, Kerry took aim.

She fired.

The rope snapped.

Slade fell forward across the horse's neck as the horse took off at full gallop towards the riverbank.

Kerry dropped from sight but kept shooting wildly.

And, mercifully, the Klansmen did what she had hoped they would—scattered to save themselves, not caring about anybody else.

They were gone in a matter of seconds.

Kerry waited, held her breath, then looked out once more.

The ground was covered with the still burning torches that had been dropped in the Klansmen's haste to flee. She ran and picked one up and took off towards the river.

Dear God, she thought, panic rising, if the horse had leaped off the bank and into the water, Slade would drown, because his hands were tied behind his back. There would be no way she could see him in the swirling, murky depths, and—

"Looking for somebody, green eyes?"

Kerry's heart slammed into her chest.

Slade stepped from the shadows, hands still bound behind him. "I jumped in time," he said matter-of-factly. "And if you'll untie me, we'll get the hell out of here before some of them muster the nerve to come back—though I doubt that will happen."

With shaking fingers, she freed him, and then his arms were about her to hold her tight as he gazed down at her in the moonlight and fervently vowed, "I love you, woman. I always have, and I always will. And I'm not going anywhere. I'm staying to finish busting up the Klan, and if Thad Albritton or anybody else comes to call on you, I'm going to chase them all the way to Georgia."

Kerry's head was swimming, and she was filled to bursting with the love for him that she had been unable to deny, no matter how hard she tried. "But . . . but what about that woman?" she stammered nervously, afraid to hear but aware there would be no peace, no understanding between them, until she knew everything.

He blinked in the moonlight. "What woman?"

"The . . . the prostitute," she said shyly. "I know you've been going to Sadie's. And I thought you were in the Klan, that you had something to do with them coming this morning to warn me, and—" She shook her head to try and clear it. "Oh, Slade, I don't know what to think."

He gripped her shoulders and held her tightly, forcing her to meet his steady gaze. "I didn't intend for you to know, but that woman is a federal agent, like me. We both work for the Freedmen's Bureau. I was sent to destroy the Klan. She's my go-between to the army. That's the only reason I went there.

"But now it's time for *you* to answer some of *my* questions," he rushed to continue. "And the first one is—do you love me at all, Kerry? Or do you want Thad Albritton?"

She had to laugh, despite everything. "I never wanted him, Slade. I only wanted you."

He kissed her, long, hard, and possessively, then released her to smile and say, "Then that only leaves one more question, and it's my last. Will you marry me?"

She wrinkled her nose and pretended to think about it, then laughed again to say, "Slade Dillon, you'll do anything to get your hands on my farm, won't you?"

He swung his head solemnly from side to side. "No," he said huskily. "I'll do anything to get my hands on *you*, sweetheart."

Epilogue

They had both wanted the ceremony to take place at the farm.

Bessie and Annie had decorated the parlor with roses made of pink and white satin ribbon.

There was no wedding gown, no wedding cake, but Kerry did not care. She was marrying the man of her dreams, the man she was destined to love for the rest of her life, and nothing else mattered.

The day had dawned beautifully, a golden sun and warm breeze promising that spring could not be too far away.

"You're beautiful," Bessie told Kerry when she emerged from the bedroom wearing the simple pink cotton dress she had bought for the occasion.

Annie chimed in to agree, "The prettiest bride I ever saw."

Kerry smiled and thanked them, then glanced nervously towards the window and the road beyond. The preacher was waiting. So were Abigail and a few friends from the church she'd thought would like to attend. There would be refreshments afterwards.

Everything was ready—except for one thing.

There was no groom.

Abigail came bustling over to nervously whisper, "Well, what's keeping him? It's way past time to begin."

Kerry managed to sound unconcerned. "He said he had some business in town."

"Well, when did he leave?"

"This morning."

"Then he should have been back. I don't understand."

Neither did Kerry. Slade had told her everything about his undercover work against the Klan. He had gone directly to the commander of the occupational forces and told him all he knew. Buck had been arrested, and he was so angry that he revealed the names of the others. He even led them directly to the two remaining leaders, who turned out to be none other than Horace Bedham, along with a man Kerry had never heard of and someone no one else would ever have suspected.

So the trouble was over. For the time being, anyway. Maybe in the future the Klan would try to reorganize, but Slade's work was over. He had a new job, he boasted to the Freedmen's Bureau. He was going to be a husband and a farmer and they could find somebody else to do their work.

Only now Kerry was starting to worry that something bad had happened. And she was almost ready to ride to town and see what she could find out when Luther came tearing into the house to happily announce, "He's comin'. Mr. Slade is comin' up the road right now."

He was wearing a gray coat and trousers, white shirt and black string tie, his boots spit-polished, and Kerry thought him the most handsome man she had ever seen.

He dismounted and strode right in to take her hand and lead her to the preacher and teasingly say, "Let's do it before she changes her mind."

Dizzy with more happiness than she ever thought possible, Kerry stammered her way through her vows.

And then the preacher was asking Slade for the ring, and she groaned inwardly to realize that in all the excitement of the past few days thoughts of a wedding ring had never entered his mind.

But, to her amazement, he grinned and reached in his pocket. "I've got it right here."

She gasped in joy and wonder as he slid the emerald ring on her finger . . . the ring she'd been forced to sell to Lorne Petrie.

"It's yours, green eyes," Slade whispered. "Forever and always."

"Like our love," she murmured . . . and lifted her face for his kiss.

Put a Little Romance in Your Life With
Janelle Taylor

Put a Little Romance in Your Life With
Fern Michaels

__Dear Emily	0-8217-5676-1	$6.99US/$8.50CAN
__Sara's Song	0-8217-5856-X	$6.99US/$8.50CAN
__Wish List	0-8217-5228-6	$6.99US/$7.99CAN
__Vegas Rich	0-8217-5594-3	$6.99US/$8.50CAN
__Vegas Heat	0-8217-5758-X	$6.99US/$8.50CAN
__Vegas Sunrise	1-55817-5983-3	$6.99US/$8.50CAN
__Whitefire	0-8217-5638-9	$6.99US/$8.50CAN

The Queen of Romance
Cassie Edwards

__Desire's Blossom	0-8217-6405-5	$5.99US/$7.50CAN
__Passion's Web	0-8217-5726-1	$5.99US/$7.50CAN
__Portrait of Desire	0-8217-5862-4	$5.99US/$7.50CAN
__Beloved Embrace	0-8217-6256-7	$5.99US/$7.50CAN
__Savage Obsession	0-8217-5554-4	$5.99US/$7.50CAN
__Savage Innocence	0-8217-5578-1	$5.99US/$7.50CAN
__Savage Torment	0-8217-5581-1	$5.99US/$7.50CAN
__Savage Heart	0-8217-5635-4	$5.99US/$7.50CAN
__Savage Paradise	0-8217-5637-0	$5.99US/$7.50CAN
__Silken Rapture	0-8217-5999-X	$5.99US/$7.50CAN
__Rapture's Rendezvous	0-8217-6115-3	$5.99US/$7.50CAN